T0156645

COCONUT SHELLS

MICHAEL ROGERS

iUniverse, Inc.
Bloomington

COCONUT SHELLS

iUniverse books may be ordered through booksellers or by contacting:

iUniverse
1663 Liberty Drive
Bloomington, IN 47403
www.iuniverse.com
1-800-Authors (1-800-288-4677)

ISBN: 978-1-4759-3266-9 (sc)
ISBN: 978-1-4759-3267-6 (ebk)

Printed in the United States of America

iUniverse rev. date: 08/20/2012

This novel is dedicated to the glory of God
and the virtue of the people of South Africa.

For Sihle, Erik, Benedict and Rowan;
I will always remember and love you.

This book is my gift to every African, whether they be black or
white or anything in between.

Published in celebration of the 94th birthday of
Nelson Mandela, 18th July 2012

Nkosi sikelel' iAfrika
Maluphakanyisw' uphondo lwayo
Yizwa imithandazo yethu,
Nkosi sikelela, thina lusapho lwayo

Morena boloka setjhaba sa heso,
O fedise dintwa le matshwenyeho
O se boloke, O se boloke setjhaba sa heso
Setjhaba sa, South Afrika—South Afrika

Uit de blou, van onse hemel,
Uit de diepte, van ons see,
Oor ons ewige gebergtes,
Waar die kranse antwoord gee,

Sounds the call to come together,
And united we shall stand,
Let us live and strive for freedom
In South Africa, our land.

CONTENTS

1

WHY I AM A COCONUT

Johannesburg, South Africa
4th June 1948

If you say it in English, my name is love. I am Lerato Dlamini, and I am a coconut. You have to say my name the African way, not the English or the American way; if you say it correctly I sound like a tomato. My name is much more African than I am, because you see, my body is black but my spirit inside it is white. The skin is just a shell, fragile and frail; you have no way of telling what lies below the brown casing and when you cut into it there is a sense of shock when the white milk is revealed. It's only a shell, nothing more than that.

I am a racial transvestite because when I was born I was sewn into the wrong birthday suit. Even when I am naked I cannot disrobe myself of my foul and abhorrent skin; the inner part of me which is correct is buried so deeply that nobody else may ever see it. I cannot simply change my clothes so that I may find a better way of outwardly expressing my inner identity. People who are born the wrong gender don't know how lucky they are; race cuts far deeper and defines you far more than a small thing like being male or female. When God gets your race wrong, the results can be disastrous. Usually it is a forgivable mistake, but I was unfortunate enough to have been born in South Africa halfway through the Twentieth Century; never in all

1

of human history has an individual been shaped and defined by the colour of their skin more than here.

I am a Russian doll. If you split my coconut shell in half and remove it you will see a completely new body on the inside; I think she looks a bit like Marilyn Monroe, only with better legs and juicier hips. I've never seen the woman inside me but I have every reason to believe that she was and is voluptuously beautiful. She has a little hourglass figure rather than this hippopotamus of a body I have been lumbered with and she has all the right curves in all the right places. I close my eyes and imagine her piercing blue eyes, her fleshy red lips and her delicate white skin. She has a sharp and dainty little nose. She has skin the colour of honey and she has toes and fingers painted crimson so they look like sparkling rubies. She turns pink and then orange in the sunshine, green when she is sick and blue when she is cold. I am the only white person in the world who can't do any of those things.

I am not, and may never be, the blonde bombshell that I should have been. My hair is not straight and golden but instead it is thick and wiry, a vast dark ball of wretchedness, and no matter how many times I brush it the curliness will not be taken away. I have big brown eyes and a wide, flat African nose. My feet are huge and wrapped up in darkness. I have chunky toes and fat black fingers made out of misery. My hands have pale palms but I have a big dark belly. I absolutely loathe this mismatched body that I have been mistakenly given. It is a vile abomination; what I really want is for my inner whiteness to shine through and for people to see me for who I really am. I hate it so much that some days it is totally unendurable and I feel like I could burst, that my shell could crack and that my coconut milk could come showering out. I avoid mirrors at all costs; they are vile, dreadful things. But everything will be alright in the end; one day I will soar into the sky because I am greater than what my untruthful and deceptive body limits me to.

Over the years of my life a lot of the monochrome people have called me crazy. They think I am deluded fool, a girl just as black on the inside as she is on the outside. They say that everything I am experiencing is because of mental illness and an inability to understand and interact with the world around me. My mother has always told me that being a black woman is a beautiful thing, a thing to be relished and enjoyed and that all black women should be immensely proud of their identity and heritage, but it is quite clear that she doesn't understand anything at all. When you read this book I don't expect you to understand me either; that's not the reason I am telling you my story. I am telling you these intimate secrets because I want you to understand how South Africa came to be free, not the psychology or biology of what it means to be a coconut. Just trust me when I say that I am one. I don't know whether or not I expect you to believe me and I don't know whether or not I care. You can call me insane if you want to; you certainly wouldn't be the first. Just make sure that you never, ever call me a black woman. I am a perfectly white woman who is completely encased in a false skin, hidden behind a mirage and a total misrepresentation of my identity. My whiteness is total; calling me black or mixed-race is utterly false. Don't lie to my face.

I am not a bluegum or a buffie, a teapot or a thicklips, a jigaboo or a jungle bunny, a spook or a spearchucker. My least favourite of these names that people found for black people was the rancid and disgusting "munter", a Bantu word which the Afrikaners used as an expletive to describe people who looked like me. My family used to get their own back by calling them "hairybacks" or "boneheads" but that didn't make me feel any better.

The reason why I know that it is not all in my head is because since my birth I have *felt* the agony of being in the wrong body. This is not a psychological condition, for my flesh screams out with the unendurable pain of being the wineskin for a spirit that does not fit inside it, chafing and itching as I struggle to wriggle free. This is not a feeling of depression or unhappiness, a cloud over my horizon that I chose to place there or one which simply vanishes whenever I decide it's not convenient to be a coconut any more. No; this is a gut-wrenching, spine-tingling, nerve-shredding physical agony which I must endure for eternity in perfect solitude. Mental illnesses don't hurt you in the flesh; they cause anguish and trauma, not physical pain. I knew you wouldn't understand, because you are a monochrome and monochromes never understand anything. I would rather die a slow and painful death from cancer than to have to endure a lifetime of being a coconut; at least then nobody would deny my unique medical condition ever existed in the first place, or worse call me stupid or foolish for bringing my doom and destruction upon myself.

I was born in Sophiatown, a township in Johannesburg, in the depths of winter on 4th June 1948. Nobody ever knew the identity, race or whereabouts of my biological parents because I was adopted as an abandoned newborn baby. My adoptive parents, Gloria and Faithful Dlamini, answered a knock at the corrugated tin door of their little shack and saw a white man standing there cradling me in his arms. They knew that I could not have been more than a few minutes old because I still had pieces of fresh placenta stuck to my hair. He told them that he was a taxi driver but to this day nobody has ever told me how he got there and whether or not he had his vehicle with him. He clearly felt very uncomfortable with being in the dangerous gangland at such an hour and he did not want to drop me off at the hospital, so he came to find Gloria and Faithful's shack and asked them to look after me overnight. He promised that he could return in the morning and admit me to the maternity unit, where I could be cared for and seen to by the social workers who would re-home me like a stray dog. The soft glow of the candlelight shone on Gloria's face as she examined the white man standing at her door in the middle of nocturnal Sophiatown with a baby in his arms, a baby with black skin. Gloria was no fool, and she must have known that he would never return for me, but I think she wanted to believe and trust him so much that her suspicions were suppressed long enough to fall in love with me. I can fully understand why, because she had never seen a coconut before and once you lay eyes on one of our kind then we are pretty difficult to forget. Faithful was sceptical and he did not want to help, but Gloria begged him.

"Answer me this," Faithful began as he took me out of the taxi driver's hands, "what is a pregnant black woman doing taking expensive taxis such as yours late at night? Where did she get her money from to pay you with? I don't believe it. You would have been too afraid to let a black passenger into your taxi because you would think she would attack you, especially here in Sophiatown where the white men fear to tread."

The driver's eyes widened with a mixture of shock and fear.

"No, sir, the only passengers that I have driven tonight have been white."

Just a few short weeks later, it would have been illegal as well as inadvisable for passengers of different colours to share a taxi together as the laws of the Nationalist Government started to bite into the multicultural skin of South Africa as though our country was a grape bursting between the teeth. There is so much about my birth that I will never know; because of that I have always felt that my identity is fragile and shrouded in secret mystery. All that I knew about my origin was the information which had been passed down to me by Gloria and Faithful, and some of the more confusing aspects of the tale gave me the frustrating sense that time may have exaggerated or changed the story which had knitted me together and constructed this coconut shell out of dust. Why was the taxi directed into Sophiatown by white passengers who would have no conceivable reason to go there? How is it possible for a taxi driver to *not notice* that one of his passengers was in labour? Was it possible that I had grown up being told a corrupted story about my birth, that the very foundation of my life was rooted in something other than the truth? I don't know at what point on the journey I became a passenger inside that little car, but I do know that the driver of the taxi never did keep his promise to come back and take me to the hospital. I'm still waiting for him.

In good time Gloria and Faithful became accustomed to the idea that they would have to be my parents. They called me *Lerato*; I'm not sure if my birth mother had a name for me but it would definitely have been something white. Mary-Jane, Elizabeth, Anna, Catherine or Alice would all have done nicely but instead they insisted on shackling me with that ghastly name of slavery. The African name clung to me as tightly as it would have done if it was branded onto my forehead with a red hot poker.

Gloria, who would have to be known as Mommy from now on, could not bear the thought of giving me up whilst Faithful was perfectly happy to abandon me immediately. He claimed that life was hard enough for the family financially and that there would not be any more room for burdens on our livelihoods. Because I had no proof of birth and my parents could not afford the relevant paperwork, I was never officially adopted by Gloria and Faithful even though they called me their daughter and I called them my Mom and Dad. I never had any proof that I belonged to them and was a part of their family. In terms of official documentation I simply did not exist and I had never been born.

So began my childhood as a misfit. I was the crazy one, the outcast and the freakish, lonely dreamer and it was all because I knew that I was not the person that everyone thought I was. I did not feel at home in the Dlamini family because I was not a member of the Dlamini family, and they did not understand how it felt or what it meant to be a coconut. It is an inherent part of human nature to look at other people and judge them by their physical appearance, but this was the absolutely incorrect way of determining who I was. I didn't match my skin at all, but nobody could see that. I bet you will be no different; you won't believe a word I say.

I was an anomaly. Sometimes you see people who like to dress up in the clothes of the opposite gender; they complain of being born into the wrong body. Their flesh does not quite feel at ease with the soul it houses and that the two of them are plunged headlong into an eternal battle which is impossible to resolve. I know their pain well, for it is not my gender that has been incorrect since my birth, but my race. My skin does not match or reflect me. I am not who I look like, and I have had to suffer a lifetime of misunderstanding and confusion as my personality and my spirit does battle with my flesh. I am like a homosexual who does not understand what is happening to their hormones, someone who is outcast and rejected and deeply hurt and confused. There is a profound agony in being the wrong colour, and my spirit sings a different lamentation to my flesh.

I have many theories as to why I am so unusual; I had to think them up myself because the monochromes were so terribly bad at understanding my condition. They would tell me a thousand different stories about how I had several types of absurd delusion all at once, that I had something called body dysmorphia or that I was traumatised by not knowing my true parents. Their theories all contradicted each other so fiercely that the only logical conclusion to come to was that everyone who had an opinion—the local witch doctor, my *forever family*, women in the street, the other children of Sophiatown; basically everyone I ever came into contact with—all of them were just as deluded and insane as they claimed I was. They were spouting their vile accusations against me to deflect the attention from the mental illnesses of their own. My theories were much more sensible: I thought it likely that my *tummy mommy* must have drunk a great barrel of tar before conceiving me, or perhaps she had munched on coal to satisfy her cravings during her pregnancy. That woman of whose womb I am the immaculate fruit, that woman who carried me into the world and that woman whose name I will never know—she must have had an appetite for cocoa, raw tea leaves, biltong and black olives. The monochromes were all flawed, broken people and I was the only one in the whole world with any sense. The misunderstandings were down to everyone else's ignorance and stupidity, not mine.

I am absolutely convinced that whiteness is derived from purity, and I am only pure on the inside. When we were made by God, we were created to have white skin. The blackness of my skin is the souvenir of the eviction of man from the Garden of Eden, the scorch-marks of the Almighty's thunder and the terrifying and beastly Seraphim standing guard at the gates of the garden. White skin is pure skin and white people are pure people. I am scorched on the outside with a pale interior, like an overcooked sausage on a braai.

Put simply, my skin and my soul do not match up. My inside is white, and my outside is black, therefore I am a coconut. The evidence is overwhelming. Gloria and Faithful are not my biological parents so it would be impossible for us to be the same colour even though our skin looks the same. The taxi driver told them that he had only carried white passengers in his car that night, and I was born with an instinctive ability to speak the languages of the white men like English and Afrikaans rather than the black ones like Xhosa and Zulu, which must be learnt and studied with an unnaturally great effort and labour. Coconuts are not mysterious or miraculous, but instead the condition is perfectly logical, diagnosable and explainable. I have absolutely no idea why this is not perfectly obvious to anyone other than me.

2

WELCOME TO AFRICA

Sophiatown, Johannesburg
9th February 1955

My neighbourhood in Sophiatown, a shanty town outside of Johannesburg, was a thriving and beautiful cradle for a culture which was being flaunted shamelessly for all to see. Sophiatown was a wonderful place to be a child, for the slum was the heart of Africa's black culture and the crucible of a new urban zest which would come to define us. We used to call it *Kofifi*, an affectionate nickname for the home that we loved so much, with all of its beauty and bleakness, all of its virtues and curses. Sophiatown was the black man's Mecca or his Jerusalem, this sacred place of cultural pilgrimage and the birthplace of the big black African family. In spite of the fact that growing up as the only non-black person there felt like being adopted by aliens, I had a great affection for Sophiatown and I loved it dearly. I still do.

Sophiatown was not so much a place as a philosophy. We did not live in that place but moreover we *were* Sophiatown; it was a living, breathing organism made of who we were and the heart and soul of that place was built out of black people. There is a southern African word which doesn't translate directly into English but it means "I am what I am because of everything we are": *Ubuntu*. As I spoke that word to myself I heard the echoing laughter, the ringing peals of joy and the sound of singing clattering down the dusty and narrow streets of the slum. We were Sophiatown and Sophiatown was us. We smiled and we sang; we loved and we lamented; we kissed and we killed each other beneath the hedonistic African sky. Sophiatown was the epitome of the African experience and we relished in the creative and political renaissance of the fifties with its eclectic mix of gangs and shebeens, jazz music and the rhythm of the slum. This was where legends were born and where warlords bled into the streets as the power shifted from one gang to the next. Hollywood had nothing on us.

I knew that Apartheid was wrong, but being born on the day that the National Party rose to power and implemented the racist laws meant that I never had an alternative to measure my life against. I simply did not know how it felt to not be discriminated against because of the colour of my skin. It was painful enough for those who were actually black inside as well as out, but because of my mismatched skin it was something I found particularly difficult to deal with even though I knew no other way. We were too poor to travel to somewhere freer, so we never left the Transvaal Province which Sophiatown and greater Johannesburg were situated in. I was a winter baby; the skies above the Transvaal were clear and bright and freezing for the whole winter long as there was never a cloud or a drop of rain. There would occasionally be mist and frost on the colder mornings but this was soon burned away by the fierce sunshine.

The sunrises in the winter were astoundingly beautiful. Even in a place of such suffering and poverty the world is still an incredible place to find yourself in. What a time to be alive. One of my first memories was of waking early in the little shack and seeing the stars out of the unglazed window above the place where I slept; we had no beds so we all slept together on the floor. In truth this was because we could not afford a larger space to call home, but it was also because the freezing winter air funnelled through our little metal house meant that the only way to keep warm was to share our body heat by sleeping in a tangled bundle of flesh beneath every blanket we could find. They were great brightly-coloured itchy things that will forever be embellished on my early memory, wiry fabrics arranged into bold geometric shapes and decorated with deep and rich hues of dark red, blue and green. I would awaken by starlight and watch the quiet hush of the sparkling frost forming on the tops of the shacks. The teeth of winter gnawed at the quietly gathering light over Johannesburg.

Sophiatown was completely dark; I remember the stifling and enormous darkness stretching out as far as the eye could see. The township had no electricity and everything was black and silent. There were no goats or cattle running down the streets made of dirt, no women lighting the fires to boil the water so that they could cook and clean, no men sitting on the street corners singing and playing their instruments and no gangsters swaggering around in stolen suits with rifles in their hands. Even the stars were quiet as their silvery pinpricks of light hung peacefully above the barely visible corrugated metal roofs of my hometown, that place which will forever have some ownership of my heart. The horizon was glowing and I could see the outline of the yellow grasses swaying on the hillsides, a heavy mist descending on the Veld as the greasy dawn began to break. The skies above the hills turned from pitch black to a royal purple and then a deep navy blue and I knew then that another day in Sophiatown was beginning. I remember feeling so unfathomably blessed, so wonderfully fortunate to find myself as a young girl ready for new adventures every day in Africa. Ours is a luminous continent and a place like no other.

The summer was hot and stormy, and the landscape became vibrant and bursting with glorious life. Everything was green and the weather was wildly unpredictable. The thunderstorms were strong and brief and the trees were unbelievably green and beautiful. But as the new year marched onwards the clouds vanished from the skies and the luscious grass died away to leave nothing but orange mud.

I remember very vividly the desolate scrubland of the Veld in the autumn and winter, and the glow of the hillsides at night when the farmers would burn the countryside in order to make the land fertile again for farming once the spring came. The ash provided the earth with nutrients that were in very short supply over the winter, and because there was never any rain the countryside was as dry as kindling and the fires blazed ferociously. As a young child the logic was lost on me and I was frightened by what I saw, with the thick smoke sailing across the skies and the fields and hills ablaze with demonic flames and the whole world seemed to be made of lava. In a township with no electricity and the candle flames flickering dimly I remember the almighty roar of light which came from the hills as they blazed. The devil lived up on those hills in the autumn, prowling around and looking for people to devour. Disease and premature death was rife. Life was hard, but life was also beautiful and wonderful.

Albert Lutuli was the president of the political party called the African National Congress, and he had promised to fight with whatever means was necessary to end the prejudice against black South Africans by the white elite. I was completely, utterly, truly, madly and deeply in love with him in gratitude for what he had promised to achieve for people mistreated by racism. Mommy asked me why I kept squealing whenever his name was mentioned. I thought it was obvious. He had that twinkly glint of genius in his eye and he made every day shine like a shiny star. He bewitched me completely.

This man would be our voice, our ticket out of hopelessness and our means of getting the authorities to listen to what we had to say. Lutuli was the star of the show but he was not the only one on freedom's team; his deputy was a strange and perfectly forgettable little man named Nelson Mandela. I remember him being a little plain and boring; Lutuli was the one who was attracting all the attention for his work to end the evil being dealt out against us and in 1960 he was allowed to leave South Africa to travel to Norway to collect the Nobel Peace Prize. He was Sophiatown's rogue champion and our runaway rescuer, the one we could trust to give a voice to the voiceless. I was so immeasurably grateful to him for the battle that he was fighting in my name, because issues concerning race were immeasurably more relevant to me than anyone else. I would get angry with black people for feeling mistreated by the evils of

Apartheid; nobody else was qualified to call themselves a victim other than me. I was the Queen of the damned.

From the age of six, when I heard Nelson Mandela speak at Freedom Square in response to the Government's ever increasing racial marginalisation, I was plagued by the sneaking suspicion that he was under my influence. I knew that he hated the fact that I was ignoring him and he went on a mission to grasp my attention. Somehow every word that he spoke seemed to resonate with me and every thought that I had seemed to echo through him. I came to realise, in 1954 as the Native Resettlement Act was being passed, that I was able to accurately predict the words and phrases that he would use in his speeches to the crowd in Sophiatown. He didn't live nearby but for some reason he kept on coming back. Sophiatown was his lynchpin, the hub of his wheel, the axis of his Earth, his beginning and his end, just the same as it was for me. Why did he keep coming back to give speeches about the Government? Here was a man absolutely committed to overthrowing the men in power and he seemed to be obsessed with coming to visit Sophiatown so that I could watch his oratory in action.

The township was dangerous, there was no denying that. I used the sound of gunshots as my lullabies every night and the sound of screaming in the streets would calm and soothe me as I lay my head down to rest. The streets were mean, cold and brutal. The shanty town was overrun with gangs, the most notorious of which was called *The Americans*. They all drove limousines and wore tuxedos, and everything that they did was inspired by the American way of life. It was so glamorous, so thrillingly dangerous, so stunningly exciting. The criminals even had their own language, called *Tsotsitaal*, and nobody else could understand them.

There was a wonderful structure and predictability to Apartheid, which was all I had ever known but was a new and terrifying thing to the older Black Africans. I did not necessarily think that it was the wicked evil monster that it was made out to be by my family, but instead it was an impossible dream for the Nationalist party, and I was living proof of that my absolutely unique mix of black and white was an exception which could find no place in the order, no section in the system to call my own. South Africa was in the grip of an identity crisis from which it would never recover. It was trying to look north and become European, trying to look west and become American, and trying to look inwards and become African all at the same time. Apartheid was its way of trying to bring order to the conglomeration of cultural chaos. It was a temporary solution for them but rather than removing the chaos and anarchy for me, the disorder doubled. I was a casualty in between the races and I was suffering because of their system, and I determinedly decided that I would end Apartheid and piss on its corpse.

One of my most prominent memories of childhood was when the policemen came to claim Sophiatown for the whites. I was seven at the time. I heard from the news reports later that there were two thousand police officers who had been sent in to evict us and to drive us away because they wanted to destroy Sophiatown, to replace it with an exclusively white suburb of Johannesburg, and they had issued us with eviction notifications before the time came but none of us actually believed that it would ever come to what it amounted to.

I remember hearing the jagged roar of the bulldozers as they warmed up their engines, the crackle of hatred and bigotry echoing loudly against the crumpled metal and hammered-together pieces of wood which made the homes. There were policemen escorting them, thousands of uniformed officers striding into our territory under the authority of the Natives Resettlement Act.

The image of my father standing defiantly in front of our little house made of metal would forever be ingrained on the white jelly of my brain. He stood there so proudly, just as he had bravely faced down the gangsters of Sophiatown's underworld and defended the pride of his family so many times before, an icon of defiance in the presence of a determined and devilish enemy. I was so incredibly proud of him, but the policemen who were closing in on our home told him in very explicit terms that the driver would fulfil his orders to destroy the house whether or not my father was still standing in the doorway. He was proud and he stood there defiantly, refusing to be moved by intolerance and hatred. I think he was a little deluded and unwise, for he thought that the authority of the white man was much less audacious and bold than it actually turned out to be. There was absolutely no way of stopping this vicious onslaught and because of this he was very suddenly in a position where he had to decide whether or not he was willing to put his life on the line for the protection of his property.

Perhaps he thought that as he stood in that doorway of his shack, his own home which he had built with his bare hands, that life would no longer be worth living in a nation which looks upon the colour of your skin as disgusting and abhorrent. Seeing my father's face crumpled with anxiety about the future did not fill me with any great hope for the dark days which lay ahead. Pessimism is like speech; we learn it by copying our parents. But then I saw him looking at my mother, the two of them silently and telepathically communicating with each other, and I saw on his face that he realised that they had built far more together than just this little shack and that in spite of the fact that they had nothing they still clung tightly to a bright future of love. They would tell one another that the love would see them through, but I needed further convincing. My father finally stood aside.

With a heavy grumble of acceleration the bulldozer bit into the gleaming corrugated metal of our home and the memories and treasures which we had spent several lifetimes accumulating were reduced to a heap in the orange African earth. The machine went in one side of the shack and our furniture and possessions burst out of the other. The dishes were smashed; the table overturned and crushed into splinters with the legs snapped like boughs of trees in a storm; the iron sink which my family had spent their whole lives saving up for was buckled and twisted and the stockpiles of food in the small pantry we had built out of wood were strewn all over the dirty road. I only had three toys; a spinning top, a rag-doll and a hoop made of metal my father had made for me out of some of the unused machinery at the gold mine, and all of them were lost when our house was smashed to smithereens. There was a cold sense of fitting correctness in the fact that my childhood died in the same moment that my toys were ripped, shredded and crushed by the merciless metal jaws of hatred. As the bulldozer worked great blue clouds of prejudice and intolerance hissed and chugged out of the rusty exhaust pipe and stained the beautiful sky above Sophiatown. Things would never be the same again.

Within seconds the house was unrecognisable even though it was still standing; all of the internal walls had been broken down and all of the furniture that we had acquired over the years and generations was broken and shattered in front of our eyes. The great metal beast reversed, like an athlete taking a run-up before a heroic jump, before ploughing again through the heap of tangled metal and wood. When the great machine came closer we could see the driver with his hands clenched against the wheel in glee; he was clearly enjoying his job. His eyes were blazing with passionate fury and his mouth would break into a wide grin every time he felt the shudder of pieces of the house being destroyed under the relentless churning of the caterpillar tracks. After being subjected to treatment like that, I knew that this struggle for correct definition would devour the rest of my life just as that machine had devoured my home.

Even at the young age of seven, I remember very clearly being roused by a sense of strong outrage at the fact that they were clearing me out of the way for the white people when I was and am white myself. Why couldn't they see what lay within me? Poverty and racial tension combine in a lethal cocktail which sculpts grown women out of seven year old girls. I was faced with a horrible dilemma: I would either be separated from my parents and our family would be ripped apart along racial lines, or I would have to suffer the pain that I was enduring at the hands of Apartheid. This was a pain that by rights I should never have been exposed to because it was an agony that was meant for black people. I would rather have stayed whilst watching the rest of my family thrown out than to go with them because they could not see who I really was. The price I paid for our family staying together was to begin on a very long and lonely road of a lifetime of misunderstanding and incorrect categorization in a nation forever obsessed with getting the racial divide precisely right. Since this line split me down the middle, with my skin and my soul on either side of the boundary, with me they had got it precisely wrong.

I felt so unspeakably humiliated and degraded to be described as black, for that single word was such a reduction of the person that I was into that one definable term. The reduction would have not been in any way blunted had the word to describe me been *white*; both were wrong and both were misleading. I honestly had no idea why people had made up their minds that I was black to the core just because that was what they saw. They didn't know anything about me and yet they presumed that they knew all that they needed to know simply from taking a glancing look at the colour of my skin. Children are endowed with a very strong sense of justice and mine was sent into overdrive as these pigs began destroying Sophiatown. They didn't destroy us with their towering intellect or the relentless power of their enlightened ideas but instead by the only means they knew how, with the cowardly and dishonourable method. The jaws of their bulldozers closed in on our home. Half of the problem of this place was the bullying policemen who were defending and protecting the strong rather than the weak. They were there to evict us and clear the way for the other white people of South Africa, but they were never there to defend us from the appallingly high crime rate in the townships or the gangland violence which reigned in Johannesburg and the surrounding regions.

There was a famine of justice in 1955 and we were starving. Sophiatown belonged to me and as a white girl I should by rights deserve to stay put whilst the blacks were removed and the whites drafted in to replace them in the new whites-only suburb of Triomf. We would be sent away to another place called Meadowlands, cast out in disgrace, and the white people would be given our land. It was outrageous enough that they would make anyone move to another place against their will just because they did not fit the residential specifications set out by a racist and abhorrent Government, but I was surely a case which should have made them reconsider the whole thing. It was deplorable that they should treat me the same as the others, a seven year old white girl in disguise categorized in the wrong section. I was neither Blankes nor Nie Blankes; I was simply me. I could be nothing else, and I was tired of trying to adapt into the prescribed colours.

A year after the destruction of Sophiatown began Mandela was arrested along with more than a hundred and fifty of his comrades. The case became known as the Treason Trial and I was out of hope; I knew that he would be found guilty and our cause would be defeated. 1956 was the end of Nelson Mandela. Perhaps now he would leave me alone; what scared me was that Lutuli would be next. Sophiatown had given my admirer a presence on the national stage and won him infamy with the Government, because it was in Freedom Square that he had first delivered speeches which advocated the use of violence as an acceptable form of resistance to what Apartheid was planning to do to us. After destroying the ghetto which was our monument to equality and freedom the elites set about destroying the people who were crucial to our fight and they arrested one hundred and fifty six people who were suspected of treason against the Government. I didn't understand what was happening until Mandela personified it for me. He was the struggle for justice, and he was fighting against everything that had been wrong with the destruction of Sophiatown. Everything within me was unspeakably outraged by the fact that upholding and defending freedom had become a crime and that unfurling the banner of dignity in the name of the downtrodden and oppressed was seen by the people in power as evil and wrong. I could smell change in the air and I did not like it.

We were forcibly relocated to Meadowlands but our new house was half the size of our old one. I hated it and I wanted to go home. Meadowlands was a horrible place and we spent five long years there before we finally moved again when I was twelve, in 1960, to Orlando West. We had a little house on Vilakazi Street and after a few days I realised that the house on the corner belonged to the man in custody, the very same Nelson Mandela. I couldn't believe the audacity of his pursuit of me; could the fool not understand that I was not interested in his romantic advances? I had a very strong and urgent sensation at the bottom of my stomach that he was extremely distressed by his arrest; this alone was not surprising but I knew that he was not half as concerned with the prospect of jail as he was with the prospect of being forbidden from seeing me again. He was *missing* me. This famous man, this political rising star, had chosen to fight my corner and his anguish at being taken away was plain for all to see. I was the reason he was fighting to get rid of the Apartheid regime. It was because he was troubled that I didn't fit in and he had taken it upon himself to rescue me.

Mommy couldn't see his motive for following me to Vilakazi Street even though it was so blindingly obvious.

"No Lerato, don't be absurd. Mandela has lived here since long before we moved from Meadowlands. He has a wife and I am sure that they love each other very much. His wife is called Winnie, hey."

"I'm twelve. I'm not ready to be anyone's mistress. If I didn't know better I would think that Mandela's a ghastly Zulu who's smooching with lots of different wives at the same time. Mommy I don't want to be a part of his harem."

She chuckled at me as she rubbed the spices into the black game meat to make biltong.

"Get your head out of the clouds, child," she laughed. "Nobody is going to come and kidnap you in the night. Besides, there's nothing wrong with being a Zulu."

"By heaven! I am far too white for that kind of nonsense."

Ever since 1923 black people had been issued with passbooks as a form of identification as the foundations of Apartheid were laid in our nation. This ghastly little book was known as the Dom Pas, which translates to English as the stupid card, and it had to be carried in order for the movements of the blacks to be monitored and restricted by the whites. It listed information about the bearer but this information was so discriminatory that it actually lost all of its truth; if the bearer was employed by another native then they were classed as unemployed. On 26th March 1960, just a few short days after that dreadful massacre in Sharpeville, the magnificent Nelson Mandela burnt his Dom Pas as an act of audacious defiance against those lunatics in power. That was what he thought of their racist little game; the foul and beastly white men were spat upon by someone who was not prepared to take it any more. My skin is my passbook, and I cannot easily burn that to show how I feel because I would look like a fool. As those flames licked around the edges of that damned book I felt a sense of validation and affirmation. I was not the only one who was able to see that this was wrong and as the raging fire charred the book from white to black just as I had been charred in the womb of a stranger I knew that I had Mandela to fight my corner. I knew he wouldn't give up on me. It felt as though the whole struggle was being fought for my benefit. I was immensely grateful to Mandela for doing this favour for me, but I did feel that it was a little cheap. I was a pretty girl and all the black boys would fight over me, but in all of my long twelve years as an African I'd never had to contend with a bid for seduction quite as badly thought out as that one.

For the first part of my life South Africa had been an effectively independent Dominion of the British Empire, but there was a greater distance being laid down every day between London and Pretoria. We were officially a self governing Dominion, but in May of 1961 there was a vote within the population to decide whether the nation should become a fully independent Republic, but they only included people with white skin in the referendum. I am not sure if they forgot about us, if they couldn't count or if they were simply choosing to ignore the blindingly obvious error but at that time the exclusively white population accounted for only nine per cent of the population. They had omitted more than nine out of every ten South Africans. The whites voted in favour of independence, and on the last day of May the nation became a republic and left the Commonwealth. Queen Elizabeth II was removed as Head of State and the last Governor General became the first State President. Our new Queen was a man named Charles Robberts Swart. I remember that in Orlando West there were great celebrations at the new independence of our nation, the separation from European colonialism and our promotion to the international stage. Clearly this was a very complex political process but most of the people in Orlando West simply saw it as an excuse to be proud to be African and to throw a big party. We are Africans, my mother would say. Partying is something that we know how to do, and the only equipment we need to set it up is an excuse for an occasion. Amidst the colourful and traditional costumes, the faces of joy and the free flowing alcohol as South Africa boasted in its enchanting rhythm, my thirteen year old self was troubled. Why were all these black people celebrating when they had been so scandalously ignored, so clearly and blatantly shunned by the minority who held all of the power? What was there to celebrate when we had been denied a voice and a place as part of the electorate who won independence for our country? I longed to join in with the party, to dress up in my colours and to dance as only Africans can, but it all felt so insincere when it was not us who had been permitted to make it happen. A white man, Dutch in ancestry, using his puny opinion to make a decision which would affect the whole of the nation forever just seemed to be wrong to me. None of my family understood, instead they had a horrible acceptance of their ghastly fate as blacks. They clearly were not quite the coconut that I was; I seemed to be the only one. Of all the billions of people in the world I was totally alone, drowning in an ocean of monochrome.

3

A WHITE MAN'S COURT

Meadowlands and Orlando West, Johannesburg
February 1962

If God had not made His mistake on me, I could have been American. The same year that South Africa had gone from being a self-governing Dominion to an independent Republic there was a new President of the United States which had made the people in the North very excited indeed. Young and charismatic, it was his wife who bewitched me, the beautiful woman who accompanied him wherever he went. That was how I was meant to be, how I felt on the inside. I never really had much of a sense of identity until I looked at her on one of the newspapers in the township, seeing her in her pearls and with her little hats and bags and gloves. I was unfamiliar with the anatomy of other white people because they so rarely dared to venture into the different townships where I lived. I am the only white person in South Africa who is not spooked by the blacks and does not feel intimidated by them. I can't really blame my white siblings; Soweto is not the best of places to be for anyone, let alone anyone white. Not seeing white people on a regular basis was difficult because I was tempted to be confused about my identity and to be unable to find something to anchor my sense of understanding to. But when I saw the American woman it was a revelation. Her skin seemed to be made of light, resonating through the grainy ink of the newspaper pages which I saw on the stalls lining the dirty roads. I am made of light as well, but sadly my coconut shell is too thick to let the light shine through.

Nelson Mandela, the militant campaigner who I had almost forgotten about, was acquitted of all charges along with all of the other one hundred and fifty five defendants at the Treason Trial on 29 March 1961. It came as a huge shock to all of us; somehow, inexplicably, he had managed to talk his way out of it even though we'd all thought that would be the end of him. This made me see Mandela in a different way; I had been wrong to count him out. When he was found not guilty at the Treason Trial it changed everything. Before then he had been a freedom fighter who had made some rousing speeches in Freedom Square in Sophiatown, but after he had been arrested and then cleared of all charges he became a very personal and heroic champion. Nobody knew the reasons why he had been released and the whispered theories in Orlando West spread faster than the malaria did as it ravaged the north of the Transvaal. To everyone else it was a mystery, but I alone knew for sure and by now it should be obvious to you as well.

The reason that he had been set free and won freedom for one hundred and fifty five other people as well was because he was a coconut just like me. From that moment onwards my relationship with Mandela changed forever because for the first time in my entire life I had a sudden rushing sensation of no longer being alone in my coconut shell. Suddenly Mandela was not quite the pathetic little man who was in love with me any longer, but instead he became somebody I respected and admired for patiently letting me know that he had empathised with my frustrations all along. If he could achieve the freedom of one hundred and fifty five people, then what untold riches and glory were waiting for me? It all made such perfect sense; all of the other arguments seemed delusional and completely irrational when confronted with the irrefutable truth that people can look one colour and be another. I had never really welcomed or encouraged his affection when it had first become apparent—he had appeared desperate, deluded and illogical—but now I knew for sure that he was inviting me to be a part of what he had already begun for himself, a war against the monochromes with acceptance and equality as our prize. At the trial he had simply let the court know that he was not as black as he looked and they apologised for the misunderstanding and allowed him to leave as a free man. That was all there was to cracking the riddle of Apartheid; there was no need for anger or confusion or heartbreakingly violent and bitter campaigns of terror, but instead the coconuts had a responsibility to stand up and be counted, because on our shoulders rested the future of the nation. Surely any fool could have taken one look at Nelson Mandela and been able to tell that he was not like the rest, which meant that Apartheid was a doomed system and that it needed replacing as fast as possible. It seemed so easy—I was frustrated that the black monochromes of South Africa had not been able to do this without my help and that they had left it all down to Mandela and I. Sophiatown could be rebuilt and we could all get on with our lives again, safe in the knowledge that racism was extinct. Rational, clear thought had won the day by proving that coconuts are the exception to Apartheid's rule and that we alone would bring the whole house of cards crashing down.

I have a thoroughly decent brain and I could definitely have worked it out for myself, but I realised that his skin condition had been the deciding factor in the courtroom because he told me that this was the case. It was a very strange experience that I had not had before, but he whispered into my ears when I was asleep in our little house in Orlando West. I cannot begin to explain it to you, but I know that he could speak to me and I could speak to him without us ever being together. Mandela used to speak to me in my dreams, passing his steadfast message of hope and optimism to my sleeping mind like a message in a bottle floating on a stormy sea.

I only learnt the beautiful American white lady's name the following year when her husband was murdered. I didn't ever read the captions below the photographs of her and I never got beyond her pillbox hats and bright scarlet lipstick to ever see her as an identity aside from her looks and her clothes, her shining and ethereal skin, her radiant and matchless whiteness. I closed my eyes and I tried to imagine how white skin must feel when the sun shines on it. I was in a jazz bar in Orlando West when I heard the news from America on the radio. The man was called Kennedy, and they kept using the word "assassinated" but I didn't really understand what that meant. It didn't instantly instil in me the sense of coldness and dread that it seemed to strike into everyone else. People were just talking about the "awful tragedy" that had befallen him but only really because of the fact that he was married and he had a young family. I sensed something else. I sensed the fact that leadership was now uncertain, and that a single man—however deranged and erratic he may be—had decapitated the government and plunged a nation into chaos and despair. Power and reputation fizzle out to nothing when a bullet goes through the brain and the sparks of life spill all over the beautiful pink Chanel suit of an immaculately dressed lady with porcelain skin. The dynamics of power were changing and Kennedy taught us all that the people in charge may not be the people in charge for very long. Power is delicate and fragile, no matter how many armed policemen they send into Sophiatown to drive us away from our homes. My mind began to whirr at a blistering pace. What would happen to South Africa if that had happened here? What if a madman had put a bullet through the brain of Mr Swart? Would they then end the insanity of it all, the unfairness of Apartheid, and the racist agenda of the Government and the suffering of the people in Soweto? Do bullets take over when words lose their strength? Our words had held no power for a long time.

It seemed to me that they used the word *assassinated* to numb the shock of what had happened to Kennedy. I wondered what you had to do to assassinate something, but all I could think of was to season it with herbs and spices and throw it in the potje to simmer away for hours in a delicious soup of creamy, hearty flavour which exploded on the tongue like a bomb. The word tasted spectacular on my fat black lips.

Johannesburg, which was also known as *Egoli* or 'the city of gold', was a vast and sprawling metropolis, an unashamed monument to commerce and selfish wealth and the relentless pursuit of capitalism with all of its glory and exploitation residing side by side. Egoli felt like the centre of the universe, a city straddling the soul of Africa and the elitist economics of the West, a city that you never felt the need to leave because it was so enormous and one which never stopped churning and whirring like a machine. The city was incredibly new and had been constructed in haste, for a hundred years before it had been the barren wasteland of the highveld but the discovery of gold in the reefs running below the gigantic plateau had fuelled an explosive development which had created the metropolises of the Transvaal in astonishing speed. Johannesburg was the biggest city for hundreds of miles in any direction and nearby Pretoria, one of South Africa's capital cities, was the most important in the region. Johannesburg was a grand mirage and nothing more, inflated with the haste of a bouncy castle and built on deluded dreams of splendour and unimaginable wealth. These fantasies were fuelled by the fact that they were achievable for the minority, and watching one man make his millions was enough to drive a thousand more to try just one more time. But for the black man, the Negro or the munter or whatever he was, his ethnicity was a gigantic pin to Egoli's inflatable promises. The land of unrivalled opportunity was available to a slender minority, and the Negro was left dazzled and stunned as the door slammed shut in his face.

Soweto was an exclusively black place and the population had grown extremely fast since the relocations from Sophiatown. No black men had anywhere else to go and no white men would dare stray away from their designated suburban areas of the city. To them the blacks were dangerous and dirty and to be avoided at all costs. Soweto had extremely few parks or reserves, museums or malls, but it was home to an uncountable population which lay in the millions. Entire families would share corrugated shacks of a single room and there was no electricity or sanitation of any kind. Ours was one of them; there were ten of us and we had a small house which we had managed to acquire after the seizure of Sophiatown.

My father was a gold miner. The outskirts of the city were blighted by enormous mountain ranges of earth that had been moved to make way for the deep shafts which tunnelled under the city, and the mounds which were the waste solids of the extraction process shone a deep yellow in the sunshine. Johannesburg was responsible for the production of one quarter of all the gold in the world, but all of the giant corporations were controlled internationally and the price of gold was determined twice a day by a group of bullion dealers in London and was quoted, even in Africa, in US Dollars. The African fingerprints belonging to my father were often found on the bars of gold which were crushed and pumped deep underground but never on the stocks and shares or multimillion dollar deals which were the other half of the industry. We were, in every sense, still a colony controlled by foreigners.

Now that I knew he was a coconut I could see that there was something so wonderful about Nelson Mandela. We heard him speak at rallies a couple of times and I remember coming home from school and seeing him from a distance, a glimpse of his kind face and electric eyes. He was a gentle, kind and lovely man who I was very fond of, but it was inconceivable to me that soon the whole world would be in love with him too. Mandela was a jealous man; I belonged to him and he did not want to share me. Why should he? I was his entitlement, his inheritance and his prize. Nobody else seemed to be able to connect with him in quite the way that I did, for the telepathy which we shared in our dreams was just for us.

I remember very clearly the day that I met him for the first time. I had been to the marketplace to buy some candles and a chicken. We needed one for the eggs and not for the meat, which meant that we needed a baby no more than a week old so that we could nurture her and raise her up to adulthood. All that the market stall had been able to offer me were old birds, huge great things which flapped and squawked and screeched in my face, and it was clear that they were ready for the slaughter and had been fed as much grain as possible so that their body weight could be maximised. These grand old dames of poultry were the African equivalent of fast food. The chickens were dirty, with the red mud clinging to their feathers, and the open cages smelt of excrement and urine. The cages had no lids because the birds were too fat to fly away, so the skies were vast and out of reach. Because of the fact that they did not have chickens young enough to sell to me for eggs they sent off a boy, of no more than six or seven, on a small bicycle to fetch the chick from a colleague that they knew of on the other side of Soweto. They told him not to stop for anything or anyone, and he scurried away along the dusty road on his bicycle.

Soweto is an enormous place, so I was waiting for a long time. Every single person in the bustling marketplace was black except for me. Some of the men would hover around me and some of them were drunk, even in the middle of the day; one of the men said that his son was approaching puberty and he needed a suitable girl whom he could one day marry, and "to be blunt, I like the look of you."

Quite undeterred by the inappropriateness of a man saying something of such an explicit nature to a fourteen year old, my response was simple and assured. "It is against the law," I began with a confidence which defied my age, "for people of two different races to marry and have children. Your son, I presume, is black. I am white. My answer is no, and it would not be permitted by the regulations of the Government."

The drunken men stared at my dark skin, confused and slightly offended. There was a moment of puzzled tension, because they had clearly never met a coconut before. They then laughed at me, brassily throwing their heads back and shrieking and cackling at each other. They could not believe their ears; a young black girl, exactly the same as everyone else, claiming to be special, the chosen one, some kind of foolish freak who had mutated far enough to grow another skin over her white body, an ethnic disguise which she hid behind. I can appreciate and understand that it sounds ludicrously fanciful, but that does not stop it from being true. I was well used to the laughter and the taunts by now, because it was how everyone reacted.

Eventually the boy on the bicycle came back, and tied to the handlebars was a small and rounded plastic bag. As the boy skidded to a halt he untied the bag from the handlebars a tiny, week-old chick poked her head out and stared in baffled bewilderment at the world outside. She was an adorable little thing, and I was glad that I was not fetching her whilst intending to kill her later that night. They handed her to me, and I gave them the money that I had ready. My mother had warned me not to make friends with my purchase to ease the pain when the time eventually came for her execution to feed our family, but how could I not? I made her a little nappy out of the plastic bag and carried her around proudly.

I decided to call her Hoender, which is the Afrikaans word for "chicken". I had to find some candles to light the family home and so I set off on my mission, weaving my way between the stalls and trying to find the one which sold what I needed. I eventually found the candle-seller on the far side of the marketplace and because I was holding Hoender in my hands I did not feel any of the aggressive and repetitive insistence that I should stop at the stall and buy something. She was too much of a distraction to the tradesmen and so they did not hassle me, they just laughed at me as I walked by. At first I thought it was because I was holding a chicken but I think a far more logical conclusion to come to would have been that they were laughing at me because I was a coconut. As I walked across the marketplace lots of strangers came up to me, all wanting to touch and stroke the adorable baby bird in my hands.

I proudly strode up to the woman selling candles, told her what my family needed and selected my purchase. The candles were all set out on a beautiful red tablecloth, embellished with gold and decorated with elephants made of black paint. The lady was trying to sell the expensive ones at the front of the table but I wanted the cheaper and smaller ones at the back. With Hoender in my hands I leaned over to have a closer look, but I was interrupted by a sharp, fiercely scolding voice.

"Excuse me Miss, your chicken is defecating on my table."

Horrified, I keeled backwards and saw a sludgy smear of watery brown liquid across the beautiful tablecloth and some of the more expensive candles. Nothing in Africa has a price; everything is done through bartering and negotiation. I was so embarrassed by my chicken's escaping diarrhoea that I asked her to give me the worst deal she possibly could. The rand vanished from my pockets like the dew on a winter's morning.

On the way home Mandela and I met on the corner of Xorile Street, and I knew that it was him well before he introduced himself.

I was fourteen, and he was forty four, and the conversation we had made me believe in love at first sight. I knew that he would come to define the rest of my life, right there and then. There is something about a small child with a newborn baby chick wrapped up in a plastic bag in her hands that was unignorable, but I knew that Hoender was not the reason he came up to me that day. I was and would forever remain absolutely convinced that he came to declare his undying love for me, one coconut to another, that intimate secret binding our hearts together for eternity. I was the apple of his eye. He had been waiting for this moment for his entire life.

"Hello, young lady."

My heart was melting with an indescribable joy. I could not believe my fortune, and I knew that I would treasure the next few seconds of conversation for the rest of my life. He reached out one of his magnificent black fingers and stroked Hoender on the head. Something about the charred blackness of his skin contrasting with the whiteness of the bird's feathers enchanted me. If she excreted again now, my life would have been over.

"Hello, Sir."

Hoender gave a sharp, shrill squawk. Mandela was taken by surprise.

"Goodness, child! Your little pet nearly made me jump out of my skin." He smiled and laughed. It was a kind smile, a knowing smile, and his heart seemed to glow within his chest.

I was laughing too. "I'm sorry Sir."

"You don't have to call me sir. My name is Nelson. What is your name?"

"Lerato Dlamini. I live on the same street as you."

"You do? What wonderful news! My house is the little one on the corner where Vilakazi joins Ngakane. Perhaps we should be friends as well as neighbours."

He shook my hand and walked away, all the while smiling broadly from ear to ear. He was singing quietly to himself as he walked away from our street on that summer afternoon, because coconuts have more soul in them than ordinary people who are either black or white. He was a magical man, with a voice which ignited the stars and sounded like a mixture between the roar of a lion and the silvery whisper of moonlight on the Highveld.

I knew that I was in love. He had won me over; he had been battering down my defences for seven years and only now did I come to realise that we were made for one another. I could not sleep, I could not eat, and my mind was flooded with him all the waking hours of my day. I yearned and longed for him more than I had done for anything else in my life. It wasn't yet a sexual obsession, for I was only fourteen, but it was difficult to focus on anything else and it was the discernable moment which every other moment of my life should be categorised as "before" or "after". It defined me and it completed me as I came to comprehend that I was not alone, for God had made me to belong to *Nelson*—for evermore I had a new name for him, an intimate name which only I would be able to use. I would never call him Mandela again. The whiteness shone from him like a lighthouse, and I knew the reason why he was so obsessed with ending Apartheid and campaigning against the Government, I knew it not in my mind but in my flesh, I *felt* the anguish of not fitting into any of the assigned categories and being subjected to a lifetime of misinterpretation. All the different races which made up our rainbow nation felt like a vast collection of Cinderella's glass slippers; not a single one was coconut-sized or Lerato-shaped. I knew and understood Nelson's pain, and I appreciated his struggle for freedom and liberty in the face of such darkness and evil.

I genuinely believed that had I never met Nelson on the corner of those streets on that summer day in Orlando West I would have given up and succumbed to the tidal wave of conformity that swept over me as Apartheid took root. Knowing that I was not alone was the oxygen that I needed to carry on with my struggle. Without me, the whole country would have been doomed. The incident with the chicken was one of the many ways that Nelson saved every South African. From that day onwards I promised that I would never call him Mandela ever again; he had personally invited me to call him by his first name in a private and intimate request which I would honour for the rest of my days. I was being personally and tenderly introduced into the inner circle of this great hero of our nation and cause, this great man who was the only one suitably positioned to end my suffering. I could feel that he wanted to relieve me of my pain, to heal me and cure me and bring an end to the injustice which was making our lives as coconuts so unendurable.

When I heard that they had jailed Mr Mandela for the second time, the bottom of my world fell away and I was left dangling into the abyss with nothing to pull me back. How could they do that? I knew why, but I didn't want to admit it; it was because he was a danger, a liability and an intimidation to the racists. He was getting in the way of their plans, an inconvenient mosquito which must be squashed quickly and brushed aside to avoid him being too much of a problem to the authority of the Apartheid government. The whispers in the community of Orlando West were that Nelson was driving back to Johannesburg with one of his allies after a political trip to Natal when his car was suddenly surrounded by police vehicles and they forced him off the road. It was the 5ᵗʰ August, 1962; I remember that it was a Sunday because my mother and I had just returned from church when the news made its way to us. It was devastating. I knew that I had to do something.

He was coming back home to Johannesburg, but this time he was coming home as a criminal in his chains. Some days later he was charged in a local magistrate's court in Egoli with numerous offences, most notably inciting workers to strike and leaving the country without possession of a valid passport. He was asked to wear a suit but instead he chose to wear a traditional leopard-skin kaross, declaring and proclaiming for the whole world to hear his own solidarity with his people, particularly those of the Transkei where he had been born, the beautiful and wonderful heritage which made him who he was. It was a middle finger at the establishment; "I am an African," his clothes bellowed, "and I will be an African publicly." He had a fantastic bravado, a great charismatic audacity to him, and he was determined to represent himself and to present the evidence for his innocence in his own unique and special way. This was Nelson's show and he was the star attraction, however he did find himself a legal adviser. This man's name was Joe Slovo.

I made it my personal mission to track down Joe Slovo and ask to present evidence for the defence in the trial of Nelson Mandela. I was uniquely positioned and I could not fail; I was, after all, a coconut and I could single-handedly stop the racists from derailing his ambitions for power and influence in the sphere of politics. If they heard me and listened to what I had to say in the dock, the men in charge of South Africa would be forced to listen up and take notice of the fact that the multiple issues concerning racism which they had raised in the policy of Apartheid were infinitely more numerous and complicated than they were ever capable of understanding.

The trial would take place in October of 1962, so Nelson's legend would have a bit of time to take root and blossom amongst his people. Support for him in Soweto at the time was enormous and it grew daily. He was our hero, our champion, our bright shining hope for a better day in Africa. Nelson and I would become a team, driving one another forwards and working hard to get rid of the baffling and confusing means of Government. I would not be left behind. I was determined that we would win, even if it was the two of us against the whole wide world.

I was permitted into the courtroom for only one day of the trial, which would be 22nd October 1962. In his opening statement to the court, I realised that as a fellow coconut of his I could understand layers of his speeches which nobody else would be able to interpret or decipher. He was whispering to me through the crowded courtroom and he was telling me the plans that he had for me, plans for our future glory together after the madness of Apartheid was over. They had denied me the right to give evidence as a keynote witness at the trial, but they could not deny me the love letter which Nelson wrote me as he spoke to me from the dock. He spoke to me as though we were alone.

"Many years ago, when I was a boy brought up in my home village in the Transkei, I listened to the elders of the tribe telling stories about the good old days, before the arrival of the white man. Then our people lived peacefully, under the democratic rule of their kings and their Amapakati, and moved freely and confidently up and down the country without let or hindrance. Then the country was ours, in our own name and right . . ."

His words trailed off as my mind closed to the wonderful sound of his voice and my imagination took flight into an endless African sky of hope and opportunity. He was not really describing the luminous Transkei in his childhood, but instead he was telling the court about his blueprint for the South Africa of his dreams, the South Africa that he would one day build for me. He was telling me that he wanted to be a king; he wanted the system of Government to be based on a monarchy such as the system which ruled the tribes of the Transkei and that he wanted the Head of State to one day be himself.

Nelson was a wise man and he would make an excellent king. He was setting down his ambition to continue an ancient tradition ingrained in the identity of Africa; nobody had a longer or prouder institution of royalty than we did. In that courtroom I cast my mind back across the millennia to the Pharaohs of Ancient Egypt, the gods in human bodies ordained to rule over their people in dynasties that spanned the centuries. I also saw the Asante Kingdom of the west with their legendary treasure of precious metals and gems; the infamous wealth of the Queen of Sheba and the audacious riches of the great royal families of Ethiopia. More recently I thought of the legendary King Shaka kaSenzangakhona of the Zulus, another King from the Transkei. Nelson couldn't fail.

Since those vile Europeans came to carve up the cake for themselves I think we have lost a lot of our reputation for razzmatazz and grandeur. This continent is the fertile womb of the world's gold and diamond supplies. This is the place where magnificent fortunes are born. With his new royal House of Mandela Nelson would now make the legendary kings of the Old Testament look like tramps. Nebuchadnezzar would be a rag-and-bone man and the renowned King David would look like a beggar on the streets of Sophiatown when confronted with Nelson in all his splendid finery. This man would be a showstopper.

"Why is it that in this courtroom I am facing a white magistrate, confronted by a white prosecutor, escorted by white orderlies?"

scolded my hero. "Can anybody honestly and seriously suggest that in this type of atmosphere the scales of justice are evenly balanced? Why is it that no African in the history of this country has ever had the honour of being tried by his own kind, by his own flesh and blood? I am a black man in a white man's court. This should not be."

Those words echoed and ricocheted through my head like a bullet from a gun for the rest of my life. *I am a black man in a white man's court.* I knew from the inflection in his voice that when he was talking about a *court* he was really talking about his soul, personality, heritage and ethnicity all at once with one substituted word. That word *court* summed up everything that made him unique, everything which was not physical about him, the part of him where the human resided. He was telling me in his own way that he was and is the same as I am; a black man in a white man's court, a coconut and an ambitious dreamer. I admired his cleverness for swapping the two halves of the phrase around so that none of the monochromes would be able to understand our own secret coded language. What he was actually saying was that he was a black man with a white man's soul; he was telling me that we were the same, that he knew how I felt and he understood the pain that I had endured for my whole life. It was an incredibly tender moment in the courtroom. I am a black woman in a white woman's court; *this should not be.* Don't believe the lies of Apartheid which vanquish the spirit of entitlement and pride, lies which declare that there is nothing wrong with the situation as it is at the moment; of everything in South Africa Nelson proudly and steadfastly declared that *this should not be.* It does not have to be this way so there is no settling or compromising to be done, no need to be seduced by the lies. There is a remedy, a cure to the injustice and the judgement, Nelson declared triumphantly, and I am it.

None of his majestic oratory was appreciated by the monochromes. For the six months after he was found guilty Nelson spent his time in jail in Pretoria. He was then handcuffed and bundled into the back of a windowless van carrying him and some other political prisoners to Cape Town, which drove without stopping for fifteen hours through the wintry night at high speed down the highways to the harbour dockyards. They were hauled out of the van and thrown into the hold of an old boat for the hour's voyage across the Bay towards the infamous and daunting destination which was no secret; it would be Robben Island, the windswept scar of land on the edge of the mighty Atlantic, a place of renowned brutality and suffering. The wardens who took charge of Nelson and his comrades would take turns to urinate on their prisoners through a manhole in the roof of the cage which they kept them in until they finally reached the island.

In all honesty I think that it took Nelson's unholy pilgrimage to Cape Town in handcuffs as an outlaw to make me realise that I had fallen in love with him. I was besotted and enraptured by the memory of the briefest of encounters with my hero, if even a hero was an adequate word to describe his matchless wonder and enthralling virtue. I was absolutely infatuated by him after meeting him just that once as a fourteen year old, then seeing him again in the courtroom where I was not allowed to testify in his defence. Every second that I had spent in his company was relived with the most delicate delight; he was my treasure, the captain piloting the course of my voyage by the patterns of the stars, the loyal guardian of my heart and the jewel in my crown. Lying in bed at night I would picture him there beside me in the darkness, grasping at his elusive black skin and moulding him into a white man beneath my fingers. We would hold each other tightly, lying in the same bed with thousands of kilometres between us, gently baring our souls to one another. The black could be seen by everyone, but the white was a precious gift just for us, tenderly uncovered with love. I was by now quite ready for marriage.

One thing that would no doubt puzzle me for the rest of my life was the question over whether or not Nelson was in control of the situations he found himself in. Was his detour via prison on the road from township to palace was a Christ-like master-plan of self sacrifice to prove his own righteousness and to make the glorious release from jail even more beautiful when the time came? It seemed like some premeditated tactic for gilding his own reputation, some

---

fanciful strategy for making his fairytale even more unforgettable when the time came. The man was a genius. His story of the journey from jail cell to throne room was at a height of superlative glory that not even the greatest of writers could dream up.

The thing which was not ambiguous was the fact that Nelson was guilty; he did not care who knew it. He was not going to bow down to the pressure of the white men who would one day bow down to him, saying the right things and answering the questions in the way they were intended to be answered just so that he could preserve his own freedom. He saw the statements that he made in the dock not as his opportunity to ensure that he would continue to be a free man nor as a chance to protest his innocence but instead to showcase his talent for oratory and as set-pieces for his political speeches to gain the attention that they deserved.

I decided that something must be done about this outrageous situation and I knew that I was uniquely positioned to be Mandela's replacement. If it meant jail, fine. If it meant the same hardship and persecution which he was facing, fine. It was an idea for which, if necessary, I was prepared to die. I knew that I had to do something, and I could not simply stand aside and let them bully us. My destiny as the leader of the ANC and the figurehead of the anti-Apartheid movement was beginning to reveal itself to me.

4

A DATE WITH HECTOR

Soweto, Transvaal Province
August 1966

In the absence of Nelson I knew what I had to do. I knew because
he would tell me regularly, nattering and chattering away across
the endless kilometres as I slept. The signals and instructions were
unignorable and he told me that the whole future of South Africa
depended fully on me. He was off in Cape Town serving out his
sentence for his perceived crimes, and the last thing that he wanted
would have been to see the struggle for Apartheid's downfall dry
up and fizzle out in a display of weakness and disappointment. Of
all the people it could have been, this coconut became the one to
realise that it could not be about just one man. We needed a team.
We needed a network, a strategically arranged group of warriors all
fighting tactically and in different areas if we were ever going to win
this war. I genuinely believed that Nelson could not achieve anything
without my help; after all, I could have saved him from jail if he had
let me. I still had not determined whether or not the jail trip was a
wonderful stunt. Just because he was in jail did not mean that the
fight was over, and now I was ready to replace him. I was angry with
Albert Lutuli for seducing me and distracting my attention when
it should have been on Nelson and I knew that I could do a far
better job of steering the ANC into power than Tambo and I would

deliver far more than his futile efforts had achieved. It was his fault we were still suffering.

Some of the more traditional members of the ANC did not like the idea of women being in charge. They did not approve of the organisation which had political ambitions being modelled differently to the blueprint of an African tribe, one which was controlled by men and supported by women. A woman stays in the kitchen and raises the children; if they work at all, they do these same jobs for other, richer women. They did not think anything of me because of the fact that I was only fourteen years old when Nelson was dragged away to jail in Cape Town. Nobody took me seriously because I was looked on as too young. I was trying to replace the mighty Nelson Mandela, who was an experienced forty-eight year old campaigner and social activist, but unfortunately an inexperienced young girl from Orlando West was not what the ANC had in mind to take their cause to the highest of heights of the Government buildings in Pretoria.

They probably could have got over their unhappiness with my age and gender if they had loved my oratory and understood that there was nobody who could have showcased the message of racial freedom better than me. Unfortunately, they hated my message and thought that I was crazy.

I became a member of the Umkhonto we Sizwe (commonly abbreviated to the MK), which translates to English as *Spear of the Nation*. It was the armed wing of the African National Congress, the militia who fought against the oppression of the Government with more than just speeches and rhetoric. The MK took over where the ANC was forced to back down, because by now political parties which opposed the Apartheid regime were banned and the only way that we had a chance of taking ownership of our destiny was to use force. Apartheid was wrong and we would do whatever it took and hurt whoever we needed to in order to make them listen to us and give us what we were entitled to. After months of persuasion I was allowed to address a political rally. It was thrilling; every breath I took was breaking the law.

"Comrades!" I began excitedly, for this was the mysterious word which all great leaders use to address their rallying troops, "I stand before you today as more than just an eighteen year old girl from Orlando West. I am a South African who is trying to regain her sense of identity and freedom which has been stolen from me by this Government and their racist agenda for the country we love."

The crowd broke out into a spontaneous applause and began to cheer for me. I had clearly said what they had wanted me to say, and my political star was rising. I could do no wrong as Nelson Mandela's appointed heir and successor, so I continued to speak with some added bravery.

"The Government wishes to segregate us into different racial categories, and to treat us with varying levels of injustice according to the colour of our skin. This, my friends, is unjustifiably wrong. Skin colour is not an indicator of virtue or goodness, and it is reprehensible to deny someone the dignity and respect they deserve by judging them by their ethnic identity."

There was another huge cheer from the crowd. People began chanting my name. My heart was swelling with pride and confidence.

"Sometimes there are mistakes with this system. It does not work, because some people are different on the inside to how they are on the outside; sometimes there is not a connection between the two. It is the height of ignorance to think that someone should be treated as a black person because they look like a black person."

The crowd began to murmur in confusion, but I wasn't really listening.

"I am a prime example of this, as is Nelson Mandela, our dear friend who is being held in a jail in Cape Town at this very moment. We are biological anomalies because we are people who have black skin and white souls. The Apartheid system has failed us because we do not fit into any of the categories that it sets out, and the system is not adequate to provide us with the identity that we deserve."

Some of the people began to boo and shout at me.

"I look at my fellow South Africans and I do not see a skin colour. I see the fact that nobody else shares the particular struggles and trials that come with being a coconut. I envy the people who have a race to belong to, a race which the Apartheid system has given them. More important than the fact that you think it is wrong is the fact that I think it does not and can never work. Apartheid is inefficient and ineffective, and it does not do the job which it sets out to achieve to an acceptable standard.

If we look across the world we will see that this nation and all of her people are far below the civilised standard which we could and should be attaining to. Racial rights are human rights. Women's rights are also human rights. Europe and America have already achieved suffrage for women, and the civil rights movement in America is gaining strength every day. I am sick and tired of Africa being a follower of the rest of the world, the last place for civilisation to touch; we should retake our rightful place as the leaders, as the innovators, and let them follow us for once. We will do away with inequality for women, and we will do away with inequality for the non-whites, but we will not stop there. We will see the task through to the end, no matter how difficult or arduous the road to enlightened justice may prove to be. This is because we are Africans and we are the very best that humanity has to offer. Africa is a leader, not a follower."

It didn't go down too well. I was shoved off the makeshift stage by Duma Nokwe.

"What are you doing, you fool? You are killing our message with every insane word that leaves your mouth. You are an embarrassing joke."

I tried to become the party leader when that moron Lutuli died in 1967; I thought that my time had come because so many of my rivals had been forced into exile or prison. I would not be challenged by Zuma, Hani or Mbeki. I thought that becoming leader would be easy but some monochrome pretender named Oliver Tambo beat me to it. Everyone said "sorry for you" as they sent me on my way, but I would make him deeply sorry for leading the ANC without being a coconut. When Nelson was taken away I thought that my calling was to lead the ANC so that I could free him and every other black South African, but it seemed clear now that because of Tambo I would need another plan.

* * *

Wednesday 16th June 1976 began like any other day, but by the end of it we knew that our lives had changed forever. South Africa would never be the same again. At this time I was working as a cleaner at Baragwanath Hospital, helping out the ward sisters with the sanitation and making sure the offices were in tidy and clean. Baragwanath was a massive complex of former military buildings converted into what was rumoured to be the world's largest hospital and medical centre. We had over two thousand patients checking in every day and more than half of these people were in urgent need of medical attention.

That morning I had a later shift at the hospital and my father had a day off from his job at the mine so we were able to eat our breakfast together as a family. The hot orange sunshine was streaming in through the window as I looked out on the world. It was a beautiful day.

We were disturbed by a commotion on the road outside our house. I looked out to see a vast crowd of people coming over the brow of the hill, marching in the direction of Orlando Stadium. I looked heavenwards and saw the birds fleeing the scene; the whole Earth seemed to be groaning and it was extremely clear that something monumental was about to occur.

I asked Nelson what was happening. "I came home," was his cryptic response. I asked him again to explain to me why the people were marching. Again he simply said to me "I came home."

Realisation dawned on me with a wonderful rush of euphoria. Nelson Mandela had been set free; today would be the day that freedom finally became ours. I knew that we would always remember what happened on 16th June 1976—for me, today would be my wedding day. In my rags I flung open the door of our house and sprinted down Vilakazi Street, closing my eyes as I did so. My spirit sang like a bird in a cage of darkness.

"Get out of the way," I yelled at the well-wishers who had come to celebrate with us. "I have to get to the front of the procession to climb into Nelson's motorcade."

The red dust was growing thicker between my toes as I ran. I could imagine it long before I arrived on the scene; Nelson would be triumphantly parading through the streets in a magnificent procession of military pomp and ceremony, at the centre-point of the motorcade in an open-top silver Mercedes-Benz 600, the choice limousine of all African statesmen. In my head he looked a little like Idi Amin of Uganda, standing proudly in a green military uniform with his chest heaving with golden medals as he waved to the crowd.

At the end of the road up ahead I saw a line of policemen. They were dressed in riot gear and they had guns and weapons. How wonderful! Nelson had arranged for the security services to protect me as he whisked me off to our wedding. They were guarding the released prisoner—or maybe they had come to join the party! My King was so kind to me.

As I ran towards the policemen they refused to let me through. "Stand aside, you fools! I am here to meet with the King!"

One of the men threw me to the ground and laughed at me. "There is no King here."

"I have come to marry Nelson Mandela. Let me through."

The policeman stopped being angry and looked at me in confusion and shock. "Do you even know why these people are here? They are protesting about the law which means that all teachers will have to speak Afrikaans in schools. Nelson Mandela is still in jail."

Soweto was a bubbling cauldron of hatred and resentment of the Apartheid system and the unfair rules which were forced upon the people as a result. The final straw for the blacks was the fact they were forced to learn Afrikaans, a foreign and predominantly white language, in their schools to tie in with the reformation laws wanted by the racists. The people of Soweto were outraged by what they were being forced to do and saw it as an attack on their culture and heritage of which language was a very clear and proud indicator.

There can be nothing more emotive, in a nation as beautifully diverse as I am, than one culture trying to swallow up another.

I just so happened to be fluent in Afrikaans, and I loved to speak it at every opportunity I was given. This proved to be problematic for those who had mistaken the war on Apartheid and what it represented for a war on Afrikaans as a language and culture which they identified me with. I loved the way that the words of the language felt on my tongue, the sugary taste of the syllables as sweet as guava juice as it cooled and soothed my throat. Afrikaans was the cure for my coconut syndrome, and when I spoke the language of the white man I felt intricately connected by my spirit to the people who were truly mine, and I felt a sense of identity and acceptance coupled with the frustration of being trapped within a body that did not belong to me. It was a trancelike state as the words germinated in my throat and I gave birth to them through my mouth, the music of a language which was exotic and soothingly familiar all at the same time giving it an almost hypnotic appeal.

By the age of twenty eight I was able to speak fluently in eleven different languages; Afrikaans, English, Xhosa, Zulu, Sesotho, Swazi, Tswana, Ndebele, Venda, Sepedi and Tsonga. The white languages have always been the ones I find the easiest; attaining fluency in the traditional tribal languages caused me considerably more difficulty. Many of these languages are widely spoken by a number of people in the Transvaal, but whilst it was very common for people to be multilingual it was almost unheard of for people to be able to speak the same number of languages as me. I was the special one, a person with an almost unrivalled talent for languages and I took this as evidence to prove the truth of the condition which I found myself suffering from. My writing was always something that I struggled with in my youth and I was unable to read coherently and fluently, but having a conversation in any one of those languages made me feel like a bird that had had the chains of frustration broken off and was now free to fly into an enormous and limitless sky. The black languages were spoken by my skin, involuntary utterances and instinctive creaking groans from my body. The white languages, notably English and Afrikaans, were instead the utterances of my soul, the entrancing music of my spirit which was yearning and striving to be released from the black tomb in which I was encased.

To think that the Soweto Uprising was about Afrikaans being taught in schools would be missing the point. It wasn't about that at all. It was an issue of freedom, or lack of it; an issue about the way in which we would subject ourselves to our Government and their racist restrictions, our response to their repeated subliminal messages that people should be judged and categorised by the colour of their skin and that one of these categories was intrinsically superior to all of the rest. It was about deciding that enough was enough and refusing to take it any more.

I was not a student at a school, and I was not being forced to learn Afrikaans against my will. I was not unhappy with the status of the language in classrooms in Soweto, but that does not mean that I was not unhappy with the way my country was being run. I was furious, hysterical and deeply wounded by the actions of the Government which had failed me so spectacularly. It was true enough that they failed all of the black people in South Africa, but I felt that Apartheid was not their biggest and gravest crime. It was not the fact that looked unfavourably upon blacks, but instead that they were willing to enforce such aggressive racial policies without even being able to tell what colour a person was, that instead of a proper and fair categorisation process I had been so badly let down by being identified as a member of a race to which I did not belong. How could it be that the racists were colour-blind? These people were desperate for the oxygen of freedom and did not want to stand for being misrepresented any more.

Some of the students reached down to the road and picked up stones to throw at the officers as soon as they saw them but they were quickly scolded by the majority of the campaigners and the group moved on peacefully, not rising to the bait of the police and holding on to their determination to keep this a peaceful protest. Some of the group continued to throw their stones, and after a few seconds of trying to shield himself one of the officers fired a shot from his handgun directly into the part of the crowd where I stood. The shot caused chaos and pandemonium.

For a couple of seconds I was hypnotised into a trancelike state somewhere between life and death as well as the usual blur of black and white. I did not know for what felt like a very long time whether or not I had been hit by the bullet, and I intermittently dreamed of the infamy that I would receive as the first death on the final day of Apartheid, but it turned out that the infamy was not destined to be mine. I snapped my head around to one side and I saw a man carrying a young boy in his arms, the stricken torso and the broken limbs losing their strength with every passing second. A little girl was with them, running alongside as they tried to find some medical help; slowly it became clear to me that the boy had been hit by the policeman's bullet and that he was dying. I was still standing as I was being carried upright on a tidal wave of human bodies as the crowd surged forwards. I looked down at my abdomen, expecting to see vast ribbons of white blood unfurling onto the ochre dust road, but my brown coconut shell was still intact and I had not been struck by the gunman.

Hector Pietersen began that day as an insignificant nobody, but he ended it as the most famous boy in the world. He was the first person killed that day in the final uprising against Apartheid, slain by a policeman's bullet dealt out in hatred. I was terrified to have been caught up in it all.

Within moments the whole township had vomited an explosion of blood. People had scattered and were running in all directions, screaming and throwing stones at the officers, and as they surged forwards the police began to fire more shots into the crowd. All of the calmness and the peaceful and resolute demands for a breakthrough had been lost in the time that it took to fire the gun which killed Hector Pieterson.

I was absolutely petrified by the violence which I witnessed on the streets of Orlando West; soon the carnage was engulfing the whole of Soweto, with millions of people forming a huge mob and turning on anyone who they deemed to be responsible for the injustice faced by South Africa's underdogs. There was a particularly grisly incident where a white man was stoned to death and a sign hung around the neck of his corpse which read "Beware Afrikaners".

The problem with this was that he turned out to be Dr Melville Edelstein, a man who had passionately campaigned for all of his life for social welfare among blacks, the same blacks who had smashed his skull with rocks simply because he had white skin. How am I to begin to fight the prejudice against coconuts given this level of madness and senselessness; how safe would I be as a fluent Afrikaans speaker with black skin and a white soul?

That was when I realised that I needed to leave Soweto and the Transvaal behind and make my way to Cape Town where they had taken Nelson to be entombed on his island in the Atlantic. The city beckoned and called me home and I could not stay. Don't worry, Mr Mandela. I am coming to rescue you, to charge your fortress and carry you off into the night in order for you to experience for the first time the delirious ecstasy of true and limitless freedom. I had to leave; I had no choice. I could not simply leave him there whilst the whole nation collapsed under hatred and anger, injustice and violence.

Besides, my plan could not fail. Nelson wanted to marry me and given that he was destined for the throne, I would one day become Queen. I will never forget the following day, the seventeenth of June, as the one that I told my father of my dastardly, brave and heroic scheme.

"I am going to rescue Nelson Mandela from jail on Robben Island in Cape Town."

"Oh yes?" He chuckled. "You have the keys to the prison, I assume?"

That response seemed to summarise so much. It was that disgusting apathy that had plagued people into accepting their fate, the tendency to dismiss any suggestion of a better life as a ridiculous and comical piece of deluded lunacy. He thought that there was nothing to be done about the trampling of one race by another. But wait! *This should not be.*

"No. I am proof that Apartheid can never work and when they see me they will take me seriously and they will listen to my request and will free him themselves. We will have a new country, a free country and Nelson I will be our new King."

My father laughed in my face. My mother was so stunned by what she was hearing that she dropped her wooden spoon into the potje and stood in a gasping, hushed silence.

"Lerato, have you gone completely mad?"

My father interjected before I could respond to her. "What are you talking about, Gloria? She's been mad her whole life. This is nothing new." I ignored him and carried on talking to her as if he did not exist.

"No, mommy, I am serious. I am leaving for Cape Town. I came to say goodbye."

"What makes you think that you are the one who can end Apartheid?"

"Like I have always told you, I am a white woman but I have a black body. The two simply do not fit together. Nelson Mandela is the same, he is the other example of the condition that I have. Because he is in prison, he needs me to go and use my freedom in ways that he cannot so that our cause is heard and respected."

My father chuckled dismissively again. He had heard many a lecture from me about my skin condition in the past but I had never verbalised the link between Nelson and I. Whilst most fathers were concerned with their children secretly experimenting with the clothing of the opposite sex my own father had spent my childhood trying to stop me finding pots of white paint which I would use to bleach my skin. In his opinion this was just the latest in a long line of fanatical episodes in my life and he assumed that it would pass as quickly as it had come about. It had been his strategy before, and it had worked. My mother was much more concerned with my sudden assuredness of my destiny in Cape Town and my connection with Nelson, joined at the skin like racial Siamese twins. Having said that, it was clear that she did not believe a word I said.

"Don't you think you could be misinterpreting Mr Mandela's beliefs and ethics? Do you have any proof that he agrees with you, that he thinks the same things about both of your bodies that you do?"

"We recognise it in each other. I can feel it in my perfectly white bones."

"How are you going to get to Cape Town?"

"I will make my way from place to place, getting a job in each town until I have the money I need to move onwards. I will use whatever methods I need to; I will walk, I will hitchhike, I will catch the train, I will take the bus, perhaps use a minibus taxi when I need to. Whatever it takes, I will get there. I must get there. He needs me and every other black South African needs me."

"She's lying again," my father said frivolously. "It's another deluded fantasy of hers. I've heard it all before."

My mother sat in a dumbfound state of shock and bewilderment. She could not believe what she was hearing, but I knew that my parents both needed me to go as well even though they were not aware of it. One day they would realise their enormous ignorance.

"Lerato," my exhausted mother began, "even if you were right, you have to understand that Mandela was put in prison for criticising and opposing the Government because he used violence to get people to listen to him. That should tell you that either you are going to be jailed in exactly the same way that he was or you will try to do it peacefully, explaining your point, and nobody will listen to you. If there was a middle ground, a way to get noticed without getting jailed for it, Mandela would have achieved it by now."

"He needs me to help him achieve it. He cannot do it without me."

"Yes he can. If it is possible to do, I don't think that you are that difference, that driving force which will make it happen."

"You are wrong."

"Do you know how to get to Cape Town?"

"No."

"You have no map?"

"No."

"How will you even get to Robben Island? Is there a ferry?"

"No."

"That should trouble you."

"Well, it doesn't. I don't need your advice or your approval, but instead I know that what I am doing is vitally important to the future of this nation. It cannot exist and improve and evolve until I make it to Cape Town and hammer on the door of the jail and they let him go. I know that I will make it; I *must* make it. I don't know how, but I know that I will and that is all I need to know to take that first leap of faith. I love you both, but South Africa and Nelson both need me too much."

I had never threatened to leave before the seventeenth of June, and that was the first time that I had revealed my intention to pursue Nelson Mandela's freedom by travelling to Cape Town, but we had talked about me being a coconut many times before this. Needless to say, I was completely alone and not even my parents would bring themselves to believe my perfectly rational and truthful account. They put my "racial identity issues" down to the difficulty that I must have had adjusting to the life of an orphan adopted into a family who did not plan to have me. I have been told many times that I was struggling even though I did not feel that it was true; it felt a lot more like the problem lay with other people who couldn't see what colour I was. Mom had always told me that the stories I would tell her about my "real" straight blonde hair and blue eyes were clear signs of delusion and perhaps even mental illness, a sure indicator that I could not recognise my body as my own. My father suggested that I was obsessed with Nelson Mandela and that I should go to a witch doctor to rid me of the evil spirit lurking within. At times throughout my childhood this misunderstood coconut felt like the only one in the world who could see the truth, the only one in the world who could see a tortured misfit waiting for medical science to catch up with her rather than the deluded and insane psycho that I appeared to people who did not understand my condition. I have learnt through so much misunderstanding to survive without the need for others to trust my testimony as truthful, so as the reader of this book you may accept or dismiss my account as you please. It matters little to me; I don't care if you think I am a crazy liar. I am telling you my story so that you may know the truth of how South Africa came to be free.

Our nation had one of the highest unemployment rates in the world. Just like everything else the statistics fell on only one side of the racial divide which separated so much; it was estimated that one in every four South Africans was unemployed and that figure was much higher among the black population. In black townships like the ones we had always lived in the figure could rise to an astonishing eighty five percent, but places such as Soweto near Johannesburg and Gugulethu in Cape Town held no accurate records of who was living there because new shacks were being built all the time and there were an uncountable number of homes which housed multiple generations of the same family. One thing which really worried and intimidated me was the prospect of not being able to find work, not being able to find any employer who would be willing to take me on and be willing to pay me a wage which would go towards the costs of my journey across the country. The future of a free South Africa rested with them and their willingness to pay me, but I was afraid that they would not recognise their duty to democracy and humanity as it nestled amongst the hundreds of other applications for the same job. I had no idea which direction my life would take from this point on, no idea what job I would be doing or where the next meal would be coming from, and I could not work out if that was an unrivalled and brilliant opportunity for adventure or a terrifying abyss of insecurity and mystery which would be the cause of a great deal of stress and tension for years to come.

5

DIAMOND DIGGERS

Kimberley, Cape Province
June 1976

Somewhat unbelievably, I was on my way. I had nothing with me and I had no idea which route I would take to get there, but I had managed to escape. I would soon be in Cape Town standing at the doors of Robben Island maximum security prison, and I would be embracing Nelson as he finally stepped out into the sunshine as a free man. It would be a glorious moment and one that would go down in the history of the nation and the memory of the world as the greatest human rights activist who ever lived was finally set free. With my help he could achieve it and he would be out of jail by Christmas at the latest, and I could see the headlines in my mind as the train thrust ceaselessly forwards: "Nelson Mandela, Free at Last, the end of Apartheid in 1976." I couldn't even begin to fathom how unimaginably wonderful that moment would taste when it eventually came.

The truth was that he had already been waiting for me and we both knew it. He would lie awake in his cell on the island, his home for the last fourteen years, listening to the crashing of the waves of Table Bay as he dreamt of me, wishing for the day when I would wash up on his shore. I flooded his head and he could not let me go any more than I could abandon and forsake him now that I had committed myself to him so completely. His every waking thought was filled with that encounter on the streets of Orlando West and now, at last, he knew for sure that I was coming to get him. He could rest easily, safe in the knowledge that his freedom was imminent.

This was my very first time on a train, the first of many new experiences that I was sure to encounter on my journey across South Africa. The carriages were all stretched out in a long, singular line behind a massive locomotive, a huge chunk of gleaming, shining metal which throbbed with the energy of the furious furnace in its belly. It was covered in pipes and ducts, dials and tubes which stretched across the surface of the engine like a network of capillaries and veins under the skin. The locomotive was one of those things which hovered between organism and machine, a vast and breathing metal animal with lungs of hissing steam, a stomach filled with charcoal and a heart which burned brightly and sent power and energy surging through the metal body.

The noises of the station were very unfamiliar; the shrill whistles of trains; the screeching breath of the steam pistons of the locomotives; the clanking of carriages being tethered together or separated. There was also the usual chatter and hubbub of any large public place which was constantly seeing a huge number of people pass through. The whole thing was bewildering and exhilarating all at the same time. As I crossed the station concourse I saw the boiler-men from the trains ending their shifts and walking towards the exits in groups as they chattered. Their already black faces were scorched with the soot from the furnace of the train. The whole station was an overwhelming crucible of human activity. I found the tellers behind the little windows in their immaculate uniforms far more splendid than my one from Baragwanath, and I stood in the line, behind all of the other people who did this every day. For me, though, buying a train ticket was a once in a lifetime experience. I stood at the back of the line, and a couple of white people who arrived after I did muscled their way past me and I was forbidden by law to resist. When I finally arrived at the desk I saw that the teller was white, and he scanned the concourse behind me to make sure that there were no white people being inconvenienced by him serving me. An elderly white lady came forward and the teller spoke to her as though I simply did not exist. Once she had bought her ticket, I was allowed to proceed with my purchase.

"Yes madam?" the man said. He didn't seem thrilled by the honour of my presence.

"I have one hundred rand," I declared proudly, "and I need to get to Cape Town by the end of the day. I am on an extremely important journey."

The man laughed at me. "No madam, that isn't going to be enough to take you all the way to Cape Town. You'll need to give me more money than a hundred."

My face fell, and I was distraught. I did not want to waste any time, and Nelson needed me.

"Where is the furthest station that I can get to with this money?"

He picked up a chart from his desk and I saw that it was a list of fares and destinations.

"If you pay me a hundred," he said, "you can buy a ticket to Kimberley."

"But that is only halfway there, and this is all the money that I have. Please sir, I am a poor cleaner in Baragwanath Hospital and I am on a very important journey."

"I'm sorry madam but that is the furthest that you can get with the amount of money that you're offering me. You need to make up your mind, there are other people waiting and you are wasting my time."

I was so disappointed. Did he not know that Nelson required my immediate assistance, and that he was sick and tired of waiting after fourteen long and unhappy years? Did he not know the enormous importance of what was resting on me? I could not give up, and I could not bring myself to stand aside.

"Sir, if you knew the nature of my journey you would give me a ticket to Cape Town in exchange for the very reasonable money that I am offering you."

The man looked up at me with a look of contempt and smiled mockingly. "Well then in that case would you mind telling me the nature of your journey to Cape Town?"

I lowered my voice and I leaned in towards the window of the booth so that I could whisper through it to him. "I am going to release Nelson Mandela."

His face turned the colour of ash, and he realised for a split second the truth of the fact that I was a valuable asset to the ANC and that I was conspiring with a man he deemed to be a terrorist and a murderer. The man looked as though he was nervous that he may have assisted my dangerous and illegal passage and was worried about the consequences for himself. I could see and feel his thoughts as they swam across the jelly of his brain. I contemplated running away, realising too late that it was a mistake to disclose the information because our enemies might impede my journey further by questioning me over this outrageous statement, but it seemed that his reaction of horror was very brief. That was the end of the dream, it was all over. Perhaps I would be arrested and sent away to jail in Cape Town and in my head I began to formulate the speeches that I would make there, but I needn't have worried about it. He burst out laughing, and swung back on his chair as he whooped and shrieked with euphoric hilarity. He shouted my story to the rest of the tellers in the office and they laughed at me too, and all of the passengers began pointing at me and screaming with laughter. I heard them joking about my delusional nature in Afrikaans and English.

"Madam I really do have to hand it to you; I have heard many excuses of people trying to buy tickets that they cannot afford, but that has to be the most outlandish thing that anyone has ever dared to say to me. You're going to save Nelson Mandela? You're the person that he has been waiting for, the one who is going to be able to spring him from his jail cell when everyone else in the ANC has failed? You think you're so special? That is the stupidest thing I have ever heard in my entire life."

"Will you give me the ticket for my bravery?"

His face fell once again.

"No," he spat.

"When the ANC takes power and Nelson Mandela is King I will ensure that you are very well remembered and provided for in gratitude for your help."

He glared at me. "Nelson Mandela will never be released. Wake up, nigger."

I didn't know what the word meant, but I could only assume that it was something synonymous with stupidity. I spent all of the money that I had on that one way ticket to Kimberley; all of those hours of hard work in Baragwanath were translated into a single piece of paper that I held in my hand in a station in the middle of the city. I took my seat on the first train which was leaving Johannesburg and with a flutter in my soul I saw that it was heading for Cape Town. I boarded with a swollen heart and found myself inside a train carriage for the first time in my life. After it had passed through Kimberley, this very carriage and my very seat would continue on across the country to reach the place where they were holding Nelson, the steam from the locomotive seeping in through the bars of his cell that I would one day make a museum detailing his journey from prisoner to Emperor.

The layout of the carriage that I was sitting in made such a profound impact on me that I remembered every freckle and wrinkle on every one of my fellow passengers for the rest of my life. I could see very clearly from the carriage that transportation was just as segregated as the rest of society; this was not a white person's train. I was the only white person in the history of the nation who had travelled by public transport. I had never been outside of the Johannesburg conglomeration before and the train was thrusting me further and further into the blank spaces on the edge of the map, and perhaps soon I would tumble off the periphery into oblivion. The billowing smoke coming from the funnel of the locomotive smelt just as strongly of adventure as it did of burnt coal; this was my time to push the boat out, to blow away the cobwebs, to leap into Africa's endless blue skies and to fill my fingers with her luminous, radiant red soil. I was grabbing life by the dangly bits and I was changing the world in my own special way, and with every footstep I took

towards Cape Town King Nelson's throne came that little bit closer
to being a firm and beautiful reality. Travel was an incomprehensibly
wonderful thing to behold. As the train rumbled forward I could
feel in the lobes of my brain that my universe was stretching and
expanding. Just as my parents had feared, I had absolutely nothing
that resembled a plan and I was completely out of money. I did not
know which route I would take, or how many stops I would need to
make, or what I would encounter on my journey to find Nelson and
exhume him from his ghastly living tomb. Perhaps I would reach
the coastline of the Garden Route and dip my fat black toes in the
Indian Ocean for the first time. Maybe I would watch the sun set
across the sea and see some variation of the thick clouds of red dust
which would smother the dusk in Johannesburg. Perhaps I would
see a lion and feel the thunder of a mighty river. Maybe I would
see a waterfall and walk in a tropical jungle. Maybe I would fall in
love with the locals, and Africa would show me just how splendidly
marvellous humanity really was. The whole journey, more than a
thousand kilometres even by the most direct of routes, stretched
out before me with a magnificently hedonistic sense of adventure,
opportunity and promise.

The golden plateau of the highveld is a place which is impossible
to describe to anyone who has never been there, with its unique
wintry mix of blazing sunshine and clear skies, yellow grasses and
soil of deep and rich ochre; the world outside of Transvaal was just
as bewilderingly unfamiliar to me. It became incomprehensible to
me that there was such a large amount of world to be explored and
I had become a woman of twenty eight without ever leaving South
Africa's northernmost province. I had never seen the ocean, and I
had never climbed a mountain. I had occasionally been into the
centre of Johannesburg but our movements were restricted because
of the colour of our skin, so my family had spent most of our time
either in Sophiatown or in Soweto. As the train rumbled forwards
my unexplored world became smaller and my imagination and my
experience of being alive expanded dramatically. If the universe was
a book, I had suddenly and wonderfully learned how to turn the

pages for the first time and Nelson had taught me to read all the words.

The journey to Kimberley was extremely long and the little train took forever to span the first half of the trip to Cape Town. It was swallowed up by the enormousness of the vast landscape which spread in every direction. The soil in the fields was as red as Hector's blood and each one seemed to throb and pulsate as the hissing pistons of the train thrust the locomotive onwards. That day, the 18th June 1976, was a wonderful day to be alive.

As the train pulled in at Kimberley, I had a glorious thought flash through my head. This train was going straight to Cape Town and I was probably halfway there by now. What would happen if I stayed on the train and I didn't step down onto the platform with the other passengers? How would my life be different if I decided not to alight the train and instead continue on as a stowaway, bounding onwards towards Cape Town with a blistering haste to wrench Nelson from his cell and to exalt him heroically to the very summit of enlightened power? He deserved nothing less. I was not a particularly sensible or predictable person and yet the fact that I did not have a ticket that extended further than Kimberley terrified me.

As the train shuddered to a halt, one of the passengers opened the old door which creaked noisily into the evening. This was the moment which the whole nation rested on. Did I dare become a stowaway and rush onwards through the night with the pounding pressure of the locomotive echoing across the arid interior of the country and the rich steam rising serenely into the starlit sky? Did I dare continue onwards to Cape Town and deal with whatever inconvenient consequences came my way when I arrived, taking the law into my own hands if necessary? I chickened out and I got off the train.

My life on the road had begun.

There was a job in a diamond mine for a laundry-maid to wash the miners' uniforms, and I applied. How hard could it be? I would simply have to shovel the vast amounts of laundry powder into the industrial scale machines, and fold and press and work on my feet for the day—to me that was easy work. Being at the mine, even in the laundry on the surface where none of the mining was actually done, was an extraordinary experience and when compared to my life in the townships of Johannesburg it was like landing on another planet. I was so immeasurably far from home and every second was a thrill.

I would hand the clean uniforms to the men in paper bags as they emerged from the tunnels and made their way back to the dormitories. If there is a Hell, surely the entrance must look something like this. The tunnel was hot and dark, crude and ugly. I could hear the roar of the machinery slow and calm to a gentle hum; feel the pulsating shudder of the heavy drills; see the glistening wet rock faces which sparkled with the valuable potential, the glittering mineral for which they were searching.

On my first day I was standing at the entrance to the mine and after the first few men arrived I accidentally dropped the pile of clean shirts into the mud. The black oil from the men's boots stained the white linen and this distressed me greatly. A lot of the men stood around waiting for me to pick them up but one of the men got on his hands and knees and helped me. After an uncomfortable silence, he spoke.

"What is your name, Miss?"

"Lerato Dlamini. I am a laundry-maid and today is my first day of work."

The man smiled at me and I smiled back. I asked him his name.

"Blessings Mngomezulu."

"How long do you plan to stay here in Kimberley, Lerato?"

"Not long. I must get to Cape Town."

"Why?"

"I can't tell you that."

Blessings gave me a look of confusion and wonder. His dark eyes were wide, deep and beautiful.

"Why can't you tell me your reason?"

"Because it is a matter of national security."

He went silent. The questioning stopped. He took his shirt and he walked away.

I saw a lot of that same miner. Wherever possible we would eat together in the canteen at lunchtimes and I would begin to slip notes into his shirts for him to find. I needed a friend, a companion in Kimberley who was on my side, but I didn't expect him to return my advances quite as quickly as he did. It all happened with a dizzying speed; he told me that he was lonely and that he had been waiting for me to come along. One night after work, as we were sitting together at the top of the hill and looking down over the lights of the city of Kimberley spread out far below, Blessings took hold of my hand. I let him do it, but I wasn't really sure why. I tried as hard as I could to save myself for Nelson, but Blessings seemed to have taken a shine to me. He became my best friend. I relished in him and I was so thankful that on the first stop of this epic journey I had found a person in whose company I was completely happy. It felt so wonderful after a long day in the mine to talk to a like-minded individual like him.

One day in December there was an accident at the mine. Profit was king here and there was very little in the way of safety regulation to protect the miners deep below the ground. Blessings told me the details; I had been in the laundry and I had not heard the explosion. The first that I had heard of it was when I noticed smoke coming out of the entrance to the mine and saw some of the miners running in the opposite direction as fast as they could. Forty eight men were killed that day.

Blessings told me about it later on. In his voice I could hear the beams falling, the terrifying sound of the earth crushing in all around him and the stifling air becoming hot and still. It was clearly a huge trauma for him and because of it he began to attach himself to me. We talked and talked. Is there any better way to spend time than in the intimate company of a friend? Finally he realised the thing about me which should be extremely obvious.

"You know, you're not the same as the other girls here, Lerato."

This statement made me more thankful and glad than I could ever express. Had he been planted in this diamond mine by Nelson himself to meet me here? I marvelled at the coincidental nature of this new companion of mine being a prophet and a fortune-teller.

How was it that he could see through my skin like no other man could? I pretended that I had not realised his marvellous secret as I revealed my own to him because I wanted to see his reaction.

"I have a secret to tell you, Blessings Mngomezulu."

His eyes brightened like a sunrise to tell me that he was listening.

"I am a coconut."

"Excuse me?"

Well there you go. That was the end of that little fantasy; I had become extremely accustomed to having my dreams shattered on a regular basis and disappointment was as natural to me as the cycles of the moon. This man was not a prophet but a demented idiot, a vile cheekyprawn. Why should he know all there was to know about being in the wrong body? How could he know how it felt? How could he feel the emotion and the symbolic power of who I am? How could he predict all of the things that were promised to me in that one word that I use to identify myself?

"I am a coconut. I am black on the outside but I am white on the inside."

"Do you mean that you can speak English?"

"It's not a metaphor, Blessings," I spat at him, slightly frustrated with the way that he was misunderstanding my words. I was accustomed to confusion from people who I was sharing my secret with but for some reason I had always thought that he would be different. "My skin is not the same colour as my soul. I was born into the wrong body."

"How do you know?"

"I just do. I know it like you know that the sun will come up tomorrow morning. I know it like you know we are all made for a reason and that fate guides our lives. I know as surely as we know that the stars are made of fire even though we have never voyaged to them. It's all about faith; it's the unseen things which we know for certain to be true."

He seemed fairly impressed with my response and he had a broad smile on his face throughout everything that I said. I knew that this was because he believed every word I said and he was admiring my clear logic and flawless rationalism.

"Is that why you're going to Cape Town?"

"Yes." My eyes darted around feverishly. "You must keep this a secret, Blessings. Nobody can know." He swore to secrecy, so with a plunging sense of trust which drenched every cell in my body, I told him my plan as concisely as I could. My bloodstream was charged with an electric thrill; telling him about my destiny was the most exhilarating experience of my life.

"I am going to use my status as a coconut to end Apartheid in South Africa by freeing Nelson Mandela from Robben Island Jail in Cape Town. They will listen to me and they will realise that they were wrong to be racist. Once Nelson Mandela is free, he will change the course of this nation's history and he will become King of South Africa."

His grin broadened and he opened his mouth wide; I thought that he was going to laugh but instead he began to speak.

"Can I come with you?"

I looked at him as though he was delusional and a little bit insane. Why on Earth would he want to come with me? What would possess him to accompany me all the way to Cape Town? And then it hit me as though it was the most obvious thing in the world and I silently scolded myself for not thinking of it before I did.

"Are you a coconut too?"

His face was perfectly composed and he did not laugh at me. "No. I'm sorry Lerato, I'm black through and through, from top to bottom, from skin to bone."

"Then for what other reason would you want to come with me?"

He smiled at me like a sunbathing warthog. "I have reasons of my own to get to Cape Town." He continued but I can't remember what he said; in good time he got back to the important matter. "Your mission to save Nelson Mandela sounds like the most wonderful adventure. I know of a coal wagon which is heading for Bloemfontein first thing in the morning. Perhaps we could hitch a ride?"

"But Bloemfontein is the wrong way. The wagon will be heading southeast, and we need to be going southwest."

"Every time we get an opportunity to get somewhere else, we should take it. We'll stay in the nearest town, hopping from place to place to get jobs like you said we would, but it doesn't matter too much if the towns are not on the shortest route. We need the journey to be short on time rather than distance. You never know, we may be able to make a direct journey from Bloemfontein to Cape Town and we'll be there before we know it. The journey will be quick but it won't be logical or direct."

Blessings Mngomezulu had a wonderful spontaneity about him that I can only put down to the accident in the diamond mine. He wanted to live a little more because of his brush with death and destruction. He was not scared of dying but he was terrified at the thought of his life ending before he ever saw Cape Town, swam in the sea or climbed a mountain peak. His spirit was so full of awe and wonder at the prospect of a journey across this great nation of ours, a great nation ruined by racism and injustice. He never considered the virtue of the reasons for doing something but considered instead the substance of the reasons against doing it and if he was unable to find anything to suitably convince himself, it would be done without delay. If there was freedom to be found we would find it and if there was life to be lived we would see it. If it was true, if we were really standing together on the cusp of a new nation and a promised land built on freedom and equality then Nelson, Blessings and I would step into it together. We would be first, followed by forty million others. Our hopes were set on the high plateau of Table Mountain and the glorious new beginning that I would win for all South Africans. A new day was coming.

6

THE WRONG RING

Bloemfontein, Orange Free State Province
January 1978

On the way to Bloemfontein Blessings asked me to marry him, which meant that I had a decision to make. I knew that I loved Nelson, and that I had sworn to myself that I would one day marry him and become his Queen when he finally vanquished the old enemy of Apartheid and claimed South Africa's throne as his own righteous property. I enjoyed Blessings' company, undoubtedly, but he had none of the magic of Nelson, none of the gleaming charisma and the towering stature of the statesman-to-be who was waiting for me to rescue him.

The journey to Bloemfontein was not an easy one, almost 180km on a minor road called the R64. It was bumpy and extremely poorly maintained. The driver of the coal wagon was very friendly, and he merrily chatted to us about life in Kimberley as we headed southeast. He would smile like a buffalo having a mudbath as he gesticulated to enhance his story, in the same way as seasoning enhances the flavours of a braai.

I knew that Nelson would not want to share me with anyone, and that was a difficult concept to stomach. I hoped that by maintaining my relationship with Blessings I would not jeopardise any shot at glory that I would be given once I had single handedly released the prisoner who would one day be King of a new nation. I knew that just as he was waiting for me, chained up in the island in the ocean and lashed by wind and rain day and night, I must also wait for him. I had need of a husband, both emotionally and economically, and I did not think that I could make it to Cape Town alone even though the cruel irony of it all was that that the reason I was going was to be with the love of my life, the man who was made for me.

Nelson was already married, but I did not let that small detail stop me from hatching a dastardly plan. I heard that the name of my predecessor as his wife was Winnie. She was the same as he was, a brave champion of the struggle against Apartheid, but she was not quite at the glorious summit of humanity and of enough merit to be called the third coconut. I had heard unfounded whispers that she had tortured children, and for that I hated her, but I hated her firstly and mostly for daring to wed the man reserved for me. Given that Nelson was married, I thought that he would not mind too much if I had a marriage of convenience of my own. I did not love Blessings but there was no denying that I needed him; we could be a team, a partnership, a duo who would one day manage to span South Africa and make it to the jail in time to release my hero. Surely it was infinitely better to arrive with a husband than to not arrive at all? I tried to picture in my head the motives that he may have had for marrying Winnie when he knew perfectly well that we were destined to be together and that I was on my way to rescue him, but I could not come to any sensible or logical conclusion. It didn't make any sense to me, and the confusion wounded me deeply. He had hurt me, and therefore I did not think that he was qualified to be disappointed if I arrived in Cape Town with a husband in tow. I would dump Blessings by the side of the road the minute that Nelson snapped his fingers and summoned me, of course, but would that be enough? Would Winnie and Blessings form some kind of demonic team and partnership to overthrow King Nelson and Queen Lerato in a violent military coup? Would our fortress at the Castle of Good Hope be able to withstand the charge of the cavalry led by the ousted spouses, their eyes blazing a fiery red and their stallions prancing as they lead their armies into battle? As I pictured and felt the sensation of burying myself in Nelson's arms in terror as we stood in the highest turret waiting for the revolutionaries to storm the castle and wrench the glittering crowns from our heads, I knew that I needed a stronger plan than the one I had. How could I use Blessings to be beneficial to the mission without having to endure the inconvenience of falling in love with him?

Throughout all of this I had to keep an eye on the line of succession to the throne that we would create together as a team, a glorious dominion which would be won by the people and for the people, all in the name of freedom. Winnie was Nelson's second wife, which meant that I would be his third wife and first Queen. The thirty year age gap was inconvenient, but love always wins.

Madiba Thembekile would have been the heir presumptive of the Kingdom if he had lived long enough as Nelson's eldest son, but he died in a car crash in 1969. He was only 23; Nelson was not permitted to attend the funeral because the Government thought he would take it as an opportunity to escape from prison. It was all very convenient really because Prince Madiba had been born in 1946, which made him two years older than me. I would have an uphill struggle as it was to put forward my case for legitimacy as Queen and my case would not be helped in the slightest by critics who would be offended by the third wife of a man on a meteoric rise to the throne being younger than two of his children. Heavens! That would have made me look like some kind of deranged gold-digger getting drunk on the fame of the ANC's celebrity figurehead. Nelson had a second child, a daughter named Makaziwe born in 1947, but she died aged nine months. Because this was before my birth, my path to one of the thrones looked clear.

The current heir presumptive was Makgatho Mandela, soon to be known as Prince Makgatho. Nelson had a total of four surviving children; two with his first wife Evelyn and two with Winnie. Prince Makgatho had a younger sister, named Princess Makaziwe in honour of her deceased older sister, and two half-sisters, Princess Zenani and Princess Zindziswa. Perhaps one day I would be given the honour of motherhood myself and be blessed enough to give the man I loved a prince or a princess of my very own.

There was, of course, a small question of the racist law to contend with as I planned my marriage of convenience to a man who I did not love. It was illegal under South African regulations for a black man to marry a white woman. I had an ingenious disguise to conceal my true identity until such a time that I could break out of my coconut shell and stun them all, the phoenix spreading her glorious white wings above the ashes of Apartheid and racism, but I still had a problem. I worried that it may take time to convince people of the insanity of Nelson's incarceration and as I made my speech at the gates of the jail on Robben Island they would believe me both black enough to sling inside as a terrorist and white enough to sling inside as a woman who was illegally married to an African man. I could not afford to do anything to jeopardise my mission and I was faced with the unenviable task of choosing which could harm the progress of the pilgrimage more: continuing on my own without Blessings' earnings or risking being arrested for my illegal marriage and having the authorities discover the exact nature of my danger to the state in the cross examinations. It was what had happened to Nelson, after all; for all of his charges of terrorism and incitement he was arrested for crossing a border without a passport.

Blessings already had a firm hold on my heart and I knew that I could never forget him. I had dragged our relationship out as much as I could have done and it was out of the question to simply dodge or avoid the subject any more. He wanted me as his wife and he deserved an answer.

I came to realise that marrying him could be a fantastic idea. There were two reasons why life was hard for me; firstly because of the incorrect misconception that everybody made that I was black and secondly because of my gender. Blessings, as a man, could do jobs that I would not be allowed to do, and this had obvious financial implications for an impoverished woman to whom the entire future of democracy and liberty had been entrusted. We could earn more together than each of us could earn on our own, and things like accommodation and food would be cheaper to find if it was for both of us. I was restricted to feminine jobs such as domestic cooking and cleaning, and I needed him so that he could do the jobs that would only be offered to men, such as working with machinery. I needed him to get there; I had spent all of my life savings on the train ticket to Kimberley and I owned nothing except for Nelson's heart now, so I was getting desperate. It would ease a lot of tension on the journey if we were married and it would probably give us advantages as a married couple that we would not be given as friends, such as being able to book double beds in five star hotels which would save us money.

The plan was devised. I would accept his offer of marriage and I would use Blessings to provide for me. When I arrived in Cape Town I would murder him and Winnie Mandela and I would then ensure that Nelson and I were married, living as an Emperor and his Empress in a castle by the crystalline sea. I smiled as I thought of it all, imagining the crown resting on my afro, sitting on my throne as the ticket seller from the station came in and begged for forgiveness as he kissed my feet. With tears streaming down his face he told me that his ignorance was immeasurable because he had failed to see through the disguise and recognise the future Empress of South Africa standing before him, penniless and in rags. My day would come, and it would come soon.

Blessings became a blacksmith's assistant to pay our way through Bloemfontein and onto the next stop on our journey. There was a workshop in the middle of the city, and the blacksmith allowed Blessings and I to use one of the tiny rooms in his apartment above the shop as our home; it was completely unfurnished, and there was no bed to sleep on, but it was a palace to us.

The days were cruel to Blessings. He was in the back of the shop most of the daylight hours and he would hammer and beat the white hot metal into shape against the anvil, the shower of sparks repeating themselves over and over in a limitless arc of light scattering from the anvil onto the floor. The coals were always glowing hot and he had to spend his day in the stifling workshop. Blessings' job gave me an interesting new perspective on the human condition and what it meant to be me. The pieces of metal that he was working with began as black pieces of wrought iron or steel, and they would be heated until they were hot enough to bend and ply into whatever the blacksmith needed them to be; a perfectly cold piece of metal would be black, and a perfectly hot piece of metal would be a bright and shining white. What, then, was I? Could it be that I was scorching hot deep down in my core but that by some biological anomaly my shell was cold, like the freezing and cratered crust of the dark side of the moon?

After searching high and low, I finally got a job. It was in a munitions factory which made handguns and bullets. I was working on the production line, moulding the metal into the distinctive shape of the bullets and fitting the casing to the handles of the weapons. I didn't know much about guns, but I soon learnt from being in that environment that guns are much like bottles of wine. The variety of different types is limitless with endless specification differences and a price range that goes from very cheap to incredibly expensive, but to a beginner like me they all looked the same. I wasn't sure of the difference between a pump action shotgun and a hunting rifle, or a revolver and a pistol, but I did soon learn how to fit the casing to the outside of a sniper rifle and a semi-automatic shotgun.

It was very difficult to spend the days on the production line in the death factory without my mind wandering to where my handiwork would eventually end up. I was giving someone somewhere a machine that they would use to threaten, kill and injure. What else was a gun used for? What other purpose did it serve? There was nothing creative about it, nothing constructive or optimistic or honourable. The nihilistic bloodbath it would cause would leave South Africa starved of beauty and virtue.

What is it that makes someone a killer? Is it something within them, an animalistic and brutal disregard for the value of human life or was it instead the equipment that they had access to? If someone is given a gun does that immediately give them a motive and an ability to murder another human? I will always remember the time that I first raised this concern to some of the people that I now found myself working with on the production line; as soon as I suggested that we were turning people into killers they responded, quite angrily, by saying that my statement was just as ridiculous as suggesting that because I was anatomically equipped to be a prostitute I probably was one. Having a penis, the women claimed, was not enough evidence to be declared a rapist, and therefore having a gun was not enough evidence to be declared a killer. Reducing the number of guns would by no means reduce the number of murders or robberies, they claimed, because people hell-bent on murderous destruction tended to be quite inventive individuals and they would find a way to do their dirty work, gun or no gun.

South Africa has always had a very high crime rate, I knew that full well. I had seen it for myself on the brutally mean streets of Sophiatown in the fifties, and I imagined the Americans, wherever they had ended up in the ensuing carnage as Sophiatown was destroyed so that white men could move in, ruling the streets with my guns in their hands. I imagined racist thugs pressing the barrels against the foreheads of terrified victims as they mugged and raped them. The racism was travelling in both directions, both from black to white and white to black. The racial divide and the hatred and distance between the ethnic groups in my country were particularly painful for me as a coconut because no matter who the weapon of racism was directed at, it was always directed at me. I was caught in the crossfire no matter where the crosshairs of racism hovered.

I imagined my guns in the hands of gang warlords, bullying and manipulating their way to the top as the police were corrupted and intimidated into silence and the drug rings grew wider and wider. How could that be? How could this future Queen be assembling the instruments of death on the production line? I raised my concerns with the people I was working with on the factory floor, and they asked me why I was coming into the company with such a closed mind. Why could I not be open to the possibility that gun ownership was a good thing? After all, how were the vulnerable to be defended if they have no access to guns? I pondered over this carefully, and came to the conclusion that my fear was rooted in that American, Kennedy, having his head blasted to smithereens by a psycho with a bolt action rifle who wanted to be famous. It was an absolutely ghastly thought; surely there could be no plainer mark of a failed society than the murder of its head of state on home soil? Nobody would do that to King Nelson in the coming era. We are not savages any more.

My thoughts then turned to Nelson and what his first actions would be as King. I knew him so intimately that I could predict his every move and I now came to realise that he would immediately ban all firearms in South Africa to reduce the crime rate. It was that magical kind of telepathy that I shared with the prisoner on his windswept island in the Atlantic, and through the kilometres and across oceans and mountains he told me that he would end the agony of the gang warfare that had blighted our land for too long.

One of the biggest clientele bases for the guns which we manufactured was as a supplier to private armed response companies. None of the employees working on the factory floor were allowed to know the details of the business plans because we were merely the ones who assembled the parts on the production line; we were black, so the financial strategy was none of our business. Following the incident at the ticket booth at the station in Johannesburg I had chosen not to disclose the aims and targets of my cross-country mission to anyone. I became something of a fugitive from the truth but there was no practical way of preventing people from detecting that for whatever reason I would only stay in each town for a matter of days and then move on towards Cape Town as fast as possible. It was in nobody's interests to disclose to me inside information on any of the corporate information of the jobs that I had on the journey from Vilakazi Street to Robben Island. On a slave ship taking prisoners to the Americas, none of the blacks who were rowing would be expected to decide on which navigational system to consult in order to make it to their destination whilst avoiding rough seas and tempests; that was a job for the Captain, the white man at the helm, not some whimsical dreamer who was merely hitchhiking a ride across the seas for her own ends.

We all knew that the biggest company which we provided equipment to was ADT, because we had to work on equipment which contained their logo and some of us were in charge of dispatching the firearms and weaponry to their company. Trust in the corrupted police force was abandoned by the South African public, so private companies who could prove themselves to be dependable were positioned to capitalise on fear. Families would take out a subscription with the armed response companies and in return they would be given panic buttons which would be activated if the home was attacked. The company would then send its own armed guards—brandishing our own weapons constructed with my own charred fingers—to the house to get rid of the criminals without the inconvenience of police corruption or slow response times.

The ethics of the industry were questionable; the product they were offering was peace of mind, but the driving force of their income was fear. They were earning money as a direct result of people being frightened. It was clearly an industry which had an extremely low moral standard and there was no glory or honour in it whatsoever. But it may just have propelled me to Cape Town and it may just emancipate tens of millions of indigenous Africans; that noble consequence had to be my reward, and I clung to that truth tightly. My promise to Nelson had been to do whatever it took to get to him, but every day of the journey I was becoming increasingly alarmed at the way that the path I was taking into his arms was evolving.

In good time, I became tolerant enough to marry my fellow traveller. It seemed fitting that it was in Bloemfontein that we committed ourselves to one another, because the city is the judicial capital of the nation; there was only legal secularism here, no Godliness in this union, it was solely for financial opportunity and convenience. I was sacrificing my virginity and my desire for Nelson in order to speed my journey and to get enough money to get to Robben Island before it was too late. We were colleagues; we could earn more money in a shorter time as a team than we could as individuals. Then, one beautiful day in the future, we would stand in this very city and instigate laws which would make the people of South Africa truly free for the first time, gloriously and wonderfully free, under the gracious Kingship of Nelson and I as a direct result of what was done here on this very day.

Given that I was getting married, I probably should have concentrated a lot harder than I did. As I made my procession down the aisle I was hatching a devilish plan in my mind of how it would all end when death would finally do us part. With each step towards the man I was marrying I pictured myself dashing his brains out with a rock when we reached the edge of Africa and finally won freedom for Nelson, grinding Blessings' skull like you would grind nutmeg with a pestle and mortar, rejoicing with a free nation with my husband gone. But that day had not yet come. We were not yet free, and so the best thing that I could have done in Bloemfontein on my wedding day was pretend to love the man who had proposed to me to speed my safe passage to justice and liberty. The journey is never long when freedom is the destination.

It was a tiny little registry office. Nobody was there to see the event; there was just the registry officer and a witness who we had found in the street and asked to sign the relevant documents so that it could all be legal. The officer asked if there was any reason in law why I should not marry him, and my white heart froze. With a chill I cast my mind over the racist laws of my country and I understood the gravity of what I was about to do; the first of my many crimes against the Government was to marry a man who was racially different to me. This was no longer simply a rescue mission; we were now fugitives running from the law. In our pursuit of Nelson's freedom we may ourselves be pursued for the crimes of marriage that we had committed. I swallowed hard as the silence echoed around the registry office. We had managed to get away with it. This multicoloured fugitive was loose and dangerous.

He had made me a wedding ring out of some of the scrap metal that he had been using at the blacksmith's workshop. It was a little piece of iron, beaten flat and rolled and cut into a circular ring shape. Blessings had told me that he had measured my finger when I was asleep; he appeared to be truthful, for it slipped on perfectly. It felt like a second skin, and that troubled me slightly because the cold and dark metal did not contrast with the colour of my finger as I had hoped that my wedding ring would. It was all the opposite of what it should have been; rather than the symbol of love and a token of my inheritance as a white woman I felt the doom seeping through my whole body beginning at the fourth finger of my left hand. It was meant to be studded with the diamonds and made of a delicate band of gold, a gleaming token of my marriage to a man I desperately loved. It was meant to illuminate and exaggerate my whiteness, but instead this great clumsy lump of doughnut-shaped metal weighed me down and felt like a shackle on a prisoner. I felt like I was a bird of paradise with her wings clipped. The wrong ring felt monstrous and ghastly and I hoped that it would not be on my finger for a day more than was necessary to get to Cape Town, kill my companion and finally put that crown on my head.

He never stopped asking me about my father. Getting him to talk was never a problem; the difficulty lay instead with getting him to shut up. Ag man! It seemed that this would be the course that the brief flicker of marriage would take while I waited for someone better and I would have to perfect my techniques to get him to stop yakking. He was desperate to pay Faithful the dowry that he owed for my hand in marriage, but I didn't really want to be the one to tell him that they weren't a part of my life any more. There would be no braai with dark meat and red wine to celebrate the wedding, no slaughtering of the fattened calf and no procession through the streets to mark the occasion. My African husband even told me that he would pay in livestock to my father's household if it was necessary. The next time I saw my family would be at the Castle of Good Hope in Cape Town and they would bow down before me in the glittering throne room, by which time I would have in all probability have already murdered Blessings in order to marry the King. Blessings would probably never meet my parents, but I often simply let him talk about the dowry if he wanted to. I wondered how much money he had and what he would offer Faithful if the two of them ever did meet; did my new husband have his own miniature armada of galleons filled with treasure chests? Did he have a private cave somewhere along the South African coastline, a great vertical string of grottos which were filled with heaps of rubies; piles of emeralds and sapphires; great mountains of gold coins; crowns and goblets encrusted with gems and pearls? It seemed unlikely, but I needed to persuade myself that the union to him would be financially worthwhile in order to justify the emotional derailment I was enduring so that I could make it to Cape Town and elope with the jailed future King. I kept telling myself that I would be killing him for magnificent jewels and treasures rather than just the wages that he had collected on the journey through Kimberley and Bloemfontein. The miners may have handled diamonds all day long but they were essentially slaves with a small wage thrown into the deal. Maybe in the lagoons along the coastline we would dash off together in the dead of night and plunder great sacks of loot from his hiding places when we finally made it to the edge of the ocean. I envisaged false graves filled with the diamonds that he had stolen from the mine and sent in wagons across the country towards the enchanted coves. There we would outwit the Coastguard and load up his galleons so that the contraband could make it all the way to Europe to swell his fortune. Was the traveller I had somewhat opportunistically married a multinational smuggling warlord, surrendering up his riches to my murderous hand so that I would be able to win a new era of freedom for our land? It was a long shot, but I thought it was worth a try. Fantasy is the highest of human virtues.

As 1978 marched incessantly onwards I began to slowly and finally realise that this journey would take longer than I had anticipated. 1976 had come and gone, but when I had set out from Johannesburg I had expected to be in Cape Town in a matter of hours and for Nelson to claim the throne which was rightfully his by Christmas of the same year. I had only been brave enough to make it to Kimberley, and I had been shackled with a husband, who I did not love as much as my future King, to slow me down even more. We had ended up remaining in Kimberley until the summer, Christmas 1977, arriving in Bloemfontein during the scorching New Year, January 1978. I had always told myself that we would take it one step at a time and that we would concentrate on making it to the next town along the route as quickly as we could afford to and that we would eventually make it. I tried to not to think about the burden of the eroding time which was passing by us with ever increasing speed, but there were short and painfully fast days in Bloemfontein where it was unavoidable. I could not stop myself imagining the number of people being killed in protests such as the one in Soweto, political prisoners dying in jails like Nelson's and opponents of the Government enduring unnecessary suffering all because I was delayed in getting to Cape Town to rescue him. It would take me a long time to arrive, and I secretly knew that I had blood on my dark hands.

Nelson was still waiting for me eagerly, I knew that full well, but I did not know how long that excitement could be maintained for or how many evenings he could endure in the disappointment of another day passing by without my triumphant arrival. I could see him holding his ear against the wall of his cell which faced Africa, imagining my white soul pressed into the cool palm of his hand like a smooth pebble from the beach of his tropical island. I felt my spirit nestling amongst the lines and contours of his rich, thick dark skin. I felt his fingerprints all over me, the beautiful stains of a lover welcoming me home, and I knew that the beating heart of Africa lay with me inside his palm. It was impossible for me to forget about him as I hurried across the country, my whole life on the road in his name, but I deeply feared that he would forget about me. I deeply feared that he would wake up one day in his cell, an abused and downtrodden political prisoner, and lose his faith in me. I was absolutely convinced that the only thing giving him the motivation to keep on enduring the hardship with the remarkable resilience that he was displaying was the knowledge that I would soon be bounding over the summit of Table Mountain towards the Bay, striding across the sea to rescue him. I was terrified that my hesitation in reaching Cape Town would crush his morale and affect his ability to rescue South Africa from itself. I hated the idea that the defeat of the ANC's grand plans for power in Pretoria would be because of Nelson losing his zealous hunger for justice, and that that would be because he was tired of waiting for me.

7

KINGDOM IN THE SKY

Teyateyaneng, Lesotho
January 1979

Rising high above South Africa far below, Lesotho is an entirely independent country made out of mountains with only one border, a nation which had broken away from the British Empire in 1966 and which was a proud kingdom under an absolute monarchy. Perhaps this was the destiny for our nation as well, with Nelson as the King on a glorious day to come. Nestled in the Drakensberg mountain range with the southeast of South Africa, Lesotho contained no identifiable highways, few well developed towns and very little technology or infrastructure. It was an African wilderness with none of South Africa's obsession with European culture and colonialism but instead this place was in possession of a very individual identity. Lesotho did not aspire to anything other than a better version of itself, an insular and very proud place where the locals swaggered with a unique sense of pride.

As lonely stowaways in the back of a donkey-drawn wagon heading for the hills I did not think that we could climb any higher, but we did and continued to do so. Every now and then I would catch a breathless glimpse down the mountainside and be left stunned by the enormity of the nation I was temporarily leaving behind, the backdrop laid out before me like a beautiful patchwork quilt. Lesotho lay on the crest of the Drakensberg Mountains like a sprawling and heavily fortified castle, her battlements made of grass and her drawbridge made of crumbling gravel and dirt.

South African authorities were patrolling the border crossing, but nobody was there representing Lesotho. Perhaps it was difficult to find the staff to patrol the crossing given that it was a Sunday, but when we asked the driver about this he told us that it was because Lesotho was so exceedingly poor that it could not afford to effectively police the borders and the ink which was used for passport stamps was too expensive for them to issue to everyone who passed through. The burden of responsibility for border control therefore fell to the South Africans who issued travellers with exit stamps. It seemed fanciful, and I was not sure whether or not I believed him. I asked if the policemen were likely to find us, but the driver assured me that it was unlikely.

"Besides," he said as he approached the checkpoint, "I can just bribe them if they do see you. We have hope, what more do we need? It should be fine."

That was the first time I had ever crossed an international border. What a thrill! I knew that I was now truly joining Nelson as he had been initially imprisoned for illegally crossing a border without the relevant documentation. I was joining him as we drove up that steep mountainside, finding my place alongside him in the history of our nation, and if I squinted I could see his magnificent silhouette striding proudly across the jagged mountain peaks. He was welcoming me into a new life as a fugitive, an existence on the run and a new identity as a pariah.

It was wonderful to be now a fully fledged accomplice of Nelson in his crimes and to be properly on the run from the law, but that is not to say that one day I would not like to be the proud owner of a passport to call my property. That magic little book of stamps and memories, that badge of triumphant adventure and heroic exploration of foreign and exotic lands, was something that I would love to own one day. If I was honest I only really understood what an international border was and that you needed a passport to cross one legally because of the trial and because of Nelson. In a strange way that mighty man, the man I had spoken to only once, had taught me most of what I knew. I imagined the State Visits that we would undertake when Nelson and I were married and we were enthroned with our courtiers at our palace in Cape Town, flying off in Royal jets to the far flung destinations where we would meet with our contemporaries in their castles and parliaments. I imagined a Royal tour of the Big Wall of China and trade relations exercises in Paris when Nelson would be meeting with the delegations at Versailles House whilst I was free to explore the city and buy fur coats and perfume in the boutiques. Perhaps we would go to America as well to complete my journey across South Africa and my transition from black to white by being a White Queen in the White House. America has a great many flaws but there is not another country on Earth which may claim to outdo it in terms of rousing grandeur and boastful pomp. Matching them in this most patriotic of senses would be a policy that I would import to South Africa as soon as Nelson was crowned King at the end of 1979.

Lesotho was stunningly beautiful in its ruggedness and natural splendour. Humans were not the self-ordained masters of the landscape but simply unsubstantial features of it, and the scenery was instead devoted to the pinpricks of rounded thatched huts, trickling streams and vast mountainous fields of emerald green grass and delicate pink flowers. It was undeveloped, but with a connotation of raw beauty rather than miserable poverty. For all of Sophiatown's romanticised American fantasies of Western excess, this place was proudly and authentically African in every sense. Lesotho was the real deal and there was no doubt about it.

The thing which filled my head was the fiendish plot to murder my husband and Nelson's wife to clear the path for us to marry. As Blessings and I bumped along in the back of the wagon hand in hand I imagined them in my heads, the fabric of their bodies disintegrating beneath my fingers, their flushing, blooming flesh moulding between my hands into stiff and brittle corpses, the emaciated skin barely covering the protruding bones. I pictured the potion with which I would commit the crime and claim my glorious prize, that sparkling crown finally placed on my black head.

The Basotho people, a name which translates into English as "the people from the sky", were indescribably different from those we had left behind in South Africa. There was something so enticingly exotic about simply being abroad, and even the air felt different as it flooded my lungs. The landscape was unrecognisable and even the skies breathed with a different texture to what I was used to back in the Transvaal. I may as well have landed on the surface of another planet; home, wherever that now was, seemed incredibly far away. My journey onwards was beginning to gain some spectacular backdrops, and our frustratingly indirect route to Cape Town seemed to be an itinerary of unimaginably beautiful places. It seemed so fitting and correct that as I travelled across the nation to Cape Town to haul my lover from his jail cell I should be spending these three years delighting in everything that this nation had to offer, expanding my understanding of the country that I was rescuing and the people who depended solely on Nelson and I for their emancipation. Fear not my love; I will be with you soon.

Lesotho made me see Africa in the same way as she was seen by the rest of the world. The Transvaal was my home and familiarity had clouded my judgement of that place; here I could see the poverty, the savagery, the exotic darkness with which this gargantuan uncivilised wilderness throbbed. I could see the strangeness in the tribal customs, the spectacular natural diversity with which our continent is so mightily blessed. If I am an African then surely the world's perception of what an African is must be tragically incorrect. If I am an African the reputation that this place has for being an impoverished continent of black people in caves is unjust and undeserved. There is more to me than crippling poverty and safaris. But alternatively I may not be an African after all; my coconut syndrome may be the last remaining souvenir of an alternative destiny, a postmark telling me I was mailed to the wrong address. Maybe all African men really are savage warlords and all African women are riddled with diseases as they live in a world starved of democracy and electricity. This contrast, cemented in the fact that I did not even know if I was an African or not, I found to be deeply troubling and distressing.

All too quickly we were required to make a plan to ensure our survival and our progress towards Cape Town in record speed. To do that we would need money, and so the search began for a job or a franchise. The economy of Lesotho was based on the exportation of water and diamonds, most of which was sent out to South Africa, but we were unable to get work in these industries because we were both illegal immigrants. We were worried that being employed by the giant companies must surely be the fastest way to be jailed in the exact same manner as had befallen the man I was solely responsible for rescuing. There was a chance that we would simply be swiftly deported which was a very attractive option, but both Blessings and I considered it to be a very high risk strategy. We could be propelled towards Cape Town with exactly the haste and urgency which we would have loved or we could have equally seen the mission for South Africa's freedom collapse forever before our eyes.

We briefly stopped off in Maseru, the capital city of Lesotho, the hundred year old British outpost for their Empire. It was the height of summer, and the coolness of the mountains was a welcome relief compared with the searing summer heat of Bloemfontein.

About forty kilometres away from Maseru was the town which we were heading for. Teyateyaneng was perched at the crown of a very high plateau, and it was renowned across the region for the famous crafts and curios which it produced. People would flock from all over the country to buy their crafts in Teyateyaneng and it was the most profitable place in Lesotho. If you wanted to get rich and you couldn't get yourself to Egoli, this was the place to come.

Just like South Africa would soon be, Lesotho was a nation with an absolute monarchy. The King of Lesotho was a man named Moshoeshoe II and he had been on the throne since independence in 1966. Because of the fact that before independence Lesotho had been a part of the British colony of South Africa the tiny enclave still used the South African rand, which was handy for us. The fortune that we could build in these rich mountains could be carried with us back over the border and could contribute directly to the funding that we needed to rescue Nelson and restore our country to peace and righteousness. I hoped to meet Moshoeshoe, but the opportunity never came.

Making the crafts seemed like a lekker opportunity to make some money to help this dream come true. The millionaires of Lesotho would soon be flocking to me and lining up around the blocks to buy my magnificent wares and trinkets, and so I set to work in making myself a stall from which I would be able to sell the products. I had absolutely no experience of making curios but I knew that I had it within me to be the very best. Nelson and I had an intrinsic advantage above every other human in the world because of the fact that we were both coconuts. The condition is the very best of blackness combined with the very best of whiteness, and being unlike every other person in the world means that there is something superiorly inhuman about being someone like me. It is humanity with a little extra added, a shell of black skin and a special cunning included in the recipe of the womb, all of which would combine to create the unique beast that I now was.

Taking the money was easy. What was more difficult was making a successful attempt at being a talented and original craft-maker and selling high quality products which were too stunning to resist. Lesotho was a nation which was famous for its high quality and quantity of crafts and we had very stiff competition. Everywhere I looked I could see weaved and painted curios, carved animals and decorative trinkets for people to buy. There were multicoloured ostrich eggs, salad servers, candlesticks, brightly coloured tablecloths and carved animals made of wood.

One day I bought a journal. It was the most beautiful book I had ever seen; made from organic paper containing whole rose petals and leaves, the cover and spine were a deep and beautiful purple colour. It was destiny, for purple is the colour of royalty. It was expensive, but I knew that it was worth it so I snapped it up on the spot. With this new book I could document my story for the sake of history, to forever preserve every last moment of this great adventure. This would be my memoir of my time before I was a Queen, a document treasured by historians for millennia to come.

Between these pages lay every square inch of my kingdom; every field, every mountain and every blade of grass.

There was something that terrified me greatly in the prospect of forgetting the tiny details of the trip. Every second of this sacred journey was precious. I have always felt as though I may have a book in me; *a book*, that most noble of human creations and that most honourable of human possessions. It was an ambition that I always held and one that I knew was within the reach of my big black fingertips. Using my considerable vocabulary I could gather together all of the elements of the universe and orchestrate them in order to tell my story; I would gather up the moon and stars and scatter them across the pages, attach the Atlantic Ocean to the front cover and the Indian to the back, and if I did it right I could span the entire circumference of the universe in one sentence. I could get from Johannesburg to Cape Town with a flick of my pen. Language is the most incredible thing that humans can do and this magical little book would be my greatest achievement.

That night Nelson told me that he, too, was writing a book about his time prior to our Royal destiny. He said that it would be called *The Big Step to Freedom* and somehow deep down I knew that he would always outshine me. But that doesn't mean I should ever stop trying. I wouldn't write to be rich or famous, I would write for fear of my words being otherwise lost forever.

Other than the journal, one of the more brilliant products on offer was a glass bottle. My curiosity got the better of me and I approached the salesman.

"What is this glass bottle doing on your table?"

"Do you want to buy it?"

"It depends on what it is. Is it a special bottle?"

His mouth curled into a grin as though he were a starving man who had just laid eyes on an almighty feast.

"Oh yes madam, this is a very special bottle and I can make you a very special price."

"What is so special about it?"

"The water in this bottle was collected from the Zambezi River at the Victoria Falls. It comes from Rhodesia."

The Victoria Falls! My heart raced as I clenched my hands around the bottle; my breath was stolen away by the thundering water and my eardrums shook with the deafening sound. The exhilaration of the spray roaring against my dark skin was stunning and thrilling. I was bewitched.

"I am sorry madam; you touch, you buy." He thrust out his hand at me.

"What is your special price?"

It turned out to be half of all the money that Blessings and I had smuggled across the border. Yes, I understood that this would slow down our trip to Cape Town but this was definitely worth it. My lunatic of a husband disagreed. He told me that I was an idiot for falling for it and that the water had most probably been filled up at the local stream to be sold to me at an astronomical profit. He said it may not have even been for sale, but a bottle that he was drinking from to keep him cool in the summer sun. According to Blessings this was the most obvious con he had ever seen. Were his ears not working properly? They had told me very clearly that the water had come from the Victoria Falls. I didn't understand his problem.

"You're not the only one who wants to get to Cape Town as fast as possible," was my husband's tempestuous reply. He was mourning the money. He needed to learn how to let all one hundred and fifty rand go. Africans are not slaves any more and our hearts should not be tied up with finance. Blessings had so much to learn from me.

I did consider it strange that the seller had told me that I had to buy the water simply because I had touched it. African tradesmen were notorious in their bullying persuasiveness and browsing was a completely alien concept to them. I tried to make it as a craft seller but I was not aggressive enough to be taken seriously and my wares were not of a high enough quality to compete with all the rivals I had.

In the end I simply gave up. I would never be an accomplished craftswoman and I could not compete with the considerable number of rival traders with much more experience and talent than that which I possessed. My tactic towards the end of our stay in Lesotho was to search around the markets to find the cheapest products that

I could and then to give them to Blessings to take to his faraway outposts and sell them at an extortionate profit which we would keep.

By the end of 1979 it was becoming increasingly clear that I had massively misjudged this tiny country. I had come expecting millionaires and mansions like you find in the north of Johannesburg, but instead we found that Lesotho was desperately poor. Their only marketable natural resources were water, which would only be sold to South Africa far below, and diamonds, of which South Africa produced far more and at a far higher quality and even this booming industry was a mere supplement to the real boom-trade of gold mining. South Africa was rich in natural resources but Lesotho's rugged wilderness was an extremely bad place to find employment. The people were desperate and far from wealthy; rumours abounded that this was the world's third-poorest nation, although nobody could tell us which two countries beat her to that less than prestigious honour.

In the winter the greenery of the Drakensberg and the rugged beauty of the mountains of Lesotho were transformed into a dazzling white winter wonderland. Some South Africans would come across the border and ski just for that same thrill that I had experienced of being in a foreign country, enchanted by this mountainous kingdom blanketed in snow and nestled amongst the stars.

I'd never seen snow before Teyateyaneng. It was a magical sight, with the thick white flakes filling the sky with a dazzling whiteness and the skies darker than the shrouded slopes. The whole world was starved of blackness and was instead drenched in nothing but crisp and freezing whiteness, every line bright and breathtaking, every inch fresh and burning in its glorious mathematical precision. I was in my element; I thought I had landed in Heaven and I half expected Nelson to come over the hill on his horse made of fire and lightning.

I stuck my tongue out and I let the snowflakes melt as soon as they touched me. I hoped that the snowflakes landing on my body would change the colour of my skin as they melted onto me, so on that mountainside I stripped all of my clothes off and stood beside the pile I had made. With my body emblazoned with all of the raw crudeness of a chunk of coal, I closed my eyes, spread my arms and stretched my fingers out in the hope that I would feel sensations I had never felt before. I stood against the spectacular backdrop of the rugged mountain range and stretched out my palms in a gesture of embrace towards this foreign land. The intense coldness feathered against my arms and face and stole my breath away. I was full of mixed feelings when the pieces of snow melted as they landed on my black skin, because of the contrast between them and me. I wanted be invisible in that scene of snow, to blend seamlessly in like a polar bear in the Antarctic with no distinction between my skin and the spectacular backdrop of the slopes which were covered with the deep drifts. As I felt the snowflakes tickling my lashes I opened my eyes.

I saw a group of children on the hillside up by the round huts. They were pointing at me with delighted expressions on their faces. I turned and ran towards them, my huge anties bouncing as I approached, knowing that they recognised the future Queen of the nation which lay beyond the only border. There was a leaping joy in my heart as I bounded towards them; I was now thirty one years old, a handsome age for an African woman, and I had not sprinted like that in years. If you were particularly unkind you would have called me an old woman, a krimpie or a sneeudier, but I knew that old Queen Lerato had a lot of life still in her to live.

As I came closer to the children they got a better view of my naked coconut shell and they began to scream and run away. Their little faces were contorted into twisted expressions of fear and revulsion; I felt sad for them. It must have been a dreadful shock to be confronted by a woman who was the wrong colour, a clear abomination of nature and a twisted evolutionary mutation. As they screamed and fled from my presence I was filled with a special kind of gladness which only comes after peaceful acceptance of your own fate as a coconut. I felt reassured that they were proving me right; had I not been of the delicate condition which had distressed them so greatly I would not have been the right woman for the job of rescuing the future King. The fact that they had recognised me for the physical anomaly that I was gave me a renewed determination to get to Cape Town and to finally get that Consort's crown on my head where it belonged. Sometimes ordained destiny is ugly and frightening to the untrained eye.

They may have been upset at my troubling racial disability, but I knew that Teyateyaneng was the first place I had ever been lucky enough to taste the addictive sparkle of freedom on my tongue and that made the whole thing worthwhile. I had no inhibitions in the snow; I could have run, childlike, through the untouched and pristine wilderness all day long. It felt indescribably liberating. After a while I remembered that I was completely naked and considered the magnitude of the fact that for the first time in my life I had forgotten what skin I was in. The mountains did not care what I looked like and there was a beautiful simplicity in that. I turned to find my clothes and saw that I had wandered a long way from the pile which was steadily being buried by the snowfall. It was only then that I awoke from my trance and felt the harsh sting of the freezing carpet beneath my feet.

Down on the Transvaal we were used to violent thunderstorms and glowing sandstorms, but never snow. It had happened once or twice in living memory, but I had never personally seen it. The temperatures, particularly at night, would fall well below freezing but the wet season coincided with the summer and so the skies were never full at the correct time to give us snowfall.

That night I had a dream. I saw myself out riding with the King in his hunting grounds in the snow, escorted by soldiers and infantrymen carrying the butchered game back to the castle on a gun-carriage made of solid gold. We had buffalo, giraffe, rhinoceros, hippopotamus and springbok. We would charge outside of the walls of the city and follow the game into the sparse woodlands. My days in rags or standing naked on hillsides were long gone; instead I was wearing the finest black fur and the coat contrasted as brilliantly with my skin as it did with the snow on the ground. I had boots and brooches and a glittering tiara on my head.

The soldiers were pristine and magnificent in their appearance as they escorted the King and Queen. Their uniforms were black with a blood-red stripe down each leg, black boots which shone like mirrors, stitched lapels of gold and immaculate white feathers on their beautiful hats. The horses were magnificent beasts, stamping and charging yet under the strictest of control. All about their mouths hung a glittering wreath of breath.

After the hunt we would return to the castle and a huge fire in the Great Hall would be waiting for us. We would warm ourselves and then head out again in the afternoon whilst the feast was prepared; the King and I would walk alone in the garden, alongside the endless evergreen hedgerows, the classical marble statues studding the gardens just as white as we were. The King would pick me a rose and put it into my gloved hands, my blue eyes bright and wide with wonder as I listened to him tell me how much he loved me.

*   *   *

The best piece of advice we learned whilst in Lesotho was to keep an eye out for yellow flags. The vast majority of the people of this tiny land in the sky were illiterate and so there were no signposts, but instead they had a system of coloured flags. The yellow one was the one that we needed to look for, because it signified that the place where it was flown sold something completely unique—they were offering beer made out of pineapples. It came as a bit of a surprise to me for two reasons; firstly that beer could be made out of such an ingredient and secondly that pineapples would grow here in the mountainous, sometimes snow-covered terrain. Was that really plausible? I pictured endless slaves squashing pineapples with their feet, dancing like Zulus do when they are going into battle with the British, finally standing back and seeing that their skinny black toes were covered in pineapple flavoured beer. We had heard rumours from the local people that a green flag would mean that the hut below would offer beer made from dagga—the local marijuana—but we had no means of knowing whether or not this was true.

We knew that the time had come to leave for South Africa and to try to continue on to Cape Town to rescue my hero. We were heading in the wrong direction but we were leaving Lesotho via the eastern border and it would be difficult to hitch a ride with someone who was going west. In the end we found a cattle truck which was heading towards Durban and we arranged to go as well. The driver wanted a bribe to smuggle us over the border, which took away a lot of our money.

At the end of our trip to Lesotho the new nation decided that they would attempt to further stamp their independent authority on their territory by introducing a new currency which was separate to the South African rand. The new money would be called the loti and I hoped that it would be simply a case of exchanging our measly savings into fresh new notes and coins in order to generate a mighty fortune. We would be in Cape Town in no time. I promptly exchanged all the measly savings we had into loti and sente and carried it proudly over the border with me. I would change it back into rand in South Africa and we would immediately become millionaires.

Gradually the map of the nation which I had grown up studying but not experiencing was being embroidered with my memories; the place-names began to be infused with more of an identity than just the marking on the paper. Every place on the journey now had a special place in my heart and that was what travel was all about. Mom and Dad had told me to get a map but this was just another example of their monochrome stupidity; I could see a map in every town we came to and therefore I did not need my own. I could feel my horizon stretching and with the most wonderful feeling of enlightenment I realised that with each day of this journey there was less of the country I would one day be Queen of which remained mysteriously unexplored. More and more of it was being claimed as my own.

As we approached the border, my heart was racing and my black palms were soaked with white beads of sweat. The whole future of my marriage with Nelson, his freedom and the liberation of all of South Africa depended on whether or not the border guards were paying attention to their jobs. I hoped that they had forgotten to drink their coffee during the long and arduous shift of protecting their country's border and that as a result they would be snoozing when we drove through the checkpoint.

As we approached the checkpoint one of the border control officers stepped out in front of us to stop the van so that they could search it. The driver stopped at the gate and stepped out to show his passport, which was blue with metallic lettering on the front and a coat of arms. He was South African, just like us. One day I would be his Queen and he would be my subject.

The guards were Basotho, and the Immigration Officer was South African. He was the master and they were the slaves; the story of every relationship between a white man and a black one, and a summary of the struggle between my soul and my body. He was responsible for protecting the border, and they were responsible for examining the dirty and dangerously unpredictable freight and cargo being transported into the foreign nation far below.

I am fluent in Sesotho, which meant that I was able to translate what they were saying to one another and warn Blessings of when they were planning to search the vehicle. As a precaution I insisted that we crouch on the floor of the van, lying beneath the bellies of the cows as far away from the rear door as was possible. The rancid smell of urine and defecation clung fiercely to the inside of my nostrils, and one of the cows had her udders perilously close to my face. The men stood at the back of the van, just a matter of inches from us, and they leant against the vehicle and lit a cigarette. They would every now and then stomp their feet loudly to denote movement and rummage with the bolts on the back door, but aside from that they did nothing. They were useless and lazy, taking every opportunity possible to avoid hard work, but that we didn't mind. I had expected them to prowl around and hunt us down like lions, but actually their disgraceful work ethic suited us perfectly.

I knew that my next venture abroad on diplomatic duty would be a much more romantic and fanciful and that I would be making my next return to South Africa in *style*. This was just a rehearsal, a foreshadow of what was coming; then I would return on the arm of the King aboard the Royal Train made of gold, swallowing up the miles of the journey from the exotic lands of the north like a crocodile swimming down the Zambezi, finally coming over the hills of the Transvaal and entering Pretoria in triumph. I would have a crown on my head and a robe of purple with white fur, and my biggest problem would be the weight of the lobe and sceptre in my hands. Nelson would roar like a lion, his magnificence on proud display for all of our subjects to see. I would raise a satin glove and wave through the windows of the Royal Train, brushing aside the thick burgundy velvet curtains and acknowledging the affection of the crowd. There would be a military band playing, the mounted trumpeters announcing the return of the King, with banners and flags and processions through the streets. Make way, make way; the King is coming home!

Yet this Queen consort, this great Empress Regent of a kingdom of peace, justice and righteousness whose reign with the King would usher in a new dawn in the history of sub-Saharan Africa, this famous political star whose life spanned the two periods of rule of the nation, was entering the country she would one day represent lying on the floor of a cattle truck, amongst the filth and the kak, hiding from the Basotho guards who were checking the trailer for contraband. Something about that did not seem quite right.

8

A CHINA PRINCESS

Pietermaritzburg, Natal Province
September 1980

The road down to South Africa was incredibly steep and treacherous. The dirt track consisted of many rocks and there were steep ravines leading down the hillside which we were afraid of skidding on. At one point we had to get out of the little truck and push when the wheels got buried in a big pile of soft shingle and mud on the steep slope.

The journey down from the mountains was uneventful other than the fact that it revealed to me the staggering vastness of the nation which I would one day come to own. We drove through the night, slowly but surely making our way towards the sea. It began in a wonderful way, leaving Lesotho and the stunningly spectacular vantage points of the mountainous roads which gave us commanding views over the valleys at sunset, the skies stained with a beautiful hue of fading glory as the great star sneezed one last time before bed. The mountains were spectacular but they soon turned into foothills, then to a never-ending flat plain which stretched out towards Durban and the Transkei, with our promised land, our Mother City and our final destination far to the west. It was a beautifully empty piece of landscape expanding on all sides like a canvas waiting to be splashed with paint.

Very early the next morning we reached the town of Harrismith. Blessings and I were filthy from our journey in the back of the cattle truck and we went off in search of a public toilet where we could wash the mud and faeces off of our bodies. Finding one which said "nie blankes" written over the door was a challenge, however, and by the time we found somewhere to wash we were on the opposite side of the small town to where we had climbed out of the truck. It was with a peculiar sense of elation that I beheld the thick layer of brown mud and dirt peeling off of my skin and into the gleaming metal sink of a public toilet, a place decorated with smashed mirrors, cracked tiles and needles in the bowls. I did not want the sensation to end; perhaps if this water was enriched with a special brand of magic it would not simply peel off the mud but it would also take off my skin with it, swirling down the plughole in great papery flakes of black flesh. I was out of luck. The mud came off but the skin stayed behind. Out, damned spot! Out I say!

Harrismith was a bleak little town on the very edge of the mountains and it was a place to drive through rather than to stop off in. There was a huge PickNPay store and some shops all devoted to the traveller and the motorist; this was the gateway to the Drakensberg and Harrismith was the last stop before civilisation ended and the rugged wilderness of the mountains began. We went to find the visitor information centre to try to work out if there was a way of reaching Cape Town directly, bypassing Durban and getting there before the end of the week. Soon enough we came to a map of the town and it pointed us in the direction of the visitor centre.

The place looked like a corporate office of some kind, a long corridor full of completely random rooms and nowhere which even resembled a help desk where we could ask someone where we needed to go in order to get to Cape Town and rescue the King. The white woman behind the desk was bored and stupid and she gave me the impression that I was disturbing her as she read her book. Perhaps she saw her job as an inconvenience rather than a blessing in a country with a cripplingly high unemployment rate. She did not say a word to us but stared with huge blue eyes, then turned her face away in a disgusted scowl and scrunched up her nose at me as though I had not washed and was still covered in slime.

Because she had ignored us, we ignored her. We walked straight past and saw a long corridor with doors to different rooms, none of which looked particularly like a tourist information centre which would tell us the way to Cape Town. We tried the first door. That was a mistake.

"Ag! What are you blacks doing in my office? Don't you know that this building is only to be occupied by whites?" He picked up his phone to call the police.

We ran. They chased us all around the tiny little town, before finally we dashed down one of the little alleyways and climbed into a bin. We lay low for a while, hoping that nobody would find us amongst the bin bags. I hoped that the rustling I could hear was just rats and not snakes. Eventually we crept back to the place where the cattle truck had stopped. It was gone; it had clearly not waited for us and had driven away to Durban with our money whilst we remained in the middle of nowhere.

We managed to find another ride as we hitchhiked our way southeast. Harrismith lay on a crucial fork in the road; the N5 went west, back around the northern border of Lesotho towards Bloemfontein and back in the direction of Cape Town where we needed to be, and the N3 carried on from Johannesburg in the north to Durban in the south. We didn't know which road we should go down but with a heavy heart we ended up choosing the N3 because we couldn't bear to waste the last couple of years on retracing our steps down an already-trodden road. We walked along the highway with our hands held out to the road until eventually a truck carrying Coca Cola bottles stopped to give us a lift.

Leaving Harrismith we drove on through the countryside. The journey was long and flavourless, with the endless plains and sparse fields stretching as far as the eye could see. Everything was going fine until the truck broke down just outside of the town of Pietermaritzburg. The engine of the trusty little truck wheezed and whirred until it could chug no more and the inside of the truck was overcome with a ghastly and ghostly silence.

Pietermaritzburg was an ancient little place which lay halfway between the port city of Durban and the rugged peaks of Lesotho. More English than England, it was dominated by grand architecture and constant reminders of this Imperial outpost from which the defeats of Zulu warriors would be plotted by men with rifles. Everywhere we were assaulted by the implication that those who look white were born to rule those who look black. We found a bank and I tried to change the loti from Lesotho into South African rand. I let my emotions get the better of me as I handed over the notes and coins to the smiling black teller; I waited for her to hand back hundreds of millions of rand in return. I closed my eyes and Nelson showed me the Castle of Good Hope, our future home, with the dungeons and catacombs stuffed with chests of gold and piles of rubies and diamonds.

"Here you go."

I looked down and saw the familiar South African money being handed to me. It seemed pitifully little; I counted it all and I realised that it was actually slightly less than the amount of loti I had given her. I called her a stupid munter and went on my way, asking Blessings why she had ripped me off so atrociously. He told me that the loti and the rand were pegged together, which meant that they were identical in value, and that the tiny difference was taken out in commission. My plan for riches had been thwarted and Cape Town felt further away than ever.

* * *

For our stay in Pietermaritzburg I found a job in a restaurant inside a large shopping mall on the outskirts of the city. Because they thought that I was black, I would have to work in the kitchen because the diners at the restaurant were exclusively white and the manager thought that they would be offended by my presence. Waitressing was completely out of the question. Financially this would prove to be difficult because the waitresses were able to boost their income with tips, but I was too black to see any of that money.

I was a dishwasher and I was responsible for clearing away the mess that other people left. I would have to scrub the crockery, removing the unwanted and uneaten food and the wasted fine wines and expensive spirits. It was a bit of a depressing job; there was no satisfaction in it, no pleasure and no enjoyment in what I was doing every day. I was not creating anything, not constructing or providing anything, I was instead simply there to clear away the remains of other people's work.

I remember very clearly the freezing winter's night in 1981 when we watched on the TV set in the kitchen as a Prince of England married the girl he loved and made her a Princess. As they emerged from the Cathedral and made their way to the waiting carriage my thoughts were solely with Nelson; the television pictures were still in black and white because it was a cheap little machine and it made the girl's dress gleam the most astonishing and beautifully radiant white. My turn was coming. My heart and soul were aching within me as I scrubbed the dishes, but the waiters and waitresses were all gathered around the blurred and fuzzy screen, half of them remembering with a dreamy euphoria their own wedding days and the other half thanking the Prince and his bride for keeping their faith in fairytales alive. My wedding day had come and gone; my finger would forever remind me of that, but as soon as I laid eyes on the new Princess I did not cast my mind backwards to the day in Bloemfontein when Blessings and I committed ourselves to one another, but instead I cast it forward to the dashing Prince I had waiting for me in Cape Town, the man destined for another throne and the man who would make me great simply by sliding my wedding ring home. I watched her smiling and waving to the crowd and I knew that she would never be forgotten. I anticipated that same destiny for myself, but I knew that I would have to wait.

The girl's dress was thrillingly, dazzlingly white. It was overflowing with gargantuan ruffles and massive romantic bows. I scrubbed the meringue off of the whisk as I kept my head down and carried on working, trying hard to get everything cleaned. Suddenly everyone wanted to be a colony again. I think I had left a piece of my heart in Lesotho, where Africans were proud to be independent; with a rustle of that girl's gargantuan train the South Africans collapsed into a blubbering herd of sentimental boneheads, desperate to be invaded again. These same people marvelling over the Princess' wedding dress were the same ones who had voted to get rid of Queen Elizabeth and replace her with a filthy hairyback. The British just had to shake their crowns a little bit, do a little parade of their soldiers in strange and pretty costumes, and the people who had once hated them were swooning. These spearchuckers hadn't seen anything yet, for my version of African Royalty would make this new princess look like an ousie. There was a word that we used to insult the English which I found extremely amusing; the English were a country of *soutpiels*—literally translated as "salty penis"—who came marching across the world claiming countries for themselves whilst trying to straddle both their homeland and their colonies all at the same time. With your hands and feet stretched out between Africa, the Caribbean and London, it was unlikely that you would be able to avoid having your penis dangle in the ocean and get it covered in salt in the process. Sis man.

The other news from abroad was the independence of the British Colony of Rhodesia, which had been granted independence in December of 1979 and split into Zambia to the south and Zimbabwe to the north, though the word did not trickle through to us until we were in Pietermaritzburg. I could not have been more thrilled for our close friends and neighbours in Zimbabwe—Zimbabwe! What a beautiful new word on my lips. The exotic and unfamiliar sound that my tongue made as I whispered it to myself to build up its familiarity sounded like independence and freedom rising out of the ashes of war. I loved the way that this was all going, the labour-pains of justice ringing out across the continent after the hurtfully squandered opportunity that the white men missed in 1961. Zimbabwean independence, at long last after so long of white domination and the suppression of blacks, was glorious news. We would be next. Africa was finally becoming African again.

Back in the restaurant, I remember that some of the customers did not appreciate me being in the kitchen as a dishwasher because they were afraid of my skin touching the plates. Somehow the air that I exhaled in an environment where food was prepared was unacceptable to some, and I could tell that there was a growing sense of resentment. When I had started my job there had been a few other members of staff who were black, but none of them had ever been in positions of power or influence. In the kitchen the chef is king, and he is always white; the Negroes would always be the ones cleaning the floors, washing the dishes and doing the more mundane tasks of food preparation such as the chopping of fruit and the peeling of vegetables. Had I not been encased in chocolate, I could have been the chef or the restaurant owner and I could have had a long and happy life. Gradually over the time that I was there I saw many people come and go, because I detected a rising resentment of the black members of staff; at the beginning that kitchen in Pietermaritzburg was the closest thing that South Africa had to multiculturalism. Thandi the sous-chef was fired, and then Zola, another dishwasher, was sent packing after she spilt some red wine on a tablecloth when she was helping to clear the tables because the waitresses were too busy gossiping. South Africa had such a hopelessly high unemployment rate—unfairly and disproportionately higher for people who were or appeared on the outside to be black—that it was with a dreadful impulsiveness that the white man had the power to ruin our lives and condemn us to a long period of austerity. I knew with every fibre of my being that this was wrong.

I would consider my greatest flaw to be impatience, which made the pain of our frustratingly long trip to Cape Town even greater. We had been on the road for four years now and Nelson was still not King as we lingered in Pietermaritzburg, snaking our way down from the Transvaal and the Drakensberg via the most impractical and inconvenient route possible. In my white brain it seemed to be completely logical that the faster I did every single piece of my job the faster the money would come rolling in, and the faster the money came rolling in the sooner we would be in Cape Town at King Nelson's coronation. When the dishes emerged from the dishwasher on the conveyor belt I could not spare the time to dry them all by hand; they were so steaming hot that they would dry very quickly by themselves and I could spend that time doing something else. I would take them in my hands, pinching and juggling them about to stop the china coming into contact with my black skin for too long and burn me, and I would pile them up as the moisture evaporated off in the steam. I would rush to have them put away as fast as possible because I figured that this would propel me to my destination quicker than ever, and carry great and unstable towers of pristinely clean dishes back to the service cabinet where they were kept. I was eager and keen because the faster I got everything done the faster I could be back at the camp with Blessings and we could plot the revolution which would be sweeping across this luminous continent. Sometimes I would be too impatient and I would burn my fingers on the searing china, my fleshy fingertips stinging and prickling with the most exquisitely delicate pain. I would shake my wrists and rub my fingertips together to try to eradicate the pain but it was useless. I had been reaching out for happiness, stretching my hands forwards into the choking darkness and trying as hard as I could to make progress as hastily as was possible but in the end all I was left with was more pain than I had at the beginning.

One of the days when I was trying to be extra fast so that I could leave and use my time after work to plan my coronation outfit I picked up the plates whilst they were hotter than usual. I thought I could do it; I thought that I had enough strength in me to take them all the way over to the service cabinet but it turned out that my coconut shell was thinner than I thought. I had always welcomed the pain in my fingertips because I thought that if it was prolonged enough then my skin would fall off and I would be white again, that the burning in my flesh was a sure sign that there was something purer deep within me just bursting to get out. But the pain became unbearable and my hands were animated with movements all of their own; with an instinctive rush of adrenaline I retracted my hands and withdrew myself from the source of the searing, burning pain. The tower of plates, dozens of them, smashed to smithereens on the kitchen floor.

This all happened before I had received my first pay-check, and then I realised that I was being paid by the hour. This meant that

Michael Rogers

I had been scrambling to finish as fast as possible and burning my fingers as I did so only to end up being paid less and being further away from Cape Town because of it, not closer to my target as I had previously thought. The way that I describe it sounds slightly grander than it really was, because even though it was calculated by the number of hours I had worked I was paid in cash and the banknotes were often stained with bits of sauce and grease because more often than not the rand had come directly from the chef's apron pocket. I was not officially in formal employment and I was also fined for the cost of the plates which I had smashed in my haste which added to the misery and made my job of earning money in Pietermaritzburg an even more daunting task. As the lost funds mounted up higher and higher, Robben Island's umbilical cord was slowly being untethered from Cape Harbour and the island found itself drifting further and further away from the shore of Africa and into the freezing, lonely and endless Atlantic Ocean.

There was a large refrigeration unit outside of the building which could be reached by walking out of the back entrance of the kitchen. One day I walked barefoot to the fridge to get some bananas for a fruit salad that the chef was making. The fridge was dark and filled with mysterious black shapes. I turned on the light. I rummaged through the fresh melons, crisp and cold beneath my fingers. As I lifted the last one up to get to the bottom shelf where the bananas were I let out a shriek and keeled over backwards. An enormous spitting cobra rose up out of the pile of food, his collar spread wide and flushed with the murderous hue of poison. His fangs were huge and his eyes blazed with hatred for his intruder. I grabbed the bananas and slammed the door. I would have to figure out a way of avoiding ever going back to the fridge after that vile rendezvous.

Meanwhile Blessings was working as a cordwainer in the local shoe shop. He also did some work as a cobbler repairing shoes but most of his main task was to create new shoes from scratch. I think he had a better time of it than me, stuck all day doing wishy-washy, because I had learned by now that my first husband liked to work using his hands. This was the reason that he had become a diamond miner in the first place. The advantageous thing for me, in my dastardly bid for royalty as I scampered across the country trying to fill my pockets with as much money as possible so that we could afford the ransom of King Nelson, was that I had been fortunate and intelligent enough to marry an extremely fast learner. With every job that he began on our trip he seemed to take no time at all to become an expert. As well as the plain black leather shoes for the men, he also was tasked with making some astounding and very expensive shoes for rich white women. Aside from their twins, each and every shoe was completely unique and custom made to the most beautiful specifications imaginable. I would go into the shop sometimes when I was not needed in the kitchen; our experience in Pietermaritzburg seemed to be introverted and mismatched. I should be here, stitching together these things of beauty whilst my husband slaves away on the wishy-washy at that hellish kitchen. Blessings made beautiful shoes. One of my favourite pairs was a wonderfully bonkers pair of platform stilettos with a vamp decorated to look like the keys on a piano, delightfully highlighting the sharp contrast between the two colours. Another beautiful pair were made of deep black velvet and wrapped in criss-crossing shining black satin ribbon. Others were red, others gold and others green. Some showed a lot of skin and some kept the foot completely covered. Before I ducked my head and stepped into that dimly lit shop I had not realised the sheer variety of shoes that one single woman could own. It was bewildering.

I asked him to steal pairs of shoes for me numerous times, but sadly his conscience was simply too immaculate and spotless to surrender to my pleading and begging. He had a very high standard of morality which gave me no use for him. It made me wish all the harder for the imminent arrival of his murder and my matrimony to come. Wouldn't it be glorious if I could kick down the vast prison doors with my sparkling, diamond-encrusted stilettos? Queens need shoes, fool.

Sometimes I felt like a pair of shoes. The Almighty Cordwainer had wrapped my pale flesh in that black satin ribbon for reasons known only to Him. If I could make it to Cape Town and make him King then Nelson would surely unwrap me from my swaddling bandages of dark doom; only he knew how to untangle me because he was mummified in black satin just like mine. I felt like we were trying to use chopsticks which were ten feet long; we could not feed ourselves but we could feed one another if we worked as a team. I didn't like wearing shoes when I was working at the sink because they would often be ruined by the splashing water, but Chef told me that I had to wear them because it would break welfare laws if I was vulnerable to be sliced by the blade of a falling knife. He could get into trouble even if I had chosen to bare my feet. I didn't know whether or not to believe him—were there such things as labour laws for black people? Did anyone care whether or not I would drop one of the cleavers with my soapy hands, then by some miraculous misfortune look down to see the sharp and curling point chopping off my fat black toes? Nobody knew I was the one who would be married to the Head of State, so their concerns over my welfare seemed doubtful.

Because Pietermaritzburg was on the main highway from Durban to Johannesburg we had many seasoned travellers coming into the restaurant. If I was cleaning a table next to a group on a night that we were short of staff I would be able to eavesdrop on the most astonishing conversations as they boasted to one another about their experiences on the road. The men were particularly entertaining because they were driven by the masculine competitive spirit. I heard wild tales of heroism and adventure as uncountable as the stars in the sky above Sophiatown, but three of the stories were unforgettable and I knew that I would carry them with me to Cape Town.

The first man was young and local, and I guessed that he was on his way back up to Johannesburg after getting off a ship in Durban. He was entertaining a group of his friends, all of them sickeningly white, and gradually I heard his tale begin to unfurl.

"I was trekking through the mountains of Colombia last summer. I had made a promise to myself that I would have an open mind and that I would say yes to absolutely everything that I was offered, no matter what it was. I figured that if I did that then by the end of it I would at least have a lot of lekker stories to tell about the trip when I got home. I met a drug baron in a jazz bar in Bogotá on one of the last days of the journey and he offered to take me to see his fields when I told him that I didn't believe his boasts. He arranged for me to come to visit him and he gave me a horse to ride through the poppy fields. It was a wonderful thing to see, believe it or not; the whole of the valley was thick with clots of red flowers swaying gently in the breeze. It was a magical, ethereal place to be. The drug lord offered me a sample of some of his wares and true to form, I accepted. He ended up giving my name to some of his customers who were guards of the local jail, and he said that if I wanted to see the 'real Colombia' I could very easily slip in and have a look at the underground. He would show me the places that tourists never see.

"The prison guards in Colombia are incredibly corrupt. We managed to bribe them into letting me and a few of my friends into the jail and have a guided tour. The place was ominous and foreboding, a vast and labyrinthine cathedral to criminal justice, and people who were convicted of drug smuggling were likely to be killed within twenty four hours unless they paid to have secure accommodation in an isolated wing. The thuggery and violence was a great source of income for the jail authorities and so they had no interest whatsoever in stamping it out."

The story distressed me greatly. I thought of Nelson, alone on his little desert island in the middle of the ocean, chained to a palm tree on the powdery white beach. Was he being subjected to the same level of abusive corruption as the prisoners in Colombia were? Perhaps South Africa was the same and the conditions on Robben Island were desperately terrible. It was by no means inconceivable that my husband should be subjected to racist and political abuse, and I suffered from a dilemma which saw me wrestle with the conflicting notions of supporting or defying the corruption. Should I continue on my journey or should I simply send him the money from my wages in the hope that I could buy him protection and make his doomed incarceration as comfortable and enjoyable as possible? I did not know where Colombia was but I made a mental note that I needed to warn the King of these stories when the time would come for us to undertake our state visit there in 1985. It sounded Asian, and I imagined that it should be next to China. Yes, I thought; China sounds right. In my head all of the prison guards were terrifyingly oriental, uniform, robotic and identical to one another so that they formed a huge indistinguishable crowd. Individualism was dead. I can no more imagine being in a country where all of the people look the same than I can imagine being a person with a body and a soul of the same colour. Colombia sounded like Hell by another name.

The second man was a German. He spoke impeccable English, which was helpful because his mother tongue was not among my eleven native languages. He was very stern and serious, but his yarn was a thriller.

"I don't even remember where we were, but if I had to guess then I would say Malaysia. We had rented an old, decrepit house to stay in because we were on a tight budget from our unexpected long stay in Australia. This house was only small and it was right on the main road of the town, close to where all the action was. The landlady was an old, mad woman who lived a few streets away and would regularly check up on the house. We had been out exploring the countryside and we came back to find some of the windows of the house smashed and a strange oily substance spread all over the building and the little wall that surrounded the front garden. When we examined it closer and sniffed it we realised the whole house had been doused in petrol. It was everywhere; it had even been spread across the flowers in the front garden with a small paintbrush. We were terrified, but it was really late so there was nobody there to help us, so we had no choice but to go inside and go to bed. It was the longest and bleakest night of my life, because we spent every painful second waiting for the mob to come for us and blow up the house. Nothing happened. We went over to the landlady's house as soon as the sun came up and pummelled on her door, yelling and shouting and begging her to phone the police. 'What's the problem?' She asked us coolly. 'Someone has put petrol all over the house,' we answered. The woman looked confused, but it wasn't because she was upset that someone would want to attack her property. 'Of course someone put petrol all over the house, you idiots,' she bellowed at us. 'I did it. There were some imbeciles sitting on the wall of the garden smoking cigarettes all last week, I told them to move so many times that in the end I couldn't handle it any more. I drenched the house in petrol so that if they sit on my wall to smoke any more cigarettes, they will be blown to smithereens."

As I was clearing the dishes away I could not believe what I was hearing. Had this woman been mad and deluded, rampaging a trail of destruction across her own property just so that she could have the most fleeting of triumphs over a group of youths who caused her some mild irritation? The image of the woman's eyes blazing in the darkness of the night as she wielded the petrol can in surely the most extraordinary of Pyrrhic victories was a memorable sight to behold and was burned indelibly into my brain. Did she seriously consider the sacrifice of her property and her tenants worthwhile if it meant that these people could be exterminated for their crime? There seemed to be a shocking lack of perspective, rationality and logic and she had failed to ensure that her reaction was in line with the situation that she found herself in. I would never overreact like that. I am sane, wise and calm. What an idiot.

The third man was an Australian. He was the first Australian that I had seen on this journey but he would certainly not be the last. Australians are endowed with a sense of adventure which was unrivalled across the rest of the world; the tourists did not venture away from the South African coast a great deal and they were severely restricted by the Apartheid system, but in the journey ahead of me I would meet many more as I made my way to the ocean. Australians are so well-travelled that later on I would come to question whether or not there could possibly be any actually left in Australia or if it was instead a people permanently in transit as they adventured across the globe.

"When I was travelling across India I found myself walking down the worst possible street at the worst possible time. There was a group ahead of me and a group behind me, screaming and shouting abuse at one another and it was very violent and aggressive.

I didn't know what was happening. I found myself on the edge of some serious gang warfare. Out of nowhere another group arrived and they were carrying baseball bats; it became clear later on that somebody had got word out that they needed backup. I had no idea what had caused all the commotion but all of a sudden I found myself in the middle of a baseball bat war."

You dreamer, I chuckled to myself. You should see Sophiatown; that would make India feel like a birthday party! And then, with a sharp pang of reminiscent emptiness, I remembered that it was gone. All I could do was to look forwards, to keep going, but that's not to say that I didn't often catch my mind drifting backwards to my happy little shack in the gangster's paradise.

I came into the kitchen and there were other kitchen hands unloading an enormous crate of oranges from the fridge and preparing to peel them. As I walked past the oranges to get to the sink I heard them all yelling at me in Xhosa, but they were speaking too fast for me to understand what they were saying. I was concentrating on their rushed words, but if I had looked down then I would have noticed black shapes darting feverishly around at the bottom of the box. I suddenly felt an acute and sharp jabbing sensation in my shins; looking down I saw a huge rat digging his claws into my legs. I suppose that I should have been grateful that the kitchen uniform included long pants to cover me down to my ankles, but I screamed as loudly as I could as my eyes bulged as enormously as the watermelons in the fridge. The rat began to climb up my leg, his beady little eyes sparkling as black as my own skin and his whiskers twitching. His rancid tail was the colour of a heartstring. He opened his filthy little mouth and I could see his teeth, ready to gnash and gnaw at my coconut shell, so I raised my creased black hand and I slapped him as hard as I could. With an almighty whack he sailed through the air and eventually came to rest in the slop bucket where we would put the rotting leftover food waste to be fed to the pigs on the local farm. This rat was plump and heavy and he landed with a splash, sending a shower of sour milk, rancid cheese, mouldy bread and stagnant casserole up into the air. By some catastrophic coincidence the Head Chef had walked in a few seconds beforehand and was standing right beside the bucket as the unhappy rat landed in it, so his pristine white apron was immediately covered in the sludge of old food. The white linen was stained a disgusting shade of brown. He had been tainted, darkened and humiliated.

After a few seconds of silent, seething anger, Chef's eyes darted around the room at all of the members of his kitchen staff.

"Is there any particular reason why a rat was catapulted into this slop bucket?"

Nobody breathed. Chef peered into the bucket and saw the unconscious rat floating in a pool of milk, his little face submerged beneath an old cheesecake and his tail resting on a roast potato shaped like Table Mountain. I didn't know whether or not to be impressed with myself that I had killed the rat with one slap.

"Who was responsible for the flight of this rat across my kitchen?"

His eyes were fixed squarely on me. I knew that he knew that I had done it. My guilt blared as loudly as a giant vuvuzela.

I was ordered to leave immediately and Chef never bothered to pay me the money that he owed me for the last few days of my job. I never signed contracts with my employers so that the secret police would not be able to trace me, but in situations such as this the arrangement definitely did not work to my advantage because of the loss of the money that the employers were not obliged to pay me. Blessings quit and we began the next leg of our journey; Durban was further in the wrong direction but it logically seemed like the next place to go.

Nelson was so good to me; he constantly reassured me that I was the same as that brand new princess in London, overcome with adoration for her new husband, garnished with adornments and embellishments to make this tramp his treasure. Across the seas, the skies and the stars my King would encourage me to come home to him in his castle. I would often think of the kilometres lined up between him and me and I could feel him running his black fingers along the line of towns and cities that lay in my way, feeling the sensation as powerfully and tenderly as I would have done if he was tracing his fingers down the vertebrae in my spine. I was so connected to the landscape that I did not know where South Africa stopped and I began.

Onwards we trudged.

9

PLEASURE FOR SALE

Durban, Natal Province
March 1982

We hitched a ride down to Durban with a young black family in a battered old Morris Minor. It was rusty and creaky and the splitting seats smelt strongly of cheese and drugs. The driver was named George, as all drivers in South Africa seem to be. "George," I said with a smile, "take me to Durban."

Arriving in Durban was the first opportunity that I had to see the ocean at the age of thirty five. Nobody deserves to live for a third of a century without ever seeing the sea. We arrived in the late evening, and the streets of the city were deserted; vast, perfectly straight avenues bathed in the hushed glow of the yellow street lamps, the buildings quiet and ghostly. We tried to catch a minibus taxi to the beach as soon as we arrived, but none of the ones that we could find were available to pick up black people. We asked if we could use one even if it was empty, but the drivers would always tell us that if they were a taxi for white people and they were seen carrying black passengers then they could lose their licence, which was a risk they were not prepared to take. I was insulted and offended because I look a lot blacker than I really am, but this was too magnificent of an opportunity to be miserable for. We ended up asking directions and walking.

Michael Rogers

The city eventually surrendered its beautiful secret beneath the palm trees on a starlit night. The Indian Ocean, unimaginably vast and dark and beautiful, marked the very edge of the African continent and the whole world as I knew it lay entirely behind me. The sheer enormity of it was breathtaking as I stood with my husband, hand in hand, the wind feathering against my bare skin and stripping my darkness away from me. I never dreamt that something so black could be so incredibly beautiful at the same time. The ocean was endless, stretching out into space and colliding with the stars, a vast vacuum of darkness stretching out before me for an infinite eternity. I felt like a termite on the snow-covered summit of Kilimanjaro.

Shrieking and laughing, we raced down into the water to touch the Indian Ocean for the first time. Blessings had seen the sea before, but I had never gone outside of Transvaal and it was a new and thrilling sensation as I submerged my toes and legs in the water. We had no possessions other than the clothes that we were wearing and a few rand in savings, and my love was trapped in a jail because he had dared to stand up for equality, stranded and waiting for me. But as I sang so loudly that I thought my lungs would burst, cackling at the stars with my first husband in my arms, I knew that freedom was near. I had never felt more content or more hopeful that Durban would be the beginning of something wonderful for us.

"I think we are going to love it here," said Blessings as he gazed lovingly into my eyes. Being in love with Albert and Nelson had taught me to recognise when I was the apple of a man's eye. I was his lynchpin, the hub of his wheel, the axis of his Earth, his beginning and his end.

I smiled up at him. I had that same feeling that I had experienced when Nelson had burnt his Dom Pas to impress me. "Durban is going to be a great place for us," I whispered gently. Then I scooped up a great handful of water and unleashed it on him, the water flowing down his back and under his shirt. I cackled and he shrieked and wailed and screamed. Life was wonderful.

Durban is the largest port in the whole of the African continent, with beaches to the eastern fringe of the city along what came to be known as the Golden Mile, and a huge container port to the south with the influx of cargo ships providing a lifeline for the province and the rest of the nation. All the money, obviously, remained white. As with everywhere else in South Africa, whites and blacks were separated like the pieces on a chessboard. There was no part of the beach which was designated as a white area which I could be in, so I had to admire them from afar instead. The women looked like Jackie Kennedy had done back in the Sixties, with their impeccable straight hair and vivid red lips. I hate mirrors. They are such liars; they don't show me as I really am, but instead they separate me from the other white people I would see on the beach in Durban. It seems to me that the Government is not the true enemy when it comes to Apartheid, but instead it is the mirror which insists on telling me that I am black. These beautiful women, people who looked how I felt, were separated from me by a simple notice on a pole in the sand. Of course, the sign was written in black letters on a white background; there could be no mixing, even on the notices.

Under section 37 of the Durban Beach by-laws, this bathing area is reserved for the sole use of members of the white race group.

Like all of the other towns and cities that we came across on our journey towards Nelson's Prison in Cape Town I had no idea what type of work I would be doing, and I spent the first few days walking around the city trying to find a job that would pay towards our journey. I asked in all manner of establishments, for the Golden Mile was rich with heavy developments attempting to transform this city into a resort which would beckon tourists from all over the world to come and enjoy the subtropical climate. I enquired in hotels and restaurants, casinos and shopping malls, expecting to be ignored but being confronted instead with a racist hatred at the unfortunate way that I looked. The managers of the hotel were concerned that I would frighten the guests with my "voodoo or whatever the hell it is you are into" and one of the managers spat in my face when I protested at his suggestion that I might be susceptible to tampering with the men's drinks in his bar.

Blessings managed to get work before I did, as a hauler in the container port. It was quite an achievement as the port in Durban had relied very heavily on international trade and by the time we got there the international community had placed tough trading sanctions on South Africa because of the disapproval of Apartheid by the rest of the world. This had an effect on the amount of trading ships that called at Durban to deliver their precious cargo. Business was slowing, but it was obviously still strong enough to maintain the valuable imports and exports which passed through the port every day. Durban was half maritime city, half exotic subtropical playground.

There was a small haulage company who offered him work loading boxes into the containers which would be lifted by cranes onto the enormous freight ships in the harbour. He would go there in the early morning and by sunrise he would be hard at work lifting the heavy boxes with his bare arms, loading up the massive containers and sorting through the cargo.

As the sun lifted above the horizon there would often be a heavy mist coming off the ocean which very few people would see as it was soon burnt off by the subtropical heat of the day. Durban has the warmest average temperature of anywhere in the country all the year long, so we were mightily blessed. It was quite a sight to see the gentle sunshine of the dawn illuminating the blanket of mist as Africa gently stirred from her slumber. I managed to see it a couple of times because Blessings would wake me as he left for work on the most beautiful days.

I asked for work in a newsagent shop on the beachfront. The dreamy views of the ocean shaded by palm trees and punctuated by beautiful people posing made it seem like the perfect place to work in the deliciously warm weather. It was August, in the middle of deepest darkest winter, but Durban's year long subtropical climate made every day a great day to be beside the beach. Unfortunately though this particular newsagent did not have any employment opportunities and he thought I was trying to rob him.

As I turned to leave I caught a glance of the front pages of the newspapers on the shelf. On each and every one was an image of

King Sobhuza II of Swaziland; as I inspected the papers more closely I saw that they were reporting his death. He was the longest reigning monarch in accurately recorded human history with a continuous period on the throne of more than 82 years.

Just like the Royal dynasties of Europe, it seemed that Africa's crowned houses were also interlinked for the sake of suitability. Zenani, the daughter of Nelson and Winnie who I would create as Princess Zenani of South Africa, had married Prince Thumbumuzi, the incoming King Mswati III of Swaziland's older brother. Her father had not been permitted to attend the wedding in Mbabane and was kept in detention on Robben Island because it had taken place during his jail sentence. As I scanned the article for a reference to him I realised something about the Swazi Royal Family that I had not known beforehand; the Royal Dynasty was known as the House of Dlamini.

When I was looking for work in a local butcher's shop they told me that they knew of a strip club that was hiring on an industrial estate close to where we were staying. I thanked them but politely declined their recommendation, but as I prepared to leave the shop they told me that they didn't need strippers. They needed cleaning and bar staff.

The club was hidden away in a place where it would be almost impossible to find it without the aid of memory and word of mouth. The outside of the building was shabby and dilapidated, but walking through the door was like transcending the heavens and landing in another world. The receptionist was beautiful, and she sat behind a polished desk of dark wood with a large fish tank set into the wall behind her. She showed me through to an office, past the suited bouncers, where some managers were waiting for me. They asked me if I had any previous experience of cleaning, and I told them that I did. They hired me immediately.

When I went into the main room, the hedonistic sensuality of it all took my breath away. It was like suddenly holding my head underwater and seeing the whole world through a kaleidoscopic lens. I had never been to one of these places before but I had always known that they had existed, and being confronted with the raw reality of women selling their bodies and access to their sexuality as a commodity and a career was a stunning and unwelcome revelation.

Psychedelic strobe lights were pulsing from the stage, and the room was set out with some low tables and sofas arranged in groups, with podiums and poles set out in the corners of the room. It was a large room, and the ultraviolet lights gave the whole place an electric, otherworldly feel.

The dancers were all white women because there was no way that a man would want to look lustfully at a black girl. Sexual attraction tends to be as racist as the economic reality of living here, meaning that white men are usually attracted to white women, and since the white men are the ones with all the money in this country, it would be white men that we had to focus on attracting through the doors. If I got up there and started peeling off my clothes whilst gazing into the client's eyes with a look of seduction, you could guarantee that any man of mine would be too black to be able to afford a piece of me at the kind of prices that they needed to keep this club running. They may well find a man to love me if I stood up on the stage with my voluptuous body priced on the cocktail menu, but they were not trying to find love. They were trying to find obscene amounts of profit.

My job was to wipe the poles after the girls had danced. There were different types of dancing that the man could pay the women to perform for him, and he would choose from a list like a drinker in a cocktail bar glancing over the delicious, succulent and juicy items on the menu. The girls would rub their legs and breasts and skin and tongues all over the pole as they gyrated and cavorted against it, and my job would be to remove the juice and saliva and grease and fingerprints. The poles were made of steel and had to be absolutely spotless, and as I looked at my black face in the brushed metal I would only be able to think of the bars of Nelson's prison cell. I was thankful for these reminders that I was being given, because they gave me the drive and the determination that I needed to see the job through and remember why I was here. The future of the entire nation's freedom from oppression was shared equally between Nelson and I, and I did not want to let anyone down.

I was very wary of doing the job, because I was afraid that I would bring shame and scandal upon Nelson through my connections with this place being in jeopardy with my relationship with the King. Would there be an investigative journalist waiting for me with his evidence at my coronation? Would my colleagues at the strip club sell their sleazy stories about me in return for millions of rand in payment? Nelson was at that very moment swimming with mermaids as they dived for starfish around his tropical island as I was working in the club. He had been humiliated enough by prison life without having to endure the shame of his future wife working in a seedy strip club.

I would stand in the corners of the club carrying a trigger bottle of cleaning fluid and a cloth, which I would use to get the equipment as clean as possible as fast as I could. Alternatively the man would be able to book a table dance, where a woman would frolic all over the table, writhing and squirming sexily as she slowly peeled off her minimal items of clothing. As soon as she was finished I would pounce, as stealthily as a lioness, and wipe away every trace of bodily contact, ready for the next girl and the next group of rich businessmen. Finally the women could invite a single man into a private booth where she would perform a private dance for him behind a red velvet curtain, and as soon as the two of them emerged with her hair dishevelled and his eyes filled with hungry love I would have to go in and clean whatever I suspected that she had touched.

A lot of the men were married. Some would take off their wedding rings but we could always tell from the tan lines on their rich white skin, but most of them would not even bother to conceal it and wore their rings proudly. I saw one man on my first night of work take off his ring and hold it against the nipple of one of the strippers as he buried his head in her bosom.

Many of the clients at the club were overweight and unattractive and clearly won sexual gratification through finance and not through virtue. They leered over the girls like a gourmand would with a piece of meat, stripping their clothes off like the leaves on an ear of ripe corn. As I watched some of them, waiting to clean the smears off of their tables, I saw the opaque glaze of lust clouding their eyes, drooling and slobbering as they took their fill not through their mouths but through their eyes.

In a way I was upset and offended by the fact that the men liked the strippers and completely ignored me. I knew that if there was some way that I was able to peel off my skin and reveal the immaculately white flesh beneath it, the dazzling and blemishless expanse of perfect tissue as pristine as the snow at the top of Kilimanjaro, then all would be well. If I could prove my whiteness to them then they would pay me enough money for a wiggle of my magnificent bangers to be able to afford a plane ticket from Durban to Cape Town and I could personally ensure that Nelson would be free within the week. The men we had were often extremely wealthy, perhaps managing directors and board members of the giant business corporations in Johannesburg, who would come down to Durban for the weekend and would make regular trips to this club as they claimed that the travel was part of their job. Durban was the closest and most glamorous seaside resort to Transvaal's cathedral of capitalism, and was the perfect place to go when time was scarce. Some of them I felt some genuine sympathy for, because for every three or so rich businessmen who could afford to have sex every night and saw no reason why they should not do so, there would be one middle aged man who had clearly been single all his life, or who had crippling confidence issues when it came to befriending women. These men were using their money to buy their way in to a dress rehearsal so that they could have the confidence to approach women who did not strip for them as a form of employment. Some were young men determined not to enter their twenties as virgins, and others were confused about their sexualities and had come here to observe the unshrouded female form as a means of finding out whether or not they were straight. A few women would come to the club too, some with fetishes for open relationships and others to get inspiration on their quest for the perfect body. Very few of them were lesbians. I found it funny and would have a silent snigger to myself as I scrubbed the table when they had left, because the white people, both client and stripper alike, had learnt to completely ignore me because of the colour of my coconut shell. Because of this they were remarkably bold in unwittingly disclosing private information to me whenever I was within earshot, and I had an unprecedented view of the seedy life of Durban and all of the colourful characters who would come through the doors. I did not know if they were being reckless or if they did not consider me important enough to care what I heard, but whatever the reason for their indiscretion I quickly became the person at the club who knew everything that there was to know about everyone else there.

The girls were careful and everything that they did was to maximise their revenue. The clients would have to pay fifteen rand just to walk through the doors of the club and then every dance and service was individually priced, and along with the alcohol would be itemised on one handy and convenient bill, to be paid either individually or by the whole group at the end of the night. The girls would greet each man or group as they entered and sit with them on the low leather sofas which had just been sprayed and wiped by me, perhaps putting one of her stilettoed and freshly waxed legs across the gentleman's lap as she asked him questions about his life and his interests and pretended to listen attentively. They used to call it the "golden fifteen," for if the man had not asked for a lap-dance or table-dance within fifteen minutes they would be able to tell that he was not in the financial league that he needed to be to claim their time and if there were other men in the club they would move away. No matter how ugly or inappropriate the other clients were, the strippers would always select the ones who paid them the most money in the shortest time.

I was never going to be best friends with these white women, and our relationship remained very basic as I wiped their slime off of the poles after they had finished. But the one thing that I did know for certain was that most of them were happy and loved their job. They loved the attention and they enjoyed the empowerment of having the masculinity and the finances of their clients at their disposal. I wondered where the girls had come from and what had led them to this most unusual and degrading of career paths.

Surprisingly, none of them were South Africans; a lot of them came from Eastern Europe and Scandinavia and obviously wanted to make a decent amount of money whilst they were here, which meant that oddly enough I was probably far closer to being a legal worker than they were even though they were earning many multiples of my wage. Some of them must surely have tainted personalities, secret addictions and desperate situations which had led them up to this point but it was not a place of wretched hopelessness and misery. I would have much preferred it if it was.

I think that I secretly wanted them to be enslaved by their profession and to hate every second of it because that would have been much easier to accept. The surprising revelation that a little girl could actually grow up wanting to do this job and living a luxurious, happy and successful life as a stripper was deeply troubling and it unsettled me greatly. I disagreed with the principle of having the women parade themselves before their wealthy clients in exchange for payment, but I was surprised to find that my expectation of them being desperately unhappy slaves who had been kidnapped for their good looks, or using the considerable income from this job to fuel their hopeless descent into drug or alcohol addiction was simply not true. No doubt those things occurred within this industry somewhere in the world at any given time but what shocked me most about this job was the fact that there were reasons other than utter desperation which would lead a beautiful young woman to choose this lifestyle. That was a difficult truth to comprehend and it was an inconvenience to the opponents of the industry who claimed that it was exploitative.

I did not like the way that sex and love had been completely separated from one another; it was a tragedy and a sad day for the beautiful virtue of humanity, as much as the dancers seemed to enjoy their jobs. I would listen as they would explain to the men the answers to questions that I did not dare ask them myself, especially by the youngest and the most nervous of the clients, and most of the time they would explain that their favourite part of the job was testing their ability to strike up a conversation and to become familiar acquaintances with a very large circle of unique and interesting people who they would encounter in their line of work. Rather than being imported in heaving slave ships blighting the Atlantic Ocean making the crossing from Europe to Africa they told the clients that they were "living the dream" in Durban and that they loved living in the warmest city in the country and had most of the sunlight hours as time off to sunbathe and relax with plenty of money to spend on themselves or send home to Europe. It was a good lifestyle, there was no doubt about that, but did that justify the questionable working environment and the commodity being exchanged for the money they lived on?

After work one evening I was coming back to the shack I shared with Blessings when I noticed that a man was following me. I recognised him as I pretended to look to the alley wall to the side of me rather than behind me and remembered that he had been a client at the club. He was a sweaty, overweight white man who had come down to Durban to play for the weekend and he would hire one girl at a time, staying with her until she took the last of his money and she moved on to somebody with a deeper pocket and a higher sex drive. Testosterone equalled cash. He had not fared particularly well with the 'golden fifteen' test and I could tell from the body language of some of the girls that he was getting a bit of a reputation as someone who was unhappy to part with his cash.

I never knew his name and he never knew mine, but he changed my life forever. He took from me what did not belong to him because his sexual desires had not been quenched by the limited funding in his wallet. He could not pay for it from them, so he took it from me after the club had closed. I felt his hands closing in around my neck and he wrenched me into a corner of the alley. We were perfectly alone and I felt like Nelson had when they had taken him and slung him into a jail cell on a rock in the South Atlantic. The storms raged on the surface of the sea surrounding my jail as he pressed my back up against the wall, sending a thrilling pain thumping through my spine as he forced himself upon me. His whiteness hurt me through the darkness. I could smell his sweat as he clung to me, his Caucasian hair smelling of money and dirtiness and his hairy arms feeling like a marble statue as I held on to them. I had, for a fraction of a second, a delicious and exhilarating sensation of the anticipation of life's imminent and permanent end. I was kept alive by the lurking instinct within me which alerted me to the danger of wrestling with him on the edge of a vast precipice, knowing that if I let him he would fling me over the edge and I would topple down into oblivion.

He had a phenomenal strength for a man of such a small and awkward stature. He was fast, warm and untidy, and he finished with a blistering haste as he rampaged through my palatial castle. He turned over the furniture and smashed the decorations, ripped the priceless tapestries off of my walls and burned the curtains and carpets. He did not feel the same as Blessings had; my first husband had been a gentle guest at my castle. This man was rough and feverish, scraping and chafing my flesh as he went, gouging at my eyeballs and tearing at my hair in a bid to keep me still. I did not cooperate, and that was very sore.

After he had finished with me, I knew that our time in Durban had come to an end and that we needed to move on. Nelson was so patient with us; he never stopped waiting and hoping and dreaming.

10

AN UNWANTED SOUVENIR

Port Edward, Natal Province
January 1985

Telling my husband that a man had raped me was the most difficult experience of my life. It was a devastating feeling knowing that my disappointingly black body had been stolen from me, but also knowing that I had offered him a service which I could have earned a considerable amount of money for which would have propelled us further and further towards our goal in Cape Town. If I had managed to be a prostitute or a stripper or a call girl I would have lowered my chances of getting sexually abused. That seemed so desperately unfair.

Leaving Durban was not a logistically simple thing to do. We never had any money but this leg of the trip was especially bad for finances and when I told the club owner the next evening that I wanted to leave he simply laughed at me and told me that leaving was forbidden. I was simply not allowed to go. I carried on working there for another three days but every time a client, any client, walked through the door I would shudder and panic and I knew that I could not continue. It was a horrible sickening feeling which swept over me like a rash, and I would stay awake panicking about how we would leave. I felt like a slave. Eventually we had to just run away from Durban, but I knew that they would be chasing us. We hopped in the back of a freight truck which was heading for Port Edward and found ourselves travelling in secret amongst packaged nappies and tubs of aqueous cream.

On arrival in Port Edward I checked myself into the nearest hospital for an appointment to see if the man had done me any damage. I felt as though my flesh had been torn and my internal organs were bruised beneath his enormous heaviness and masculine might, and I wanted to know if I was still ordered correctly inside my abdomen. I told the doctor with rushed and untidy boldness about every grim and gruesome detail of my ordeal, and he seemed overwhelmed at the bravery which I displayed and the frankness which I employed when returning to the memories of the assault. But in reality I was not being unnecessarily brave. It needed to be done, for I was not in the slightest concerned with my personal safety but more for my ability to reach Cape Town and save Nelson so that together we could save the nation and save the continent in the name of freedom. The doctor did not have good news for me.

"You are pregnant, Mrs Mngomezulu."

The word sliced through my heart like a rusty dagger. How were we going to be able to cope with a baby to burden us as we made our important pilgrimage to Cape Town, another mouth to feed and another bed to find each night? I did not want to be a mother, I did not have any desire to see my body through the trials and tribulations of labour, I did not have any objection to my womb being forever sealed over and abandoned to bleak desolation. That would have been fine. I simply sat on the bed with my mouth wide open, the size and shape of Lake Victoria, and after he had given me a few seconds alone with my thoughts he continued with his barrage of scandalous news.

"I also have the result of your sexual health test," he said with a revealing gravity in his voice. "We believe that your attacker has passed a virus on to you. You have an aggressive virus in your system, but we are unable to identify exactly what it is."

I was not sad, but stunned. How could that be? How could a white man, a man so ethnically perfect, give me this wretched physical curse? Can white men even get sexual diseases; is it not surely a black man's scourge? How could he have been infected, and how could I now be infected as well?

"Wait," I said, finally moving my mouth. "I'm pregnant?"

His answer was short and devastating. "Yes."

"But how can that be?" I spluttered. "We were standing up when he attacked me. I was pressed against a wall. How can he have impregnated me when I was not lying down in a bed?"

The doctor looked confused. I could not believe that I was in the position of attempting to educate a doctor on medical phenomena and the biology of human reproduction. It was a wonder that he had ever passed his exams before he met me.

"You do realise, Mrs Mngomezulu, that pregnancy can be the result of unprotected sexual contact of any kind between the genitals of a man and a woman?"

I sat on the bed with my mouth wide open. This was a shocking revelation and, I hoped, an untruthful one.

I pictured in my mind the little life inside of me, the jumbled mass of cells and flesh seething like a tumour beneath my skin. It was a hellish thought to comprehend that there was a living thing lurking in my belly, a new and unwanted life inside me that was not my own. The baby, if a baby it may be called, was a demonic souvenir of the man who had attacked me and to imagine it festering within me was something that I could not bear to comprehend. It felt like a parasite, a vile leech inside me, sucking the life and energy out of me as though the umbilical cord was some kind of ghastly drinking straw. My immediate reaction was that the pregnancy should be terminated as fast as possible. We could not afford to have a baby; we could not afford to survive ourselves and we needed to be saving every precious cent for the journey, not wasting it on food for a child who was not ours who we did not want. This was a vitally important chapter in the history of our nation and I could not let Nelson's shot at glory be jeopardised by a drunk white man on his way home from a strip club. It was such a seedy, pornographic and incredibly demeaning way for the enlightened struggle to come to an end, not in a spectacular finale as I had planned but instead in a humiliating and embarrassing defeat. A grimy alleyway on an industrial estate in Durban was no place for freedom to die.

The doctor recommended that I go to the dispensary on the ground floor of the hospital and collect some medicine for the virus that the man had passed on to me. The line was very long and people were getting hot and frustrated. Every so often a white patient would arrive at the dispensary and was able, by entitlement, to walk straight to the front of the line and collect what he or she needed from the desk. I felt just as mistreated as the rest of the black people in the line, but my objection was altogether nobler. I was once again exposed to the brutal and searing pain of remaining racially anonymous and unrecognised, where people treated me to less than I was rightfully entitled due to the misleading colour of my skin. I was the only white South African to ever remain at the back of the line and wait my turn, the only white South African to submit to other whites and to take my place among the blacks. Being raped and infected with a mysterious virus was degrading, but because I had already lived my life as a coconut I was well accustomed to humiliation and shame.

Nobody knew exactly what to call the virus that I was suffering from so any form of pharmaceutical treatment was very difficult for me to learn how to trust. They had made it very clear to me that the medicines were in their infancy and I knew deep down that they were little more than a placebo. The days of being able to slow down this infection were far ahead of us. If only that man had raped me in the 1990s then maybe everything would be better.

*   *   *

As I got back from the hospital I found my husband with the journal I had bought in Lesotho in his hands. It was perfectly clear that he had been reading it.

"*Coconut Shells*," he said to himself calmly. Is that the title of a book you are writing?

He clutched it tightly and examined every inch of each magical piece of paper. Horrified, I dashed over to snatch it out of his miserable black hands but I was too slow. He turned away from me and opened my book, *my precious and beautiful book*, at a random page and began to read from it.

"The day I met Nelson in Orlando West was the great divide between the eras of my life. My life before Nelson and my life with him now are like my morning and my afternoon, my BC and my AD, my night and my day." He closed the book and he looked over it with an angry curiosity.

"What is this?"

"It's my book. I am writing about this trip." There was a sense of defeat in my voice; I had never wanted him to find out.

"Why are you writing it?"

"I am writing it for the sake of history. I am going to change the world, Blessings. I want everyone to know how it came to pass."

His eyes blazed angrily. "Do you think you can just write what you want about me? Am I some kind of shadow? Some sort of ousie, perhaps? Why have you written about me as if I am a weak follower of yours, too deluded to do anything but follow you wherever you go? Is that really how you see me?"

I said nothing, so he began to read.

"This man was not a prophet but a demented idiot, a vile cheekyprawn. Why should he know all there was to know about being in the wrong body? How could he know how it felt? How could he feel the emotion and the symbolic power of who I am?"

I have always had a burning hatred of listening to people reading my work to me. I was overcome with embarrassment; I wanted everyone in the world to read this book but I did not want to be with them when they did. He was the last man on Earth who should have read it and he looked up at me with an expression of horror agitating his silly little black face.

"What's wrong with you, Lerato? Why can't you see anything from a point of view other than your own?" He slapped the page of the book with his palm. "You're so obsessed with me understanding you, but you have never tried to understand how I feel! Why don't you write about the real reason why I am taking you with me to Cape Town? Why don't you write about my father?"

Die dof, flou moegroe was losing his mind. I think the poison of his black skin was seeping through his skull and polluting his brain. I was dismissive of his intelligence and I snatched the book away from him, but I would be a liar if I told you that I wasn't worried about what this meant. How much of this sacred document, this cornerstone of literature, had he read? Would he be honest about the revelations he had been exposed to? Thank goodness he had not discovered that I was in love with Nelson and that I would one day be Queen. It was a stroke of luck that he did not realise that I planned to have him killed and he sailed onwards towards the Mother City in blissful ignorance.

I did get some good news to cheer me up after the trauma of realising that I had a new illness, that I was going to be a mother and that my husband may have uncovered every one of my secrets. My old neighbour from Orlando West, Desmond Tutu, had been given the Nobel Peace Prize in recognition of his steadfast opposition to the Apartheid regime and his tireless campaigning for the release of Nelson Mandela. My own new dawn of promise was coming soon; compared to me this Archbishop of Cape Town was a failure. He had fought valiantly for freedom and equality and if he had been a coconut he would have been able to manage to release Nelson from jail. Everyone was looking for their hero in the wrong place and the wrong person. Their champion had been here all along in the form a pregnant woman with a mysterious virus more than a thousand kilometres from home. What was wrong with the monochromes which prevented them from recognising me for who I was? When I saw the Archbishop again I would be wrenching my prize out of his grubby little hands, make no mistake about that.

Just as my child was beginning to form within me, my husband began a hideous job as an undertaker. To begin with he was not permitted to deal with the corpses but instead was given a shovel and told to go and dig holes for them to rot in. The earth beneath him was cold and fresh and as he turned it over it was an intense, rich ochre colour. Blessings dealt mainly with the bodies of people with no families or people who had no money for a large funeral, so the coffins were wooden and simple and Blessings' hole in the ground was all the monument they would be given.

When he came home from work he would tell me all the stories of the day. One of the odd observations that he made was the fact that the corpses, even after death, were known as "clients". The funeral would be conducted in the name of the client and the file and all correspondence with the family would be in their name. It was a curious technique that was used to endow these complex bundles of flesh and bone with a sense of identity and dignity after the spirit within had flown away. When Blessings would ask to speak with a member of staff, quite often the reply would come back as "they are just dealing with a client at the moment." This seemed infinitely more sensitive and respectful than to describe the task at hand as, say, washing the bloodstained machete-wound which had killed them or drenching the corpse in solution to keep the maggots at bay.

During our brief stay in Port Edward I managed to land my most unusual job yet, taking up work at a wigmaker's shop. If I was going to have an abortion it would undoubtedly cost a lot of money if I did not want to get badly injured in the process. Only the very finest abortion would do for the future Queen of South Africa. There could be no rusty spears, no swallowing of chlorine and no gouging of my womb with a butcher's cleaver. The child would be disposed of using the tap of a magic wand on my enormous belly and with a streak of glitter passing between my legs the whole sorry episode could be forgotten and we could walk forwards together into the promised land. The thing would be removed from me on a bed strewn with white rose petals with a string orchestra playing quiet concertos in the background as we feasted on mangoes and pomegranates. Blessings kept whining about the pain it would cause me, but he obviously had not been listening when I had told him that I was on my way to rescue the King. Little did he know that very same King would be his replacement as my husband; with the assurance of Nelson I was absolutely convinced that the abortion would be so painless that I would barely notice it. In simple terms this coconut was too good, too rare a specimen, for the curse of abortion to wound her body.

We would have huge sacks delivered to us from the barbers and I would have to sort through the hair, wash it and arrange it by colour and texture. I was instructed to get rid of all of the hair I could find which was from black people because it was too wiry, too thick and oily for the wigs. My manager never told me explicitly but I suspected that it was because he assumed the hair would be dirty. He told me that the texture of the black hair was completely wrong and would be too difficult to knit together coherently and flush against the net at the base of the wig. The truth of it was that we all knew that nobody in their right mind would want to wear the hair of a nigger in a wig on their head. It was the economics of fashion; there was a certain amount of revenue needed to keep the company afloat, and black hair was simply not popular enough to bring in the amount of money needed. It simply was not worth the time and effort, so I sorted it into a separate sack to be used as kindling for the fire although it didn't burn especially well. If the barber sprayed it with hairspray before it was delivered to us, however, it would burn very nicely indeed. Half of it was burned in the shop in the winter and half of it was given to Blessings and I to burn at home so that we could get a little fire going. Not having to pay for kindling, the wigmaker told us, was a perk of the job. He never took any home for his own wife and family; he didn't like to touch it because of the peculiar sensation he felt when he held it between his fingers. Sis.

There was a parrot in the workshop where I would sit, sorting and stitching my way through the human hair. I asked the wigmaker why he had a parrot in a cage and he told me that he liked to have another living thing in the room where he spent lots of time alone because the parrot kept him company. I was spooked by the ugly bird and we spent much of the day with our huge eyeballs locked together in a stare to the death. Had I not been pregnant and in the middle of the most important rescue mission in African history I would have issued the vile green bird with an ultimatum; either you go or I go. The bird told me that he was really a flamingo inside and that by a cruel mistake by his Creator he had been given the wrong body, but I laughed his outlandish claims off as an attempt to unnerve his opponent and insensitively mock my rare condition. This devilish green-feathered enemy would have to do considerably better than that to beat me.

Our clients who would buy the wigs from us varied greatly. Most of the money would come from party shops and fancy dress retailers followed by film and television costuming departments. Very few of the wigs, I was surprised to find, were sold to people who had no natural hair, whose heads gleamed like mangoes ripening under a juicy African sky. But there were some. Some of the customers would come in individually, bald as a gem squash and as curious as a meerkat, and would pay for the ornate wigs to turn their heads into fashion statements. From Port Edward our wigs would travel a great distance and end up in the cities right along the coast. This country seemed to be getting bigger and bigger every day of the journey.

The little shop also made hats, although not very many of them. I would make fascinators, which were headpieces which would be worn as fashion accessories but only by the extremely rich and adventurous. I would stitch together the ostrich feathers to a headband or a hairclip in a riotous explosion of colour and texture and shape. It would sometimes end up looking like a cross between a star and a crown, and we would dye the feathers in starchy vats of ink to create fashionable styles. I thought that the feathers which had been dyed red made the wearer look a little bit like Kennedy on his final day, his head crowned with unhappy streaks of crimson. I would have loved to have known what they used to dye the feathers with but they never told me. After I kept repeatedly asking, my boss turned around and simply said "magic, Lerato. It's magic."

Where was I to get some of this magic from? How could I obtain it? I was downhearted to know that none of the mysterious vats contained any white ink, for if there was such a thing I would have crept in during the night after my work was done and plunged my naked body into the cleansing white liquid, allowing it into my every pore and orifice, the thick ink seeping through me and into the thing within my womb. It would surely be a means of removing all of our troubles to sink myself into an enormous pot of paint.

It would rid me of this ghastly virus, it would end my agonising dilemma and it would assure my ascension as Queen.

As I was making a black and green Halloween headpiece I thought for the first time about the colour of my baby. Surely it would be white, taking my soul and the skin of its father. The bundle of cells within me would be bleached with beauty, adorned with pale splendour and endowed with a hue of glory when it formed itself into being. Given that both the parents were white, I could not think of any more logical conclusion to come to than the baby having white skin. It was an undeniable and unshakeable fact and at first I did not give it any further thought.

One day, as I was stitching curly blonde hair together into a wig, the parrot called me a munter. I was quite taken aback at the spitefulness of this vile little bird. As his owner came into the room he immediately went back to chirping and dancing on his stand in front of the mirror in the cage, the ghastly little sod.

*　　*　　*

Blessings was not happy when I told him about the thing lurking inside my womb. How could he be? I reassured him that there was every possibility that the thing could have been his, but there was no way that it was convincing enough for him to believe. We both knew, and yet I kept up the pretence with the steadfast professionalism of any of the actors wearing wigs knitted by me. Eventually he confronted me over the fact that I was in denial that I was carrying a rape baby in my belly. I was not in denial at all, but instead I was too ashamed of the obvious and inevitable truth of the hellish matter that I could not bring myself to admit to another, not even my husband, the fact which I knew to be true.

After a few short days of pretending that I had every intention of keeping and raising the child as our own dear and beloved baby, I gave up and I asked Blessings if we could have a conversation about the plausibility of an abortion. He seemed displeased.

"I will not permit the murder of a baby which could be mine."

"How come you are suddenly now so sure that you are the father of this child? Who was the one challenging me over the fact that I was in denial? It's not yours, Blessings. We both know that. The baby isn't yours. I am pregnant because I was raped."

"You can't kill your baby, Lerato. This baby was meant to be born for a reason and it is wrong for us to stand in the way of that."

"This child could be the difference between us making it to Cape Town and managing to release Nelson, or us getting there too late and the Apartheid system being in place forever. The whole future of this nation depends on us, and we depend on being as employable as possible so that we can make it to Cape Town as fast as we can. Nobody is going to want to give a job to a woman with a tiny baby."

During this time of indecision and hopelessness Nelson appeared as an apparition to calm and soothe me. The Government had offered him his freedom in exchange for a promise to end the militant struggle for universal democracy and the violent campaigns of the ANC against the authoritarian state. If you go quietly, they said, you are free to go. Zindziswa delivered a response speech which had been written by her father. In it she declared proudly that he would never negotiate his own freedom with the freedom of his people and that he would never give up the fight until the freedom of all South Africans was secure. "Why do they come to me to negotiate? Only a free man can negotiate."

The parrot laughed at me, calling me a fat, useless slag. He told me that I did not deserve hair as beautiful as the wigs I was making for the white women. I was doomed to darkness for the rest of my days.

There was a dilemma which we were now faced with which was incredibly troubling. What were we to do with the baby? I knew that Blessings did not want an artificial abortion, but in all honesty I did not know of a credible alternative. We had no resources to support a family and we had a mission to complete which was of extreme and monumental importance for the future of millions of South Africans. The baby was mine, not even ours, and the shred of love that I felt for it was immediately extinguished by the reminder that its unborn life was a drop in the ocean of promise and opportunity that lay ahead of us without the foetus in my belly. We had so much to hope for, so much to expect from the hedonistic sense of opportunity which glimmered beautifully on the African horizon far ahead, that I could not logically justify preserving the life of my child because it meant giving all of that up. I could not abandon Nelson in the way that the rest of the world had abandoned him, leaving him to die in a jail cast adrift and geographically separate from the rest of the country. I was faced with a direct choice between my baby and my fantasy and it was an incredibly easy decision to make. Human life, unfortunately, is subject to economics and at the moment I simply could not afford to be pregnant. My motherhood could not go ahead, but it seemed slightly unfair that this child should be condemned to death by the pregnancy not going ahead either. Was there some sort of amicable compromise that could be reached?

The parrot mocked me and tormented me as I stitched, laughing and shrieking as I embroidered the ribbons into the hat on my desk. You're not a Queen, he said. Mandela doesn't even know who you are.

Enough! Unable to endure another second of his relentless screeching I stood up, throwing my chair over in the process, and waddled over to him. I flung open the door of the cage and grabbed him by the wing, spinning him around my head and thrashing him until his bright green feathers started to sink silently to the floor. As I swung his squawking little body around he began to blur into a single green wheel before I finally released him and he went shooting headlong into the wall. Upon impact he stayed still for a split second before he slid down to the floor, and I was ready with my raised foot to stamp on his head as soon as he landed in his crumpled heap. I didn't notice the wigmaker creeping up on me as the parrot's infernal screeching came to a raspy end.

"What are you doing to my pet parrot, Lerato?"

"I am killing him, sir."

"Why are you killing him?"

"I am killing him because he called me black, sir."

The wigmaker was too aghast to know what to say first in response to this unexpected turn of events. There were so many things that he could not understand, so much that he saw as wrong with what I was doing. The poor white man did not understand my reasoning at all, which meant that he was a man of monumental stupidity.

"But you *are* black, Lerato."

"Don't you dare say that to me, sir," I said with my eyes blazing as I scraped the blood and feathers off of my foot, "or you will be next."

"Lerato are you aware that this parrot cannot talk?" I remained silent. He continued. "I have never trained him to chat to me and I have never heard him speak."

"That's a lie. You told me that he kept you company."

"It's a figure of speech to say that I appreciate him being there, I didn't mean that we literally have conversations. Do you have these hallucinations regularly?"

"What hallucinations do you mean? I am perfectly sane. I heard the devilish little beast speaking to me with my own ears. He told me that he is a flamingo trapped inside the body of a parrot."

Rather than thinking that I was hallucinogenic the wigmaker decided from that comment that I was insulting him and being unimaginably rude and disrespectful. I was fired with immediate effect and his final words to me as he threw me out into the street were to let me know in no uncertain terms that he did not care whether or not this "daft whore" was pregnant. In the coming days I could not work out if his judgement of my sanity was a blessing or a curse, because if I had been admitted to a psychiatric hospital then my journey would have been considerably hindered but I would have had access to a safe abortion. I wanted both speed and safety but realistically I knew that each of these aims would make the other impossible.

I thought about the colour of my baby often. Perhaps it was progress to think of the thing within me as a baby at all; if the baby would be white, then that would surely prove it and secure my status as a coconut and prove to me once and for all that I could indeed continue with my mission towards Cape Town and the future of the world that came with it. If the baby was white I knew that it would instantly be able to justify and validate our epic and pivotal pilgrimage to the mother city, because none of my skin colour would have been passed down through the genes and it would confirm my suspicions that my black skin is an aesthetic hiccup, a blemish which is restricted only to the outside of my body and one which was not a true reflection of who I really am. My blackness would be proven to be nothing more than a racial disguise and it would be so overwhelmingly obvious to the whole world that I was telling the truth that Nelson would be released and I would run away with him to have a crown thrust onto my head immediately.

But if the baby was black, that would seal the fate of the whole journey. I knew the inescapable fact that the father was white, and so if the baby was black then that would prove that my soul was as charred as coal because the baby must get its blackness from somewhere. Two white parents cannot make a black baby; that's madness. My black baby would kill off the dreams of a united South Africa, and would destroy the perception that I could end the injustice dealt out upon Nelson. I felt the pressure of the baby as it kicked and writhed in my belly. Did he or she know that the whole nation rested on me, and that he or she held the influence over whether or not I would continue with my one woman mission to wrench Nelson out of his cell and exalt him as the Emperor for whom our wounded and battered nation had been waiting for so long? The baby held its own life in the palm of its unfinished hand, fingering the destiny of the world between its fleshy stubs of digits. I imagined my child choosing between all the colours of the human race, some kind of foetal chameleon who would tense all of its muscles and flood its barely formed mind with the incandescent hue of human skin, stretching and straining and willing and hoping until finally its minuscule body would transform into the colour of its choice. My baby was confronted by the toughest decision it would ever face before it had even made the dangerous ten centimetre journey out of me and into the world. I hoped and prayed that the baby would get it right when God had got it so wrong with me, choosing the perfect shade of brilliant white within which to clothe itself upon the beginning of life and allowing me to remain a coconut, a woman uniquely positioned to free the champion of our people and to end the Apartheid which had so enslaved almost eighty per cent of the population. I rubbed the fat black skin of my belly, as bloated and gargantuan as a warthog's. This little baby needed to get it right.

We came to our conclusion in good time. I would wait, and I would carry the baby to full term and deliver him or her in the normal, natural way. Abortion was out of the question; I was of absolute importance to the destruction of Apartheid and I was too important to be put at risk by the backstreet abortionists who would be unable to assure me of my safety throughout the ordeal. My body, this unhappy jumble of black and white, this ornate and astonishing blur of races and colours and the extremes of humanity all knitted together into one physical incarnation, was the Achilles heel of the whole Apartheid regime. My physical wellbeing would be the difference between the tower of racism reaching further and further heavenward or being ripped out of the sky in a dazzling and pulsating shower of fire and cloud. My mismatch of skin and soul was Exhibit A in South Africa's version of Nuremburg and I needed to make it to the trial in one piece at any cost. If I had a black baby I promised myself and Blessings that I would abandon the dream and raise the child in a loving and stable environment, because it would be proof that I am not the coconut that I thought I was. If the baby was born white, I would know that my suspicions were true all along; I really am a coconut and the birth of my child would affirm my belief in myself which told me that upon arrival in Cape Town my presence alone would be enough to topple the Government. We would march onwards to Cape Town and rescue Nelson from his birdcage; we would dispose of the baby by whatever means were most convenient to us in order to speed our journey towards enlightenment and freedom.

11

SOMEONE ELSE'S NELSON

Coffee Bay, Transkei
July 1985

South west of Durban and the gleaming, shining beaches which
stretched out along the coast was the ancient kingdom of the
Transkei. This was Nelson's country, his pride and joy and his
ambitious dream for the future of South Africa. I could smell him
in the air, I could hear him in the rushing wind and I could see him
in the clouds which floated above the hills like fluffy white Afros.

My baby decided that it would be here that he would enter the
world; I had no choice in the matter. I wish that I had, for Coffee
Bay is the very worst place to give birth to a child. I was not so
fond of the place, for it did not hold many good memories for me.
It is and always will be, however, a place of matchless beauty and
wild majesty, with the sweeping rugged panorama of restless sea and
enormous sky. There were many differing rumours and legends to
explain how this little cove on South Africa's most forgotten piece
of coastline came to have such a visually evocative name. The most
popular of these was the tale that the village had been built on the
location of a shipwreck, where a massive vessel stuffed with coffee
was smashed to splinters on the rocks in a storm. The bountiful cargo
was swept overboard as the great ship gurgled beneath the churning
waves, turning the whole bay into a giant frothing cappuccino and

staining the sand on the beach a dark mocha brown. The whole coastline of this region was bristling with the masts of shipwrecks at low tide and the water was littered with lethal rocks. One day I would be on the flagship of Nelson's fleet, a great and proud African galleon, escorting the King around the great sea-ports of his country. I would look ashore to Coffee Bay and remember my brief stay in that place like someone remembering a half-forgotten nightmare. As for Blessings, I didn't know if I would even remember him at all by then.

Coffee Bay is a tiny place, and the remoteness which was so undeniably beautiful in its own way was a curse for us. We needed people, and this little village had only a couple of hundred of them, and for the baby we needed a hospital with a decent maternity unit, but in reality we were trapped in a tiny village that we did not want to live in with no feasible means of escape. Of all the towns and cities that we visited on our entire trip, none of them could compare to Coffee Bay for the enclosed feeling of stifling entrapment. The large amount of empty landscape stretching in all directions from the sea when all we needed was a large number of people from whom we could find help led to me suffering for the first time in my life from simultaneous agoraphobia and claustrophobia.

The village was not safe either. Coming from Sophiatown, which had been ruled by gangs; Johannesburg, rumoured to be the world's most dangerous city; and Durban, where I had been raped, had not quenched my feeling of isolation and my desire to be back in a big city surrounded by people. Perhaps there was something deeply primeval about my instinct to keep myself and my child in a large group of people, because given my track record of keeping myself safe in larger towns and cities a fear of the rural isolation of Coffee Bay did not make a lot of rational sense. Because of the stunning and empty beauty of the area, Coffee Bay was an optional if inaccessible stop for tourists and there were a couple of tiny hotels dotted along the hillsides overlooking the rugged cliffs and the Hole in the Wall. The influx of money had caused problems, as it always does, because by the time we found Coffee Bay it had become overrun with drug dealers who were intent on selling their goods in as forcible and aggressive a way as possible. They were almost as inventive in their malice as they were in their manufacture; they offered all kinds of potions and pills, powders and fungi, weeds and leaves and technicolour liquids. To the very few white tourists who would pass through the hamlet they were very polite and deceivingly enticing, often talking about something completely irrelevant until they had the victim in a situation from which there was no escape.

To us, however, they were extremely aggressive and intimidating, and I knew that it was because they thought that we were both black. They would stand in the dirt road in a pack, prowling and slinking around like hyenas around a zebra carcass and guarding every entrance and exit to the village. Coffee Bay was the perfect place to do this because of the large numbers of tiny alleyways and the parts of the village which encroached on the dense forests of the surrounding area. Coffee Bay was very small but it was an untidy jumble of tiny roads in very poor condition and the buildings were scattered wherever flat ground was available.

The birth was excruciating. I had known that he was coming for days before he actually did. My body was clenched with seizures and overcome with an incredible burning, relentlessly scorching pain in the very depths of my body. Because of my medical status as a coconut I knew that I was anatomically different from every other human in the world other than Nelson himself; I did not know how this would affect the baby. Would the baby be monochrome like his father, or would he instead be a coconut just like me? Is this condition hereditary? Can it skip generations? Does it cause damage to the baby as he develops in the womb? My birth was a mystery to everyone; there was nobody that I could reasonably hope to ask this side of Cape Town.

I had never before known the feeling of staring into the jaws of death. In that moment death and life were inextricably intertwined, with the beginning of the child's life wrapped around my own doomed demise. Perhaps my attacker had recognised in me the most dangerous man in the world's explosive attraction to me and had raped me as an assassination attempt to derail the cause of freedom. In raping me he had committed the single most destructive act of vandalism and terrorism against the black population in the history of our nation, and I didn't even know his name. If I did not survive the trauma of giving birth to this child, nobody would know my name either. My chance at history and destiny, not to mention the marriage that was waiting for me to the man who loved me endlessly, would be squandered and lost forever.

I knew that the births of my subsequent children, the princes and princesses that I had promised to Nelson when we had conversed across the stars and seas, would be born in much more grandeur than this forgotten child in the middle of nowhere. Now I was in a small hut in the Transkei; then I would be in our summer palace in Pretoria and I would have my choice of the cottages on the estate, riding my horse and strolling through the gardens to induce the contractions. I would deliver South Africa's most important child in a birthing pool sculpted out of a single block of marble beneath a chandelier, with rose petals floating on the surface of the warm water. There would be a harpist playing a gentle serenade to welcome the heir to the throne into the world. Nelson had already promised me that upon his ascension to the throne Archbishop Tutu would annul his previous marriages and declare them void, meaning that Makgatho, Makaziwe, Zenani and Zindziswa would have to renounce their claims to the throne to make way for my own pure bloodline. As the descendants of the only two coconuts in the world the princes and princesses I would make with Nelson would be immeasurably more suited to sovereignty than the children of Evelyn and Winnie. My children would take precedence over them as descendants of a King rather than descendants of a prisoner and the line of succession would be altered accordingly. Their births would be greeted by the canon on Signal Hill leading a 21 gun salute and a military flypast over the capital city, with the day after the birth being declared as a national holiday of celebration. We would be given gifts from dignitaries from all over the world and the child's face would appear on commemorative stamps, coins and china to mark the joyous occasion. To honour the mother of the future King of South Africa Nelson would ask me what I would like as a gift of his gratitude for providing him with an heir; I would ask him to rebuild Sophiatown on the site of the former suburb of Triomf and to rename it Leratotown so that I would always be remembered. Yes. That would be lekker.

None of that was happening today; I had expected to spend my first day as a mother after my coronation as Queen, not before. I had never expected the process of welcoming a child into the world would be painful and dangerous. How could I possibly have guessed that this would be the situation that I would find myself in if nobody had bothered to tell me? Why did nobody think to mention that it would not be romantic at all but a grisly, agonising trauma which would cause great harm to the future Queen of South Africa?

My child was facing downwards when he began to emerge from me. Blessings had a rusty machete to hand which he had kept hold of to defend us against wild animals I begged him to use it to slice the cord as he took the baby up in his hands, but he wouldn't. He told me I would bleed to death if we didn't wait for the placenta which would follow soon afterwards and that I needed to learn to be patient. Watching the placenta follow my child out of me was like seeing the stitching unravelling on a sack full of cracked rubies. The gems of my womb then spilled out all over the floor and congealed like crystallised fruit.

Mwanyisa, as we named him, was as beautiful as any rape baby can be. The name was chosen because it means "accept defeat", in reference to the fact that I had never wanted to fall pregnant with him and that he would be a serious burden on our progress across the country in pursuit of our dreams. Just as my body had accepted defeat to the man who had attacked me so too did I accept defeat in my obligation to love and care for him. Blessings was never a part of his life; this was my journey, my mission and my cross to bear. He asked to hold him but I always refused to give him permission because Mwanyisa was nothing to do with him. The baby was merely an extension of my own womb and it was mine to do with whatever I pleased.

Nelson's future kingdom was also dangerously close to accepting defeat as I carried my foul cargo to Coffee Bay and the fate of the whole world rested on the colour of this child's skin. Mwanyisa was half black and half white. He had curly black hair but a pale little face, and his skin was dark in huge patches on his back and legs. The lesions looked like bruises and I worried that people would accuse me of beating my child. I am a great many things, but I am not a bad mother.

I wanted to be a shepherdess to earn some extra money but nobody would hire me. I thought that it would be easy, that I would be able to just spend the whole day sitting down on the hillside with a dog I could shout to, resting whilst my overstretched vagina recovered. The dog would then go about doing all the actual work of rounding up the sheep and protecting them from predators whilst I pocketed the money which would send me to Cape Town. How hard could it be? Any potential employers that I could find, of which there were considerably less than I had envisaged, thought that I was mad. Why would anyone employ a woman who had so recently given birth, a woman who was still experiencing fresh bleeding from her wounded body? I was so angry and frustrated that they could not see that I was a coconut and that I was destined for Royalty. Being misunderstood so regularly was an exhausting and exasperating ordeal and there were times when I did not know how much more I could endure.

Mwanyisa had done his work; he had proven to us that I was a coconut and that our mission must continue; I had a white soul and on that merit alone I needed to be in Cape Town standing at the door of the prison and screaming at the top of my lungs until someone listened to me and let my hero go free. I had a private wager with Nelson that if the baby I bore was black then I would go quietly, that I would abandon my ambitions to be the one to rescue him and that I would instead pursue a life of private happiness with my husband and bastard child, all of us surrendering the fight for justice and equality by coming to realise that there was simply nothing we could do about Apartheid.

But the child was white. He had proved to me beyond all doubt that I had been chosen and selected by my almost unique ethnicity and that I would be able to free my hero from his incarceration on an island in the ocean and to help him onto the podium of glory. I knew that in Mwanyisa's birth the universe was trying to send me a signal that I was a Kingmaker, not through beacons, cannons or smoke signals, but through the innocence and helplessness of a baby boy. We had no place for him in our family, and I would be leaving him here on his own whilst we went forward to rescue the future of our nation.

Blessings was having none of it. He forbade me to abandon the baby, telling me that we had fought for Mwanyisa's survival against abortion and that now we had to take him with us to give him a chance at having a life.

"If you abandon this baby he will die. He deserves better than that. He has a right to live."

"You don't understand; we can't keep him."

"What would have happened if your own mother had said the same thing about you when you were born?"

"I *was* abandoned, you fool. I am here, I am fine."

"No Lerato, *you* don't understand. You are not going to abandon this child. I will not allow that to happen."

My temporary husband was an unfathomable idiot. In that second I hated him more than I have ever hated anyone else; I hated him so fiercely that it eclipsed all of my hatred for the State Presidents and the guards who were holding my lover in his prison in the sea. As quick as a flash I thrust him up against the wall just as that man had done to me in the alleyway in Durban and I threatened to take his life away from him. I knew that he wanted to get there just as much as me and I was desperate for him to open his brain and see the economic truth of the fact that we could not keep this baby. This was important enough to justify me killing him; nothing would be allowed to come between Nelson and me.

My mind was spinning. All of a sudden it would explode with all of the unpredictability of the blowing of the wind—one second I would be calm and serene and the next I would be embroiled in an ocean of unquenchable rage. Blessings' lunacy made my mind lurch from one extreme to another and it made me hate him all the more.

I wrapped my hands around the machete that we carried with us on the journey and I thrust it up against his neck, pressing the curled blade into his neck tenderly and gently so that the skin was dented but not torn. His death was a long time coming and I knew that the hallowed hour of my widowhood had come upon me far sooner than I would have expected it to. I pictured Nelson in my mind, smiling and welcoming the demise of Blessings Mngomezulu, because in the moment that he was killed I would once again become fully available for the King's pleasure.

"We are not taking this baby with us when we leave Coffee Bay, Blessings," I said sternly. "If you don't swear to me that you will drop your insistence that we take Mwanyisa with us then I will slit your throat here and now. Every black African needs me; you can very easily be replaced. I will happily slice you from navel to nose."

On pain of death, he agreed. I was shocked and surprised; how could it be that he would allow me to have my way and agree to abandon this baby? I wasn't complaining though, because I had thwarted my enemy's attempt to prevent me from getting to Nelson. To be truthful, I would rather have killed him straight away to save time.

I hated Coffee Bay and we left at the earliest available opportunity. Even then it was far too late for us and we felt an oppressive sense of claustrophobia knowing that we had to remain in Coffee Bay against our will. Access to the highways and the rest of the country was very limited and our escape was frustratingly elusive. Finally we saw a horse with a small cart tied up outside the local tavern and, with a dash of outlandish spontaneity, untethered it and took off into the evening. We had a precious little window of the time as the traveller drank his beer and rested beside the fireplace, watching the dying embers glow with an outlandish beauty, and we hoped that his concentration had been blunted by the alcohol which would hinder him from realising that he had been robbed. He probably thought that we were being selfish, but in reality Blessings and I were noble heroes. The stolen horse and cart were helping to usher in a new dawn of freedom and justice. I wish I could have had some means of explaining to him just how much his sacrifice meant to world history but with a heavy heart I realised that there was no way of me telling him now. So I untied the horse and we scampered away from the tavern. Sorry for you, you shameful dronkie.

Only one thing was remaining to do before we left. Blessings said that he wanted no part in it and he rode on ahead of me, leaving me alone in the gathering darkness. I knew that he was disgusted with me. He promised me that he would wait for me with the wagon further up the road but I wasn't sure if I expected him to be there or not. The sky over Coffee Bay was stained with a blood red sunset and the trees were mourning as they swayed in their vigil as I passed through.

I left my baby in a dustbin on the outskirts of the village. I found the bin beside a small bridge crossing the trickling brook, where the tiny track snaked its way out of Coffee Bay and up on the road to Umtata. I did not kiss him on the forehead or cry as you might assume a mother would, and he made no sound as I wrapped him in a blanket which I folded so that it would feel like a hug. The bin was mostly empty, but there were a few sealed bags of rotting food in the bottom which gave the whole thing a sour and rancid smell. I hoped that there would not be many rats. I was in two minds as to whether or not to leave the lid of the bin open or closed; I did not want any wild animals to come prowling around the roadside at night-time and so I resolved to keep it closed. I knew that his only hope was that someone would hear him cry and come to his rescue, and so I hoped that they would be able to hear him crying in spite of the closed lid. We all have our Nelsons, our loved ones to rescue and guide away from certain doom, and the simple fact of the matter was that Mwanyisa was someone else's Nelson and not mine. I had my mission to focus on, the life of one man in the palm of my hand, and someone else must play their part and take Mwanyisa home and raise him as their own. I debated whether or not he had ever even really been mine in the first place; he had, after all, been created in Durban in the squalid hole of depravity where the man with a libido larger than his wallet had seen me as nothing more than an opportunity to relieve himself. He was an inconvenience and he always had been. It was the unfortunate truth which meant that he would always be denied a place in our family.

I closed the lid of the dustbin, and I wondered whether or not I should say anything to the baby. The last glance that I ever had of him was to see his little white eyes closed; his perfect little face as angelic as a cherub and looking as though he was made out of pure and blemishless ivory. I decided not to, for if he was going to make his way in the world without me it was for the best if he did not have my memory tangled around his ankles and making life immeasurably more complicated. I wondered what kind of a world this baby was being born into, what his welcome into existence would be. Given the external colour of his skin, I presumed that he would be soon inheriting glory, privilege and riches.

I walked up the little track as fast as my exhausted and bruised body would allow. The gravel prickled on the soles of my feet, scratching and scraping against my dark coconut shell. As well as being a former mother I was also a thief, so I kept looking back down the road to the thatched rooftops of the village of Coffee Bay half-expecting the angry owner of the horse and cart stumbling after me with a beer in one hand and a machete in the other. Finally I found my husband and his chariot at the side of the road behind one of the trees, trying to remain incognito. By some miracle, the drunkard had not yet realised what had happened.

"Is it done?"

"It is."

Blessings dismounted the horse and helped me to climb into the small wagon. The planks were bare and uncomfortably hard on my wounded body. He then climbed back onto our horse and gave the reigns a tug as he carefully guided the wagon back onto the road and we set off along the coast in the direction of the mother city. I caught him looking back over his shoulder for any sign of the drunken traveller and the sunset was reflected in the shimmering trail of a tear down his left cheek. The man was an oversensitive and sentimental fool.

I felt a joyous rush of freedom and elation surging through my veins as I left the baby behind. Rape can never be forgotten, but the trauma of it all somehow eased as I turned my back on the thing which had sprung from it I was leaving the pain of my pregnancy and the little village which had been so cruel to me and moving onwards in pursuit of a better tomorrow. I was unburdened in my onward quest for the future of South Africa and I did not have the child to shackle me to this wretched, hellish spot any longer. I was free, and I could go. Cape Town was close; I could smell it in the evening air as the horse picked up speed.

12

A FULL BELLY

East London, Cape Province
December 1985

On the road going through the wilderness of the Wild Coast, I was plagued and troubled by the spectre of my child. Mwanyisa stayed with me as we journeyed onwards even though I had left him in that dustbin and he clung to me with an iron grip as we crossed landscapes on our journey towards Cape Town. I know how odd it must sound, but I think I was beginning to fall in love with the child I had borne. What was wrong with me?

For three days after the birth of my baby my body secreted a strange white substance from my nipples. I was overcome with joy and delight; was this not the ultimate proof that I was indeed a coconut after all? My coconut shell was cracked and tender and my tiets were the parts of me where my inner body was coming to the surface to break free and taste the air of the outside world for the first time. Soon this whiteness would spread and my whole body would give way to the glorious white core I had within me. I felt an enraged sense of retribution and affirmation; I wanted all of my doubters in Sophiatown to see me now. I wanted to show my parents the mysterious white liquid dribbling out of my breasts and to hear them begging for my forgiveness for their crimes of doubt against me when it mattered the most, I wanted to hear them apologise for my ruined childhood and my painful experience of being forced to be black. I wanted to show the teller at the station in Johannesburg how stupid he now had been proven to be. My destiny was never in doubt for a second. My eyes blazed with furious and passionate rage; I dare you to call me a fool now. I dare you to tell me that I am black to the core. I dare you to tell me that Apartheid can succeed in separating people across racial divides. I dare you to tell Nelson Mandela that he will never be released. When I am Queen I will make you sorry for your ignorant and deluded stupidity, every last one of you. I will hunt you down and right that wrong. You'll see.

Before I was raped I often considered the women who would abandon their children to be monsters and demons. The Transvaal and specifically the Johannesburg area was blighted by an extremely high incidence of violent crime and together with the poor standards of living this combination often left the most innocent of victims at the height of helplessness. Staying alive is an expensive business in Africa, and human life is not immune to the mathematical laws of economy and finance. When the budget is heavily pressured and stretched, something has to be sacrificed in order to survive. When an illness is involved the human body makes its own opinions very clear indeed, just as my own body did with Mwanyisa, who was born after just seven months of pregnancy. Pregnancy beyond the seventh month is almost impossible as the immune system fights ruthlessly for its own protection and survival. Biology is a cruelly selfish thing; when life is under threat there is no opportunity for sentimentality and all unnecessary burdens are thrown off. This includes a foetus in the womb, for the energy spent sustaining the life of an unborn child could instead be better spent on fighting the effects of the illness. It is through no act of hatred or revulsion for their children that the mothers come to abandon their babies, but instead of desperation, necessity and hopelessness. Through no fault of my own, I had joined their number.

The Transkei was incandescent even as we left it. The homeland of Nelson Mandela, the kingdom where he was born and raised and the blueprint for our future together at the head of a new nation, a new Empire, a new and wonderful promised land set out in our inheritance. I had never left the Transvaal and I was a stranger in these majestic surroundings, but I felt like I belonged here and that this place could stake a claim on my soul. It was a pilgrimage for me, a ride through Nelson's hometown of Umtata on the long road leading west. Umtata was the capital of the Transkei region and the largest town in the area. As we passed through I knew that this was a famously dangerous area for white people and they were extremely vulnerable to violent crime, and I was afraid that they would be able to smell my internal whiteness just as my rapist had done and that they would batter me to death for the few rand I had in my purse.

The village where Nelson had been born in 1918, a place called Mvezo, was close by and lay to the south in the direction we had just come. Nobody was exactly sure where it was and the locals gave confusing and contradictory directions, which meant that the mythical status of the place was heightened more and more. It was my own personal Valhalla; with a rousing sense of joy I looked at the hills and the trees around us, knowing that just beyond them may be that sacred little village, that hallowed turf and that consecrated ground. I had never seen it but I knew that it must surely be the most beautiful village in the entire world. We had come all this way, but there was no way for us to find it on our own and so we resolved to continue. I was upset by this and a tear ran down my cheek as we headed west, but I did not lose my hope. I would make it to Mvezo one day, and the next time I would come into that village I would be the Queen of South Africa.

A horse is simply the best way to explore this beautiful place, exhausting as the ride was. It was so natural and beautiful to be a part of the landscape, but I would be a massive liar if I told you that it was painless. Having just given birth to my baby I was in absolute agony as the rickety little cart bounced along and I felt every stone on the old road shuddering up through the wooden wheels and chassis and finally pounding against my exhausted body. I would spend most of the journey lying flat on my back to make the ride a little smoother, staring at the beautiful white clouds over the Transkei and imagining all of the carriage rides I would have to endure as Queen, ghosting down these same roads in our State

Landau. At least three different people on this leg of the journey thought that they were watching a makeshift hearse speeding by. We were pieces of driftwood being dragged along the coastline by the currents of the ocean. Soon we would be home.

My arms felt empty as we travelled across this incredibly beautiful place. The silence and stillness of it all took my breath away; the lack of humanity in the wilderness stretching out in all directions made me feel dreadfully alone. Loneliness is an old enemy and I know him well; until I met Nelson I came into the world believing that I was the only coconut in human history, and I knew that nobody understood the wrenching pain of my medical condition. I felt alone every time I would catch sight of myself in a mirror and detest what I saw, wishing I could somehow rip all of my skin off and start again. I felt alone every time I would see white people living their lives of immeasurable wealth and happiness, luxuries I was entitled to but I was always denied. I would feel a deep and angry hunger every time I saw their perfect bodies, their beautiful skin mocking and taunting me as I remained trapped in my cage of darkness. But somehow this feeling was different, this was new. I would wake up with the unforgettable sensation of having fallen asleep with my arms around someone who was no longer there by morning, giving me the constant impression that my companion had made a very recent departure. Blessings, of course, remained at my side the whole time but the hungry yearning was not for him. At first I had thought that my body was preparing the way for Royalty and the future Queen was in need of the company of the King who defined her title, but very soon I came to realise that my womb was in mourning. I had abandoned my child and my body was scorning me for it. It was agonising.

We spent the first half of 1986 in East London. In May, an announcement was made which gave a name to the illness which I had. It was to be known as Human Immunodeficiency Virus, which was commonly abbreviated to HIV. Because my blood tested positive for traces of the virus, I was to be identified as being HIV positive, a new coat of arms which would come to summarize everything I am in one concise name. The old was gone and the new had come, and my life as a human like the rest of them was over. I was the same Lerato, the same coconut that I had always been, but in South Africa humanity was being strategically divided between those who were HIV positive and those who were HIV negative. As well as colour, HIV status would also be a divider of the people of the land I loved; I would never be viewed by other people in the same way again. Once I was infected with HIV the ultimate clinical consequence would be *acquired immunodeficiency syndrome*, commonly abbreviated to AIDS. It was a new illness and had not been widely reported before 1981, and the anonymity of it was terrifying. The medical profession had not known that HIV was the cause of AIDS until we arrived in East London in 1986. Knowing that I was positive and that this would eventually evolve and mutate, finally becoming AIDS, gave a satisfying sense of resolution to a very frightening ordeal. Being told that I was positive could never be described as good news, but it was the removal of the confusion and the mystery of the illness which I was suffering from and for that I was incredibly thankful. The man had raped me and murdered me in a matter of seconds but the second of these crimes would take decades, years if I was unlucky, to take shape over my life. As my life was ending, the life of his child was beginning in a dustbin in Coffee Bay. The tragedy of the whole thing was the waste of it all, the simmering potential of a human life as yet unlived being put to one side for the sake of this unholy pilgrimage to the Mother City.

Mwanyisa would not loosen his grip on my heart. I could not forget him and I could not shake off the sense of shame and regret which clung to me as I came to realise the magnitude of what I had done and what it had meant. He would not allow me to forget and I did not want to think about whether he would forgive me or not. Would he one day be able to bring himself to the place where he could find some compassion in his heart for his mother? I wondered who had come to find him and who would be raising my child as their own. Nelson told me that a family would find him and take him back to their home south of Johannesburg. He told me that the farmhouse would have yellow walls and a green roof and there would be a mother of Dutch descent who would raise abandoned black children alongside her own. As well as envious I was also immeasurably thankful to the Dutch lady and the people helping her for the part that they were playing in raising the future generation of South Africans and the rescue mission that they had been performing on my baby. As I was rescuing Nelson, they were rescuing Mwanyisa. It made me see the King in a different way, and in my spirit my relationship with him became maternal.

I gradually became more and more furious with Blessings as time went by and Mwanyisa lingered further and further behind us. Eventually I could hold it in no longer and I confronted him. I needed answers. I held my husband completely responsible for the situation my child now found himself in.

"How could you let me abandon my baby?"

He looked at me, exasperated by his perception of me as a deluded lunatic.

"Don't you dare say that to me, Lerato! You know that I never made you abandon Mwanyisa. I wanted to keep him, not see him die in a dustbin in Coffee Bay. I wanted to bring him with us on the journey to Cape Town."

My eyes widened in horror. "Mwanyisa is dead?"

"I don't know that. But you abandoned him at the side of the road. His chances of survival do not look good, you must have known that when you did it."

"But you should have stopped me! You should have done something to protect him when he needed you. Why did you just stand by and let me do that?"

"I did try to stop you. I told you not to have an abortion and then I told you not to abandon the child. You held the machete up to my throat because you accused me of squandering our chance of completing the journey and seeing Mandela go free. You claim that this baby was not mine and that he was nothing to do with me; if that is true then you have to face up to the responsibility for what you did."

"You know," I scolded him; "if I didn't know any better I would think that you were working for the Government and that you wanted me to fail. I think you are happy that Nelson is in jail and that Apartheid is alive and well."

"You think I like being treated like a second class citizen because of the colour of my skin? Do you think I don't want the change that the ANC can offer me? Don't you dare tell me that I am a racist just because I'm not telling you what you want to hear! I fought for that little boy's life but I knew that you would abandon the journey if we kept him. I knew you wouldn't let us continue if we kept him because that would have made you think you're a monochrome and the mission was in vain."

I never came closer to revealing to Blessings my deepest secret than I did that day. I never did tell him that I would one day become Queen and that I would have him executed with a snap of my black fingers as soon as I had stopped spending his money on the trip. He knew that I was uniquely positioned to free Nelson and to be his leverage on his way to the throne because of my status as a coconut, but I had been very careful to prevent Blessings from finding out that I was in love with the man I was attempting to save from jail. He knew nothing of my plans to marry the King and he knew nothing of Nelson's long-standing infatuation with me. Blessings was making the common mistake of underestimating me without knowing what a powerful woman I was about to become. This matriarch of the Royal Family was not somebody to be messed with, but Blessings was too much of a *moegoe*, a stupid weak coward, to realise this.

"You know, Lerato, you're different now. Everything changed when that man raped you."

"Don't talk about that *man*, you fool," I bellowed at him, "you have no idea how painful that experience was for me. You never will, because you are a monochrome and therefore you are an idiot."

"Do you think it was easy for me? To endure the shame of having my wife raped? I'm not claiming that I suffered more than you did but it certainly wasn't an easy thing to endure. Since he raped you, you're twice as selfish, twice as short tempered, twice as illogical and twice as deluded as you were before. I know that you are not like anyone else; at first it made you interesting and charismatic, but now you are hurting people because you are determined to get what you want. When I met you your coconut syndrome made me love you more but now I am struggling to love you at all."

* * *

In Zulu mythology there is a mischievous and evil dwarf-like sprite called a Tokoloshe which could have caused my slumbering baby some trouble. He is able to achieve total invisibility by swallowing a pebble and is called upon by malevolent wizards to cause mischief. His favourite type of harassment was to creep up on children as they slept; he could bite off their toes and cast illnesses over them with a snap of his extremely long, bony and hairy fingers. In extreme cases he could rape women and cause death. I did not know what was more unthinkable: that this hairy little devil could be creeping up on sleeping children or that humans were raping and murdering one another and then blaming it on a mythological gremlin. Whether or not he existed, he was an unimaginably horrible enemy for Mwanyisa to contend with. Could this beast be prowling around that dustbin in Coffee Bay, feasting on the corpse of my baby? There was nobody with him who could call the *n'anga*, the witch doctor, to come and banish the spectre from his bedside, because I had left my baby to face the demon on his own. That moment of realisation was the most distressing moment of my life. What had I done? How could I have done that to my own baby? My claim to be a coconut had cost an innocent baby his life, regardless of the crime committed against my body by the man in Durban.

Being positive made me see the world in a different way. I worked as a cleaner in a hospital back in Egoli, but I realised that I knew nothing at all about the human body and the way that it worked; I had never heard of this virus before and it would only be later in the 1980s that the virus would garner its terrible infamy. Surely coconuts were immune to this monstrous enemy? It was a terrifyingly mysterious enemy to have to contend with; it was like dancing with a partner who had no discernable face, duelling with an invisible enemy soldier on the battlements of a vast ruined castle.

It was like a blind man suddenly being jolted with electricity and having his sight miraculously restored. Whether for good or for bad, it was becoming increasingly clear that I would never be allowed to see the world around me without the watermark of HIV indelibly attached to it, stained onto my eyeballs like a tattoo.

More than the actual illness, the problem with HIV is that the whole world has an opinion on something that very few people comprehensibly understand. I knew at that moment that I would never recover from it and that it would continue changing my body until the end of my life, but that did not mean that my life was over as soon as the diagnosis was official.

How would I be Queen now that I was positive? It troubled me greatly and I had enormous difficulty sleeping in the days that followed the announcement of the identity of the illness lurking inside me. Would the stigma which was attached to this mysterious illness be a hindrance to my performance as the spouse of the Head of State of South Africa? Would I be allowed to make love to Nelson or would the Royal Protection Officers consider this tender act of affection a risk against the life of the King which they could not justify and would not tolerate? Even worse, would I be allowed to bear children? Would the heirs to the throne be permitted to be carried through pregnancy by a Queen with a tainted womb? The future Princes and Princesses were likely to be born negative, given that God made three quarters of positive women with a particularly unlikely ability to swallow the virus up into their placentas and deliver babies who did not inherit that curse. If this was to be the case then perhaps they would escape; I would have at my disposal the best wet-nurses that money could buy and the nannies and bodyguards would ensure that my children were able to live a completely sterilised life in the court of the King. Still I worried and sweated over it; HIV is one of those things whereby the mysterious legends and rumours surrounding it are more poisonous than the infectious virus itself.

I imagined myself on a state visit to the White Palace or Buckingham House, visiting Kings, Queens, Prime Ministers, Presidents, celebrities, statesmen and politicians. I pictured in my mind the way that they would shun and reject me, clamouring and elbowing each other to get their hands on the great Emperor Nelson but silently refusing to touch or look at me because of my polluted blood. Most of the job description of a Queen is to wave at and shake hands with many millions of people as I represented South Africa at the very highest level. How was I to do that if it became public knowledge that I had a contagious disease? Yes, it was true to say that I could only infect people by having sex with them or breastfeeding them, but in spite of the laughably small odds of this happening the thought that they could suspect me of infecting them with what they thought was a death sentence was the most terrifying idea that I could have held in my head. The fact that people would see their Queen as a plague rat was a thousand times more terrifying than the vision that I had in my head of my own gruesome death when they had told me the nature of the illness, or of the anguish I felt every time I was reminded that the man I loved was in prison. I deserved better than this.

No. Perhaps I was a fool. I liked to think so; deep down I held a far greater hope and faith in the goodness of the human race than I sometimes remembered. My unruly imagination sometimes allowed me to forget that humanity, with all of its splashes of drudgery, is a beautiful thing to behold.

Just because I found myself to be positive did not mean that I was not the same Lerato as I had been before. I was the same person and I was every bit as deserving of respect, love, happiness, dignity and self worth as any other person. Let me tell you that the majesty of human life is not snuffed out the very second that somebody is declared to be HIV positive. It is not an instant death sentence; it is not a vast shackle of doom around the ankles and it does not make life impossible to endure. Positive or negative, life is still an incredible gift and it is always worth living.

I am not asking for respect because I love HIV, but because I hate it. I want to curse it with my wicked spells and stamp on its miserable head like a snake. I want to see the downfall of this virus only slightly less than I want to see Table Mountain on the horizon up ahead. But as we wait for the day when AIDS is a memory we must end the ignorance, end the hopelessness and end the shame. When I become Queen I promise you that I will stamp out HIV as soon as I have stamped out Apartheid. It is the middle of the 1980s. This madness has gone on for an obscene amount of time and it must end now.

The world would look at me and decide for itself what the effects of the illness were, and there were some outrageous rumours and gossips about what it meant to be positive and how you can catch it. Rumours spread much faster than the truth did; I heard that sharing bathwater, kissing, shaking hands, sharing toothbrushes, breathing in the same air and touching the same food could all infect someone else; none of this was truthful. The doctors had told me that the only way you could catch the virus from someone else was by transferring your bodily fluids to them, and the two most common means of transmission were sexual intercourse and the nursing of infants. I asked them if it made any difference if you had a shower after having sex with someone, meaning that if Blessings cleaned himself thoroughly he might be spared the same fate as me, but the doctors laughed in my face. They said that I was stupid and naive for thinking that anything that ridiculous could be true. It became very clear to me that if I had sex with him he would in all probability be doomed. In the beginning I had thought that making love to my husband would in some way damage and deform his genitals, but what I could not fathom yet which transpired to be true was that I was dying, and I would drag him with me to my grisly fate if we made love. It was a heartbreaking dilemma.

"I want to have another baby, Blessings." If he knew his place as my temporary accessory then he would hold my head against his heart and ease my agony. I was surprised by the way that he actually responded.

"No. Absolutely not. We must go back to Coffee Bay and find Mwanyisa if you want to have a child. We had our chance to be parents and you willingly threw it away." I could sense the anger in his voice. He was furious with me for taking until now to recognise that abandoning Mwanyisa was a terrible thing to do. "How can it be that you can change your mind so quickly? How is it that you suddenly want a baby so soon after abandoning Mwanyisa? You are temperamental and unpredictable, and you have to admit that it looks like the people in the ANC who called you crazy may have been able to see something that you couldn't."

I wanted another baby so desperately. There is nothing illogical or irrational about the love of a mother for her baby. Children don't get abandoned through any lack of love. It seemed so perfectly clear to me that I had been overcome by the trauma of losing a baby and I wanted to make it right by having another baby as fast as I could to take the pain away. I didn't care that we couldn't afford another child; I felt a great burden to atone for what I had done. I knew that I had squandered my chances at motherhood and that I had carelessly tossed my child into the rubbish bin as though he was an inconvenience and a wasted commodity rather than a precious and divine gift which revolutionised my identity just as radically as the coming coup d'état would revolutionise Cape Town.

One night, Blessings asked if I would let him make love to me. Now who was the fickle one? I had told him that if we had room in our family for a child then we should take that opportunity and that Mwanyisa's demise should not prevent the miracle of life from taking place, but I didn't realise that he was listening to me and taking on board what I was saying. My eyes were full of wonder and surprise; he knew me so intimately, and he knew that if he were to lie with me he would contract an illness from me and would never recover. He also knew exactly how much I missed Mwanyisa and he could feel the regret and grief which plagued my heart. He knew how much I wanted and needed to be a mother again, how much my body craved for pregnancy and how much my spirit yearned for a baby to hold in my arms. It was a hungry feeling, an urgent groan of my biology, and I was desperate to quench it. Blessings was the only way that I could. I had learnt a thing or two about him during our marriage, and I knew that even though he wouldn't admit it he wanted to be a father.

The tenderness of his act of love was the most overwhelming thing I have ever experienced. He knew the risk involved, and he knew that he was creating a child who would no doubt share the same virus that we would soon both be suffering from, but he prioritised my need for motherhood above his need for a healthy body. Love is about sacrifice and surrender, and I could think of no greater demonstration of love than what Blessings did for me that night in East London. My head was full of Nelson, and I still intended to murder him, but I realised for the first time that my husband was deeply in love with me.

It was a thrillingly biological exchange, the passing of the virus from my body to his and the fertilization of my body, the infusion of my womb with the glorious miracle of lush and abundant life, which was the gift that he took great pleasure in physically giving me. I could feel the chemicals rushing within me as we connected.

Miraculously I soon discovered that I was pregnant. I was feeling very nauseous and tender but I didn't care. This was glorious news. I had assumed that the combination of being positive and pregnant at the same time would mean an inevitable and natural termination of the pregnancy as my body would be unable to carry the foetus to full term, my sick womb flushing it through in an attempt to preserve my own life and health. But this baby was a fighter, and the pregnancy showed no signs of ending early which was a bit inconvenient as it would have saved us a great deal of money. My virus had not yet evolved into an illness and at the beginning I felt exactly the same. There was morning sickness, which often made me hurl the contents of my stomach into the gleaming toilet bowl, but none of the deathbed scenarios which I had envisaged. It was a relief to know that a positive pregnancy was not the death sentence that it could have been, but it did cast a light on the fact that I did not understand anything about HIV and what it meant.

In East London Blessings found a job vacancy at the zoo as an assistant to the chief zookeeper. The zookeeper was a bizarre old white man, enormously fat with a curly handlebar moustache and half-moon glasses, who had been in the job for decades and who had a deeply conservative mindset. White people rule, black people serve. I never met him, so quite what he would have made of me I will never know. He always wore a full morning suit and carried a large pocket-watch on his breast, and Blessings told me that he smelled of "cigars, money and power".

We kept the horse for as long as we could, but because he represented everything that we owned in the whole wide world we were unable to feed him. The plan had been to ride all the way to Cape Town but it soon became clear that hitchhiking would be a far cheaper option because we would need to pay to provide him with food. Breaking into fields risked the possibility of being shot by white farmers.

Blessings tried to offload the horse to the zookeeper, but he was more interested in the altogether more exotic varieties of animals than the humble horse. If we were offering him springboks and hippopotamuses then the story would have been very different, but for the horse he laughed in my husband's face and he ridiculed him for imagining the people of East London paying to see a horse in a cage. "What a *ludicrous* idea, you blithering fool," he said. My husband did not altogether abandon our plan and we instead decided that perhaps we could sell it to tourist attractions so that they could do horseback safaris. I had heard that there was an elephant sanctuary close to Port Elizabeth; what could be a more romantic notion than riding out through the forest of stripped trees in the hazy light of an African dawn on horseback, drunk on the anticipation of seeing some of the elephants up close in their natural habitat? It was a wonderful idea, and the park would instantly love it. They would pay us a gargantuan sum of money and we would be able to buy a pair of one-way train tickets to Cape Town for Blessings' final journey.

The horse and the little wagon eventually were stolen from us just as we had stolen them. One day we simply woke up and found them gone. That was the end of that. The elephant sanctuary would forever elude us. I was very upset by this, because I would have loved to have experienced a rendezvous with a real elephant.

There was one particularly memorable occasion which stuck in my mind well after Blessings had finished telling me the story that night. He was, for the first time, assigned to feed the lions; the adult lions had carcasses flung over the sides of the enclosure because they understood how to hunt, but the cubs would be used to their parents teaching them to hunt in the wild and so the zookeeper decided that his staff would have no hesitation in feeding them just as their absent parents would be naturally. There were inoculations to be administered as well, and the adults would be shot with a tranquiliser dart from the edge of the enclosure but, true to form, the zookeeper decided that his staff would enter the enclosures of the cubs and administer the vaccinations by simply holding the cubs still. Presumably this had something to do with the fact that the zookeeper was the one making the decisions but not the one carrying the actions out. About three minutes before he had entered the enclosure, Blessings was told that it would not be the newborn cubs but instead the seven-month-olds, who were pubescent, hormonal and extremely large.

Blessings was terrified of lions. There was nothing especially unusual about that, but I still found it something to chuckle at as I pictured him sweating and trembling as he stood at the entrance to the enclosure with his hands filled with syringes. What a fool.

He went in slowly, my very own Daniel facing down the lions in their den; he had been told that they were lion cubs, and this was not technically incorrect, but they were definitely the oldest lions in the long history of the world to be described as babies. A few of them were beginning to grow short wispy manes and they looked absolutely nothing like the baby cubs which he had envisaged when he had been given the task.

The eyes of a young lioness were fixed firmly on my husband as he approached with his syringe of medicine. They were great, deep marbles of life, heart, truth and vibrant passion, real windows on the soul of this most incredible of African animals. Blessings was so close that he could see his face in them, but all I could think of as he was telling me this story was Nelson. All three of us were fighting as hard as we could for the end of Apartheid but Nelson's fight had not taken him into a den of lions yet. He had not been to any strip clubs in the name of freedom, nor had he made wigs or shoes on his journey to Cape Town. Blessings found himself face to face with a baby lion and he was doing it all so that I could get closer to Nelson and my glorious destiny. It was ironic when you think of it logically, that Blessings' job at the zoo dodging deadly beasts was bringing the day of his murder closer and closer.

As he navigated the eyes and the teeth of the lion in front of him, sprawled out on a wooden pallet with its face perilously close to his own, he suddenly felt a very sharp pang of acute pain, a crunching, clamping, searing pain which gripped the left hand side of his ribcage. He turned slowly to see another lion cub, a large male, wrapping its jaws around his side, grappling with his ribcage and steadfastly refusing to release his grip on my husband's flesh.

When he came home that night he looked lost and dishevelled, broken and exhausted. I asked him what had happened to him at the zoo to make him look so upset and traumatised and he told me that one of the lions had bitten him when he was trying to vaccinate one of its siblings. I pictured a ferocious beast, enormous and majestic, with rippling muscles and a huge tousled mane of masculine fur, holding his ripped shirt against the floor and pressing its massive teeth against the black skin on Blessings' face . . .

"No, Lerato, this was a lion cub."

"A lion *cub?*"

The huge and terrifying lion in my mind vanished as quickly as he had appeared. I was confused, but I asked to see the wound. I had one thing on my mind; we needed to make sure that the wound was dressed properly because we needed to contain the spread of HIV which lingered in his poisonous blood. Blessings lifted his shirt and he pointed to his ribcage. I could see nothing, and I glanced up at him in concern.

"Look!" he protested, pointing at two small marks on one of his ribs. "The thing felt like it was ripping great chunks of my flesh away, and you're telling me you can't even see anything?"

I carried on staring for a few more seconds, but I could not contain myself any longer and I collapsed on the floor, screaming in laughter. Tears were streaming down my cheeks, it was possibly the funniest thing I had ever seen and heard in my life. He was genuinely upset, genuinely traumatised, and I cackled with glee as I asked him if we should spend our savings not on the journey to Cape Town but instead on a microscope so that we would be able to see the wound. His pathetic masculinity was indescribably hysterical.

"What kind of man are you?" I laughed. "You are meant to wrestle with lions in your sleep. And as for being my husband and protector, I hope that we don't get attacked by any lions because you will be absolutely useless at keeping your family safe." I cackled at him, the shrill sound of my laughter echoing against the corrugated tin of the roof of our makeshift house. I pointed to my freshly infused belly. "What a joke you are. You will be a terrible father, a terrible role-model for our son. When I write Nelson's coronation speech I will make sure this one goes in it, it will make them all laugh so much that they will forget that Apartheid ever happened."

I pictured in my mind the little life inside of me, the jumbled mass of cells and flesh which had miraculously arranged itself into a human being. I imagined my baby's fingernails gently being infused with shape and texture, the eyelashes being knitted together beneath the skin of the miniscule eyelids, ready to grow. The small heart with all of its chambers and vessels, the intricacy of the shape of the ear, all of it made with astonishing attention to detail. The majesty of creation was a stunning thing to behold.

I pictured the tiny fingers wrapping themselves around my thumb, the rising and falling of a miniature chest as the baby lay asleep on me in the evening. I imagined how it would feel after the birth, to be so intricately connected to another human who relied on me and my husband for absolutely everything. Surely there can be nothing more wonderful than that.

I tried to imagine what colour my baby would be. Could it be that there was a black child inside my white womb? Perhaps there would be a chance that this child, like Mwanyisa, would be half caste as well so that my suspicion that I am a coconut would be inescapably proven. This baby would deserve and receive all of my love and devotion, and in return would be the perfect proof which the guards at Robben Island would need to understand the unique condition shared by Nelson and I which would mean that the Apartheid regime would come to a swift and spectacular end.

It was when I was considering my child to be a Prince of the realm, imagining the titles that I would one day bestow upon him or her as I sat on the throne of South Africa with my King beside me and a crown of enormous rubies on my head, that I suddenly realised that this could be an act of treason by Blessings. Could he have suspected my plans to murder him? Could he know of the scheme which I had plotted, the erotic fantasy which I was harbouring to replace my husband with the world's most famous prisoner? Perhaps he had impregnated me because he was attempting to infiltrate the Royal circle with his own children, and because of the influence of his genes in the creation of the child he was hatching a plan even more dastardly than mine to dethrone King Nelson and Queen Lerato. Perhaps it was jealousy, perhaps it was an attempt to prove me mad or perhaps he was secretly a huge supporter of Apartheid and what it meant for Africa. Whatever the reason for Blessings' crime against humanity, I would not allow it to slow me down. We entered a tense and uncomfortable period in our marriage and I became very suspicious of his motives to install his biological offspring in the line of succession. If I needed to bring the murder forward to secure my claim to the throne and to oust the impostor then I would do it without hesitation. I was pregnant. I had no further use for Blessings now.

13

TREASURE

Grahamstown, Cape Province
May 1986

The journey out of East London was made by minibus. My belly was enormous and I knew that the baby would come soon; I was exhausted and as bloated as a black beached whale. The winter was beginning to bite and the cold wind off the ocean was bitter and bleak.

Public transport in South Africa was something of an oddity to white foreigners like me. The trains had something resembling a timetable to make the operation of the tracks more practical, but the buses ran on what we affectionately dubbed "Africa Time". This was the time-zone of a parallel universe and one completely unrelated to hours, minutes and seconds. Nobody in Africa is ever in a hurry for anything and when you want to get somewhere your life can be exceptionally difficult. How on Earth could we ever expect to trade ourselves out of poverty if we did not understand the basic principles of efficiency and timekeeping? When I became Queen I would whip this unruly bunch into shape, but today I could do nothing.

I felt a contraction. Mwanyisa had made me an expert and I knew that I didn't have much time.

"Sir, when does the bus leave?"

He shrugged his shoulders and carried on munching on his bag of *Simba* chips.

"We leave when the bus is full."

"I am having a little trouble here, bru. When can we get underway?"

"Just now."

"No, I need it to be *now now*. We have a very important reason to be getting on with our journey to Cape Town. Why is it taking so long?"

He sniggered at me dismissively. "Welcome to Africa."

We waited for extra passengers on that dirt road for four hours. It was so frustrating that I could have cried; all the kilometres that we could have travelled in that time vanished before my eyes. When we finally did set off my labour began to accelerate faster than that scruffy little bus. With a horrible sense of irony I realised that this baby could enter the world just as I had done; is there some law written out in the stars which declares that coconuts must be born in moving vehicles? I'd been hoping to travel far that day but a couple of hours in I had to get off. The driver dropped us off in the nearest little town and then carried on his way. Monochromes are unbelievable.

I gave birth shortly after we arrived in Grahamstown. It was a quiet night in a shack in one of the tiny townships on the outskirts, which disappointed me. After the glory of Mwanyisa, my divine white child borne of my black body, the last place that I wanted to give birth to the child I would *choose* to love was a place where black people were contained to preserve the integrity of the whites-only areas. This was Triomf by another name and the wounds of Sophiatown still stung sharply in my painfully black skin.

It was a painful birth, but I knew that it was over when I heard the gulp and cry of a child as the unused lungs were suddenly filled with air for the first time. It was a girl. Blessings took her and wrapped her in an old rag, holding her in his cradling arms and gazing on her with eyes filled with an overwhelming sense of love and hope.

Her name would be Siphiwe, meaning "we were given". The beauty of her story and her conception was at times more than I could bear and I loved her more than I could possibly hope to express. I had waited so very long to be a mother, to hold my child in my arms again, and I knew that my purpose was once again completed. All of the pain of the memory of Mwanyisa was suddenly and deeply healed from within me.

As I watched Blessings hold her in his arms, I suddenly felt a wrenching pain as a new contraction began. What was happening? I knew that this could not be normal because of my memories of Mwanyisa and the birth which I had already performed for him. As soon as he had left my body I knew that the labour was over and intense relief established itself in the place of the clenching pain of the contractions, but there was the same feeling of a foreign body lurking in my belly, making agitated movements. I knew from my previous encounter with motherhood that this was not a normal birth. As Blessings comforted me, I felt the kick of a tiny foot.

"Lerato you are having another baby. I can see the head."

Nangila came five minutes after his sister. We gave him the name which meant "born on a journey", because that was the very best way to describe the conception which had ignited him into being. It was a tribute to me and my part in the most important journey in South Africa's history, the epic pilgrimage across the country from Johannesburg to Cape Town and the journey upon which the entire future of the people rested. Whether or not Nelson would be freed was being decided by every step we took to the south west.

Nangila was also born on a much more personal journey for me, one from a rape victim to a mother. I began it hating every second of pregnancy, every waking moment an unendurable agony as the thing within me germinated and festered as it grew. I ended it as a mother, a woman who loved her children and a human blessed enough to be able to endow the gift of life upon another. My womb was now holy and consecrated ground, a blessed and sanctified place where miracles were made.

He did not cry. He did not gulp and breathe and scream; he did not wriggle and writhe and suddenly flush his skin with fresh, oxygenated blood. He did not struggle in Blessings' hands as he lifted him out from between my legs and was instead extraordinarily limp and flaccid.

Nangila was dead. It was questionable whether he had ever truly been alive; he had never revealed himself to me during the pregnancy and Siphiwe was much bigger and stronger, determined before she had even begun her journey. It was a journey that would conclude with us getting to Cape Town as a family and beginning our new life in a gloriously free new country, a place where I would have an instrumental place in Nelson's new administration and a place where we could be the envy of the world. If Nelson became the South African King then perhaps he would endow upon me a reward of aristocracy for my instrumental contribution to his successful overthrow of the evil government of Apartheid, and Siphiwe would become a lady of the realm, a countess or a duchess, an honoured daughter of the Queen Consort.

I had dreamed of great things for my sons, but sometimes the things that we plan do not come off as successfully as we had hoped. I knew the truth of the matter was brutally mathematical; we could not afford to have two children slowing us down, and I had been given a wonderfully graceful gift of not having to either choose one of the children to leave behind or to risk arriving in Cape Town too late to set Nelson free. I was so incredibly blessed to have shared those precious moments with Nangila, to get to know and say goodbye to him, to hold my child in my arms and to show him the love that he so deserved before we needed to let him go.

We buried Nangila by the side of the dirt road. Blessings took off his shirt and cradled our little boy in it, covering his face and kissing his forehead, and lying him down amongst the bulrushes. He had an unhealthy knowledge of burials and I trusted that the burial of his son would be the best one that he had ever done. When we could embrace him no longer we committed his body to the Earth and Africa began a new embrace in our absence; a new physical intimacy as he was enveloped in the sandy red soil. She was holding him, caressing him, welcoming him home. It was a moment of unbearable tenderness and I could not watch; instead

I turned my back on the two of them, the men whom I loved, and instead faced Cape Town with tears running down my cheeks and a precious daughter in my arms. I never loved Mwanyisa during the time that I had him all to myself, but I loved Nangila with a passion as fierce as the white lioness that prowled around within my heart. The red sand of Africa began to throb and pulse as it chanted the requiem for my sons, my boys, my *Bafana*.

Blessings managed to get himself a job as an assistant to a chandler in his shop in Grahamstown. Candle production was a vital industry and a staple of any family who had no access to electricity and a necessary backup for the rest of the country as the electricity system was extremely temperamental and the infrastructure of copper wires was prone to theft as criminals would dig up the cabling which they would sell as scrap. The townships of South Africa were bleak, cold and dark places and the work that Blessings did helped a great number of people to see. That was a wonderful thought; just as my husband was helping people to see their own homes after dark, I was helping to illuminate people's souls, to dispel and banish the darkness of Apartheid and to illuminate instead a path of justice and righteousness.

The candle wax once came from the slaughter of sperm whales along the coastline between Plettenberg Bay in the middle of the south coast and Lambert's Bay on the west coast, with the Indian and Atlantic oceans meeting at Cape Town and providing South Africa with some of the best harvests of whales of any nation in the world. Spermaceti was frequently extracted from the heads of the whales and ferried up from the harbours of the region to townships along the railway lines where it would be made into candles to light the homes. By the 1960s, however, the whale populations were running low and the sperm whales had almost been eradicated from the area. In 1979, seven years before we had arrived in Grahamstown, whaling in South Africa was comprehensively banned.

This particular chandler made the candles from beeswax. It was a good ingredient to use but it was fairly expensive to obtain, and because of that the business was not as busy as it could have been. Blessings would mould the candles predominantly into the standard white pillar shape but every so often he would be allowed to make one which was designed for ornamental rather than practical use; there would be animals, moons, stars and globes to name but a few.

The two of us were feeling very creative. I knew that he was proud to have managed to father a child with me and he put a lot of this pride into his candles. They were all shapes, sizes and colours, and as he lined them up I can only imagine that he saw them as representing a new South Africa, a new place of freedom and justice where all the people of all different ethnicities are also lined up side by side. We are all candles; no matter what colour our wax is, we all have the same wick running through the middle.

Is there anything as beautiful and wonderful as the fragility of a newborn human life? Siphiwe was as pristine as a sparkling mountain top covered with untouched snow, her intact spirit untainted by the drudgery of the world we live in. I saw the majesty of the world unfurled before me in a fresh and exciting way now that I was really a mother again. I saw the glory of Africa and the divinity with which life is endowed to us through a new lens; the grandeur lay in the sparkle of the stars and the majesty of the African wildlife but also in the delicate beauty of my daughter's eyes. Life is undoubtedly hard—I had been separated from the man that I loved by racists and I had lost two baby sons—but in equal measure that very same life is wonderful. Life is indescribably, immeasurably, gloriously wonderful, even here in Africa where the suffering seems to never cease. Surely there was as much awesome wonder in the immaculately created fingernails and eyelashes of my daughter as there was in all of the constellations of the heavens, all of the treasures of the court of the King. I was so blessed that I felt like I would burst open in a shower of coconut milk; my reward was waiting in Cape Town, for this was just the beginning of the adventure. I was a mother again. Siphiwe put the moon and stars to shame. My fruitful womanhood had been restored.

I often wondered about her future; what kind of South Africa were we building for Siphiwe and her contemporaries? Would she ever go back to Soweto and meet my mother and father, the ones who had done for me what I was now doing for her, and would she ever rest in the shade of the power station towers in Orlando? Would she ever see the skyscrapers of Egoli, or would she instead commute with me between the capital cities of Cape Town and Pretoria and never set foot in my old homeland? I wondered where she would go first, to my birthplace in the Gothic ruins of Sophiatown or to the King's in the peaceful wilderness of Mvezo.

One thing that was not a mystery for very long was her HIV status. I had never known Mwanyisa for long enough to determine whether or not he had inherited my ghastly infection but Siphiwe was one of the lucky ones who had not become infected when I gave birth to her. One of the commonest myths about HIV and AIDS is that it will be passed from mother to child in the womb; the reality of it is that this happens only in about a quarter of all cases. The human placenta is a marvellous and miraculous thing and I don't think people rave nearly enough about its magical capability to shield the baby from the virus. The problem came once she was out of the womb and needed feeding. The doctor told me that my coconut milk being secreted by my spectacular tiets was for the baby to drink, but at first I thought this was a joke. He told me that he was serious and also that my milk, my baby's food, was saturated with the poison of Mwanyisa's father.

I would have to infect her; there was no way around it. At first Blessings tried stealing milk from the local dairy on his way back from the candle shop, but it proved frustrating and inconsistent because my daughter did not need much milk but she needed it often. We had no way of keeping the milk fresh and we could not go out and steal from the dairy every three hours when she was hungry, so at first I fed her the stale and curdled milk to save her from my most bleak of magical curses. The milk would quickly turn watery and a greenish-yellow with flecks of pure white solid on the surface, but I still fed it to her because I was so reluctant to feed her from my own tainted body. I figured that it should be fine but it turned out that Siphiwe did not take to the rancid and sour milk, and even when I persuaded her to actually take it into her mouth she would scream and cry in distress. I didn't appreciate her selfishness; did my child not realise that I was bound by destiny and we did not have the time or the finances to waste on her welfare? Babies are such inherently egocentric little things and screaming is their strategy for solving all of the problems of the world. I was hurting too, for it is not easy waiting to be Queen, so perhaps I should have more success if I sat down in the middle of the road to Cape Town and simply screamed until my lips turned blue.

That night Mwanyisa came to visit me in a dream and he scolded me for my wicked heart. He reminded me of my crime against him in Coffee Bay and of my regret and heartache at letting him go, and then begged me to learn to feel compassion for his half-sister. The world does not revolve around Nelson Mandela, he would say. There are others, and now my job was to love Siphiwe and give her all that she needed in her hour of infantine helplessness. Mwanyisa told me to give up the dream and abandon my ambitions as readily as I had abandoned my child. He told me to turn around, return to Coffee Bay and find him in that little bin where he would be waiting for me so we could make a forever family; Nangila had died, but Mwanyisa had not, and my son implored that all the while he remained alive in that dustbin the bid for South Africa's freedom must be put on hold.

With a burst of brilliant white light I beheld my future husband descending out of the clouds on horseback. He held in his hands a sword of solid gold and he charged on Mwanyisa, the two of them battling for my honour and fiercely defending their own claim on my heart. Eventually Nelson drove Mwanyisa away and began passionately begging me not to abandon him to his fate on Robben Island, pleading with me to remember my promise to chase his freedom wherever the trail may lead. He told me that he loved me and reached out a hand to touch the side of my face, but as he did so I suddenly saw enormous bars coming down between us and we were held apart by a great divide, with him a captive and I a free woman. There were a thousand things that I wanted to tell him, secrets and whispers and truths, and I badly needed to feel the physical sensation of having him in my arms. But it was not to be;

I awoke from my slumber sharing in Siphiwe's aching, excruciating hunger.

In the end I knew that if Siphiwe drank rancid milk or refused anything I offered her that she would soon die so with a heavy heart I took the decision to feed her from my breast. Cursing her was the most difficult decision that any mother could ever take, and as I held my poisoned nipple to her lips I knew that I held her whole life underneath my maternal fingers. She had been very hungry and she was screaming for a feed, and as I slipped my teat into her mouth and felt the comforted suction on my breast the tears streamed down my cheeks. I was nurturing and destroying her all at once, slowly murdering her just as that ghastly White Man had already murdered me in Durban, forcing her to ingest a microscopic bomb which was set to detonate years in the future. What was even harder was the fact that she was so thankful and satisfied for the curse that I had given her. As she suckled from me she gave little whimpers of pleasure and although my heart was breaking I was so indescribably reaffirmed by the fact that perfectly white milk was being secreted by my ghoulishly black body. This undercurrent of purity, this magnificent emblem of a white soul bubbling up within me and breaking through the darkness of my coconut shell was all the assurance that I needed that I would make it to Cape Town on time, free Nelson and save the world.

Blessings and I found a mail wagon which was being loaded onto the train waiting in the deserted siding. The young worker was black, and he was unloading the wagon and inspecting the bags before hauling them onto the open carriage. I looked down at the addresses on the envelopes in one of the open sacks, and it became quite obvious from the ones he was loading on and the ones he was leaving in the wagon that the train was bound for Cape Town, which meant that the next station stop would be Port Elizabeth.

Blessings was a very smooth operator when he needed to be. He strode confidently up to the worker and he began to explain what was going to happen. His confidence was ostentatious.

"Shub shub bru."

The man looked bewildered and perplexed.

"I'm sorry?"

"I said shub shub."

"Don't you mean sharp sharp?"

"No, I mean shub shub. My wife and I are waiting for a late connection coming just now and we have nothing to do. Do you mind if we help you?"

The young man looked very uneasy about being in such close proximity to strangers when he was working, perhaps suspicious that we would try to steal something based on the fact that we looked black. His movements were jerky and agitated. Blessings explained to him that we were fugitives who had been framed for a murder on the highway, and we needed to find an alibi to cover our tracks so we could escape the clutches of the racist, corrupted police force. We would tell them that we had been here the whole time. Blessings begged and pleaded with the stranger to help us and implored him as a black brother, wordlessly evoking the passion of the pilgrimage of freedom which we found ourselves on. This was a man for whom we would be improving South Africa, and we needed his help. He had probably been accused of being a tsotsi as well at some point in his life.

Eventually he relented and he allowed us to help him to load the parcels from the cold gravel and onto the train carriage. As I held them in my hands for the briefest of moments I wondered who they were for and where they were going, for the names and addresses on the envelopes and boxes meant nothing to me as I loaded them on. The mystery of this property of countless strangers was thrilling and exciting, and I felt drunk on the power that I now held over them.

When the man had turned his head away we leapt onto the carriage and hid in amongst the mail. It was pitch black, so nobody would see our dark skin. I was terrified that Siphiwe would cry, so I held my hand over her mouth as tightly as I could.

14

ZEBRA STRIPES

Port Elizabeth, Cape Province
August 1986

We had arrived in Grahamstown as a couple, but we left as a family. I treasured Siphiwe, held her tightly to my chest and loved her to the very best of my ability. We jumped off the train at Port Elizabeth when the driver became suspicious; our journey was long and exhausting. Port Elizabeth is one of the largest cities in South Africa and is positioned right in the middle of a large bay on the south coast. There were now less than eight hundred kilometres lying between us and the Mother City. The bay on which this city sits is a great wonder and I decided that this beautiful place should be named Queen Lerato Bay in honour of my achievements in ending Apartheid.

If the fight for the freedom of our people and the emancipation of Africa was described as an animal, it would be a zebra. That was the part of it all that the Government loved; the clear and defined separation of the whites and the blacks, made into distinct and separate lines on the strong and thick hide.

Even though I knew that the best way to describe myself was by declaring myself a coconut, sometimes I would think that the zebra was a little like me. We had so many things in common; I was black and white all at once, and these animals could not be divided into a dazzle of black zebras and another dazzle of white zebras. It was absolutely incorrect to describe any zebra as black *or* white; each and every single one of them was both black *and* white in equal measure. That was how ridiculous this law of Apartheid was and that was how impractical it was to begin the task of separating people along racial lines. I was just as outraged as the zebra was when I was described as black, because it was as far away from my true identity as it was possible to be. I wasn't completely white but nobody ever really made that mistake because people were always quick to judge me by what they could see. Being described as black was incomprehensibly, indescribably and disgracefully *wrong*.

If I was a coconut then Siphiwe was a zebra; I was externally black and internally white but my daughter was black and white simultaneously, with half of me and half of Blessings uniting in flesh to mould and sculpt her little body. Zebra skin is intriguing; looking at the animals you would think that each and every one was the product of crossbreeding between a black father and a white mother. My daughter's skin was darker than Mwanyisa's had been and she didn't have the blotchy complexion that her brother Nangila had done when he died, but instead she had a thriving, flourishing skin tone as rich and wholesome as dark chocolate. I never thought that I could ever come to love someone with black skin but I looked on Siphiwe with a pure and fierce love, the love of a lioness. I adored everything about her and thought she was perfect just the way she was. Her eyes sparkled like shooting stars and her smile made me melt. I was in awestruck wonder at every part of her miniature body: her tiny fingernails, knuckles and palms; her soft lips and supple toothless gums; the perfectly smooth skin; her tiny toes and her miniscule ankles and knees.

She had been created out of a yearning hunger for affection and love, the collision of two souls who were travelling far and wide on an endless pursuit of justice, righteousness and peace. I had wanted her so very badly and I knew that she understood that when I looked at her. It was a truth wholly unlike my telepathy with Nelson; that truth was rationally and logically provable, whereas my evidence for my daughter understanding how much I loved her was simply that deep within my white spirit I knew it to be true. As I held her in my arms that shred of flimsy proof was all that I needed. That splinter of hope was enough to see me through.

Nelson waited.

Every time I fed my daughter from my breast I knew that I was killing her as well as nourishing her, but what other option did I have? After the tragedy of Bafana I would never let my child go and I would never let her go hungry.

Parenthood is a wonderful thing to be cursed with. Blessings had been infected with HIV, a virus that none of us understood in greater detail than it was incurable, but he had never been so happy in his life. He was able to find himself a job in the Ford Motor Company's assembly plant in the city centre, working on the production line and spending the whole day on his feet fitting the components together. He often told me that it was exhausting, dirty and gruelling work.

My husband's job was to assemble the components of the headlights on some of the models which were manufactured at the plant in Port Elizabeth. It was painstaking and it was a frustrating job for him to be doing and he told me that he didn't like it, but his boss seemed to think that he was doing a good enough job. With my temporary husband working on his temporary job of manufacturing cars, I thought often of the splendour and opulence with which Nelson and I would travel once he had been crowned. I imagined the gleaming limousines, the deep and soft leather seats and the curtains on the windows, the engine sculpted of solid gold. That day would come soon. Nelson told me that the day when I would ride in an expensive limousine was closer than I thought; given that I had been born in a car I was unusually preoccupied with all things automotive.

I stayed with Siphiwe, nursing her and helping her to grow. We lived in a tin shack in one of the local slums and we sat on the side of the road most days. I held out my hands for the passing strangers to give us gifts. I didn't have particularly high hopes for success but the generosity of the people we came into contact with put me in a mood of surprised optimism.

Just the same as all of the other places in South Africa at the time, Apartheid was keenly felt in Port Elizabeth. There had been relocation policies similar to the ones which had set me on this miserable journey from Johannesburg when Sophiatown had been destroyed in 1955. The blacks were kept in one area and the whites in another, with a vast and invisible curtain coming down between them keeping them apart. Because of Blessings and Siphiwe I was shackled to the black half of the people of my country and so we could only stay in the areas where blacks were permitted to be.

We decided that the best way to continue our journey was to hitch a ride along the N2. After a few hours of waiting, one of the cars pulled up. It was a big Mercedes saloon, and the driver was a young white man. The perfection of his pale skin was so beautiful that it made me queasy.

"Are you going to Cape Town?"

"No Miss, but I can take you as far as Plettenberg Bay."

It was better than nothing, and we accepted. Perhaps there would be work there for us to do.

"We have no money and nothing to offer you, my friend, but we mean you no harm and we are very grateful for your help."

He welcomed us into the car, explaining that he was interested in doing us a favour rather than taking our money and we were happy to be on our way. I wondered what would happen if someone saw a black family and a white man sharing a car; I did not know the law well enough to determine if it was illegal or not but what I did know was that this man was taking a huge risk and that he taught me that compassion is multicoloured. That brand new Mercedes was the nicest and most expensive car that I had ever travelled in, and the wayfaring stranger was very good to us. We never learnt his name, but he explained that he had been visiting his sister in King William's Town and was on his way home to Plettenberg Bay, a famously wealthy resort town where the South African elite enjoyed themselves beside a beautiful stretch of coastline. We sped through the night along the highway and I smiled to myself as I sank down with my daughter into the cold leather seat, knowing that this would probably be the easiest of all the legs of the journey so far. What fortune had befallen us to make the decision to hitch-hike from Port Elizabeth and also to come across this kind natured stranger! We talked about the weather and his sister, and he was very pleased to see Siphiwe and hear all about her.

The night was dark and we could not see, but the traveller decided to give us a little tour of the countryside surrounding his home when he realised that we were from Kimberley and Johannesburg. It was with a great sense of pride that he told us when we were crossing the new Bloukrans Bridge, the highest single span arch bridge in the world, which had been opened three years earlier. The roadway floated more than two hundred metres above the valley floor and as we looked out on the cliffs which dropped away from the edge of the road with a thrilling suddenness, it felt as though we were accelerating along a road through the heavens. The windscreen and the rear view mirror were filled with nothing but starlit sky. The valley which the bridge spanned marked the beginning of the final stretch of our journey, the crossing of a great and vast divide; we were now only six hundred kilometres from home.

We stopped at a robot at an intersection, and I heard a rustle in the bushes alongside the road. The man locked the doors of the car and I gripped Siphiwe tighter, my eyes as wide as a deer's caught in the headlights on a dark road. After a couple of seconds of silence I suddenly heard a furious pounding of footsteps closing in on the car and a masked man tried to open the driver's door. Discovering that it was locked, he began punching the glass until the whole window caved in on the driver, collapsing all over his body in a shower of sparkling glass. He slammed his foot on the accelerator and the engine roared back into life, throwing us all back in our seats as the car sped quickly through the red light and we swerved to avoid the other cars crossing our path.

I heard three gunshots from a Ruger LCR .38 Special calibre revolver. On the third shot the car was thrown into a violent spin and I heard and felt the grating of the metal wheel hub scratching against the surface of the road as the view from the windows was obscured by smoke. He had deflated one of the tyres of the car with his bullets. We skidded to a halt and a group of men rushed towards us, some of them with guns. Aiming his weapon at the driver's head, the leader of the gang reached through the smashed window and with a chilling calmness pulled up the knob to unlock the door and opened it. The darkness of the night flooded into the car.

"Get out," he said coldly.

Blessings and I did not need any convincing, and we undid our seatbelts and attempted to open the door. The driver, however, was much more reluctant to surrender his beloved car and refused to move, telling them that it was his property and that they had no right to take it from him.

The leader of the gang pushed the gun against the side of the driver's head, pressing the tip into the flesh of his temple. The gunman cocked his head to one side and peered deeply into the man's soul. It seems that people do not truly reveal themselves until the stakes are so high that life is hanging in the balance. "Are you afraid?"

The driver gripped the steering wheel with both of his hands and clenched his teeth.

"No."

The gunman pulled the trigger and the driver's head exploded, sending a shower of brains, flesh and bone across the car and into the empty passenger seat. There was a splash of blood on the speedometer and a piece of skull was wedged in the bottom of the passenger's foot-well. The shining metal of the interior doorhandle was soaked with the jelly of his brain, and the gear stick was covered in clumps of flesh. I had never seen the inside of a white man before. As I looked at the gore-soaked interior of the car, I could not help but wonder whether my white soul would have meant that my guts would have been the same as his, or if instead my brain floated in pure coconut milk.

The leader of the gang reached around the torso of the corpse and unstrapped the seatbelt. He pulled the body out of the car and carried it over to the grass verge where he unceremoniously dumped him with what was left of his severely disfigured face pressed into the gravel and mud. Then he turned his gun on me. We had been silently debating whether or not it would be a good idea to flee from the scene; in all probability they would try to shoot at us and would hit their target before we could elude them. In the end we remained, and we decided to try to talk our way out of this messy situation. With his accuracy at training his bullets on the tyres of the car, it didn't seem likely that we would have been able to escape.

Two of the gunmen came over to us and they waved their weapons in our faces. "Give me all the money you have," said one of the men in Zulu. I decided against my wiser judgement and opted to plead; I couldn't lie to them because if they saw through it they would surely kill all of us.

"Sir," I began, "we are trying to reach Cape Town and we do not have enough money to get there. I have a baby daughter," I opened my coat and showed him my hands, wrapped around Siphiwe resting against my chest, "and we need the money we do have to feed her. Please, good sir, I beg you to let us go."

"As I said," he replied, "give me all the money you have. I don't care about your daughter. Give me the money, or you die." He waved his shotgun in the direction of the driver's corpse, his blood and brain leaving a trail from the open car door, and in my mind he suddenly became Blessings, the skin morphing from white to black and the head transforming into that of my team-mate. I could not let that happen. Blessings reluctantly took out the ball of money that he had been keeping in his coat and handed it over. The men thanked him and turned away.

The leading gunman who had shot the driver clearly had a change of heart as he turned back to us a couple of seconds later. I was pleasantly surprised at his honesty and virtue, and I held my hand open to receive the money back from him with a smile of gratitude. But instead he grabbed me violently and thrust the pistol up against my jaw, clutching me roughly with his other hand. "Before I go," he hissed aggressively, "you will satisfy my manly needs."

Oh God, not again. My head was filled with Mwanyisa as much as the driver's head was filled with a shining steel bullet. He rummaged in his pants and with one hand he took out his dick and aimed it at me. I was still holding my daughter as the black scumbag considered it. With the other hand he still held the gun to my throat, the cold metal of the barrel sending a stimulating chill through my dark skin.

"I am HIV positive," I said harrowingly and coldly with tears in my eyes. It was a horrible thing to have to say, and I have never been so embarrassed and ashamed of anything in my whole life. It was as though by saying it out loud I was verifying its truth, and I didn't want to do that. Blessings knew that there was nothing he could do and he turned his back. "All of us are HIV positive. You will be infected if you have sex with me, and for the rest of your life you will fight against this illness until it eventually kills you. Every day from now on may be your last, and there is no cure."

The gunman's eyes widened as he contemplated what he was about to do, and I could see the mechanism of his brain processing the idea and weighing up the risk. He eventually came to the right conclusion and he put his weapon back where it belonged. The five of them changed the most damaged wheel of the Mercedes and drove away into the night. The red glow of the tail-lamps faded slowly and we were left horrified and alone in the middle of the night at an intersection in the middle of nowhere. It was with a dazzling sense of ironic wonder that I realised that it had been my illness, the withering curse of HIV, which had saved my integrity and my life.

Carjacking had always been a problem for South Africa, and several international gangs would steal cars to order for "customers" both at home and abroad. In a country that was already blighted by an extremely high incidence of violent crime the economics of Apartheid was always tipped in favour of the opportunistic criminal when people who had nothing were side by side with the extremely wealthy, and because of the racism in government which side of the divide you fell on was determined by the colour of your skin. Because I cannot drive a car I did not ever expect to be involved in a carjacking. Mrs Kennedy had nothing on me now.

15

MONSTERS IN PARADISE

Plettenberg Bay, Garden Route, Cape Province
January 1987

We were very distressed from our ordeal on the road, and we had faced the daunting task of completing the journey with all of our money taken and being stranded on the roadside, alone and terrified of the motorists speeding past in their cars. As each one rushed past my frail little body I was rocked down to my core and I was tense and afraid. The headlights shone magically in the opaque, stifling darkness of the night. The world shimmered in a murky stillness and the stars shone like phosphenes sparkling on the underside of my eyelids during a migraine.

We camped on the side of the road in the ditch on the Robben Island side of the place where the corpse of our deceased driver lay. We could not continue on in the darkness because we were too afraid of being attacked and so eventually, when my illness began to get the better of me, we found a place to hide ourselves and settled down for the night against the mud and foliage, taking care to be well out of sight of the road.

The next morning we decided to be brave and hitchhike again. Our experience the second time was much better than the first; there were no murders, no embroidered blood on leather seats, that sort of thing. We were eventually picked up by a trucker who was delivering ingredients to a restaurant in Plettenberg Bay after a couple of hours of walking with nothing but Siphiwe in our arms by way of possessions along the dusty and dirty tarmac of the N2. The journey was relatively short and there were two of them in the truck but we did not speak a word throughout the whole time we were together. We had hoped that the driver would be able to take us further than Plett, but when we arrived in the town we changed our minds immediately.

Discovered by early Portuguese sailors, Plettenberg Bay was named *Bahia Formosa* or "beautiful bay" probably because they were too dumbstruck to think of anything else. This was a land of private castles along the beach, an unbroken sweep of perfect sand and sprawling palatial villas on the hillsides above the town. The whole bay was encircled by mountains and lush valleys and forests. We were now just six hundred kilometres from Cape Town, and we had landed in paradise.

When we were dropped off at the restaurant the first thing we did was to go to the beach, just as we had done in Durban. Somehow it had lost some of the otherworldly magic, undeniably beautiful as it was, and I let the cool crystalline sea wash over my fat black toes as I dipped them into the Indian Ocean. I stared out at that elusive horizon guarding the sea and sky, trying to imagine the thousands of kilometres of ocean spread out before me, unbroken until the next piece of solid land which was Antarctica. I closed my eyes and I saw the clean, eye searing whiteness of the snow and ice, the thumping blizzards and the atmosphere drenched in ice-dust, the sharp and mathematical precision of every brilliant line and edge. I felt a deep connection as I pictured it in my head; the fact that I did not fit into this world of blackness and whiteness made me know that the most probable explanation was that I was made for more. I was created for somewhere different, and I knew that the only person who could take me there was Nelson.

The daydream about my perfect life in Antarctica was interrupted as Blessings woke me and told me that I had fallen into an exhausted sleep for half an hour on the sand. I looked behind me and the dramatically lowered tide appeared to confirm his accusation; Siphiwe was crawling in and out of the waves far away from me and I could see her between my toes which were standing to attention as they saluted the vast and endless sky. They looked like a little line of black soldiers standing guard for their Queen. Blessings held my hand and touched my arm to help me up; as his foul black skin came into contact with mine I felt a burning pain shoot through me as though his masculine hands were made of fire. The excruciating sensation was matched by one of elation and jubilant anticipation; perhaps this was the moment that I had been waiting for all along and that this sensation was the unfamiliar feeling of having a coconut shell peeled off of me. It wasn't. I was mistaken; the sensation that I was feeling was sunburn. Blessings and Siphiwe had been in the sunshine just as long as I had but their skin had not been burned. My temporary husband told me that my HIV had turned to AIDS which was causing my skin to become more sensitive, but he was a dangerous idiot and I would not be easily deceived by his poisonous words. I would be lying if I told you that the sunburn in Plett did not trouble me, however. If I had been wrong about this physical sensation which I took as proof that I am a coconut, what else might I be mistaken about? Could I be more wrong than I realised? The indecision did not last for long; whenever I doubted my mission and my identity I always took great comfort in the indisputable fact that Nelson was still in jail and still waiting for me. He could not be free until I arrived in Cape Town. If he did manage to be free before I reached him I promised myself that I would abandon the dream and return to a quiet life of anonymity, but I knew that the chances of him being free without my help were miniscule. He held my royalty in the palm of his hand and I knew it.

We set about finding somewhere where we could sleep that night and we found a short, steep hill leading up from the beach. We followed it until we got to the top, and the view as we turned around every so often when we lost our breath on the way up was nothing short of spectacular. Sometimes we were not tired at all, but we were just gawping at the stunning panorama that we now had of Plettenberg Bay.

The hill was a short cut to a private road and it was lined with enormous mansions and castles. Perhaps the largest and grandest of them, an ostentatious mock Georgian house with massive Palladian pillars and statues of lions guarding the front door, caught my eye more than the others. The front garden was enclosed behind massive electronic gates which were garlanded with great wreaths of razor wire and walls with anti climb paint. As I looked through the gates, I saw that all was not well. Some of the immaculately manicured shrubs had been ripped out of the beds and there was a smashed window on the ground floor. Blessings had been more attentive to our pilgrimage and our lack of luck on the N2 whilst I had been distracted by the opulence and grandeur of the way that the people live here; he had noticed a sign which was hung on the gates. It said "Help Wanted".

The house was nothing short of magnificent. The sign told me to come back at the weekend when the owner of the house would be back, and we waited for him. I made sure that our family set up camp outside of the gates and waited for our hero to come home. Saturday came, and he arrived mid-morning in a chauffeur driven limousine which made that Mercedes driver look positively impoverished.

As he pulled up at the gate of his mansion he told the driver to stop and wound down his window so he could speak to us. As we caught a glimpse of him for the first time we saw his perfectly white skin encased in a suit of the finest materials available. He had a sumptuous aura of cologne that glowed against my husband's blackness.

"Move away." His voice was deep and gruff and he spoke with a very thick Afrikaner accent.

"Sir, we are here to ask you about the job that you have posted on the gates of your house."

Our rescuer looked bewildered and suspicious. "Why have you been loitering outside of my home?"

"We were not loitering. We were guarding it. We knew you were not here until Saturday and we were afraid that someone may try to break into your property."

The stranger did not know what to say. He got out of the limousine, paid the driver, and the car drove away. Our rescuer unlocked the gates of the mansion and welcomed us inside. "You would guard my home for me when I was away before I even asked you to?" I gave him a little curtsy, and affirmed his suspicions that I was indeed an outstanding employee. I did not like to bow down in submission to another white person, least of all a man, but I did it when I needed to in order to get my way. It is wrong to think that whites should be superior to blacks but it is stupid to deny the cruel nature of the South Africa that we lived in and it is foolish to not manipulate the situation to your advantage at every available opportunity. Our white rescuer loved being exalted by our black humility. Blessings and I were hired on the spot.

"You," he began, waving a large and hairy hand in my general direction, "will be my ousie." I was shocked and offended as his words cut through me to the bone. *Ousie* is a word used to describe a female black servant, someone who would take control of a household and carry out general duties as a maid. I would be expected to clean when the family were away and to cook when the family were there. How many times would I have to explain over the course of my employment that I am not really black?

"And you," he said, turning to Blessings, "will be my tuinbooi." *Tuinbooi* is an Afrikaans word for a black male servant who was hired to tend to the grounds of a large house. He would be the gardener for the Van Der Merwe family and he would also have to feed and groom the horses that would soon be driven down to the mansion's stable block from Johannesburg so that his wife could ride them at the weekends.

The man's name was Christiaan Van Der Merwe and he was the chief executive of one of the banks in Egoli. The company had its own skyscraper in the middle of the business district of Johannesburg and operated in dozens of countries all across the world although the backlash against Apartheid was beginning to hit him hard. His family owned an apartment in Cape Town and a large house in Sandton, the affluent and exclusive suburb to the north of Johannesburg, so this was their third home. It had eight bedrooms, a swimming pool, tennis courts, a gym, a "small" and as yet empty stable block which "only" included space for two horses and a few luxury Italian sports cars. The mansion in Plettenberg Bay had been ransacked the previous month and they were looking for people to take care of the house so that it would be always occupied and hopefully this would deter the criminals. The house had panic buttons fitted which were linked directly to a local private armed response company who would send security guards to the house if any trouble arose, and they needed someone there all the time so that these could be activated when necessary. He showed me the controls for the armoured gates and the electric fencing, and I was bewildered. They were ADT. The guns which I could now send for at the touch of a button had in all probability been made by me when I had been at the munitions factory in Bloemfontein.

Plettenberg Bay had its own airport, and the family would spend the weekdays in Johannesburg where Christiaan worked and the children attended school, and they would fly down to the coast on a private jet for the weekend. I wondered how much a plane ticket to Cape Town would cost; perhaps this would be the last stop before the glorious reunion with Nelson. The mother of the family was Ida Van Der Merwe, and she had told him that she wanted some horses to be kept in Plettenberg Bay so that she could ride along the beach during the weekends away from the city.

Christiaan and Ida had four children: three sons and one daughter. Heinric, their eldest, was eighteen at the time and was training to become an officer in the South African Army. His younger brother Ralf was sixteen and at boarding school in Johannesburg, and their sister Natalja and brother Jaap were twelve and ten and at private schools in the city. All of the children owned at least one horse and were keen equestrians, and the boys were all talented rugby players and golfers. Ralf had also been a successful fencer in his school's House Team. The family regularly went on surfing and skiing holidays and owned a yacht which was moored in Cape Town; that magical city; that hallowed ground; that sacred spot.

The thing which entranced me the most about the possessions and the lifestyle of this family was that little jet which ferried them between South Africa's cities and made the journey which had so far taken us ten years in a matter of hours. Some nights as I was lying in bed and waiting for sleep to come and drench me I would consider a particularly outlandish plan to somehow hijack the plane and pilot it myself to Cape Town's airport, getting Blessings to navigate our course using the stars. We would be there in no time, and perhaps the plane would be put in a museum one day as the chariot which had carried me triumphantly to my destiny as Queen, the battle horse which I had used to break the siege of Robben Island. I wondered how it would feel to fly. Would we be able to feel the sensation of the air rushing past us at very high speed when we were up in the sky, charting our path through the constellations and the slumbering heavens?

I did not even know what surfing was until I arrived in Durban, and I had only seen snow a couple of times in my life because of the perfectly dry winter season in the Highveld of the Transvaal. It was, quite simply, a different world from the one I had known. Everything about Plettenberg Bay was to do with the ocean, from the fashion on display by our wealthy hosts to the fact that every single building seemed to face the sea, almost like a crowd of Muslims facing Mecca as they prayed. Looking up at the hillsides from the beach reminded me slightly of the way that plants bend towards the sunlight, for every building seemed to have grown out of the lush and fertile soil to give spectacular and far reaching views of the shining sea.

I remember walking around the mansion in an awestruck silence on the first day that we worked for the family. Blessings and I were given use of one of the bedrooms and an old cot which had belonged to Jaap, and as she showed me our new home Ida apologised for the "cramped abode" that she was offering us. Perhaps this woman's eyeballs did not work correctly; the room was enormous and palatial, and beautifully and sumptuously decorated. It was easily the size of our shacks in Sophiatown and Soweto which we had shared between an extended family of ten people but it was only for our tiny and new family of three. The room had a vast and comfy double bed, carpet, curtains, glass in the windows and an electric light-bulb behind the shade in the centre of the ceiling. It was beautiful. Ida said that she had wanted to give us an en-suite bedroom but of the three spare rooms in the house she wanted to give the other two to family and friends. I was not even used to using a bathroom inside of the house, but clearly a woman like Ida could not survive without a bathroom adjoining her bedroom which meant that she assumed that I was exactly the same as she was and would view this palace as a dump. I will never forget the way that Ida Van Der Merwe smelled. It was a hedonistic cocktail of fine clothes, jewellery and extremely expensive perfume which mixed together to give a blisteringly strong, deep aroma. She was fabulous and extraordinary. Was that what I would look and smell like if I could shed my black skin and disrobe myself of this miserable coconut shell I was entombed within?

We had a dinner together on that first day to celebrate the start of something new. We had expected a feast of grasshoppers with pap or the slaughter of one of the family's chickens but what we got instead was the invitation to clink our glasses together whilst they were filled with a drink called Champagne. Apparently the drink comes from France, which was a shock to me because I was convinced that Champagne was the capital of Liberia. These little differences in culture convinced me even more that I had spent far too long as a black woman and that I needed to change without delay. The thought that I may one day forget about my whiteness because I had been overexposed to black culture and starved of white culture for too long was the most terrifying idea that I could imagine.

It was in Plettenberg Bay that I realised that racism is not evil or wicked, but instead it is stupid and ignorant. It comes from a place of misunderstanding rather than one of judgement; hatred is normally reserved for what we are not able to fully comprehend. The Van Der Merwe family did not like black people and they were perfectly supportive of the Apartheid system, thinking that it was in the interests of the nation to keep the people separated along racial lines, but that did not make them devilish monsters. I think that the thing which proved this to me was the way in which they treated Siphiwe. A child is a child regardless of the colour of their skin, and the way that the Van Der Merwe children especially accepted

Siphiwe was something which was beautiful to behold. We arrived shortly before her first birthday and it was here that she took the first unsteady steps and tumbled many times despite the whoops and cheers in support of her until she finally managed to learn how to walk. She was so proud of herself; she would clap and give herself little cheers when she eventually came tumbling down and that was because the Van Der Merwes were so supportive of her as they clapped and cheered and smiled in encouragement. Humanity, for all of its selfishness and drudgery, is a magical and miraculous species and one which is endowed with great virtue even in the most unlikely of places. Living in this mansion with our multi-millionaire employers was one such scene of improbability.

Natalja, who was twelve, had grown up as the only little girl in the family and she relished the chance at getting a new baby sister for the weekends, even if that sister was black. She would lend Siphiwe all of her toys, dress her up in white girl's clothes, take her for picnics in the garden and take her for trips to the seaside. In her young mind Siphiwe was just another toy to play with; this millionaire's daughter was well used to being provided with things to keep her occupied. I could not help but think of Natalja as being a little bit neglected and forgotten in the testosterone filled environment of that family, with her three brothers muscling in on their parent's attention and affection and leaving no room for her. For all of the boasting of the brothers, I was absolutely transfixed by her. Something about her was electric and I found her fascinating.

I would watch Natalja and Siphiwe walking around the garden together and think of the speeches that I would make to crowded stadiums when I was Nelson's Press Secretary, Vice President or chief speechwriter. That would be the enduring image of South Africa in the future, these two young girls cultivating a friendship in the most unlikely of circumstances. It gave me proof and it restored my faith that two races living in mutual respect and harmony was possible and achievable and close. As the two girls held hands, I felt stirring in my soul a rousing sense of peace and justice at last. Everything that was beautiful and unique about South Africa was summarised beautifully in Natalja's hand meeting Siphiwe's. It was a premonition, a prophecy, a shadow of the glory to come and the freedom which I would hep to usher in.

The daughters of our respective families continued their close relationship every time that the Van Der Merwe's flew down from Johannesburg for the weekends. Natalja would even try to brush Siphiwe's hair but neither we nor the family had an afro comb and she would not have had a clue how to use one anyway. It didn't take a rocket scientist to understand that you push the comb in against the scalp and scrape the hair vertically until it is soft and fluffy, but it is not something that you can understand without having practised before. This was the frustration that I had found with my own body many times; I longed for straight hair to brush with a white girl's hairbrush, but instead I had an unhappy ball of black wire, a tortured and tragic bob of misery which was indelibly stained with the demonic and dark hue of an African. I hated my hair. To flick my hair with a swing of my neck and to feel my straight hair flowing in the wind would be something that I would never experience and Siphiwe could never know either. Instead I had hair which bounced rather than flowed and that tortured me. I deserved whiteness, but a white body would be something I was forever denied.

That hairbrush summed up our potential for failure in ending Apartheid. The image of sisterhood and reconciliation which these two girls displayed was not a celebration of the black culture which had been murdered in Sophiatown in 1955 but instead an attempt to turn black people into white people in order for them to get along. It was the expectation of the people to surrender their culture and their heritage to their supremacist masters; in the Van Der Merwe's slice of paradise in Plettenberg Bay we saw the exact same situation unfolding as the riots in Soweto in 1976 which had killed Hector Pieterson. Then it was about sharing a language, now it was about sharing a hairbrush.

I could never be happy until I was in Cape Town and reunited with Nelson again, but I think that Plettenberg Bay was the closest that we came to complete happiness simply because of our unbelievable good fortune. We lived in a mansion in one of the most beautiful places in the country, enjoying an incredible lifestyle with the treasured daughter for whom we had dreamed for so long. The Van Der Merwes would arrive late on a Friday night, and we would all be together in Plettenberg Bay until Sunday evening when they would take their jet back to Johannesburg. There were often times when some members of the family would miss the weekend by the sea, as sometimes Ralf would have a rugby match on a Friday or Christiaan would go to Europe to do business. They also had servants at their house in Sandton so the remaining family members would not be left alone whilst the rest of them came to Plettenberg Bay to stay with us.

One of the weekends when Jaap was in town he asked me if I would play him at a game of chess, but I declined because I could not bear to have to bring myself to choose between being black or being white. By selecting to have black soldiers represent me, would I be condemning the white half of me to death? Which was more important and which was more disposable? It was an extremely distressing and troubling conundrum, and so I agreed to referee a game between him and Blessings.

We had what we financially needed fairly fast, but we did not leave and move on to the next town on the way to Cape Town at the earliest opportunity as we had always done before. The Van Der Merwes were a very generous family. I tried to convince myself that we did not make a move was because we were saving up for three plane tickets to Cape Town and that this would be the last stop on our journey across the nation to rescue him, but I wasn't even sure of that because I didn't know how the Apartheid laws applied to aviation. Were blacks and whites meant to travel on separate planes, or did they have to sit on either side of the same aisle? The truth of it was that we were enchanted and bewitched by the enrapturing beauty of Plettenberg Bay and the kindness and hospitality offered to us by our employers, and we were in danger of losing our focus and failing to make the progress that we needed to. We were getting comfortable in our mansion by the sea and we were unable to summon the sense of urgency which had propelled us across the country as far as we had come. Could it be that we were losing focus on the prize which we had spent so long obsessing about, the objective which was so important to so many and which we were in a unique position to achieve and to avenge Sophiatown? I felt as though the whole of Soweto, millions and millions of people all piled into tiny shacks of corrugated tin, were relying on us to pack our bags and leave and continue in our quest to free Nelson. But as we dined in our mansion on the weeknights when we were alone, using a table and metal cutlery for the evening meal for the first time in our lives, it seemed as though we had discovered our Achilles heel.

I thought of Nelson often when we were working for the Van Der Merwes. It seemed so unbelievably unfair; we were living in a mansion with an unbroken sea view, riding horses in our spare time and he was locked away in the dungeon of Robben Island, lashed by Atlantic storms and starving to death on his own, tantalized by a glimpse of land on the horizon and the false hope of us imminently and triumphantly rescuing him. It showed me that all the justice in this country was destroyed when the Nationalist party swept to power in 1948. Apartheid had failed to install logic and justice into a hurting world. Life was still painfully random.

A couple of years passed. The summer of 1989 arrived, and Siphiwe was almost three years old; she was walking and her words were becoming sentences. We knew that her first memories of life would inevitably be of this place, this hallowed ground in the history of our family, this beautiful backdrop to my daughter's childhood. But now the air was beginning to turn sour. It began when I was horrified to learn that Natalja had been taught by her parents to operate a shotgun in the hope that if she was alone in the house in Johannesburg that she could shoot and kill any black man she saw on their property. Next she would run into the kitchen and fetch the biggest bread knife that she could see, place it carefully in his hand and *then* call the police. Apparently they had a huge guard dog that was trained from a puppy to identify black people by their scent and to only attack the dark visitors. Whilst being deeply uneasy about this new revelation I was also a little curious to experiment with the dog and see how it would react when faced with a conundrum like me.

I was in the kitchen preparing a fruit salad for that evening's dessert and Blessings was outside washing Christiaan's new Ferrari. I remembered how much he had been looking forward to washing the headlights because he thought they were the most beautiful headlights that he had ever seen. Ida's line of conversation hit me like a bolt of lightning.

"Are you HIV positive, Lerato?"

I was stunned and I could not speak. My throat was dry and I could not articulate myself; after a small eternity I roused my voice into action. It seemed so cruelly spontaneous.

"You have known me for almost three years now, Mrs Van Der Merwe. What makes you ask me a question like that?"

"Because it's just that I wouldn't really want anyone with HIV preparing the food. The virus might seep through their skin and into the ingredients that they were touching and we could all end up infected." She gave a high pitched cackle. "I don't want my kids getting HIV, thank you very much. They deserve better than that. Can you imagine Heinric with HIV? That's the most absurd thing I have ever heard in my life. My baby is too precious and I love him too much."

"No, Mrs Van Der Merwe, I am not positive." I gave her a wry smile to help the lie go down a bit smoother. "Did you think I was?"

"Oh, you can never be too careful nowadays. It's spreading like wildfire amongst your people, you know, the black ones. Perhaps you caught it from the monkeys when you were living in trees. I guess that those places like Soweto are infested, and there is just nothing that anybody could do about it." She seemed thoughtful. "It's quite sad, really. Those poor people, all swarming with sickness and disease. Perhaps it's a part of being black and you just have to accept it. Doom runs in the bloodstream as thickly as the illness itself does."

She looked up at me and smiled kindly. "I'm sorry dear, you must not know what I am talking about. Do you know Johannesburg at all?"

"No Ma'am. I have never been there."

"You have never heard of Soweto then. How silly of me, I'm sorry. It's a slum, a shanty town, a hellish little place on the outskirts of the city on the other side from us, thank God. You never want to go there if you can possibly help it. No culture, no soul, no quality of life, all just a big and dreadful black hole of seething, infested scumbags. It's a vile place, Lerato, and the people in it must be kept separate from the white people. That separation is the lifeblood of our civilisation and the future of humankind."

"I'll try to bear that in mind, Ma'am."

"What about your husband? Does he have HIV? Or your daughter?"

I pulled my fat black lips into a small smile.

"I am curious to know what you would think if they did."

Ida went green. It was a special shade of green that only white people can manage to turn, and I gazed upon her queasiness with wonder and curiosity. She filled her cheeks up like a hamster and I thought that she was going to vomit. I quickly reassured her that none of us were HIV positive, but I knew that our Utopia had been shattered beyond repair. We would have to go soon, but I was worried that we could not leave quickly enough to stop them suspecting something. HIV was a shackle of shame and I was terrified of them discovering our secret.

Ida told me so many untrue things that she believed about HIV that it was my turn to feel sick. I disguised my questioning by asking her to share with me some tips on not catching the virus from someone. She told me that it was possible to contract it from using the same toilet seat, and so she suggested that I carry a toilet seat around with me if I ever had to go into a township. She never would, but I had this obscene woman's permission to enter somewhere like Soweto because "you're the right colour and they won't try to kill you or rape you or something else ghastly." She told me that she was afraid of her children contracting the virus because their friends at school would think that these multimillionaires were a family of drug-dealing homosexuals. She tried to give me advice about how to cure myself if I ever got infected; apparently you can flush out the virus by making love to a virgin, or in an appalling ritual called the 'zoophilic cure' she suggested that my family make love to farm animals to get rid of the stain of shame within our bodies. I would be Queen of South Africa one day, and I considered for a split second abusing my power and forcibly subjecting this ludicrous woman to her own suggested cures to demonstrate to her beyond all denial that her brain was seriously malfunctioning.

The ignorance of the Van Der Merwe family terrified me. I was shocked at Ida's willingness to pass comment on places that she had never been and people that she had never had anything to do with. Jaap asked Blessings one day why his skin was black, and before he had a chance to answer he asked him if it was because he did not clean himself properly. I'm the only one qualified to speak in that way; nobody else fully understands both black and white the way that I do.

The final straw came one day when the family arrived on the plane from Johannesburg, and Ida asked me if I recognised the name of Nelson Mandela, and in a feverish and impulsive burst of optimism I asked her why, wondering if it was because he had left a message for me on the telephone. My brain flashed at the speed of light, wondering if I would be able to manage using the contraption as I had never used one before in my life. What would the message be? How would I react if he told me that he loved me?

I didn't expect Ida to know who Nelson was, but it turned out that she did. He was clearly not only famous to the blacks but also to the whites, which came as a shock to me. The reason that she had asked me if I knew him was because she was about to embark on a vile racist attack on my beloved Nelson. She called him a terrorist and a murderer, a dangerous criminal and the gravest threat to South Africa's national security. He was a disaster for our country and he was a deluded fanatic who would stop at nothing, even murdering innocent white people, in his pursuit of his treacherous and wicked schemes.

The Van Der Merwe family made me reassess my desire to be white on the outside as well as the inside. They were perfectly reasonable people when race was ignored or forgotten, but the problem was that race can never be truly forgotten in South Africa.

This nation is obsessed with it, completely and utterly gripped by the fanatical fixation with the colour of the skin and the constant friction which only comes when there are dozens of people groups, eleven official languages and extremely strict laws which meant that they could not intertwine in a natural way. People who claim to have forgotten or traversed issues of race are liars. It reminded me constantly of Nelson, which could only be a good thing, and in my head I would sail across the skies to the romantic paradise of Robben Island and dream up the democracy that we would build together, the new nation that we would construct together from scratch. In the vibrant and glistening sand of Africa we would take up a stick and begin to draw, letting our dreams and ambitions spill out in great unfurling ribbons of beauty and promise. I imagined a new flag to signal the dawn of a new era for this place, a design whose colours would boast of our triumphant ability to cleave one nation out of many different groups of people. That was the thing which nobody else understood, that it was the barriers which were causing the friction, and Nelson and I promised each other that we would remove them together as a dream team. That was the only way to bring peace to our land.

One Saturday night Christiaan discovered some pills amongst our clothes when he was in our room looking for the keys to his Ferrari which Ida had told him Blessings had stolen. They immediately assumed that the pills were medication for the HIV, but this was only partly true. I had stolen them from the medicine cabinet in the bathroom and they were to soothe itchy and chapped skin, which both of us had because of the virus surging through our veins. The family was extremely angry with us for lying to them and Ida threatened to braai Siphiwe to make us sorry for contaminating her children. We all thought that it would be best if we left. Within the hour we were on the road again, getting closer and closer to where Nelson was waiting for me.

16

THE OYSTER AND
THE ELEPHANT

Knysna, Garden Route, Cape Province
January 1989

Just twenty five kilometres west of Plettenberg Bay lay the small town of Knysna on a large lagoon which was home to a bustling quayside. We made the trip on foot, walking through the day and staying on the side of the road by night, taking turns to sleep so that we could keep watch for highwaymen who would often prowl the lonely road through the Garden Route and pounce on unwary and exhausted travellers. I was not sorry to leave the Van Der Merwes behind, but I did not adequately prepare myself for the shock of moving out of a house made of bricks to sleeping on the side of the road once again. Just like Plett, this too was a place of vast palatial villas and mansions guarding the African coastline and arranged to give the most commanding views of the Indian Ocean and Knysna's lagoon behind it. We were not tempted for a second to go up to one of the massive gated residences and ask if they needed a maid or a cook, but I did find my mind leaping over the electrified fences and nestling amongst the sports cars and the manicured gardens. They were all arranged with commanding views to the south, but sadly I don't think that we would have been able to see the coast of Antarctica even from the attic room of the highest mansion. But I'll never know, because we never tried.

I knew that time was precious. It was now the beginning of 1989 and soon we would be entering into a whole new decade under Apartheid at the hands of racist bullies with a would-be King in a prison in the middle of the Atlantic Ocean. This should not be. After the loss of focus in Plettenberg Bay and the three wasted years in bed with the racist enemy, I declared to Blessings that we would have a new strategy for getting to Cape Town. We would not be wasting any more time, but instead leaving as soon as possible by whatever means was necessary even if it was illegal. I should never have got off that train in Kimberley and I would not be making that mistake again. We needed deadlines; we would travel at least two hundred kilometres at a time and we would endeavour to spend no more than two months in each place along the way. Every day that the white South Africans were suppressing the blacks a little more of the spirit of the nation that I loved so dearly was killed off. Enough was enough. This would be the year that it all ended.

As if to encourage me, it transpired that whilst we had been with the hairybacks in Plett a war hero named Robert Gabriel Mugabe had won the presidential election in Zimbabwe and had replaced Canaan Banana. I could not have been more thrilled at this perfect demonstration of justice and righteousness; I promised myself that the moment I became Queen I would invite Mugabe to the Castle of Good Hope and give him a huge slobbery kiss on his beautiful black face for winning such a monumental victory in the evolution of Africa from a colony to a kingdom of peace and harmony. He was a heroic champion of equality and he was at the very forefront of what was possible for human achievement. He would have the finest of all state visits to South Africa and I would see to it that his wife, Sally, would be kitted out in the finest diamonds that the Royal Treasury could provide for her. I would take her on shopping trips to Paris and relaxing long weekends in Hong Kong. Unless, of course, she arrived from Harare wearing a better dress than me, in which case I could not rule out sending a hitman up to her room in the tallest turret of the castle with a crystal dagger in his hand. I imagined Nelson and Robert becoming the very best of friends, taking many holidays together and going on safari trips in the national parks of South Africa, travelling through the bush in fabulous varnished and embellished sedan chairs carried by the Van Der Merwe family in the unbearable African heat. Perhaps we would buy private overseas palaces in Mauritius and Zanzibar and take retreats there with our courtiers. We had an unimaginably luxurious life spread out ahead of us and I was excited for it to begin with a strong ally like Robert Mugabe there to support us along the way. Under his leadership Zimbabwe would flourish as a beacon of justice, prosperity and democracy in the region and Mugabe would be a close and treasured friend. Should I make him godfather to the babies I would deliver for the King?

I was edging closer and closer to that wonderful prospect, and we were now in a new town. Knysna's lagoon was guarded by two rocky cliffs called the Knysna Heads, and one side of the entrance to the lagoon was built upon whilst the opposite side was raw forest, and the town was surrounded by beaches, rivers and mountains. It was a breathtakingly beautiful place to arrive in; the orange and white bleakness of Soweto in midwinter seemed a lifetime ago as we walked along the beach together and dipped our toes into the chilling waters of the lagoon, feeling the reeds caressing our skin and trying to make out the reclusive forms of the seahorses and starfish who hid between them.

Seafood farming was a huge part of the economy of Knysna, and it was not long before we were offered jobs doing manual labour on the oyster farms, collecting the molluscs from the lagoon. They were always looking for extra help, which was fortunate for us, but we did not want to ask what had happened to the other harvesters who had gone before us alone with a basket out into the lagoon to see what aquatic treasures they could lay their hands on.

The sunrise and sunset over the lagoon was nothing short of sensational. Africa is so wonderful at putting on a show at dawn and dusk because of the high levels of red dust in the atmosphere and I feared that on the coastline the sunsets would lose their hazy mystique, but thankfully I was wrong. Each and every night the haunted sky would turn the colour of an oil stain on concrete with twisting yellows and deep oranges mixed in with the blue of twilight. As I watched the sky become encrusted with stars I saw that the surface of the lagoon would gleam like the inside of a pearl. I remember one night the moon was a tiny slither of a crescent in the sky and the whole spherical shape of it was visible as if illuminated from behind. There was a planet close by, a huge and bright light in the evening sky and it shone in the dark dome of heaven like a diamond had done in the dark mine back in Kimberley where I had met my first husband.

The days harvesting oysters were quite lonely, even with the man I was about to murder by my side and the daughter I had waited for so long to meet splashing about behind the two of us in the cool water of the lagoon. But in spite of the emptiness I found something intensely thrilling and wonderfully satisfying in the work of plunging my hands into the deliciously cold water to reach for the oysters, slicing through the tough dark shell with my knife and finally reaching the prize that I had been working so hard to find. The stunningly white pearl was cold in my black palm. I held it between my finger and my thumb and lifted it up to orchestrate my own total eclipse of the sun. The vast and endless skies and the sense of the wide open space of the lagoon made my heart race. I should have left Sophiatown earlier than I did just to spend time in this exquisite dorpie by the ocean.

About half of the oysters that we produced in Knysna were for pearls and the other half were produced for seafood restaurants. The meat of these little shellfish was perfectly black and it made me remember the peculiar dietary habits of my tummy mommy. Was it one of these ugly little strips of slime that stained my skin this disgusting shade of brown?

We had to defend against the predators who would want to destroy the oyster farm, notably the starfish and the stingrays in the lagoon. Siphiwe would enjoy looking through the shallow waters of the lagoon for starfish and she would peel them off of the multicoloured rocks and leave them on the shore to bake. Once they were dead she would keep them in a little wicker basket that I had managed to steal from one of the traders on the N2. Perhaps we could paint the starfish and sell them to tourists along with the great strings of pearls I had stolen from the farm.

One day I was walking through the jungle and I had my first encounter with an elephant. There were rumours around this town that the elephants in the jungle had somehow managed to evade the poaching which had wiped out all of the others; I knew the legend well, and the story went that three of them were unaccounted for and that there was no conclusive proof either way to determine whether or not they were still roaming the forests around the coastline.

The elephant was a magical and mystical thing, a legendary fable which had transcended the generations to endure in popular culture. We did not really believe in the thing in the forest and I did not particularly expect the elephant to believe in us. Humans and elephants had never had a great deal of interaction and they did not have much interest in one another.

In all of my years on Planet Earth as an African, I had never seen an elephant before. That sounds wild, but I don't think that foreigners really understand that there are no elephants wandering through the streets of the cities in the Transvaal. There were no elephants in Orlando West, no rhinoceroses poking their heads through the windows when I was cleaning the floors in Baragwanath Hospital and no giraffes peering into the office towers in the business district of Johannesburg. I was not familiar with the countryside until I had the fanciful idea to rescue King Nelson and had decided to embark on my trip through it all to Cape Town. At risk of sounding detrimental to the cause of freedom, as I wandered through the jungle of Knysna I was thankful that I had not been able to afford the cost of a flight from Johannesburg to Cape Town; if that had been the case I would have been able to rescue Nelson in two hours but I would never had been able to see the beauty of South Africa, the exquisite and extraordinary contrast in scenery within its borders, to grow accustomed to my dominion in advance of my coronation as Queen. Nelson's prolonged suffering was undoubtedly heartbreaking and I wanted it to end with immediate effect, but my desire to free him did not eclipse my unbridled sense of adventure. There were new discoveries to be made every single day, and in marching on Cape Town I was falling more in love with everything that Africa was made of. The rhythm of life which pulsated through the countryside had infected me, and I could not let it go.

I wandered alone through the forest until I had lost my way. Then I wandered even further.

The elephant was standing in the middle of the pathway through the dense trees, guarding the way through. The canopy above us was quite thick and the sunlight was dappled, shining brightly on the ground and contrasting strongly with the darkness of the soil.

The elephant was just as shocked by my presence as I was by the surprise it gave me. I know nothing about elephants, and I could not tell if this magnificent specimen was a male or a female, but I assumed that it was a male because of its gigantic size for he towered over me and he made me feel like a termite. Besides, this elephant was not wearing any lipstick or mascara, and everybody knows that lady elephants take drastic action to look their best.

The nose was very long; drooping down in a long and skinny tube from the beast's head until it almost touched the ground. The end of the nose was perfectly flat and triangular with two incredibly inquisitive nostrils sniffing and snaking along the jungle floor, sightlessly feeling their way around and stripping the vegetation off before smoothly lifting it to the mouth and munching. The lips and tongue were large and ripe, and as he gnashed his jaws I caught sight of the flat yellow teeth. Ah! Huge.

I nervously reached out a hand and very slowly touched the skin on his nose. It felt like sandpaper; scaly but not slimy, bald but not smooth. It was very slightly warm to the touch, just like mine, but it did not feel soft or plump. It was covered with tiny bristles of hair that could only be seen up close, extremely coarse and wiry in their texture and appearance; the hairs were the only thing which let me know that this enormous specimen standing before me was not reptilian. For all I knew it could have laid eggs, for it was very large with rustic skin the colour of gravel. Do elephants shave? Could this beast have once had an afro to rival my own? The elephant and I came to a peculiar little agreement that we would choose to suspend our mutual disbelief and that we would for a surreal moment entertain the idea that the legends we had heard about the other might just be true.

As I touched the rough skin, I was struck by a wondrous thought. What if this thing was a coconut as well? What if lingering beneath the coarse surface of the rough skin, if skin it may be called, was a spirit as perfectly white as my own? Could there be any way of telling what was inside the body of this creature, what colour was the soul that lay lurking beneath the bizarre and unusual physical case in which he was trapped? If I were trapped in an elephant's body rather than a black human body, would anyone ever be able to rescue me or liberate me? Was it better or worse to be a coconut disguised as an elephant than to be a coconut disguised as a munter? Had he accepted his own fate whilst I had been given a false sense of hope by my ability to articulate my own unique condition to the people around me and thereby persuade them to end the Apartheid which was so unjust, the cruelty of an expectation that my outlandish dreams may one day come true? I hoped not. Hope is the strongest of all things.

The elephant had beautiful eyes. The lashes were just as coarse and bristly as the hairs scattered across his skin, each strand very long and filled with soul. Perhaps when Nelson was King and I was Queen I would send my soldiers into this forest, and tell them to hunt him down and bring him home to my castle by the sea and I could keep him in my menagerie with the flamingos and white tigers. We would need a name for our pet, of course; almost instantly I decided that this elephant should be called Mashumbi. The three coconuts could live together in perfect bliss; the Emperor, his Consort and their pet elephant. I imagined Siphiwe chasing the elephant down the endless and labyrinthine corridors of the Castle of Good Hope when she became bored of entertaining foreign Royalty and Presidents at our court, dressed as she was in perfectly white miniature corsets, petticoats and ball-gowns. I imagined riding on the elephant with King Nelson at the reigns as we galloped through the royal parks to hunt springboks, kudus and impalas for the feasts in our castle. Could the elephant swim? Could this very elephant be the one which would take me to Robben Island, the one waiting for me tied up at the jetty like a loyal dog as the King and his Consort dashed through the cobbled courtyard of the prison, dodging bullets and rushing to get back to Africa for his coronation? I pictured this elephant with its extraordinary nose, using it as a type of snorkel and swimming across Table Bay to save us. This could be the lifeboat coming to the rescue of freedom itself, the torchbearer for the new South Africa and the new system of government which would ensure that equality and dignity was fully protected. This could become the most famous elephant in the world, the perfect addition to our little family and I would ensure that upon its death it would be stuffed and put in a museum for all to see. It was a wondrously flamboyant and eccentric thought, but as a symbol of Africa I felt that this gift-wrapped wedding present of an elephant from Knysna suited Nelson as a reward for his outstanding achievements for the people of our country. Surely, if I knew nothing else about the man that I was in love with, I knew that he deserved an elephant as a wedding gift.

I think Mashumbi could read my mind. As soon as I pictured him as the plaything of my daughter, with Siphiwe dressing the elephant in enormous frocks and hats and sitting down in the gardens of the castle amongst the roses and lawns to drink afternoon tea from a china cup and saucer, he began to rear up on his hind legs and prance and bellow at me.

I tried to argue my way out of the confrontation which was erupting before my eyes. "Hush, Mashumbi," I told him gently. "It will be a good life in the menagerie of the King. You may have your own little palace in the Castle gardens and I will have the rooms painted whatever colour you choose. I will give you a troupe of little black slaves and you may have more golden goblets of the finest wine than you could ever dream of."

Elephants are teetotal. Why didn't that idiot Blessings tell me this vital piece of information? Mashumbi was furious with me for my foolishness; he thrust his nose towards me like some demonic trumpet, blasting my hair back so it tugged at my scalp and showering me with a deluge of moist breath. My eyes slammed shut of their own accord; I should have kept them open so that I could focus on this ludicrous beast.

The nakedness of the sheer organic power that this monster had over me took my breath away and rendered me stunned. The raw and brutal enormity of this massive animal suddenly became apparent to me and I knew that I was in great danger. I was simply too important to die; my death here, crushed beneath an extremely angry and proud rogue elephant, would be a national tragedy which would change the course of the history of Africa forever and chain the corpse of freedom inside the dungeon of Apartheid. At first I was rooted to the spot in terror as the elephant rose up above me and began his angry protest, but soon enough I came to my senses and I realised that if the country that I cared for and the man that I loved were to be set free, I needed to run. History was depending on me and I knew that if I was trampled to death here then Sophiatown would never be avenged by righteousness and peace.

I have never run as quickly as I did that day when Mashumbi turned on me; I did not wait to see what would happen, and I did not attempt continue with my planned journey through the forest, but I turned on the spot and I sprinted back the way that I had come as fast as my legs would carry me. AIDS is not an easy thing to have when you are trying to sprint away from an angry elephant, and I could feel the exhaustion burning in my lungs and heart, a vast wall of pain pounding in my legs and feet. I ran as fast as I could back to the lagoon and the safety of the town of Knysna, and as I approached the edge of the lagoon I finally summoned the courage to turn and look my attacker in his extraordinary face once again. He was gone; apparently too afraid to leave the relative safety of the dense jungle. Completely overcome with exhaustion, I collapsed into the shallow edge of the lagoon and I lay on my back with my ears below the surface of the water, gazing up at the endless hot sky of Royal blue and listening to the shrinking sounds under the lagoon, the echoes of the current shrouded in otherworldly noise as they swirled around me. I knew in that moment that there was nothing that I could do to convince anyone that my encounter with the elephant had really happened at all.

For the first time I began to wonder if I was seeing the world in the way that the monochrome people were seeing it. There had been nothing to tell me that this encounter with the elephant in the Knysna jungle was anything other than an illusion or a hallucination, given that the mythical beast seemed to melt back into the trees just as stealthily and mysteriously as he had appeared to me. Had it been some troubling daydream, some untrue vision or ghostly apparition? I began to wonder about the words of my parents during my difficult, mismatched childhood; they had told me that they did not believe that I was a coconut even though they could find no other rational account which would explain the mystery of how I came to meet them that freezing night. I wondered if I was a woman particularly prone to delusion, hallucination and the effects of apparition, but then I remembered as I always tended to that Nelson's incarceration in prison was all the proof that I needed that I was a coconut and had been one all along. If he could have escaped without me, he would have done so already. He had had twenty six years to win freedom by himself; the fact that he had not managed to do so was firm proof that he was incapable of breaking free without me. My identity as a coconut depended on his identity as a prisoner. I promised myself once again that should he find freedom without me, I would give up this audacious campaign. It made me chuckle to myself; I knew how close we were now and the chances of him getting out before my rescue attempt being executed were laughably small.

Even though I reassured and then convinced myself that I would soon be Queen of this nation, there could be no denying that, for the first time in the journey of thousands of kilometres which I had travelled in resolute certainty of my identity as a coconut, doubt had become a companion of mine.

17

THE FEATHERED
DINOSAUR FACTORY

Oudtshoorn, Garden Route, Cape Province
April 1989

We were so incredibly close. Cape Town was just around the corner and we were doing well with our money so I knew in the bottom of my heart that I would be in Nelson's arms soon. He was still in jail and he still needed me there with him so that the people could see that I was different and realise that Apartheid was an unsustainable system of population management. Let me loose on the reigns of power, you filthy colour-blind cowards. You had your chance and you squandered it.

The thing which Oudtshoorn was famous for was its ostrich farms. These incredible animals were astoundingly beautiful but also extraordinarily bizarre. Oudtshoorn had a population of humans only in the dozens of thousands but it was rumoured, according to a local legend, which we heard almost as soon as we arrived, that there was not another place on Earth which contained a higher population of ostriches. It was difficult to know if this was a human town containing pet ostriches or an ostrich town containing pet humans who were enormously deluded by thinking that they were in charge. The meat was a very reliable staple which was served in restaurants and to families across the country, but I was surprised at how versatile the uses of a dead ostrich can be. The feathers were used for decoration and for making feather dusters, and the skin could be used for leather. Ostrich-feather hats were very fashionable in Europe and America in the early twentieth century and so this had fuelled a booming trade which had still not calmed down. I remembered the times when I had snuck into Ida's walk-in wardrobe and seen all the feathered hats on the top shelves.

Every morning we would go to the coop to check for eggs. The eggs were sold as food, or they sometimes had their yolks drained out and were sold just as shells for the simple novelty of being the largest egg in the world. They were so enormous and heavy that every time I picked one up I would expect a small newborn dinosaur to emerge to open its eyes for the first time and devour me. Perhaps this was a dragon's egg with the fiery lungs being formed and nurtured beneath the fragile shell separating the embryo from my fingertips. The cratered, dappled surface of the eggshell felt as though I was holding the whole hemisphere of the moon in the palm of my hand, my fingers stretched around its poles and my thumb guarding its equator. This other planet, this gargantuan bulb of life held between my fingers reflected me as though I were holding a mirror in my hands; the shell was only thin, and beneath it lay something unrecognisable. This, though, was the perfect and exact opposite of who I was, for the shell was a dazzling and brilliant white and the creature which would hatch out of it would grow and change and eventually become dark. Yes. The feathers would be dark.

Only very few were fertilized, with most of them being produced with factory-style efficiency and dispatched quickly. They were transported across the country in great cargoes on trucks and on freight trains, some going towards Cape Town and some heading northeast in the direction of Johannesburg. An omelette made from one of these eggs could be enough to make a meal for a whole family. They were also traditionally sold as ornamental souvenirs, although the international economic trading sanctions were having an effect on the demand for trinkets from South Africa, but there was enough to keep production steady. We would send them all across the country and local curio sellers would paint them or carve them into different shapes and patterns. Some had animals on them, others maps, others still were made into quite expensive and exotic light bulbs. I remembered that some of the local people in Sophiatown and Soweto had sold them to people on the sides of the main roads into Johannesburg, far away from the squalor of the townships and where there were more likely to be white drivers keen to stop. If you follow the whites in this country, you follow the money. That will never change.

One of the attractions of Oudtshoorn for tourists was the offer from many of the farms of the chance to ride one of these magnificent animals and it was a strong source of income to see the farm through the year. I tried it one day, and I was not quite prepared for the experience that I was given. The ostrich was very sturdy, surprisingly so considering its awkward and disproportionate shape. I sat with one leg on each side of the neck of the bird, holding on to the long and fragile neck for dear life at times, and the vast and scaly legs of the thing would thunder and pound beneath us. The sheer speed of the bird was mesmerising; you felt it as much as you saw it. The birds looked fat but really it was a great pillowy mass of fluffed-up feathers, and when you sat on the beast's shoulders you could feel every single muscle of its lean body tensing as it ran. Each step began to blur together as the bird gathered speed and the feet moved at a phenomenal rate. The head of the bird would move backwards and forwards with all of the rhythmic hammering of a woodpecker as the neck muscles expanded and contracted in time with the steps taken by the reptilian three-toed feet. The eye of an ostrich is bigger than its brain. It says a lot really; they can see you wherever you are, but they are unfathomably stupid. It was beyond all doubt that this bird was the avian equivalent of a monochrome.

As well as the saddled ostriches there were also little ostrich-and-trap sets where the birds would pull a small cart for rich children and people who were not brave enough to put one leg on each side. There was a little racecourse set up around the perimeter of the farm and the visiting children would squeal with delight as these most bizarre of God's brainwaves would swagger and waddle their way around at often terrifying speeds. Oudtshoorn was becoming something of a tourist attraction for the ostrich farms and there was soon a small cafe for them to make use of. There was also a little gift shop with small stuffed ostrich toys, key-rings, fridge-magnets and hollow ostrich eggshells to buy as souvenirs. Colour reigned supreme even here. The chef in the cafe was almost as white as his apron and hat, and I never once saw a black child lead their mother into the gift shop to ask if they could buy something.

I stole one of the cuddly ostriches from the gift shop for Siphiwe. It was a bizarre little thing and it didn't really look much like a real ostrich, with a weirdly misshapen beak and terrifying boggle eyes, but she treasured it forever. I've barely seen her happier than when I emerged triumphantly from a long day at work and I produced my magnificent piece of contraband from its hiding place under my skirt. I had nowhere else to hide it but when I presented myself to Siphiwe it must have looked as though I was giving her a brother or a sister, not a cheap stuffed ostrich toy. I had taken it when I saw the stockpile being unloaded from the truck that delivered toys and merchandise to the gift shop, and because I was a member of staff nobody really suspected anything when I walked in and loitered. My daughter deserved a souvenir of our time in Oudtshoorn and I also was wary of the Museum that Nelson was planning to open which would document my life. I needed to begin gathering items which would be suitable exhibits for the story of my journey to Queendom. I closed my eyes and I imagined the dignitaries of other nations visiting the museum on their way to the Castle of Good Hope, both during my reign and long after I was gone.

Our farm had an abattoir. The birds were herded into the building which stood on the far side of the vast coops and the makeshift racetrack, and they would all stand in a line of dumbfound confusion as they patiently waited their turn. Blessings was often the one to do it, and he had a thick set of boots on and was wearing an apron as white as I am as he prepared to begin. The birds were so beautiful, powerful, majestic and elegant, and it seemed to be an act of brutal economics to kill them for their meat, bones, feathers and skin. The heart and soul were thrown out with the tiny brains, the vast and globe-like eyeballs, the legs and the bowels. As he chopped them up Blessings would fill up plastic white buckets which had once contained Fox laundry powder with the blood and guts from the entrails. The gleaming white plastic would be splattered and tainted with clumps of blood and flesh. I would often wonder quite where the miracle was, where the housing was for the symphony of life endowed to each and every creature—this was a question I had also asked myself when that poor driver had his brains blown out and his head had opened like a book for me to browse the contents and consider whether I wanted to read. There was no soul-stain on that leather passenger seat, no fleshy lobe of conscience or imagination emblazoned against the shattered glass of the Mercedes' window. I often wondered if they were intelligent enough to understand what was happening to them and if they had enough thinking time to become nervous and afraid of their doom. It was undoubted that they were not unaware of Blessings as he pulled on his pristinely white apron and gloves, but I did wonder if that tiny little peach-sized brain of theirs was able to understand what it meant. Did they equate Blessings' distinctive clothing to their imminent demise? Could they smell the clotted atmosphere of death in the slaughterhouse, and did they have time to figure out how ergonomic the killing machines were and which part of their clumsy bodies they would be attached to? With a buzz and a twist and a slice, it was smoothly and cleanly finished. Sis.

Siphiwe needed to be put to good use, but we could not think of anything for her to do. I had contemplated selling her but Blessings told me that he would not come with me if I abandoned another one of our children and leave me to do the work myself. It was shameless blackmail; regretfully I did not have any choice but to keep Siphiwe because Blessings knew that I could not do it without him. Ag, I was barely managing to do it even with him! It was already 1989 and we were still loitering in the far flung countryside surrounding the Mother City, miles from home, wandering in the desert like Moses had a dream ago. We were flirting with freedom and dipping our toes into the water of justice, too hesitant or terrified to plunge in. The years incessantly slipped between our fingers, as fleeting and fragile as the summer haze.

In the end we decided that Siphiwe should sing. She would be a busker at the farm for people who came to ride the ostriches, and she would have a little bowl laid out in front of her so that they would have somewhere to dispose of their rand. She would dress up in whatever we could find for her to make her fit the mould that we needed in order to make the most money; we would pluck out some of the ostrich feathers and make a dress for her from them, and I was upset when I realised that it would be an investment rather than a free gift to us because we were flaunting the stolen feathers in such a public way that paying for them in order to keep our jobs would be unavoidable. Blessings said that he was amazed that we were permitted to use Siphiwe to beg on private land, but he's a man and he doesn't have half the brain he thinks he does. She would just be wearing her knickers and the ostrich-feather skirt, and to make her look a bit more ethnic we would mix the red dirt with water and then paint it on her torso in stripes which made her look like more of a native than she really was. I spoke to her in a mixture of Zulu and Afrikaans and so she had a confused and incomplete grasp of the languages of South Africa, so she did not know any songs all the way through to the end.

I began to teach her *Nkosi Sikelel' iAfrika*, but it was a risky strategy. It was the underground anthem of the ANC and it was seen as a song which represented the struggle for Apartheid to be ended and the ushering in of a new era. We were making that journey together as a family and there was nobody who deserved to sing it louder and prouder than this future Princess, but I did not know how much I would be able to trust a three year old to keep our identities anonymous. Would she blow our cover and reveal the nature of our mission simply in the choices of songs that she sang? I would slit her throat if she did.

But she was only three, bless her, and she was only halfway through learning how to control her body and was still moderately incontinent. When she danced in that ridiculous little outfit of hers she sometimes had inconvenient accidents and would dance whilst covered in her own filth. The sight of wealthy white tourists crowded around my daughter as she sang her tribal songs and danced her "native routine" was difficult to stomach given our memories and experiences in Plettenberg Bay, but it kept a steady stream of rand coming in. That was the most important thing and we could not lose focus on the mission in hand because of a little thing like the dignity of a child. The freedom of King Nelson could not wait and would not wait for us. We needed to get to Cape Town as fast as possible and all of the coins that were thrown into that little hat in front of my daughter were a contribution towards the ultimate aim of seeing him freed, however small or insignificant. Thirteen years into this journey I was losing my sense of pride and now it simply did not matter to me where the money came from in the same way as it once had. The important thing was that we had money of any description coming in to build up the funding for the most important rescue mission in the history of the African continent.

The ostriches taught me how to be a good mother, and as I looked at them I realised how much I missed Mwanyisa and what I should have been doing for Siphiwe. The mothers were so fierce and protective of their eggs, even the unfertilized ones, that even if Blessings' lion had come to clamp his teeth around their babies they would have bravely fought them off. I had heard rumours that the kick of a giraffe's legs could decapitate a lion, and it did not seem particularly inconceivable that these ostriches at our farm could do the same thing. Surely they would maul and maim any predator that would be prowling around looking for a feast of eggs or chicks. I imagined the mother ostrich roaring like her prehistoric ancestors, bellowing her threatening disapproval and shredding an enemy with the ferocious talons on her bizarre and scaly toes. Where was I when Mwanyisa needed me to defend him? I had abandoned him in a dustbin and left him to be eaten by the dogs, the very beasts that I should have been protecting and defending him from. These Jurassic birds were giving me a masterclass in fierce and proud motherhood and I slowly began to comprehend the scale of my immense failure. I should have squawked and flapped to his defence, building him a comfortable nest to hatch in, but instead I let him go. Siphiwe was now in the same position as these whelps; she was a fledgling, a weak little chick and I was keen to follow the example of the ostriches and protect her in the way that I had failed so spectacularly before.

We were getting close to Cape Town now, I knew that much. I could smell the ocean and I could feel the zesty rhythm of Africa's best city seeping through my skin and tickling my white bits. I could hear the voice of Nelson against the rushing winds of racism as I held Robben Island against my ear and cradled its heartbeat in my hand. I could hear Nelson smiling. I realised that the island was the same shape as an ostrich egg. We both laughed.

I would creep into the coop on my own, often late at night, to simply admire and play with the birds. They were astounding animals and I was completely bewitched by them. One of the more amusing things to do if you ever find yourself alone with an ostrich is to put a whole lemon in their beak and watch as the magnificent bird swallows it. You can follow the bulge in the neck as it slides down towards the stomach of the animal, stretching the skin above it and creating a huge knuckle halfway up the ostrich's neck.

It got me thinking of other things to give the ostrich to swallow to distort the shape of her long neck. Perhaps a coconut was an obvious next step, given that it is a larger lemon of a different name and re-coloured to look like human skin, or perhaps a pineapple would make an interesting shape in the neck as it slipped softly down the oesophagus. I realised that perhaps my wish to see an ostrich swallow a grand piano whole may be slightly too ambitious, so in the end I resolved to feed the bird a large unpeeled banana instead. The crescent in her neck would be quite a sight to behold. She opened her beak, but as I forced the banana lengthways into her mouth she gagged and reared up at me. Her beady little eyes blazed with a fiery fury and she began pecking furiously at my face and beating me with her wings, throwing me to the floor. Blessings heard the commotion and came rushing into the coop, bundling the bird away from me with a strength that I could not find in my own ravaged body. Quickly hiding the banana I told my husband how the bird had attacked me without any provocation, a sure sign of some kind of demented insanity and of a great danger to anyone else who came into contact with the bird. Blessings listened to my complaint and immediately stunned the bird with his fingers, hauled the great weight of her onto his shoulders and made off for the abattoir. Doom clung to my unconscious enemy like Mwanyisa had tried to cling to me.

As I lay on the floor of the coop, covered in bird kak and blood from the lacerations and beak marks on my forehead, my terror was replaced with a rushing sense of hedonistic power, ambition and anticipation. My bleeding lips curled into a wicked grin, showing my black gums and my white teeth. Blessings was a lowly miner, a drifter and an anonymous munter who was as perennial as the grass. His replacement would be a magnificent King-Emperor, an eternal statesman and the new South Africa's glorious founding father who would be remembered until the end of human civilisation for the victory he won in the name of freedom. If I could whisper in the ear of my first husband and command him to rid me of an enemy, surely I could do the same with my second husband as well? I imagined myself in the Castle of Good Hope, counting the stars from my four poster bed, the curtains embellished with justice and the sheets and pillows embroidered with truth and peace. I would whisper across the pillow to my lover, beseeching him to send his little soldiers in their resplendent tunics across the wild plains of Africa to cast death and destruction upon the heads of the people I took a disliking to with a swing of their swords. They would spread east from Cape Town like a vast black cloud of plague, swiftly destroying those who stood in our way and dispatching them with a ruthless and cold efficiency. If he held the power to bestow a title and make me a Queen, I had the power of seduction over him and I found myself in an incredibly influential position within our nation. I would soon be above everyone except His Majesty the King.

18

HAVE YOU EVER WONDERED HOW IT MUST FEEL TO BE A GIRAFFE WITH AN EXCEEDINGLY SHORT NECK?

Mosselbaai, Garden Route, Cape Province
June 1989

Mosselbaai was at the very end of the Garden Route, the golden stretch of coastline which we had been navigating our way along since we had crossed the end of the Tsitsikamma National Park going from Port Elizabeth to Plettenberg Bay. It had been around this area where the Garden Route began that we had suffered the hijacking of the car we were travelling in. The whole of the Garden Route was popular with rich white tourists and because of this our three year old daughter was able to undertake her next job of the trip after proving how delighted she was to have been exploited in Oudtshoorn. There were three of us in the family workforce now, not just the two of us, and this made me regret abandoning Mwanyisa even more. The boy could have made us a fortune, and we would have been in Cape Town in no time.

Siphiwe's job for us was to be a beggar. I had wondered whether or not it would be more financially practical for us to amputate one of her limbs, but Blessings passionately objected and asked me to get a grip on reality. There isn't anything special, unusual or heartbreaking about a fully healthy little girl, and wealthy white tourists who have had a lifetime to accustom themselves to the practise of ignoring beggars on the street would not even bother to give her a second look. I pondered over the economics of charitable giving, and how much of a proportionate increase would be attained by an amputation; how much more would an amputated arm earn than an amputated leg? Would it be worth the disability that my daughter would be left with? Would one missing arm be more profitable than two missing legs? I was simply applying my white brain for business and money to the situation which we now found ourselves in; we needed to make the largest profit possible, in the shortest amount of time, so that we could charge to Cape Town and rescue my King from his prison cell.

"You are behaving monstrously. I will not allow you to slice off my daughter's limbs as if she is some sort of commodity. I took HIV into my body so that I could give you the baby you claimed to have always wanted, so if you think she is there to be exploited then you have a surprise in store."

"Oh shut up you stupid munter," I replied. "You are a deluded fool and you should get your head checked."

For all of my bravado I never did slice Siphiwe up into pieces after he said that. Her father had become far too comfortable in Plettenberg Bay and he had lost sight of the glorious, incredible future promised to this nation under the kingship of Emperor Nelson and Empress Lerato, and he had instead been seduced by the comfort of living in a mansion on the beachfront and being able to wake up to the sound of breaking waves, and walk in the jungle after riding the horses to the highest hill and surveying the magnificent view far below. I had given him a good life with all of my crazy dreams and outlandish ambitions, but the tragedy of the whole thing was that he had lost his focus and prioritised a child that we had not begun wanting until East London above the journey that we had to make in order to secure the future of the human race. If Africa was condemned and abandoned to the funeral pyre of a healthy and thriving culture of Apartheid, where would be the next place to fall under the wicked spell of racism? Humanity had begun its journey in Africa, and I feared that humanity was beginning to end its journey in Africa in the same way. Johannesburg was first, and then Asia, then Europe, then America and Australia were to follow our lead just as they had in mankind's infancy. The situation was gaining importance with every passing day, and we had been wandering for far too long now. I needed to have that crown on my head, and I needed to be brought under Nelson's rule along with the rest of the nation with a heightened sense of increasing urgency. The future of the human race depended squarely on me.

Blessings pleaded with me and begged me to consider putting Siphiwe on the street to see how much money she could earn with all of her arms and legs intact, and then we could reconsider and renegotiate if it proved to be unsuccessful. She's three years old, he would say. That has to count for something in the sympathy stakes without the need for limbs to be sliced off. I was not so sure about that, because in the begging industry sympathy is money.

I was proud of Siphiwe. She would gallantly march off to work every morning, collecting her wages and bringing them dutifully home to me every evening, happily surrendering the money as I wrenched it out of her hands. With a profound sense of irony I came to accept that there was very little in the way of work for me in Mosselbaai. I was a Queen in disguise and the people who did not recognise me would continually turn me away. I tried and I tried over and over again, asking in every shop and marketplace I could find, but the tactics which had served us so well all the way since leaving Johannesburg seemed to be running dry and I was running out of ideas. Having grown up as a coconut I was used to the familiar feeling of shame but I was quite taken aback by the humiliation of unemployment. I did not expect anyone to recognise my Royal pedigree but at the same time the frustration and sense of hopelessness that came with being rejected over and over again was a shock which I found difficult to deal with.

Perhaps I should try prostitution. The idea of it suddenly transported me back to being in the club in Durban, the smell of the grease on the poles and tables and the psychedelic pulsing of the strobe lights as the skin of the white girls shone in the darkness, their womanly flesh on display for all who entered and paid for it. What a wonderful way to spend some of the money used by randy men on their adulterous orgies, that it may no longer be used to fuel the drug industry and be able to be manipulated by violent criminals but instead that prostitution would be directly funding the path to freedom and hope for the black majority of South Africa, that the money from their high sex drives would be pushing me further and further towards the completion of my mission and the end to one of the great evils threatening human civilisation. Using the revenue from such debauchery to fund the implementation of such righteousness; I could think of nothing that would taste sweeter than that.

Blessings was unhappy with this as well. He told me that he could not bear to imagine me with another man again after the rape in Durban, that his masculinity was under threat and that he felt very sensitive and insecure about my faithfulness to him because even the fact that I had given birth to another man's baby brought him tremendous shame. I was getting tired of it, and I quenched my immense frustration with his inability to comprehend how important all of this was by plotting his murder as I lay down at night to sleep. I held in my hand the phial of poison, perhaps lying to him and telling him that I had found a cure for his HIV, standing with him on the summit of Table Mountain on my pillow and lacing my fingers around the back of his neck as I held him there, gently pressing the phial to his lips as I whispered into his ears. The wind sang to us as I did the deed, and I gently felt the life ebbing away from him and his flesh losing its vitality beneath my fingertips. Finally he fell, collapsing in a heap on the plateau of the mountain that we had taken so many long years to reach, and his body became lifeless and inanimate before my eyes. I lifted the hem of my magnificent and multicoloured skirt to reveal slippers crafted entirely of glass, and I raised one of them and pressed the heel into the small of his back. In my dream he had suddenly lost all of his clothes, but I was unsure as to why, and his skin shone with the colour and texture of coal as he lay lifeless at my feet. I pushed him gently with my foot and he began to tumble down the edge of the mountainside to the city bowl far below, his spinning and naked carcass overcome by clouds and puffs of dust as he hit the rocks on the way down. I breathed in the glorious and enrapturing air of widowhood, the oxygen for my lungs which I had needed the whole trip long, and I dreamed once more of Nelson. I grew a tail like a mermaid's and I made the heroic swim across Table Bay towards the island prison where he was being incarcerated. As I hauled myself up on the rocks I stood at the gatehouse of a magnificent and enormous castle, the steep and jagged outlines of the turrets emblazoned against the moonlit sky, the portcullis kept tightly shut to keep the freedom in and the ruined battlements guarded by dragons and trolls. I knew where Nelson would be. I hammered on the portcullis and shouted through the holes the details of my condition and a handful of guards were struck down dead by the power of the revolutionary ideas they were hearing. As one of them came towards me with a gigantic bunch of keys, I was roused from my slumber. Never in Africa's long history had there ever been a more disappointed wife and mother to wake up in the morning beside her husband and daughter.

Blessings managed to find a job as a fisherman on a local crew who would supply the elite of the Garden Route and the surrounding areas with their quota of expensive seafood. I decided that in spite of my rather vivid and gratuitous dream that I would hold on to him for a while longer rather than slaughtering him as soon as we arrived in Cape Town. A husband can be a very useful utility to a woman on a mission to end a tyrannical regime and replace it with liberty, justice and freedom, especially if that husband has previously experienced the command of a fishing boat. Perhaps I would not need to swim across Table Bay after all and navigate the hazardous rocks and shipping lanes if Blessings knew how to navigate a fishing boat towards the island. I had not quite worked out how we might foil the South African Navy as they chased us across the bay to the jail, but I knew that it would be a wonderful thrill to be chased across the waters in my first husband's boat. We would have the authorities hot on our tail only for Blessings to propel me into the arms of his replacement and rescue him in the way that he deserved to be rescued.

The Port of Mosselbaai is the smallest commercial harbour on the South African coast. The revenue from the fishermen's hauls had once been the driving force of the local economy and it still played a big part in the lives of the town's workforce, but in 1969 there had been the discovery of natural offshore gas fields and the two decades which had ensued in the meantime had been devoted to the pursuit of harvesting and refining the gas to make diesel.

The town was small, but it was surrounded by incredibly beautiful scenery even though we were now used to the stunning landscape of South Africa's coast since we had spent so long travelling from place to place. The most memorable features of the surrounding area were the huge sand dunes towering above the lagoons and beaches in the surrounding area; they must have been hundreds of metres high, like vast yellow mountains which were the colour of ripe mango flesh. It was a stunningly beautiful place to be.

Blessings was out at sea for most of the days but he only very rarely was gone for more than one day at a time on the voyages, and the boat was only small and was operated by a crew of three. One of their crew had been lost at sea when he had been diving because one of the nets had become tangled and the ropes had jammed; nobody told us, but there was a whispered understanding that he had actually been attacked and devoured by a shark as he plunged into the water. I have never been particularly familiar with the ocean but apparently these beasts had a ferocious reputation and their infamy spread through these coastal communities like wildfire. It was hard to verify whether all of the rumours that we had heard on our journey were true or not, for we had heard some outlandish things; I cast my mind back to the Van Der Merwe family and I could not remember whether or not they had haboured any noticcable fears of the ocean. There wasn't really any way of gauging the opinions of all of the locals at any one time. Perhaps we should

put it on the ballot paper if we were to have an election after the end
of Apartheid, so that it would have question one asking who they
wanted to be the new Emperor and question two asking whether
or not they were afraid of sharks. Maybe then we would know for
sure.

In my mind Nelson would send me a herd of giraffes to count to
send me to sleep. Giraffes were strangely magnificent creatures and
their stampeding arrival in my slumber was a sharp surprise. They
thrived in the Transvaal but the Garden Route was completely the
wrong habitat for them and so I had not seen any since setting off
from Johannesburg in 1976. I was fascinated by the way that each
and every individual giraffe had a completely unique pattern on
their coat. Looking at one made me feel special again and it restored
my hope in the beauty of life; just like the hide of another giraffe
in the herd, there were new and unique adventures to be had every
single day in Africa. Each day and each place had its own unique
pattern, etched like a fingerprint and completely unlike any other.

I had been bewitched by the tales of Hannibal riding over the
Alps on his elephants, marching triumphantly into battle across
the blizzards and the mountains, leading his mounted troops in
the magnificent procession of tusked beasts. I imagined his shining
standard bearer carrying the gleaming flag, resplendent in its dazzling
beauty as it was emblazoned against the searing white snow.

I decided that King Nelson would have a fleet of giraffes to
lead him into battle. They would have armour plating around their
bodies to guard them from attack and they would have painted tunics
around their long necks. I imagined their headdresses which would
be tailor-made to match that of their knight: a protective covering
of shining steel with holes for the eyes and a magnificent plume of
coloured feathers rising up from between the horns. My husband
would have a deep purple ostrich feather both on his helmet and
the helmet of his giraffe. Tyrian purple was the most appropriate
colour for the King to wear as he led his army into battle because
it would have been extracted from rare sea snails and the intensity
of the colour would increase rather than fade in the strong African
sunlight. Eight and a half thousand of the snails would produce a

harvest of one gram of pure dye. My captive King deserved only the best.

I imagined them charging, plunging and neighing furiously as they carried the soldiers into battle. Nelson's enemies would be on horseback and they would be unable to reach up and attack the South African soldiers who would be more than two metres above the ground. It would be like playing polo, that most regal of sports, and with a casual swing of the weapon at the target the helmeted head of the enemy far below would be sliced cleanly off and roll along the ground. In my dreams Nelson told me all about the nature of such a weapon; it would be a large mallet, embedded with razor sharp spikes, which the knight would reach over and swing low alongside the giraffe. The force of the blow, amplified by the pendulum effect of the long handle, would smash the body of the enemy to smithereens. Perhaps he would build me an Empire, invading the new Republic of Zimbabwe and spreading our Kingdom of Hope northwards. Maybe he would name a colony in my honour and use the Queen's Regiment to lead the invading navy across the sea to Madagascar.

Could a giraffe prance in triumphant victory above the smashed body of its vanquished foe? It seemed almost comical to me that nobody had come up with the concept of a giraffe cavalry before I had teamed up with my fellow coconut and invented this marvellous concept.

If I were a giraffe, I would in all probability have a very short neck. This would make me nothing more than a multicoloured horse; I was never the one who fitted in or followed the convention. What was to say that not a single one of the millions of horses that roam the earth do not contain a misshapen giraffe trapped beneath their skin, their beautiful and unique coat entombed forever within the body of a horse? I understood the unlikelihood but I was absolutely certain of its truth and there was not a single person who could prove me wrong. Being unlikely and being incorrect were two vastly different things.

19

FABRICS AND FIREWORKS

Swellendam, Cape Province
August 1989

We were in Mosselbaai for six weeks. The time came to move onwards and we left after our brief stay in the town by getting a bus to the small settlement of Swellendam. Swellendam is the third oldest town in South Africa, and it felt like the bronze medal being hung around our necks as only Stellenbosch and Cape Town were older and they were both within the short distance that we still had to cover. It was an absolutely beautiful little place, one of the picturesque highlights of the whole of our trip so far, and we were immediately enchanted by its quaint and serene charm.

Swellendam's population is more than fifty per cent white in ethnicity with large swathes designated as being white only. We found it to be a very rich, very exclusive community and had it not been for our experiences in Plettenberg Bay we would have been positively overwhelmed by the apparent hostility towards people who looked like us. We were deep behind enemy lines and we had no choice but to pretend we were black and find a job so that we could get ourselves to Cape Town as fast as possible. One of the things which delighted Siphiwe the most was the Oefeningshuis, built a century and a half before as a school for freed slaves, as it had a clock on the side of the building which was designed with the illiterate in mind; when the time painted on the sculpted clock face matches that on the real clock below, then we would all know it was time for worship. I think that was when I realised that Siphiwe really was turning into genuine Princess of South Africa material; of all the places in the town she chose this as her favourite, a school for freed slaves, seemingly in recognition of the pilgrimage for freedom that she had been born on. Her mother would be the one to free the greatest slave of them all, and it would happen soon. Siphiwe could feel it in her soul. When liberty is close, the human spirit is able to detect it from a long way off.

In one of the ancient streets of this pretty little town lay an old gunpowder factory housed in one of the cottages. They would manufacture fireworks and then sell them to the shops and customers in Cape Town to help them with celebration. I didn't know what a firework or a barrel of gunpowder was or exactly how it would help you with celebration, but apparently it did. I was thinking that maybe the fine grey powder was intended to be snorted or inhaled, a drug which would pump through the bloodstream with twangs of ecstasy and sparkles of pleasure. Blessings eventually told me that the firework would be lit with a match and would explode in the sky in a dazzling array of kaleidoscopic colour. The product that the little factory was selling was a decoration to be hung in the sky, an ornament to garland the darkness with. It made a bit more sense after he had explained it like that but I still thought that my version of a firework was better than the real thing and I still wanted it my way. As the woman who was about to be crowned as Queen of South Africa, I felt that my demand for the firework drug was not particularly unrealistic. I was preparing myself for Royalty by getting used to demanding what I wanted; I wanted a splash of colour and a thumping explosion to ricochet through my body, my veins illuminated by strings of sparks and my skin the black canvas of the sky onto which the technicolour lightshow would be etched like a tattoo.

I became a seamstress. A small shop on the side of the highway was doing an unpredictably solid trade with the local community. The shop was called *Sew It Seams*, which the white people found funny and always talked about with me but I never really understood what they meant. It was a fairly easy job for me to do because I have a keen eye for detail and a steady hand, but the painstaking and often frustrating work of stitching dresses was arduous when done for a very long time each and every day without a rest. We made costumes and formal outfits for wealthy women and, if we could find the time, we would mend the battered old clothes of people too black to be able to afford anything new.

There was nothing especially African about anything that I was doing, and that troubled me greatly. For all of my European desires and my feelings of not being able to fit in with my family or my community in Sophiatown, something seemed tragically incorrect about the elite of South Africa constantly striving to surrender their own culture in favour of European ones. For the first time in my life, I really missed being an African. I had expected to be making multicoloured cloaks, garish reds and greens, bold and brash geometric patterns swimming psychedelically across the rustic, distressed materials. I expected sandals with the raw fur of wild animals of the bush, huge necklaces of beads piled on top of one another in great riotous chokers of colour and ethnic heritage. Instead we were doing what all white South Africans always do, which is to look north and pretend to be European. We were casting off our African garments and trading them for the more attractive, more acceptable alternatives offered by the foreigners. The dismissal of African identity was a stormy sea and I sensed that the tide was coming in.

But I for one was standing firm. I am *African*—how can I be anything else? To wear these clothes would rip out half of who I was. That was the very reason why I was going to Cape Town to rescue Nelson; the whole system was deeply flawed and badly needed changing. I did not feel comfortable being mistaken for a black woman, but I did not want to be merely white either; I am a coconut, and I am proud to be both. The Government must recognise and respect my claim to both races and *this* was why Apartheid was wrong. I would not settle until they did recognise my condition, but deep down I knew they would not. We needed a transplant at the very top. De Klerk, Blessings and Winnie all had to die.

Yet at the same time there is nothing African about me at all. I had spent my entire life being so deeply confused and distressed by the whole ordeal, and even now at the age of forty one I had no idea what colour I was. There was not the steadfast resoluteness that there had been within my white spirit on earlier occasions; I had veered from believing that I was black to believing that I was white, all against the agonizing backdrop of Apartheid which had been ripping me in half since the day I was born. Sometimes I wished that skin was as simple as these clothes that I was stitching together, that when I needed to be white I would just take it off of the hanger and slip it on to cover me up. I imagined a great racial wardrobe which I could dip in and out of whenever I needed a quick change of clothes; perhaps I could have slipped into an Indian number in Durban so that I would not be identified as a stripper or a slag, or maybe if I had been white in Plett then Ida would never have questioned me about my hygiene when preparing the guava and pineapple in her kitchen. I would run my fingers down the seams at my sides, the stitching perfect and flush against my white soul, the smoothness of the shell calm and delicious beneath my naked fingertips. And when I was bored of being white, when I needed to fit in with my contemporaries in the streets of Sophiatown once again, I would simply peel it off like a banana skin and replace it with the blackness I had once left behind, leaving a crumpled heap of white skin on the floor behind me.

I never did instruct Siphiwe to go out begging on the streets again because she did so before I had the chance to order her to go and collect money to fund our rescue mission which would make her a Princess. She dutifully took up her begging bowl and she headed off into the town, taking care to identify the places where she would be noticed by the white locals but at the same time ensuring that she did not stray outside of the boundaries dictated by the colour of her coconut shell. I was so proud of her, for she was learning so quickly. Three already! You are growing so fast my gorgeous girl, I would say. In reality I should not have been surprised at her eagerness, for there is not a girl in the world who does not harbour a secret desire to be a Princess of the realm, a fanciful and secret kingdom, a wondrous city of gold.

Following on from our adventures in Plettenberg Bay, it was impossible to make fashion items such as these without picturing them being worn by rich white people. The only rich white people who immediately sprang to my mind in the backroom of the shop were the Van Der Merwe family, and I imagined myself working for Ida again.

We had a lot of mannequins in the shop which we would dress to display our proudest creations, and as I arranged one of the dresses on the plastic person I imagined Ida Van Der Merwe, her linen-white skin and her angry, misguided hatred of everything that she did not understand and everything which was different and foreign seething within her as though she had swallowed a burning red hot coal.

It seemed that Ida was the complete opposite of me. I am black with a white core, but Ida had a beautifully white shell with a core as black as death. She was withered and shrivelled on the inside, dead and cold as a never-ending night, and as I arranged the neckline of the dress over the bust of the mannequin I knew that my hands were hovering over a heart of stone. We had lived in their home for three years which meant that even now, on the cusp of Cape Town as we were, I found her an impossible woman to forget.

Nelson waited.

The gunpowder factory was dimly lit and was not dramatically different from the bilges of a huge naval warship. Even the air seemed to be stained with the sepia hue of explosive powder as Blessings painstakingly filled the barrels with his poisonous wares. He would spend his days stuffing the vast barrels full of multicoloured sparks and plumes of fiery smoke, great folded ribbons of shimmering light and sound. He would painstakingly stitch together the different colours and weave the textures of the smoke trails. Some of them would whoosh, some of them pop, some of them squeal and some of them bang and boom, a deep pulsating thud echoing through the dark sky above the hundreds of delighted faces on the earth below.

He gathered up the trails of multicoloured smoke, scrunched up the glittering sparks and bundled up the dazzling pulse of the explosion and inserted them all into a barrel. The precious ingredients were all wrapped up in light and packaged in booming electroluminescence of the ignited skies. I often wondered if handling the gunpowder would burn his fingers, imagining the glittering sparks sifting through his hands like shining grains of sand on the beach at Durban. I wondered how it would feel to scoop up great handfuls of light, the scalding droplets slipping between his fingers and spreading out in etched lines on the dark sky, pour them into a barrel and seal the lid.

There was something so wonderfully Promethean about it all. He had stolen the gifts of fire and light from the Heavens and he had audaciously made off with them in the night, bundling them under his greatcoat and dashing through the darkness with the white hot treasure held underneath his clothes, sending crepuscular rays through the buttonholes and the stitching of his lapel. I imagined him making his break for freedom and shining in the darkness like a powerful beam of sunlight reflected in a brilliant diamond on the top of a heap of coal. That diamond was me. The great shaft of sunlight which was the raw ideological genius of my future husband sliced through the omnipresent darkness and was reflected on my perfectly white spirit. The rest of them were all chunks of coal but I was a big fat diamond. I basked in his glow and I relished his phosphorescent shimmer.

I knew that as I was approaching Cape Town I was getting blacker on the outside. It was almost as though my brittle coconut shell would tighten around me until it grew ashen and scorched, crumbling off in large flaky pieces and revealing below it a perfectly white core. If my skin was getting blacker then it was surely a sign that I was getting whiter on the inside. The patches of crocodile skin on my arms and legs were growing at an alarming rate and the condition of my skin was growing worse and worse the closer that we came to my new throne and King. My body was giving me signs and signals that the King was coming and that his everlasting rule was close at hand. My tissue was aching and crying out, groaning and murmuring its praise of my future husband and yearning for the day when I would be released from my fleshy black prison.

Some of the time in the workshop I would imagine Siphiwe as an adult woman. Would I ever see that happen, given the virus which was surging through my system and gaining strength with each passing day? When she was a princess in the court of King Nelson would I see her make her debut at the palace ball, descending the staircase like a white china statue in an enrapturing gown of satin and gold stitching? As I embroidered the dresses in that little shop I thought of the finery which she would one day be embellished in, the tiaras and the ballgowns, the satin sashes and the fur coats. Time was running out for my womb to produce its heir to Nelson's throne; I did not know if I would have the eloquence left in me to present the case which would alter the line of succession in favour of Siphiwe when Nelson already had a male heir.

Blessings would explain to me what the gunpowder that he made would be used for and I slowly gained an insight into his work over the days that we stayed in Swellendam. The dynamite that he would bunch into different sticks and tie them together at the stem like a bunch of tulips was used not for spectacular fireworks displays but instead for something altogether more destructive. Dynamite would be used for demolishing buildings and for shifting enormous amounts of rich red earth in mines and construction sites. Perhaps the very sticks of dynamite that Blessings was now knitting together would be sent back up to Kimberley and used to move the earth in the very same diamond mine which he had been working in when I had met him at the beginning of our journey to Cape Town. Perhaps they would be sent all the way up to Egoli and used in the gold mind which my father had worked in a dream ago, when Nelson was free and Hector was living. It was a wonderful thought to consider that the dynamite may be making a journey back in time as well as a geographical journey back to Johannesburg, weaving its way along the Garden Route to the motor factories of Port Elizabeth, up through the graveyards of Port Edward and the strip clubs of Durban, the hills of Lesotho and the munitions factories of Bloemfontein.

Christmas was fast approaching, and we knew that we had to move. The time was near; I knew because I could feel it in the depths of my soul. Nelson's freedom was coming, and it could only come through me.

I didn't know if we could make it to Cape Town all in one go or if we would have to make one more stop before I swam to the island prison after the murder. I was under no illusions that this would be a difficult and testing battle. I never knew exactly what Blessings was thinking of the mission which we must confront before the new dawn of freedom could be ushered in; I hoped with everything that I had that he was not some deluded fool who thought that our journey would end simply and safely. We were the most dangerous assets to the ANC's battle for the rights of the masses, the scourge of a Government at the very peak of its power. I would not be surprised if the secret agents working for De Klerk were now in Plettenberg Bay, turning over the mansion of the Van Der Merwe family because they had been given a tip-off of our location but had failed to get there in time. I imagined the scowling chief of police, his vile white face contorted by a fit of frustrated rage as he realised that I had slipped through his fingers once again, that with devilish cunning I had eluded his efforts to ensnare me and I had continued with my audacious scheme to get Nelson out of prison.

With a sickening sense of dread I realised that there would be wanted posters of me in all of the taverns across the country. We must now avoid all of the public places where people may have heard my mission statement and manifesto. I was Africa's Lenin, Cromwell and Washington all rolled into one, and I was an unignorable threat to national security and the elite establishment of Government. They were coming after me, but soon the day would come when I would be going after them.

20

THE KING AND I

Stellenbosch, Cape Province
December 1989

We arrived in Stellenbosch on Christmas Eve, 1989. The skies were dark and it was uncomfortably hot with the faint whine of mosquitoes always close to the ear. We came across an old farmhouse in the middle of an endless vineyard, and we enquired as to whether or not the inhabitants would be able to provide us with accommodation. We didn't really care about work any more; if we could have enough to eat, then we could walk the short distance to the fabled city of Cape Town. We could be there very soon and we knew for sure that 1990 would be the year that Apartheid came to an end and the year that Nelson Mandela stepped out into the sunshine as a free man.

After the fall of the Berlin Wall the break-up of the Soviet Union was inevitable, and like the great wall which divided black from white and spirit from body in my country it was all just a matter of when the end would come. It was a race to the finish, and I desperately hoped that South Africa would be free before Russia would. It was time to be a leader, for Africa to give the rest of the world a lecture in political integrity and the end of suppression; we still had the racist agendas of the white elites enshrined in the law many decades after the Civil Rights Movement had gripped the American South, centuries after the Africans had been shipped around the world as slaves. How could it be that this madness was continuing into the 1990s?

After a few days of asking for work we soon came to realise that the entire industry of Stellenbosch seemed to be based on winemaking. It was a beautiful place to be; all around us endless fields were given over to vineyards and the grapevines tangled their way up the scribbled hillsides.

I had been on this journey long enough to be able to tell what was worth pursuing and to detect Nelson's whispers in my ears as he told me which paths I should follow. As I walked up the long, dusty pathway towards the farmhouse of one of the wineries I heard his voice thudding in my ears with every bare footstep I took. I knew that he was telling me that here was where I should be. We were so close now that we probably could have walked to Cape Town in a day; the journey was simply not long enough to have any more stops than this final one. The farmhouse was beautiful and ancient, a grand single storey whitewashed building with a large Dutch-inspired gable above the entrance, with the roof curling and rising in fancy crest. The house bobbed on a churning sea of green leaves, spreading out like the sea around Mosselbaai had. This vineyard was my Table Bay and this building was my Robben Island. I turned to look back at the road; it wasn't so far. I could easily swim the distance of the pathway and drag his body back to shore to freedom, carefully keeping his crown above the surface of the raging water. I needn't worry about the journey to come.

The winery offered us work as grape-treaders, and we asked if it would be for a wage but the farmer instead offered us a place to stay and food to eat in exchange for our work. There would be no money changing hands; the revenue from the wine would go to him and his family. We would not see any of it, and taste precious little. The vintner was an old white man with half-moon spectacles and receding white hair. He had a plump white wife and a pair of unattractive white children. I didn't bother to listen to him as he told me their names because I knew that we would not be staying long and the only white man that mattered to me was Nelson. We quickly found out that the treaders who lived here before us had died of AIDS one day whilst they were working on the grapes and their corpses had been found in the vat, half-submerged in the barely crushed grapes.

The days were spent treading the grapes into must, which was the raw juice containing the skins and the stalks. I sometimes thought back to what Ida had said to me, and I remembered her squeamishness when it came to me handling food, and when I was feeling weak I would sometimes think back and wonder if her fears had any truth in them. I know the truth of HIV transmission but that did not mean that the doubts did not have their own place in my tortured, incandescent mind. I would stare down at my fat black toes and the ghastly lesions and demonic marks on them, the stained reminder of a brief and violent encounter, and wonder if the virus would find its way through my thick dry skin and turn the wine into poison. I was in two minds about the staining of my feet by the crushed grapes, celebrating on the one hand the fact that the lesions and aching wounds of AIDS were covered, veiling my shame in a film of purple and green juice; at the same time I wondered if my skin really was shedding like a snake and that the day was coming when all of my skin would fall off altogether. I did not want the slime of the grapes to steal my glory or shroud my coconut shell.

The days were long and extremely arduous, but I did not find them tedious. It was perhaps the first time on the whole of our trip that we could all spend the time together as a family, splashing and dancing in the vat of grapes. The only one missing was Mwanyisa. I valued and treasured the time that I could spend with Blessings before his imminent murder, before Siphiwe and I would begin our new life as African Royalty in the stifling social claustrophobia of the court of the King.

The most vivid of all of my memories of the farmhouse in Stellenbosch was of being in the cellar where the fermentation was done. There was a vast storehouse of all of the wine which we had helped to make, kept in enormous barrels and stored in huge avenues of shelving where they were stacked horizontally on shelves which were three barrels high. The rich, sulphuric smell of the place was indescribable. It was enthralling, mesmerising and unfamiliar. This was like being deep down in the belly of the Earth, with the dark room and the ancient stones in the walls combining to create a rich atmosphere and to provide the visitor with the sensation of the wine being the crushed-up juices of Africa itself. I closed my eyes and I was back in the diamond mine in Kimberley again, the warm and moist mud of the caves around me now catacombs of solid brick, the treasure itself now a liquid and not a precious stone.

I noticed that the red wines would be stored in bottles of green glass. This would completely change the colour of the bottle from a rich green to a midnight black. Was this what was happening to me? Was my skin made of glass and the black hue created by my alcoholic blood which filled me up? How could I pour myself out, to rid myself of this abhorrent curse and to once again return to the clear colour of my white soul within me?

The rumours about Nelson being transferred to a prison in Paarl persisted, even though I knew with everything within me that they were false. Nobody knew Nelson like I did and so there was no way that any of the information about his prison sentence would reach someone else before it would reach me. He was on Robben Island, the glamorous castaway shading himself beneath the palm trees on the sandy beach, drinking the coconut milk as he gazed across the water to see the majesty of Table Mountain guarding the Mother City. I can't explain how I knew. All I can say is that I closed my eyes and I had never been surer of anything else.

On the evening of 2nd February 1990 we were given some news that we could not ignore. After decades of pressure coming from both within South Africa and from the rest of the world, our President F.W. De Klerk made an address to the nation to tell us that the ANC would no longer be a banned political party. Blessings came to fetch me and we went into the farmhouse to watch the address in which he laid out his plans to open up South African politics to all the people rather than the white minorities. This was the speech which we had been waiting for and searching for on the whole of our journey ever since 1976, and I knew that the moment was coming. If I did not swim for Robben Island now, I knew that the President would beat me to it. It was de Klerk, not I, who stood at the door and hammered on it whilst the guard approached with his enormous bunch of jangling keys, demanding the release of the world's most famous political prisoner. As I listened to the excitement surrounding the President's speech I could feel the opportunity for glory slipping between my fingertips, my Queen's crown slipping lower and lower down the back of my head as it tumbled off into the red dust at my feet.

"Our country and all its people, have been embroiled in conflict, tension and violent struggle for decades. It is time for us to break out of the cycle of violence and to break through to peace and reconciliation. The silent majority is yearning for this. The youth deserve it. For the steps the Government has taken it has proven its good faith and the table is laid for sensible leaders to begin talking about a new dispensation to reach an understanding by way of dialogue and discussion. The agenda is open and the overall aims to which we are aspiring should be acceptable to all reasonable South Africans. Among other things those aims include a new, democratic constitution, universal franchise, no domination, equality before an independent judiciary, the protection of minorities as well as of individual rights, freedom of religion. A sound economy based on proven economic principles and private enterprise. Dynamic programmes directed at better education, health service housing and social conditions for all. In this connection Mr Nelson Mandela could play an important part. The Government has noted that he is willing to make a constructive contribution to the peaceful political process in South Africa. I wish to put it plainly that the Government has taken the decision to release Mr Mandela unconditionally. I am serious . . . I am serious about bringing this matter to finality without delay. The Government will take the decision soon on the date of his release. Unfortunately, a further short passage of time is unavoidable. Normally there is a short passage of time between the decision to release and the actual release of prisoners because of the logistical and administrative requirements. In the case of Mr Mandela there are factors in the way of his immediate release of which his personal circumstances and safety are not the least. He has not been an ordinary prisoner for quite some time; because of that his case requires particular circumspection. Today's announcement in particular goes to the heart of what black leaders, also Mr Mandela, have been advancing over the years as their reason for having resorted to violence. The allegation has been that the Government did not wish to talk to them and that they were deprived of their right to normal political activity and the prohibition of their organisations. Without conceding that violence has ever been justified, I wish to say today to those who argued in this manner that the Government wishes to talk to all leaders who seek peace. The unconditional lifting of the prohibition of the said organisations places everybody in a position to pursue politics freely. The justification for violence which was always advanced therefore no longer exists. These facts place everybody in South Africa before an equal standard by which they are judged. On the basis of numerous previous statements there is no longer any reasonable excuse for the continuation of violence. The time for talking has arrived, and whoever still makes excuses does not really wish to talk. Therefore I repeat my invitation with greater conviction than ever; walk through the open door. Take your place at the negotiating table together with the Government and other leaders who have important power bases inside and outside of parliament. Henceforth everybody's political points of view will be tested against their realism, their workability, and their fairness. The time for negotiation has arrived."

I could not believe it. Nelson was going to be set free within the week and the President would enter negotiations to bring a legal end, once and for all, to the Apartheid which had blighted the landscape of our culture for so long. We were here in Stellenbosch, just a few dozen kilometres away from the conclusion of our journey, and the fate of Nelson Mandela and a free South Africa was being decided without me. It had to be some horrible coincidence; I was still a coconut, but the rest of the plan had been ripped apart before my eyes. Nelson had managed to win his freedom without my help. Flabbergasted I turned to Blessings and I felt a burning anger at the injustice of it all rising up inside me. The road which stretched out for fourteen years behind us was disintegrating. It was all so desperately unfair.

"Nelson was let out before we arrived to rescue him."

His eyes were huge and kind. They showed that he understood me like nobody else ever had. "Yes, my love. He was."

I wanted to break free and run away from the unignorable truth. I would not stop running, I could never stop running. Nelson's whispers had been wrong all along. How could this be? I had tears in my eyes.

"Why didn't he wait for me?"

"I think you need to remember the promise that you made in Knysna. He was able to break free on his own. That means that he was never waiting for you in the first place."

I gazed deep into him, trying to work out if he was just another stupid monochrome. Every truth I had ever known was now exposed as a lie. I didn't know what to say, so he kept talking.

"I guess now it's just the three of us."

He took me by the hand and drew me in towards himself, kissing my forehead as he did it. The tenderness of the moment was unbearable.

"I think you have to consider the possibility that you have always been black."

I pushed him aside, for my husband had angered me. I shrieked and screamed at him.

"How dare you, Blessings! How could you say that? You know that's not true, you know that I am halfway between black and white . . ."

He interrupted me sternly with the only argument that I could not contest.

"If that were true, Nelson would still be in prison waiting for you."

It made me wonder for the very first time in my life whether or not Nelson had been listening to me for the past fourteen years, across the endless journey that we had made to Cape Town and which we were now so desperately close to completing. I felt an agonising sense of heartbroken betrayal, for the President's speech to the nation was the one which I should have made, standing before the leaders and declaring to them that the era of legalised racism had come to an end. It was indescribable to fathom what was happening, that he really had been able to do it without me after all. I felt as though I had been mugged and robbed; did nobody recognise my birthright, my prerogative to be the one who ended Apartheid? Surely when they saw me they would know once and for all that the system cannot possibly work if white souls are contained within black bodies. How are you to separate black from white if you cannot separate body from spirit?

In my bed that night I walked across the sea to Robben Island to meet with Nelson. I held him in my arms through the bars of the window of his tiny little cell, the place he had spent twenty seven years of his life; I couldn't bring myself to believe that he would finally be free after so long. I refused to believe that he was in Paarl because it went against everything that I felt within the loins of my soul; love takes its lead from the guts, not the mind. I held his black head against my white heart, and I soothed him exactly as I had soothed my children. He was my father, my lover and my child all at the same time.

I remember watching on the news as the live television cameras followed Nelson Mandela's release from jail in Paarl. The famous scene which would indelibly remain on the brains of this nation was of Nelson Mandela and his wife Winnie, emerging from the prison in Paarl together, walking up to the gate and holding hands, holding their fists up in the sunshine in a defiant gesture of freedom. At long last, he could once again call himself a free man.

My eyes were on her as much as they were on him, for I loved her and I hated her all at once. I envied her, I envied her wedding ring and I envied her position as she took my place, walking down the street with him, waving to the adoring crowd as one of the biggest victories for freedom in the history of humankind was won completely without me. I did not know what to think of Winnie Mandela; there were widely circulating rumours that she had been indulging herself with other men whilst her husband had been in prison, she used violent and brutal rhetoric in her speeches which had included advocating the torturous practice of "necklacing" in which the victim was executed by having a burning tyre placed around their neck and torso, and she had been charged multiple times with corruption. I was coming to recognise that I would never be Nelson's wife and Queen, but it seemed difficult to accept the virtue of his alternative choice. Perhaps I should have murdered her after all so that we could mark a truly fresh start independent of hatred, but deep down I knew that my personal battle for the wedding ring of her husband had been lost long ago. With a heavy heart I came to the decision that if Winnie was not to be murdered then there was no plausible way that I could justify killing Blessings as well, so I came to the heartbreaking conclusion that my husband should live.

It was in that moment, that nation-shaping moment which was the end of one era and the start of another that I finally came to the realisation that I never had been and never would be a coconut as I had thought. It was all a gigantic illusion, just as the promise of wealth in Johannesburg had been to the black men moving there for prestigious employment; my belief in who I was had been a magnificent inflatable mirage, and now it was running out of gas. I am not white. I am not filled with coconut milk, a black bell-jar carrying white treasure, a white wine in a black barrel. I am black from my skin to my core. There could scarcely have been a better day for me to realise this than the day when Nelson Mandela, the man I had loved and dreamt of for thirty long years, finally won his right to be a free man. He had done it without me and without, I suspected, having ever been a coconut either.

My whole world was crumbling before my very eyes; with a jarring pain I was realising that I was not at the centre of the universe and that the struggle for freedom from Apartheid did not revolve solely around me. I was struggling to see the sense or use in anything; you may dismantle the stars now, for I have no further use for them. Wrap up the moon and fold up the seas, take down the mountains and pluck out the trees. The whole world seemed bland and colourless in comparison to when my dream of being a coconut had flourished when Nelson had been in prison. I realised that I hadn't actually wanted him to be free after all.

I may as well have been in that jail cell on Robben Island, that holy and sanctified place of pilgrimage and unyielding and audacious hope, for the battle had been won when I was in the kitchen, the laundry and the strip club, not on the front lines fighting for the right to be included and accepted. I was consumed by an indescribably overwhelming sensation of waste; my life and my epic journey had come to nothing. Mwanyisa, my beloved baby boy, had been abandoned on the premise of a lie, and I was subjected to a heartbreaking and unnecessary agony as my soul was ripped in half when I realised what I had done to him. We could have been so happy; we could have made a life together in Coffee Bay, growing old as a family and enjoying each other's company as we ripened in the African sunshine.

That was that. I was not the coconut that I had always thought I was. My soul was as black as my skin. Nelson was free but would not become King. He would have no Queen, but if he had it would have been Winnie and not me. Blessings and Winnie would both live after all. The numerous interconnected events which would now never happen created a chain of disappointment which tumbled like a line of dominos. My heart was the last one to be knocked, wobble and fall.

It was very difficult to arrive at the conclusion that the most popular and charismatic man in the world may not be interested in me, a married and impoverished mother who was dying of AIDS and was one of the millions and millions of faceless and anonymous black citizens of the nation that surely now belonged to him. I had missed my chance; when he was released all of my uniqueness evaporated from me like the thundering steam from the Victoria Falls for I was no longer the unique pillar of the campaign against Apartheid that I had spent a lifetime considering myself to be. I would not be remembered above Tutu, or Tambo, or De Klerk or Pietersen; I would not even be remembered alongside them. I would not be remembered at all.

Even more difficult to contend with was the realisation that Blessings and I were approaching our twelfth wedding anniversary and it was not until that day, 11th February 1990, that I finally fell in love with him. I fell in love with him because I knew that he loved me when Nelson had not and never would; I fell in love with him because he had risked everything that he had to be a part of my adventure and he had asked nothing of me in return. I was awestruck by the steadfastness of his love for me, and I cast my mind back to that night when we had made Siphiwe and Nangila. He had willingly accepted the curse of HIV and a lifetime of illness and misery just so that he could grant me my wish to be a mother again; a real mother, a mother of more than just biology who does not leave her baby in a dustbin. The sacrifice he made for me was overwhelming. He had stuck by me through thick and thin, through black and white, never leaving me and never giving up on me. By heaven, I knew that I deserved to be abandoned to my hair-brained scheme, my outlandish plan of delusion and fantasy, but he never did the obvious thing and he had remained at my side honouring his promise 'until death us do part'. I could not believe it. What was so lovable about me? What was so deserving and virtuous and worthwhile about Lerato? I was a mess, a shambolic disaster zone, an unlovable and hopeless catastrophe. But his love never failed, never gave up, never ran out on me.

I didn't need to be a Queen or an Empress, a dignitary or a First Lady, a world changer or a statesman like Nelson. I was only just coming to realise that I had already found my king and had married him more than a decade before. The man who was perfect for me had been with me all along; I had been running for all this time, chasing a hero and a saviour when I had one by my side the whole time. It seemed such a dreadful shame, such a brutally depressing way for my story to finish as we watched Nelson prove that I had been deluded for a large proportion of my life, to have made the long and arduous journey all the way from Johannesburg only to have missed our chance just a few dozen kilometres from Robben Island, then to discover that we were heading in the wrong direction anyway. But all that I felt that day was joy. My black soul sang hymns of rejoicing as I realised, finally, that I had been deeply loved for a very long time and that my husband and daughter cherished me. Is there any higher honour in the whole world than to love and be loved in return? I was so busy looking for what was mythical, fantastical and frankly delusional that I had been running towards Cape Town for a quarter of my life without ever really noticing the Blessings which I had been given. I could have mourned the time I had wasted but I knew my end was coming, and that there was no more time left to waste on regret. So I spent it in the best way that time can be spent, the way that time was made to be spent; I spent my days being in love. Adoration by another really is the best blessing possible, and there is nothing more wonderful than that. I had all I needed. How could I not be enraptured by the wonderful shape my life had taken? February 1990 was not the month I lost my shot at glory and my Nelson, but the month that I gained uncountable blessings.

Being a political prisoner on Robben Island was not a compulsory requirement for being a South African hero, but it does help. All of the new political elite would be drawn from the cells on the little island; I knew that I would not be among their number because I had never been there.

For the first time since leaving Johannesburg I was given regular updates on Nelson's condition and the exact nature of the progression of our nation towards full democracy, a struggle that I was no longer involved in. The secrecy, the hushed and censored confusion over the details of his life in prison, came to an abrupt end. They kept on using a pet-name, a nickname, to mean Mandela. They called him *Madiba*, which they said was the tribal clan name that he was known by back in The Transkei in his childhood. With a heartbreaking and crushing encounter with the reality of the situation the newsreaders would tell me, it felt like only me, that it was *close friends and members of his own family* who would be able to use this term to address him affectionately. It was an incredibly tender and intimate term, and one which a stranger would not be permitted to use casually. I stood on the shore of Robben Island, preparing to stride proudly through the gateway and into the gloomy courtyard crowned with Gothic watchtowers to rescue my lover after my gruelling journey and marathon swim across Table Bay. Fear not my love, I called through the gaps in the portcullis, I have arrived and I have come to take you away on a long walk to freedom. As I spoke the mighty wooden doors of the jail slammed in my face, the vast wooden doors with black iron studs heaving shut with a massive noise. Scrawled above the doorway in perfectly white paint were the words "Madiba is in Paarl". At that moment I knew that I was a stranger and an outsider, rejected and cast out of the inner ring of Apartheid heroes, devoting my life to search for a jail where Mandela was not being held and with writing above the gateway in a colour that I would never be. I thought back to that conversation that we had shared in Soweto in 1962 and how he had never let me call him by the tribal name, and whilst he was appearing so loving and affectionate he was giving me a cryptic message of distance and rejection. He had never once told me that his name was Madiba in all of the telepathic encounters that we had shared over the decades but instead had introduced himself as Nelson, and from that I could garner only one logical conclusion. Real as he undoubtedly was, in my world I had been talking to an imaginary friend.

Without me they drafted a new constitution, and my idol made speeches detailing the most tolerant, progressive and enlightened human rights bill in the world. The changes to our country under Nelson Mandela would be enormous, and his popularity was overwhelming; Blessings and I definitely saw the imminent election as a formality with a completely foregone conclusion. I was so incredibly proud of Nelson and what he had already achieved as well as the things he had promised to accomplish in the future for South Africa. The satisfaction and affection that I felt for our nation's champion deep within me glowed like Jacqueline Kennedy had in that photograph in Soweto in 1961. That glowing sense of pride was the closest thing I will ever know to being truly white. Since that day we had both made the journey across the nation and we had seen and experienced extraordinary things. Now that his long walk to freedom had been completed the time had come for a new chapter in the history of the nation and the narrative of humanity to continue. To see journey's end, I came to realise that Nelson was a better version of himself without my unruly imagination attempting to guide him and if I left it to him he could achieve far greater things when he did it his way. He had been right to run for President; an absolute monarchy would not have been the correct way of stepping out of the darkness of racism and into the glorious sunshine of freedom. I loved him; I really and truly and desperately loved him more than he will ever know, but as he stepped out into the sunshine of freedom and changed the course of South Africa forever I knew that it was finally the time to let him go.

21

ON TOP OF THE BOTTOM
OF THE WORLD

Cape Town
27th April 1994

Lerato, Siphiwe and I made it to the Mother City in January 1992 after two years spent trying to survive in the vineyard in Stellenbosch. My wife was getting frail and weak, but we eventually completed our journey by walking most of the way on foot and catching a minibus taxi when we were in range and when Lerato was too exhausted to walk any more. She had done so incredibly well and I was so proud to have her as my wife. She was a deluded nutter, fiery and flawed, but she was so lovable that I couldn't help myself. You'll tell me that I should have left her ages ago, but I don't regret a single step of our journey together from Baragwanath Hospital.

I will never forget the majesty of the moment of our triumphant arrival. The Mountain was visible ahead of us as the road curved and bent around it and eventually ended up in the City Bowl, and it was crowned in crepuscular rays of golden light as the sun was partially obscured by the Tablecloth. The world simply could not have looked any more beautiful than it already did. It was almost as if Cape Town was prepared for her wedding day, garlanded in her finest and shimmering with untold treasures of splendour. I had my wife and my daughter at my side and freedom and democracy was finally ours after so many long years of waiting and fighting. Cape Town had been preparing for us the whole time, knowing that we were coming, making herself beautiful and welcoming for our arrival. Glory.

As the taxi sped towards the city bowl I felt a deep recognition of every street and every palm tree. There was something familiar, something comfortable about it all and there was an immediate sense of belonging. The seas rang out with the sweetest symphonies and the spirit of Africa carved itself on the sky above the city that I had never been to but that I already loved like no other. We were home.

My father, Sibusiso Mngomezulu, had been arrested in Johannesburg for acts of violent demonstration against the Apartheid regime. He had been taken to Cape Town for incarceration and eventually found himself on Robben Island. I had been sending him letters along the journey, telling him that we were getting closer and closer, but after Mandela's release I realised that prisoners in my father's category were given one letter every six months and they would be completely indecipherable once the censors had finished with them. I am almost certain that he never knew that I was married and even though I kept telling her I am sure that Lerato thought I was going to Robben Island for the same reason that she was. Prisoners were segregated by race and because my father was black he was given the fewest rations. Hungry and heartbroken, he had died of exhaustion and dehydration in the limestone quarry after being forced to work as a slave alongside Nelson Mandela. He had died in a small cave in the quarry where the prisoners rested and which also served as their only bathroom. It was in this cave that the prisoners would meet in secret to draft what eventually became the South African constitution. Dad is buried in the island's graveyard which was begun when it was used as a leper colony, a simple white cross serving as a headstone. I had promised myself that I would one day lay eyes on this little island, and I am a man of my word.

The profound irony of Lerato's struggle was that she was actually extremely racist. She saw her black skin as dirty and unhygienic, a monstrous birth defect she could not wait to be rid of. She got a lot right and she got a lot wrong; in the end she was trying her best to do a great and noble thing but she was doing it for wicked and evil reasons. It is absolutely right and proper to hate Apartheid because it is an abomination against human rights but Lerato hated Apartheid because as an institution it failed to recognise her unique racial identity. Presumably if the South African Government had recognised coconuts as their own ethnic group then she would have given the racist regime her full approval. Being in love is not always pleasant or enjoyable, but I hoped it was worthwhile.

Lerato had never been a coconut. She was just as black as I was; through and through, from top to bottom, from skin to bone. Snapping out of her deluded fantasy would never be a fast or easy process given that this would have been her identity for her entire life up until the speech made by De Klerk in 1990 and the release of Nelson Mandela from the wrong prison. It was a moment of huge transition for everyone who calls themselves an African, but for her it redefined the very core of who she was. For so many people Mandela's freedom was the making of their dreams; for my wife it was the shattering of them. Over the four years between Mandela's release and the first democratic elections of our country Lerato would lurch violently between her old colour-blind self and her new rational, calm and reasonable persona. It was as though she was two people at once; some doctors I spoke to suggested bipolar disorder but I think that her flashbacks to the time when she was a future Queen were simply episodes of denial and confusion. Mental illness is a cruel beast to have to wrestle with and there is infinitely more to curing it than simply waking up from an intense daydream. Everyone, myself included, had been telling her the truth of her condition for her whole life and she had always found a convenient reason to deny it, so letting go of those reasons would be far from immediate.

I could not be more thrilled to have completed our long and epic journey across the nation, but I knew that Lerato was disappointed to have missed the release of Nelson Mandela from Paarl. I remember the absolute ecstasy that flashed across Lerato's face when the rumours began in 1992 that Nelson and Winnie Mandela were going to separate. She cheered and danced on the table when the announcement was read out on television, and everyone who witnessed it was astonished by a woman who was all but crippled by the ravaging effects of AIDS suddenly finding the enormous inner strength to leap onto the table and sing and dance with tears running down her face. But I watched as her face fell when the newsreader told us that the couple had no plans to formally divorce and that he intended to run for President with Winnie Mandela as his wife and First Lady. It baffled me. Why on earth would she be happy that the Mandelas were separating, but be sad that they were not divorcing? If she really and truly loved him as much as she said she did, she would never have reacted to the news quite like that. She managed to be happy at a more appropriate time when Mandela won the Nobel Peace Prize alongside President De Klerk in 1993.

Siphiwe loved Cape Town as soon as she saw Table Mountain looming on the horizon from the taxi. It is the perfect city for a child to grow up in and this truth did not help to ease the regret of our journey taking just that little bit too long to complete. If we had been here sooner Siphiwe could have cherished more of her golden days of childhood beside the Twelve Apostles and in the shadow of Lion's Head. We could have had longer to enjoy the view from the lighthouse on the Cape Peninsula, longer to talk to the penguin colony at Simon's Town and longer to explore the wilderness of the coast of False Bay.

Cape Town is quite simply the most breathtakingly beautiful place in the world. The Mother City's skyline is constructed not of steel and glass like the cities in America or Europe but of stone and cloud and soul. The mountain ridge looming large across the bay, the iconic sight of Devil's Peak, Table Mountain, Lions Head and Signal Hill standing proudly together as they guard the mighty port; something about the natural grandeur of this city welcomes a stranger home as a long lost prodigal son even on the first visit. After being given the worst news possible in Stellenbosch, we had expected Cape Town to be a place of bitterness and disappointment for us as President Mandela began his new life of elitism whilst we were left in the miserable agony of poverty, but it was almost impossible to be unhappy here. The spirit of the place was breathtaking and mind-blowing.

Before Lerato became too fragile and frail I made sure that we made a family trip to the summit of Table Mountain. We spent hours and hours in the sweltering summer heat climbing up the face of the mountain, following the trails that had been established by goats and other Africans. Lerato was weak and I tried my best to fight the fatigue but the hike up was extremely gruelling and the AIDS inside all of us was a burden and a drain on our energy.

Every so often she would become too ill and weak and would collapse into a breathless heap on the side of the mountain. I would turn to her to nurse her and encourage her to rise once more. We had promised one another that we would not look at the view below us until we had reached the summit of the mountain. Siphiwe had an admirable strength in her and she put both of us to shame, and she was the most rigid enforcer of the family promise. She would never stop and she would never look down until she had reached the plateau, not like we had when our surprise was ruined as we climbed the hill up to that mansion in Plettenberg Bay. That time we had got it wrong, but this time we got it right. The importance of a noble intention was very clear to her.

We struggled onwards for hours and hours and eventually we reached the top of the bottom of the world. Standing on the huge plateau we did a slow, three-sixty degree turn to confirm our suspicions that we had in fact just landed in Nirvana. Lucky us! That view and everything in it was our inheritance, our entitlement as Africans on the brink of a beautiful future endowed with democracy. With a pang of pain we saw that Robben Island was clearly visible from the summit, the scarce and tiny buildings dotted across the scrubland like scars on black skin. It was absolutely nothing like how Lerato had told me it would be; she had described a vast fortress with Gothic towers and bristling turrets rising out of the sea, a gloomy cobbled courtyard far below and a huge gatehouse where she would plead her case for liberty. Instead it was a rugged little oval speck of wasteland given over to concrete exercise yards, limestone quarries and anonymous whitewashed buildings containing prison cells. The island had appeared in Lerato's dreams as a gloomy and foreboding castle rising out of the tropical sea, surrounded by a ring of powdery white sand and palm trees where the prisoners would be allowed to shade themselves and swim in the technicolour fishbowl of Table Bay. She had told me that Mandela went swimming every day, finding himself dancing underwater with the dolphins and the stingrays, waiting for her arrival. I knew she was a dreamer—I knew my father was being held in far more bleak conditions than she ever dared to admit. The most shocking and sobering revelation I was confronted with when I laid eyes on Robben Island was that it was real. Seven kilometres of deep, cold, violently churning ocean lay between the coast of the island and the African mainland; swimming would have been impossible. When I saw it I saw not a token of triumph or of beauty but one of suffering and hatred. It was a monument to Nelson Mandela's steadfast and unswerving ability to forgive in the face of injustice and evil and of my father's desire to sacrifice his own freedom for the freedom of the rest of us.

Lerato finally died on 27th April 1994. It was Election Day, the day that would go down in history as the day when South Africa finally laid to rest the ghost of Apartheid and finally reached the enlightened summit of democracy. It was a day when people who had never been truly free were seen queuing in serpentine miles around the blocks from the voting booths, the red dust of Africa between their toes, black and white and Indian and coloured all together in one winding river of humanity. She had been very sick the night before Election Day but she had been adamant that she wanted to brave the enormous lines and cast her vote. She told me that she had spent her entire life fighting for change, fighting for equality, and if she could not achieve it by declaring to the world that she really was a coconut she would instead achieve it by choosing the destiny of the nation by deciding between the names on the ballot paper. As a woman dying from AIDS, it was the most powerful gesture that she had left in her. She never once told me who she wanted to vote for as a mark of respect for the significance of the right she now had as a South African citizen to an anonymous vote, but it was not the easiest secret to keep; we all knew who would win and we all knew who she had spent the last thirty four years of her life being in love with. It wasn't me and it would never be me but I didn't care. I had always known that she would never make it to Cape Town on time and I had known that she did not hold the power to release Mandela, but I never once let that stop me loving her. I shared her with the most famous prisoner in the world and it was the most affectionate and tender declaration of love that I could offer her and I never once regretted what I did for her or lamented her lust for Mandela. I have always been an optimist, and it was immeasurably better to have had a little piece of her for the sixteen years that we were given together than to have never had her at all.

We stood in the line for hours and hours, under the fierce African sun, but towards the end of the afternoon Lerato lost consciousness. I kept her hand in mine and I kept wiping her brow, telling myself that I would take what was left of her to the booth and I would wrap her sleeping hand around a pencil and press it to the ballot paper, a final kiss for Mandela from us both as we ushered in a new and beautiful era for the country that we loved so much. There were men, women, children, the crippled and the maimed, some with their dogs, many with their babies, all of them standing in the brutal heat of the African sun and waiting to do their duty at the ballot box.

By the time there were five other voters in the line ahead of us waiting to enter the hut where the votes were being cast, with an awful inevitability, her chest stopped moving and I could no longer detect a pulse through her paper-thin skin. My wife was dead. I begged the election officials to grant her the final dignity of allowing me to press a pencil into her quiet hand and cast her vote, but they refused to let her into the little shack until I could prove to them that she was still alive. I was breathless, and Siphiwe was crying hysterically, but the officials were completely calm as they explained that no voter may cast a vote on behalf of another person, so if she was incapacitated to the extent that she was unable to independently cast her vote with no help from me then her vote would not count in the election. I felt very strongly that they had no right to deny her something she had fought harder than anyone else for. Was this the new nation that we would be ushering in as our inheritance? Was this the type of place that we would be condemned to, a place shackled to bureaucracy and rulebooks and obsessive legalism? Suddenly the future which we had given our generation of Africans to fighting for seemed a little less rosy.

I tried my hardest not to forget all about my dead wife as I stood in the voting booth, the coolness of the shade quenching my burnt skin, but it was difficult. I stood at the very summit of my nation, race and continent, the absolute pinnacle of all that is promising, achievable and possible for humankind. The magnitude of the moment was difficult to take in. As I stood in the booth and prepared to cast my vote, a widower for less than three minutes, the whole journey flashed back through my mind as I contemplated how far we as a nation had come and how great the sacrifices had needed to be just to secure my place on the electoral register. I remembered my father and his fight for equality. I remembered the evictions in Sophiatown, the bulldozers looming on the horizon as the racist rulers tried to stamp out the culture of the black communities. To them Sophiatown was a termite's nest and the black inhabitants were vermin whom they would attempt to exterminate. As I stood here, finally having reached my destination more than three thousand kilometres from the start line, ready to cast my vote, I proved to the world that they had failed and my father had succeeded. I held in my fingers white paper and a black pencil; the paper was the polling card, and the pencil was a nail for the coffin of racism which we had been waiting for so long to slam shut. I knew that the delusion of the Van Der Merwe family had been finally set right and the indignity had come to an end. It was exhilarating. All of the candidates had their images on the polling card for the benefit of our compatriots who were illiterate, and so I scanned it until I found Nelson Rolihlahla Mandela's shining black face smiling up at me from the ballot paper and the ANC logo beside him. I could not read English and so I did not recognise the strange hieroglyphs but I knew what they meant. As I planted my X on the paper next to his name I joined the more than twelve million others who ended it, who really and truly ended it, by speaking together with one voice to propel him to the Presidency.

Mandela would go on to the glory that he was destined for and had been assured all along, but for all the soaring rhetoric of the Long Walk to Freedom and the difficulty of the struggle which had spanned decades and continents, it would be vindictively untrue to grant him all of the credit for the miracle of democracy arriving in our nation. People started talking about Mandela as though he was some kind of messianic saviour, but the genius of Nelson Mandela lay in his soaring humanity, his compassion and his determination to never settle for second best for the people he was representing, his patience and endurance which had seen him walk out of jail as twice the human he had entered as all those years ago. The true brilliance of the man, for a man is all that he ever was and is, lay in the fact that he was a person of extraordinary grace and forgiveness which had enabled him to emerge from prison without any hatred in his heart, without any agenda for vengeance or retribution to be poured out on the people who had committed crimes of such evil against him. He was not jealous or embittered, and he did not take the ample opportunities he was given to exalt the blacks above the whites and implement discriminatory laws against them to make them sorry.

His supporters were faced with two temptations. Firstly, many of them were enticed into the violent fantasy to vanquish for the black African race that which had been so cruelly and brutally taken from them for forty six years under the nationalist Government, which revealed in them a truth which they should not have been proud of; they did not actually want to end Apartheid but inflict it again on the elite which had exploited them for so long. They wanted to see the white men pay for what they had done to Mandela and the rest of us; after all, they would say, whose country is this? Who was here first, and who has been endowed by God with the skin of a true African? Who are the visitors, the tourists who must now be sent home to where they belong? Just because Nelson Mandela had announced his candidacy for President and was almost guaranteed victory did not mean that we were on a safe and steady road to peace. It is my firm and clear belief that South Africa will never have a white President again. I worried that Mandela's mission of reconciliation, forgiveness and peace had not yet reached its conclusion, especially when the anti-Apartheid campaigner Chris Hani was assassinated on 10th April 1993 and the nation, as Mandela put it at the time, "now teeters on the brink of disaster".

The second temptation for the ANC campaigners, the majority of the country and the watching world was to glorify him as some immortal and eternal God and King. It was a crime that Lerato was guilty of, but she was not the only one. We had travelled across the nation, working hard for the entire period of Mandela's incarceration in prison to end the injustice which had blighted our country at the hands of racism and hatred. We had learnt that we were two drops in an ocean of dissatisfaction with the rules that our tormentors decided to impose, a mighty torrent of passionate uprising which no army could ever resist. It was a great achievement to see Nelson Mandela walk free because it was something that we had all achieved collectively, an achievement for South Africa as a whole rather than by any one man. Just as we had endured the shame of Apartheid corporately for the part which we had all played in standing by and allowing it to happen, we now should share in the glory of the miraculous direction that our nation had begun to take after the end of the injustice. Some people were only willing to award that glory to the superhuman, immortal and divine figure which was fictionally constructed of Nelson Mandela. To construct this alternate reality of who Nelson Mandela is was every bit as delusional and incoherent as Lerato's completely bonkers idea that she held the destiny of the whole region and its people in the palm of her hand, as we stretched our family across the decades and the kilometres, in the quest to free Mandela from his jail cell.

My wife suffered from a mental illness called erotomania, a monstrously torturous condition which means that the victim is convinced despite a huge lack of logical evidence that someone else is in love with them. This subject of the obsession is usually a person of immense stature, fame and influence and the victim is often deluded into thinking that greatness awaits them because the subject will return their obsessive love and bestow a huge amount of privilege or wealth on them because of their status. The sufferers usually interpret flimsy evidence such as particular lines or phrases in speeches as being solely directed at them and many of them believe that they have a telepathic relationship with their subject. In particular, the victim often believes that dreams are mediums whereby deliberate messages can be transmitted from their subject, with neurological love letters going backwards and forwards over a prolonged period of time. The condition is similar to obsessive and unrequited love for a person of stature but the crucial difference between Lerato and the rest of Mandela's crazed fans was the fact that Lerato never lost her firm conviction that he was far more in love with her than she ever was with him. In her mind she was merely rearranging her life so that she could make him happy by giving him what he wanted. Obsessed fans choose their targets; in her mind Nelson Mandela had chosen her.

Lerato was also a compulsive liar. An example of this would be that she never met me in a diamond mine, even though she would tell everyone that we had met whilst working at the mine in Kimberley. The Big Hole Diamond Mine had closed down in 1914 and I had met her when I was selling mangoes outside the gates of Baragwanath Hospital. She had been a toilet cleaner in Bloemfontein; there was never a firearms factory in that city and some of the branded guns that she claimed to have manufactured did not exist. In Coffee Bay she told me that she was taking Mwanyisa to doctor to treat his ringworm, but she came home on her own. This unusual juxtaposition of deception and delusion presented me with an unusual dilemma, because for the whole of our marriage I was never sure of how aware she was over the lack of truth in her brain; was it a finely constructed fairytale, a conscious disregard for the truth and an active denial of what she knew to be real, or instead did she genuinely think that she had been on the production line in a factory making machine guns? Did she deliberately ignore the truth or did she simply never experience it?

"Coconut syndrome" as she would have me call it was in fact something called a somatic delusion, where the victim believes something about their body which is not true based on medical symptoms which they are unable to understand. She had been convinced that her body did not match her soul but the groaning from within and the periods when the shell seemed about to burst open were all neurological. Mwanyisa had been white because babies are only flushed with the rich dark skin tone once they begin to grow, although we did not realise that at the time. The patches of skin which looked like an inside-out pomegranate, which she interpreted as her coconut shell cracking and splitting, were in fact a symptom of AIDS called Kaposi's sarcoma. By a cruel coincidence she also suffered from vitiligo, a condition which causes the cells responsible for skin pigmentation to slowly die and cease to function, causing the extremities of the body to have a blotchy complexion. It only became apparent in her thirties; by the time of her death all of her knuckles, her entire left thumb and all of the toes on her right foot were completely white. If this had never developed perhaps she would have abandoned the lie a little sooner.

I felt a connection of my own to Mandela, because he knew how it felt to be touched by the curse of AIDS. His son Makgatho lost his battle with the illness in 2005. He sat in front of a microphone and he sliced open his broken heart: "Let us give publicity to HIV and not hide it, because the only way to make it appear like a normal illness like TB or cancer is always to come out and say somebody has died of AIDS. Then people will stop regarding it as something extraordinary." He didn't shy away from revealing the loss of his son and I won't shy away from revealing the loss of my wife. You have to hear her story.

I never quite knew the finer details of Lerato's plans. A marriage is meant to be based on trust and even though I gave her all the trust that I had inside me I had to live every day with the reality that she did not put any trust in me at all. All of her hope was in Nelson Mandela and I was a piece of driftwood tumbling off the edge of her horizon. Once he had been set free there was a dangerous question lingering in my mind over how she would react to her dreams being shattered; I worried that she may try to visit Nelson Mandela at his rallies in Cape Town between 1992 and 1994 when he was campaigning for the Presidency. How would she react when she confronted him, when he became irritated by her infatuation and vehemently demanded that she leave him alone? How would Mandela feel to be imprisoned for twenty seven years for being a proud black freedom fighter and then have a mentally ill woman insult him with her theory that he was in possession of a white soul after all? It turned out that I needn't have worried about her emotional welfare, because she believed that he was concealing the love he kept in his heart for her from the outside world. She did not need any outward proof to cement her feelings in him and give her satisfaction; in all honesty, if she had then she would never have had enough evidence to begin her obsession after meeting him with a chicken in her hands. I did worry that she would try to attack him because of the strength of the illness's grip on her mind, but that day never came. In the end, the illness in her body was stronger.

The fact that her fantasy of reaching Cape Town, swimming across Table Bay to the island jail and declaring that because she was a coconut the whole house of cards that was Apartheid would come crashing down with a click of her black fingers was ludicrous did not mean that she did not play her part in bringing about Mandela's release. The fact that she did not see him become the overarching Emperor of a new nation solely because of her recommendation did not mean that she was not a valuable asset to the campaign for justice and she did not play her own role in setting the captive free. We all had a part to play in the miracle of 1994. Lerato had claimed her place in history but it would be false to claim that she was the only one to have ended the racist administration, and in the same way it would be untrue to credit Nelson Mandela with being the only political prisoner who had suffered unspeakable evils at the hands of the Apartheid regime. The great crime of the transition to freedom was limiting the achievement of our country in reaching the summit of freedom and crediting it all to one man.

Nelson Mandela won the Presidential election with remarkable ease, securing more than sixty two percent of the votes. Finally, after twenty seven years of incarceration, he was not only a free and innocent man but he was now the Head of State of the country which had banned his party and thrown him into jail. He was inaugurated as the new President just thirteen days after Lerato died. Everyone expected him to be embittered and full of hatred because of what he had been subjected to for the deplorable crime of daring to dream of freedom and equality, but he was a bold and beautiful beacon of forgiveness and grace. He even went as far as to invite three of his prison wardens to his inauguration ceremony. President Mandela was everything that Lerato hoped he would be but never had the chance to see. I felt my heart swelling with pride as Nelson Rolihlahla Mandela was sworn in as the first President of our new nation, partly out of respect for his towering humanity as he preached a message of hope and reconciliation after decades of abuse but also partly out of love for my wife, the crazy and reckless woman who had stolen my heart and dragged me across the whole of South Africa chasing the man who had stolen hers. "Never, never and never again shall it be that this beautiful land will again experience the oppression of one by another . . . the sun shall never set on so glorious a human achievement. Let freedom reign."

*   *   *

The first thing that people want to know when they hear about my story is exactly why I was so patient with Lerato, why I remained faithful to her and followed her all the way to Cape Town on her ludicrous campaign as she tried to change the world. I had made a promise to myself that I would lay eyes on Robben Island to lay my father to rest and her delusion gave her a determination which I would be able to take advantage of. When she first told me on that sunny day in Soweto that she was going to Cape Town, I jumped at the chance to go with her. It would be easier for a man and a woman to get to the Mother City together than it would for them to get there individually, and I knew that this woman may provide me with an encounter with my father. As the journey continued I began to fall in love with her; I knew that she was a delirious fool and my affection

Michael Rogers

was probably as much to do with the claustrophobia of spending all those years together as it was to do with being soul-mates. But I am a good man and I keep all of my promises. If I am going to love her, I declared to myself, I am going to love her properly. The thing about Lerato was that she was ravishingly beautiful, but she never knew it because she was convinced she was the wrong colour. Her eyes were mesmerising and her skin was wonderfully rich and dark. She had the most incredible cheekbones I have ever seen; high and strong and striking. My wife was a stunner and I could not help loving her any more than she could help loving Mandela.

I knew that she was settling for second best when she accepted my proposal of marriage. I knew from the look in her eyes when she heard news of Mandela and when she spoke about him; I am no fool, for I knew that her mind would wander to Robben Island at every opportunity and I would be a liar if I told you that it didn't hurt. But who are we to decide the ones we fall in love with? And in what way does that even slightly diminish my own love for my wife? Just because she hurt me, and just because she believed in that mad, "white", brain of hers that Nelson Mandela was the perfect man for her, it didn't mean that she was not the love of my life.

Surely there can be few higher demonstrations of love for someone than to follow them for more than three thousand kilometres across the whole of the country, to go with them on an outlandish and doomed crusade destined for failure, to know deep in your heart that you are made for one another and to pursue that end wherever the road may lead even though your partner does not know it to be the truth. My wife was raped by a stranger whilst she was in love with another man, and so her body belonged to one and her heart to another all the while she was married to me. It wasn't a good union; we both had one eye on Robben Island the whole time, but I felt sorry for her because, although we both had a loved one on the island, I was the only one who was loved by a prisoner in return.

She was simultaneously a mesmerising genius and a deluded fool blinded by love and absolutely fixated on a mirage which was false. She was not a coconut. She was not able to speak with Mandela in her dreams and in her thoughts. He did not love her and long for her; he did not even know who she was. I didn't even know whether or not I believed that she had ever met him on the corner of that street in Orlando West, holding that defecating chicken in her hands. It was all a delightfully fabricated sham.

Lerato was a brilliant and exceptional person on the very cutting edge of what it meant to be a human being. She was fiery, flawed and deluded, but she had so much passion inside her that she spent most of her life thinking that she would soon burst. My life with her was not boring. She was overwhelmed with love for Nelson Mandela and she never lost her sense of zeal and determination to see Apartheid's destruction. In her mind she was construed by her maker in a ludicrous accident which meant that she had been born into the wrong body, she lay entombed within her sarcophagus of charred skin for almost forty six years and had to endure the shackles of mortality and illness and the tragic fragility of human life. She weathered the curse of HIV and AIDS and she remained as steadfastly focused on her goal as any of the greatest heroes of the struggle.

She never knew a free South Africa; born in 1948 as the Apartheid regime was being instigated, she was a newborn at the same time as racism and segregation on the mean streets of Sophiatown entered an infancy of its own. She was there for the violent and brutal evictions, the destruction of her home in favour of the exclusivity of Triomf, the foundation of Meadowlands and Soweto and the rallies against the oppression. She was there when Mandela was arrested, thrown into jail for daring to dream of equality and freedom, and she campaigned heavily against his incarceration even though nobody believed her wild and fanciful tales of being uniquely able to straddle the races in her own special way. She watched a boy named Hector Pietersen get shot by policemen who were angry with him for objecting to learning the language of the white man.

She made the journey across the whole of the nation, scraping together enough money in each of the places she ended up in to continue on the next leg of the trip. Cape Town is a two hour flight from Johannesburg but it took Lerato sixteen years to travel those thirteen hundred kilometres, gaining a husband and three children along the way. She never lost her zeal and sense of determination in seeing it through to the bitter end, and that I admired greatly. We had seen all of South Africa, all of her luminous beauty and her bitter drudgery, her colourful people and her majestic, matchless natural scenery. I would never regret that. Nothing that could have befallen us would have made it a bad experience. Grace never fails. Love always wins. Life is beautiful.

I am an old man now, but I'm not as old as Mandela. As I lie here on my deathbed with my notebook in my trembling hand, I hear the news that the failed segregation zone of Triomf is to be renamed Sophiatown as a mark of respect for what went before the cruel madness of Apartheid. Lerato's home was destroyed for nothing; the houses were cleared to make way for white people who never moved in. Leratotown never did come to be and I know that she was angry about that even though she thought I didn't know about that particular ambition. But with any luck she will feel a renewed sense of peace, wherever she is now, that the home she once loved was given its identity back. Today is Tuesday 12th September 2006 and I know that my time is drawing near. Down in my beautiful black heart I know that today is my last day. I knew Gloria and Faithful very well indeed and they became a second family to me after my father was taken away. But the day we left for Cape Town was the last time I ever saw them and I never did discover if they made it back to Sophiatown, but it doesn't seem likely given the number of years that have passed since their proud little house last stood there. In spite of that I'd like to imagine them there, a part of the place where they belong. I'd like to think that Mwanyisa managed to escape from that dustbin and went home to Sophiatown to be adopted by the Dlaminis. I close my eyes and I see them strolling hand in hand along the wide boulevards of red mud, with the sound of jazz music in their ears and the warmth of the African sun on their backs. Perhaps the old grandparents chuckle together under a veranda as Faithful smokes his pipe and Gloria knits clothes for Mwanyisa and all his cousins, sitting on her old rocking chair watching the world go by. After more than half a century, Sophiatown can now resume from where it left off.

It seems that the old saying is true: the darker the berry, the sweeter the juice. As the reader of this book I want you to remember Lerato, to hold her story in your heart and to be troubled when humanity is reduced to the indignity that it was here, on the streets of Cape Town and across the country which I love and have sacrificed everything I have for. Remember Sophiatown and the way in which culture was oppressed and then destroyed. Remember the liberation which the non-white population of this country was denied over the long years of struggling for an equal distribution of justice. Remember Nelson Mandela and the way that he was denied his dignity as he rotted away in a prison cell before defying the odds to claim the Presidency. Remember South Africa; her matchless beauty and her unparalleled heartache, her triumphant history and her brutal, violent oppression of the many by the few. Enjoy the rights of democracy and the hedonistic joy of liberation, but the world must never forget the suffering and the pain, the blood which was shed, in order to win that prize for all of us and make that dream a reality. As the reader of this book you must never take that struggle for granted, but consider what it is that makes dignity a birthright rather than a gift.

And then go and enjoy your freedom.

ACKNOWLEDGEMENTS

This book is my gift to the people of South Africa in gratitude for their gift to me of some of the most unforgettable experiences of my life. I only hope that it is enough to cover the debt.

Thank you to the Jarvis family with all its miraculous members of every size and colour. I will be forever grateful to you for showing me what a free, equal and Godly South Africa looks like. To Mommy Thea: thank you for rescuing all those Mwanyisas from all those dustbins and seeing them for the treasure that they really are.

For everyone who has ever volunteered at TLC Ministries in Johannesburg. The babies will never be able to say thank you, so thank you.

To the people who shared any individual part of this journey with me. Thank you for making it such a good one and I hope it changed your life as much as it did mine.

To the English wayfaring traveller named Danny who told me what became The Pietermaritzburg Stories in Livingstone, Zambia in July 2011. You are one of the coolest people I have ever met and I salute your sense of adventure.

Finally, Nelson Mandela, we are all forever indebted to you for your achievements in the name of human rights. The world is an immeasurably better place because you dared to stand up and say that enough is enough. Thank you.

Also by the Author

Burnt Fingers
Michael Rogers

Alice looked back at the man who had killed her daughter, apparently studying his face in close detail for the first time. Doom clung to him stubbornly as he took his place on Death Row, the first in the queue for the great renaissance of capital punishment. His eyes were set back into his head, with dark circles around them that seemed to have nothing to do with tiredness or the light in the room; the eyes had a dark and foreboding evil around them and the actual irises themselves were an electric and bionic blue. Looking at his eyes reminded her of the photos of Rasputin in her history books at school, where even the most passing of glances appeared as a haunting and bone-chilling stare, of windows on a soul containing unspeakable evil. He seemed to be permanently unshaven, with messy and rough stubble across his cheeks and neck, and great tufts of chest hair climbing out of his shirt. His skin was greasy and dirty, and although his hairline was receding and he had an enormous forehead his hair was wildly tousled. Obviously she guessed that the conditions in prison were not such to keep him in peak aesthetic condition but it was a look of scruffy ruggedness that she had remembered from the courtroom and he had a deeply disturbing presence, with more than a hint of psychological abnormality and madness. She pondered his name, which meant *lion*; he had none of the majesty of his namesake but there was the same sense of raw physical power about him, the same instinct to hunt and kill and the same disparity from the human race. Staring deeply and thoughtfully into him, Alice was unsure of whether he was extending or reducing her understanding of what it is to be a human. From an evolutionary point of view, she wondered, was he a terrifying prototype, a hellish vision of what happens when perfectly normal sexual feelings are driven out of all control and breaking out of the confined space within restrictive boundaries that society would call the normality? Or perhaps, as her instinct told her, was he more of a relic and a psychological antique, a man so basic in his primeval and prehistoric filth that he had not yet advanced and evolved far enough to warrant being called a human? She knew that he was a vile monster, but she was unsure of whether he was horribly more or horribly less of a human than she herself was; the depth of his feeling for Joy certainly transcended her own, and with morals and goodness out of the question it seemed as though she may have been mistaken and that he may in fact have been more. His fingers were pressed far more firmly into the electrical current of humankind and he felt a fuller force of the sexual kaleidoscope than she ever did.

"In answer to your question, the reason that I came here to see you is a matter of unfinished business," she said, looking at and then pointing to the guard who was standing watch, slapping the truncheon against the palm of his hand. "It is very important to me that I know what they are doing to you here. I want to see justice being done to you."

"Ah," said the paedophile, the halogen lights of the dungeon ceiling reflecting in his eyes. "You wanted to see them hurt me."

Author biography

Michael Rogers studied English Literature and Journalism at Roehampton University in south west London. He was a volunteer for 9 months at TLC Children's Home in Johannesburg, South Africa, caring for abandoned newborn babies affected by crime, illness and poverty. He has travelled extensively around Southern Africa and has also worked for the secretariat of the British HIV Association in London.

This is his second novel; his first was entitled *Burnt Fingers*. He lives in Bournemouth, on the south coast of England.